Once Upon a Time in . . . Donnybrook

Once Upon a Time in . . . Donnybrook

ROSS O'CARROLL-KELLY
(as told to Paul Howard)

Illustrated by Alan Clarke

SANDYCOVE

an imprint of

PENGUIN BOOKS

SANDYCOVE

UK | USA | Canada | Ireland | Australia
India | New Zealand | South Africa

Sandycove is part of the Penguin Random House group of companies
whose addresses can be found at global.penguinrandomhouse.com.

First published 2022
001

Copyright © Paul Howard, 2022
Illustrator copyright © Alan Clarke, 2022

The moral right of the copyright holders has been asserted

Penguin Books thanks O'Brien Press for its agreement to Sandycove using the same design approach and
typography, and the same artist, as O'Brien Press used in the first four Ross O'Carroll-Kelly titles.

Set in 12/14.75pt Dante MT Std
Typeset by Jouve (UK), Milton Keynes
Printed and bound in Great Britain by Clays Ltd, Elcograf S.p.A.

The authorized representative in the EEA is Penguin Random House Ireland,
Morrison Chambers, 32 Nassau Street, Dublin D02 YH68

A CIP catalogue record for this book is available from the British Library

ISBN: 978-1-844-88552-7

For Derek Foley, the original One F

Contents

Prologue   I

1. Hill, Bill   7
2. Moo Romance   44
3. The Hateful Number Eight   82
4. Man Go On Chained   116
5. Yankee Brown   156
6. From Ruck till Dawn   192
7. Reservoir Underdogs   230
8. Win, Glorious Passers   270
9. Prop Friction   307
10. Once Upon a Time in Donnybrook   343

Epilogue   385
Acknowledgements   392

Prologue

The old man looks a complete state. Yeah, no, his face is literally black and his hair – slash, wig – is all *over* the shop? He looks like the old dear on the morning of the Commodore's lunch in Howth Yacht Club last year, after she fell asleep in front of her desktop tanning lamp with a bottle of Miraval Rosé and six fingers of Beefeater inside her.

Focking raddled, in other words.

But then, the rest of us don't look much better and I'm possibly including *myself* in that? It's, like, eight o'clock in the morning and none of us has had any sleep. We've been standing around all night, watching Leinster House burn.

The fire is out now, although all that's left of the building is a shell. The roof fell in just before midnight and the windows were all blown out, leaving just, like, holes surrounded by mascara smudges of black.

I heard Sorcha say it was as if the place was weeping for the death of Ireland's democracy. Like I said, it's been a long night.

The girl is still in literally tears, by the way. Yeah, no, she's wrapped in one of those tinfoil blankets and she's sobbing into the shoulder of Simone, her Special Adviser, telling her that she – oh my God – can't believe that the European Union would do something like this, that she cried tears of happiness the day Ireland joined the single currency and that she was once proud to say that she'd been on city breaks in seventeen of the other twenty-six EU capitals.

I notice that Simone is just, like, staring into space and shivering – like she's in basically *shock*?

The smell is horrendous, by the way – like when you pour water on top of ashes, except multiplied by a thousand. The firemen are packing away their hoses and the rest of their bits and pieces. Their work here is done.

There's, like, a crowd of thousands – I want to say – *thronging* Kildare Street? Some of them have been here all night. Some of them have swung by on their way to work to see the shit that's been made of their, I don't know – the word that everyone keeps using is, like, *porliament*?

I'm looking at their faces, pressed against the railings. They're all waiting for someone to make sense of what they're seeing. And that's when the old man steps forward, one orm around the shoulder of an exhausted fireman and a megaphone held to his mouth.

'Ireland, today, is on bended knees,' he goes, 'in a prayer of thanks that nobody was killed or even hurt last night! The nation sends its thanks to our brave firemen – and, indeed, women, because I'm sure I saw one a moment ago – who battled the flames until the early hours of this morning! We lost a building last night – but I want you all to know that we did *not* lose what that building represents!'

Through the railings, some randomer shouts, 'I can't hear you!'

But the old man goes, 'Well, I can hear you! And the rest of the world can hear you! And the people who burned down this building will hear *all* of us soon!'

There's, like, a loud cheer, followed by a round of applause.

I suddenly spot Hennessy to my right. I tip over to him. He's got a Montecristo like a roll of wallpaper burning between his fingers.

'The fuck are you looking at?' he goes.

I'm there, 'I know it was you.'

'Me?'

'Yeah, no, you and the old man. As in, I'm saying you burned it – yourselves.'

He takes a long drag on his cigor, then he goes, 'That's a very serious allegation to make.'

And I'm like, 'I'm well aware.'

'You got proof to back that up?'

'I do actually, yeah. Ronan told me you were going to do it. *They're godda burden Doddle Airdint.* His exact words to me. At the airport last night.'

Hennessy is instantly thrown by this. He storts looking around him for presumably Ro.

I'm like, 'He's gone, Dude.'

'Gone?' he goes – not a happy rabbit. 'Where's he gone?'

I'm there, 'America, the States, whatever you want to call it.'

He stares at me like he wants to tear out my Adam's apple with his fingers. I think that's what he's actually considering.

I'm there, 'He's out of your clutches. He's away from you and that dickhead up there with the megaphone. You can't corrupt him any more.'

'I'm the Attorney General,' he tries to go, 'the highest-ranking lawman in this country. You think I couldn't get him arrested at JFK and sent straight back?' and the dude whips out his phone.

I'm there, 'Except that he landed – oh, what – four *hours* ago?' and I make a big show of looking at my watch, even though I'm not wearing one. It doesn't matter. Because he smells what I'm stepping in. 'Right now, he'll be sleeping off the jetlag in a hotel on the Upper East Side that Erika sorted for him. In a day or two, he's going to stort his internship at a proper law firm, fighting for people's – it wouldn't be *my* thing? – but civil rights, instead of doing your dirty work.'

He goes, 'One phone call and I could have him picked up and deported by the end of the day.'

'Yeah, you do that,' I go, 'and I'll tell the world who was behind last night's firework show.'

He just, like, stares at me. From his expression, I can tell that he knows I'm not shitting him here. He sucks another inch out of his Montecristo, then blows the smoke in my face.

'You want me to say congratulations,' he goes, 'for ruining your son's life?'

But I'm like, 'Er, *no*? Because I *saved* my son's life?'

He laughs.

'Your old man was right,' he goes, 'when he said the brains in your family skipped a generation.'

I'm there, 'Excuse me?'

'I mean, doesn't it bother you that the man had to look beyond you to find an heir?'

'I've never really thought about it.'

'Well, think about this, you little shithead. Ronan could have been the next Charles O'Carroll-Kelly. And you've taken that away from him.'

The old man is still talking into the megaphone – not that he's ever needed one.

'I don't wish to make political capital from this outrage,' he goes, 'and our wonderful democracy precludes me from making campaign speeches on the day of a vote! But what you see behind me, the chorred ruin of our national porliament, is a reminder of just how fragile our freedoms are – and the lengths to which sinister forces will go to take them away from us! They! Will! Not! Succeed!'

There are, like, raucous cheers from the crowd beyond the gate. I notice that the famous K . . . K . . . K . . . K . . . Kennet is raising the tricolour on a badly blackened flagpole.

'You can let them *know* they won't succeed,' the old man goes, 'not by standing around and cheering – but by voting today! This, my friends, is Ireland's Ground Zero moment! Quote-unquote! It's a day for sombre reflection! But it's also a day for asking ourselves who our real friends are!'

My phone suddenly beeps. It's a text message from the famous – yeah, no, blast from the past this – Laura Woods, asking me, in typical Laura Woods fashion, what the fock that voice message I sent her was all about? I suddenly remember my conversation in the kitchen with Fionn, my highly sensitive conversation, which was recorded by Silas – that focking voice-controlled personal assistant thing that Sorcha brought into the house – and sent to everyone in my contacts list.

In all of the excitement of getting Ronan out of the country and then trying to stop the old man and Hennessy from burning down the Dáil, I nearly forgot that everyone in my phone – from my daughter, to my in-laws, to the great Robbie Henshaw – will probably know by now that I rode my old dear's best friend and my daughter's teacher from the Gaeltacht.

'And while I'm loath to start pointing fingers at this early stage in the Gorda investigation,' the old man goes, 'I want to make a promise to you – we will hunt down those responsible for this outrage . . . all the way to Brussels!'

Hill, Bill

Sorcha says she still can't believe it. Yeah, no, we're sitting in the back of the limo and Kennet is driving us home.

'*Dáil Hair-khinn*,' she goes, really ramping up the Irish pronunciation – like she used to do when she was debating against Coláiste Íosagáin at *their* place. '*Dáil Hair-khinn* . . . is gone.'

I tell her I know. I watched it burn *with* her?

Kennet says there's going to be a lot of anger out there today. He goes, 'The T . . . T . . . T . . . T . . . T . . . Teashocked says it was the EU what d . . . d . . . d . . . dudden it,' and I tell him to shut the fock up and just drive.

A Gorda cor flies past us, going in the opposite direction, its blue light flashing and its siren blazing.

Sorcha shakes her head. She says she once interviewed a former speechwriter for Jacques Santer on Transition Year Radio and I tell her I remember – even though I don't. I've no idea who the fock she's talking about.

I'm there, 'Where is he now? That's what I'd like to know. The focking nerve of these people.'

'*She*, Ross.'

'*She*, then. My question still stands.'

'She told Sister Adalsinda afterwards that she thought I was a true Europhile,' Sorcha goes. 'A true Europhile! And to think that I took that as an actual compliment. Oh my God, she even sent me a signed copy of the speech that Jacques made when he won his Vision for Europe Award in 1995. If I knew where it was, I'd actually rip it in two.'

I'm there, 'And I'd help you – gladly,' trying to deflect attention away from myself.

My phone beeps. It's a message from Robbie Henshaw, asking me if I *meant* to send him that voice message yesterday and is the Delma that I mentioned in it the same Delma who runs the Taste of Décor interiors shop in Ranelagh?

Sorcha goes, 'I honestly can't believe the EU would resort to those lengths to stop us from leaving.'

I probably should tell her the truth, that the fire had fock-all to do with them, except I don't because – classic, classic me – I can suddenly see a way back into her good books.

'Still,' I go, placing my hand on her knee, 'at least it puts everything into prospectus.'

Another Gorda cor zooms past. There's a definite feeling of paranoia in the air.

She's there, 'Excuse me?' swatting my hand away.

'Prospectus, perspectus?' I go. 'Am I using that word right?'

'What does it put into *perspective*, Ross? You having sex with our daughter's Irish teacher? And – oh! my God! – *Delma*? Jesus, how old is she – sixty?'

'Yeah, no,' I go, chuckling to myself, then rolling my eyes, 'that's being kind to the woman.'

I've no idea why I'm laughing, since it was me who rode her.

'Oh my God,' Sorcha goes, 'I can't believe I was going to ask her to supply all of the soft furnishings for my office refit. I feel like such an idiot.'

I'm there, 'If it's any consolation, Sorcha, *she* was the one who made a move on *me*?'

She's like, 'Yeah, I don't want the focking blow-by-blow details.'

I notice that Kennet is watching us in the rear-view mirror, obviously loving every second of this.

I'm there, 'I'm just making the point that I was only trying to comfort the woman – like you said, a mate of my old dear's, going all the way back to the stort of the Move Funderland to the Northside campaign – because that dickhead she was married to has got his much younger girlfriend up the stick. But she threw the lips on me in my old dear's side passage and the next thing I knew she was unzipping the front of her dress and I was lifting her up onto that anthracite jumbo storage box that the old dear uses to keep all of her *gordening* gear in?'

She lets a roar out of her then. She's like, 'ROSS, I SAID I DON'T WANT THE BLOW-BY-BLOW DETAILS!'

Kennet goes, 'Evoddy thing alreet, M . . . M . . . M . . . M . . . M . . . M . . . Ministodder?' just letting me know that he's following every twist and turn of the conversation.

Sorcha's there, 'Yes, it's fine, Kennet. Just get me back to Honalee. I need to sleep.'

'Been a l . . . l . . . l . . . l . . . long neet,' he goes, the stuttering fock. 'Idn't that reet, Rosser?'

I totally blank him and he drives on through Dalkey village. As usual, my rugby tactics brain kicks in then and I decide to switch the angle of the attack.

I'm there, 'Sorcha, the only reason you know about any of this is because that piece of shit – which *you* brought into the house, by the way – recorded a *supposaly* private conversation that I was having with Fionn and sent it to everyone in my phone.'

Speaking of which, my phone suddenly beeps. It's a text message from, like, Lorraine Keane – Jesus, they're all coming out of the woodwork now – telling me that she got a really random voice message sent to her from my phone and I should check if I've been hacked.

'So, what, you're saying that it's *my* fault?' Sorcha goes.

I'm there, 'No, I'm saying that if this was a court of law, the evidence would be, I don't know, *unadmissable*. Because it was, like, illegally *obtained*? And I'd walk – on a hopefully technicality.'

'Well, you *won't* be walking on a technicality – not this time. You know Sea-mon thinks I shouldn't even let you back into the house?'

'Yeah, See-mon's not who she pretends to be, by the way.'

'Excuse me?'

'She's a plant, Sorcha. She's reporting to the old man and Hennessy – just like focking K . . . K . . . K . . . K . . . Kennet there.'

'You'll say literally anything to avoid taking responsibility for your actions. And, by the way, her name is pronounced Sea-mon, not See-mon.'

'You think she's advising you – she's actually *controlling* you?'

'Yeah, Sea-mon knows more about climate change than anyone I've ever met. She's just finished a Masters in Environmental and Natural Resources Law.'

'Banning cows and sheep wasn't even her idea – it was my old man's. He's trying to wipe out the formers and destroy rural Ireland so that he can give their land to the Russians to dump their rubbish and build power stations on it. The entire population is going to be moved to the coast, where everyone will work for multinational tech companies and sleep standing up in rented wardrobes.'

'Ross,' she goes, 'stop deflecting.'

I'm there, 'I'm not deflecting, Sorcha. It's all true. Erika figured out the entire thing. The EU didn't burn down the Dáil last night. It was my old man and Hennessy.'

I can nearly feel Kennet's eyes boring into me in the rear-view mirror. I don't give a fock if *he* knows that *I* know.

'After listening to that voice message –' Sorcha goes.

But I cut her off. I'm like, 'It wasn't a voice message. And I repeat, Delma made all of the early running – before I even knew what was going on, she'd pulled my plonker out of my trousers – and it was pretty much the same story with Honor's teacher.'

'After hearing what I heard,' she goes, as Kennet pulls into the driveway of Honalee, 'do you honestly think I'd ever believe another word that came from your mouth?'

I'm there, 'Okay, don't believe me. But ask Ronan. He told me the full story at the airport last night.'

'The ayer p . . . p . . . p . . . powurt?' Kennet can't stop himself from going.

I'm like, 'That's right, Kennet – the ayer p . . . p . . . p . . . powurt. I dropped him off. He's gone to New York – to live.'

Kennet is just sitting there with his mouth flapping open and closed – a bit like me the time in UCD when I crashed a first-year Philosophy lecture to try to chat up Melissa McCrory and I ended up being asked to describe the ways in which Plato challenged Socrates on his assumptions about the nature of virtue.

I'm there, 'So you can tell that so-called daughter of yours that her husband is storting a new life for himself in the States. And hopefully he's going to be riding all around him.'

Sorcha throws open the back door and gets out. I get out too and I follow her into the gaff, still trying to get her to see reason.

I'm there, 'Sorcha, I honestly don't think this is as bad as some of the stunts I've pulled in the past.'

We head for the kitchen. Honor is sitting at the island with the boys. I'm there, 'Morning, Honor.'

But she just goes, 'Eat focking shit!' and then Brian, Johnny and Leo say the exact same thing to me.

They're like, 'Eat focking shit!'

I try to do the whole tough love thing then. I'm like, 'Honor, maybe don't speak to me like that. Why aren't you dressed for school yet?'

She goes, 'We don't have school today because of the referendum – and I'll speak to you any way I focking want.'

I realize that it's going to take longer than I possibly expected to chorm my way out of this one.

'Oh my God, the referendum!' Sorcha goes, putting her hand to her forehead. 'I wanted to be there when the polls opened. Okay, I'm going to bed for a few hours, then I'm going to get up to vote.'

I'm there, 'I'm going to do the same. Except for the bit about voting. It'd be nice to get my head down – and I don't mean that in a sexual way.'

'Ross,' Sorcha goes, 'come with me.'

I'm like, 'Er, okay,' and I follow her out of the kitchen.

But she leads me, not up the stairs, but into what used to be her old man's study, until me and Honor burned all of his books one day, just for shits and giggles.

I'll have to keep reminding the girl of all the good times we had together.

Sorcha takes a key from a hook on the wall and brings it over to a door in the corner that's, like, hordly ever used. She puts the key in the door and turns it.

I'm like, 'Sorcha, what are you doing?'

But she just goes, 'Follow me.'

The door, I already know, leads to one of the two round towers that her old man had added to the house when Sorcha and her sister, whose name I can never remember, were apparently going through a princess phase – which, if you ask me, never *really* ended? This one was Sorcha's one and the second one – on the other side of the gaff – belonged to . . . I don't know, it will come to me.

Sorcha reefs open the door and storts climbing the winding stairwell to the top. I follow her, at the same time going, 'Sorcha, what the fock is going on?' my voice echoing off the bare brick walls.

She's like, 'When I was a little girl, I used to spend hours and hours sitting at the top of this tower, looking down on the Vico Road, dreaming that a prince would one day come to rescue me.'

'You told that story at a family dinner in Fitzpatrick's Castle,' I go. 'I'm pretty sure it was the night of your eighteenth – and I seem to remember you saying that the prince was me.'

She's there, 'And I was wrong. Our relationship – including our marriage – has been a sham from the very stort.'

I'm like, 'It's not as bad as some others I could mention. Do you remember Josh Peasley – he played loosehead for King's Hos back in the day and was their only decent player? Well, his wife found out that he was wanking into her shoes every Saturday morning while she was out playing golf with her old dear in – I want to say – *Woodbrook*? Yeah, no, he used to, like, film himself blowing his muck into her good work shoes, then post the videos on some, I don't know, foot fetish website for other perverts to watch.'

This story seems to cut no ice with Sorcha. I don't know why I thought it would.

I'm there, 'I'm tempted to say typical King's Hos,' refusing to accept defeat. 'The point I'm trying to make is that they're still together – although I'd imagine she locks the bedroom door when she leaves the house now.'

We finally reach the top of the tower. It's – like I said – round and there's barely room to swing a basic cat in it.

I'm like, 'Sorcha, what are we doing up here?'

She goes, 'This is where you sleep now, Ross.'

I'm there, 'Excuse me?'

'I don't want you sleeping in the house any more,' she goes. 'But I understand that it's important for the children to have you around. So this is the compromise.'

'What, you're banishing me to the tower?'

'It's either that or you can go and find somewhere else to live.'

'So where am I supposed to sleep – on the hord floor?'

'No, you can drag a mattress up the stairs. And bring your sleeping bag.'

'Sorcha, are you not listening to what I'm telling you about Josh Peasley? I think you know his wife, Edel something or other. She might have even gone to Andrew's.'

'Ross, *you're* the one who's not listening to *me*. This is the only way you're staying in this house. You're here as a father to our children, but our marriage – if that's what it ever was – is over.'

'Including the physical side of it?'

'*Especially* the physical side of it. From now on, Ross, you're going to be Bill Clinton to my Hillary.'

Yeah, no, I'm wondering if that means I'm allowed to have sex with other women. But in the end I decide not to ask.

What the fock? What the actual –

There's something in my sleeping bag. Yeah, no, I can feel it nibbling at my–

I end up screaming – as in, like, a proper *cortoon* scream? We're talking: 'Aaaaaarrrrrrgggggghhhhhh!!!!!!'

In one fluid movement, I unzip the bag and scramble to my feet, then I lean against the wall, shaking, my breathing all over the gaff.

Suddenly, a mouse – literally – sticks its head out of my sleeping bag, sniffs the air and makes a run for it across the floor.

Again, I scream. I'm like: 'Aaaaaarrrrrrgggggghhhhhh!!!!!!'

Then it disappears through the tiniest of cracks into the actual wall of the tower.

'Oh, Jesus!' I'm going, stamping my feet up and down because I've got, like, the *major* ick now? 'Oh, Jesus! Oh, Jesus! Oh, Jesus!'

All of a sudden, my phone rings. I end up answering it without even checking the screen.

I'm like, 'Hello?'

'Rosser?' Ronan goes, talking in a whisper. 'Thee really dud it – thee burdened Doddle Airdint?'

I'm like, 'Yeah, no, who told you?'

'It's arthur been on CNN.'

'Jesus.'

'It's all oaber the wurdled, Rosser. And Cheerlie's saying it was the EU what dud it?'

'He's a dick. I've been saying it for years. On the record.'

'Rosser, what he's arthur doing – it's threason.'

'Treason? Jesus, is that still a thing?'

'You bether belieb it's stiddle a thing. If thee foyunt out it was him, he'll get thoorty yee-ors. Thee'll thrun away the key.'

'Well, all this goes to prove is that you didn't know your grandad as well as you possibly *thought* you did? He made you think you were about to be chorged with illegal possession of a fireorm, bear in mind, just to stop you from going to the States.'

'I stiddle say it's the wig – it's like he's under some koyunt of speddle.'

'Some kind of what?'

'Speddle.'

'Say it again?'

'Speddle.'

'*Speddle?*'

'Yeah, like a *magic* speddle.'

'Oh, a *spell*! No, he was always a dodgy focker, Ro, long before he ever put that thing on his head.'

'The fedda on CNN says the foyer is probley godda swig it in Cheerlie's fabour – Ine thalken about the referdenduddem.'

'I'll be honest, I know fock-all about politics, Ro. Except that there's no doubt a lot of anger out there right now. And that Sorcha went out to vote about an hour ago wearing what, from up here, looked like her good Stella McCortney pant suit.'

'I joost caddent belieb he did it, Rosser. He burdened the Doddle.'

'Look, you're better off forgetting about him, Ro. You've got your new life over there. How's the hotel?'

'It's lubbly, so it is. Foyuv steers, all the way – feer fooks to Edika.'

'Yeah, no, nothing but the best for my sister. Always the best hotels. The best cors. The best clothes. God, I love some of the stuff she wears. Especially when it's leather trousers.'

'Rosser.'

'Sorry. We meant what we said, by the way. We're going to come over to see you before Christmas.'

'Hee-or, me ma is looking for you, by the way?'

'Oh – er, really?'

'She's on the bleaten warpatt, so she is. She says you kiddled Tom McGahy.'

Yeah, no, he's talking about Tom McGahy – as in, the former Principal of Castlerock College.

I'm there, 'I hordly killed him,' which I *didn't*, by the way? I just happened to mention to him that Tina, who he had a fling with back in the day, said he fell very short of satisfying her in a sexual sense – which is literally what she said, very nearly word for word – and the dude keeled over shortly after I left the office and, yeah, no, sadly died.

Again, I made the mistake of telling Fionn about it in the conversation that half of Ireland seems to have heard at this stage.

'She says you geb him the *heert* attack what kiddled him,' Ronan goes.

I'm there, 'Two very different things, Ro. Two *very* different things. So when are you storting the new job?'

'Ine godda rig them tomoddow. Ine joost wonthering about Shadden.'

'Who?'

'Shadden.'

'The name's not ringing a bell, Ro.'

'Shadden – me wife, Rosser.'

'Oh, *her* – what about her?'

'Well, I'd lubben her to come oaber – and brig me thaughter wirrer.'

'I'm not sure if that's such a good idea.'

'Soddy?'

'Ro, you're storting a new life for yourself over there. You don't want that focking family getting their claws into you and dragging you back here, do you?'

'Ine arthur leabon her a loawut of voice messages, thrying to explain to her why I had to leab in a huddy.'

'You left in a hoodie?'

'In a *huddy*, Rosser. In a *huddy*.'

'Oh, in a hurry.'

'That's what Ine arthur saying. But she woatunt rig me back. I think she's in a snot with me.'

'Like I said, there's plenty more fish in the sea. I always did well in New York. Did I tell you about the time on my J1 when I rode a Rockette?'

'You did, yeah – maddy, maddy toyums.'

'Well, there you are, then.'

'Rosser, if you see her, will you purra woord in for me?'

'As in?'

'Shadden, Rosser. Will you ted her why I had to go? And that I lub her. And that I'd lubben to steert a new life wit her and Ri oaber hee-or.'

'I don't know, Ro, that's a lot of things to remember. Maybe if I just tell her you said hi?'

'Rosser, please.'

And being too nice for my own good, I end up going, 'Yeah, no, whatever.'

There's, like, silence on the end of the phone then.

He goes, 'I cadn't belieb he did it, Rosser. Thoorty yee-ors ago, thee'd hab executed him for it.'

I'm like, 'Fock.'

And he's there, 'I stiddle lub him, but.'

The dude on the radio says the European Union has angrily denied any involvement in the blaze that destroyed the Houses of the Oireachtas.

'As fire investigators continue to sift through the chorred remains of Leinster House,' he goes, 'the Taoiseach, Charles O'Carroll-Kelly, has accused Brussels of burning the building as a warning ahead of yesterday's referendum on Ireland's continued membership of the EU. In a joint statement issued yesterday, the leaders of all the other Member States called on the Taoiseach to either substantiate his claim or withdraw it.'

The traffic on the Stillorgan dualler is, like, bomper to bomper. There's a woman in a white Ford Explorer who's trying to join the lane in front of me, except I'm refusing to *let* her? Yeah, no, every time a space opens ahead of me, I just inch the cor forward, blocking her off. It's funny.

'Here, Honor,' I go, 'look at the face on this one beside me here. She looks like she's licking the top of a battery.'

Usually, Honor would be all over it, telling me how hilarious I was being and even giving the woman the finger. But this morning she doesn't say shit to me. She just looks over her shoulder at her three brothers in the back and goes, '*Dein Vater ist ein Arschloch.*'

I have literally no idea what it means, but the boys stort shouting, '*Arschloch!*' at the top of their voices. '*Arschloch! Arschloch! Arschloch!*'

The dude on the radio says that the counting of votes in the referendum is due to begin this morning. He says that exit polls suggest that the vote on whether or not to repeal the Third Amendment to the Constitution is likely to result in a Yes vote.

The woman in the white Ford Explorer gives me an angry blast of her horn. I wind down the window and I go, 'Sorry, is there a problem?' with a big innocent face on me.

She winds down *her* window and she goes, 'Yeah, I'm *trying* to change *lanes.*'

And I'm like, 'I didn't see you there.'

'Well, will you let me in front of you now?'

'Yeah, no, be my guest.'

A space opens up between me and the silver Renault Sandero in front. As soon as she goes to fill it, I lean on the accelerator and I block her off again. She gives me, like, *three* angry blasts of the horn this time and I crack my hole laughing.

I'm there, 'That was vintage Ross – right, Honor?'

'*Dein Vater ist ein Wichser,*' she goes to her brothers. '*Ein kompletter und absoluter Wichser.*'

I'm like, 'Vintage, vintage Ross.'

We eventually arrive in Clonskeagh. I pull into the cor pork of St Kilian's and Honor gets out and – yeah, no – helps the boys out of the cor. She gives them each a little hug and a kiss on the top of the head and goes, *Bis später, Johnny! Bis später, Brian! Bis später, Leo!* and then off the three of them fock, shouting, *'Wichser!'* and *'Arschloch!'* at the top of their literally voices.

Honor gets back into the cor. I point it in the direction of Mount Anville and I keep trying to make conversation with the girl.

I'm like, 'That, em, tower is freezing, by the way. As in, there's no actual *radiator* in it? I've got to get back into your old dear's good books before the winter sets in.'

Again, she leaves me hanging.

My phone beeps. It's a text from, like, Dan Leavy, telling me that he got a voice message from me the other day and I should check if my phone has been hacked.

I'm there, 'There's, like, mice as well. Yeah, no, one ended up in my sleeping bag last night.'

And that's when Honor suddenly turns on me.

She's like, 'What are you looking for – me to feel sorry for you? Because I focking don't!'

I'm there, 'Look, I know you're angry with me. By the way, can I just ask you, Honor, is *Wichser* the German word for wanker?'

She doesn't say anything for a good, like, sixty seconds, then she goes, 'Why the fock did you do it?'

I'm there, 'As in?'

'Are you *actually* going to make me say it?' she goes. 'Why did you have sex with my teacher?'

I'm like, 'Oh . . . er, that.'

'Yes, Dad – *that*!'

'Well, first of all, what I *would* say in my defence is –'

'Don't you focking *dare* tell me that she came on to you!'

'She made it very difficult for me to say no, Honor – *very* difficult.'

'You know, you sound just like *him*.'

'Who? Reese?'

18

'Yes, Dad, Reese.'

Reese was her ex. One of the biggest rugby wankers I've ever met, and I mean that as a compliment.

I'm there, 'Honor, I know you're upset about getting dumped, but I want you to know that all men aren't like him.'

She goes, 'So how are *you* any different? You're a cheat. You're a liar. You hate women.'

'I don't hate women. Jesus, if my record is anything to go by, I'd say the *opposite* is the case?'

Suddenly – this is, like, totally out of left field – she goes, 'Why wouldn't you let that woman change lanes?'

I'm there, 'What woman? The one in the white Ford Explorer?' obviously wondering where this conversation is going.

'Yes,' she goes, 'the woman in the white Ford Explorer.'

I'm like, 'Er, I don't know – you'd usually find that funny, Honor.'

'What if that woman was me,' she goes, 'and some man was being an asshole to me like that?'

I'm there, 'I'd want to deck him. Two hits, Honor. Me hitting him and him hitting the floor.'

She's like, 'Well, that was somebody's daughter in that Ford Explorer.'

'Honor,' I go, swinging the A8 into the cor pork of Mount Anville, 'I genuinely thought you'd laugh.'

She's like, 'Have you ever heard the phrase toxic masculinity?'

I'm there, 'Errr . . .'

And she's like, 'Look it up, Dad!'

Erika looks well in jodhpurs – always did, in fairness to the girl, although I'm trying my best not to look at her orse, portly because of what Honor said to me this morning and then portly because – yeah, no – she's my sister slash *half*-sister?

'Here, Erika,' I go, 'you speak German, don't you?'

She's like, 'I did it in college – why?'

I'm there, 'What does toxic masculinity mean?'

She goes, 'What?' like she can't believe that anyone could be so thick.

'Am I saying it right? Toxic masculinity?'

'It's not German, Ross!'

'Isn't it?'

'It's English.'

'Fine – so, like, what does it actually mean?'

'It's a bunch of typically male behaviours that most people consider anti-social. Bullying, aggression, violence, emotional repression, the sexualization of women, getting an erection because your sister is wearing jodhpurs – that kind of thing.'

'Okay, I get the point – no need to hammer it home.'

'Where did you hear the phrase anyway?'

'Yeah, no, Honor told me to look it up.'

Erika ends up laughing in my face.

I'm there, 'It's not funny. She's not talking to me at the moment.'

'I wouldn't blame her,' she goes. 'You had sex with her teacher.'

'I'm well aware of what I did, Erika – as is half the country at this stage.'

'And you lied to her about it. You've no idea how much that girl idolized you, Ross.'

'I want that back. How do I get that back?'

'I don't know if you ever will.'

Erika suddenly storts clapping, going, 'Well done, Ri! Perfect round!'

Yeah, no, we're in, like, Enniskerry, where she keeps her horses. Rihanna-Brogan is riding Chiaroscuro, Erika's black-and-white thoroughbred mare, around a sort of, like, horsey obstacle course and we're leaning over a wooden fence, watching her.

'Can I do anutter rowunt?' the girl goes – the accent is pure Ronan.

Erika's like, 'Of course you can, my pet. We'll do this one by the clock,' and she takes out her iPhone to time her.

'Is she any good?' I go.

Erika's there, 'She's an absolute natural on a horse.'

I'm like, 'Makes sense, I suppose – given that Shadden's old man is a focking cowboy.'

Erika laughs, in fairness to her.

Then she's like, 'Okay, Ri – go!' and off the girl shoots again.

I'm there, 'Sorcha's making me sleep in one of the towers, by the way.'

Erika goes, 'I can't believe she didn't just fock you out on the street. That's what I would have done. I suppose it suits her to keep you around. Did you talk to her, by the way?'

'About?'

'Er, about our beloved father burning the Dáil down?'

'Yeah, no, I tried to tell her, but she refused to listen.'

Erika stops the clock on her phone, then goes, 'Whoa! Fifty-eight seconds and no time penalties, Ri! That's amazing!'

Rihanna-Brogan rides over to us then.

She's like, 'Reedy?'

'Really,' Erika goes.

'Ah, tanks, Edika! Howiya, Grandda?'

I'm there, 'You can just call me Ross, Ri – or Rosser.'

'Fifty-eight seconds!' Erika shouts over to Helen – as in, her old dear, who's, like, mucking out the stables. She tips over to us, pitchfork in hand. I can't help but notice that she knows how to fill a pair of jodhpurs as well as her daughter.

I think there might be something wrong with me.

She's like, 'Well done, Ri,' because she's such a nice woman. I don't know what she ever saw in my old man. 'How are you, Ross?'

I'm there, 'Never been better, Helen,' because I've always been a glass half *full* kind of goy? 'I'm actually in scintillating form.'

'Sorcha has him sleeping in one of the towers,' Erika goes, letting me down in a big-time way. 'You remember her dad had them built onto the house when she thought she was a princess?'

'Why are you sleeping in there, Ross?' Helen goes – she's a fan of mine, in fairness to her.

I'm there, 'It's complicated. Probably shouldn't talk about it in front of –'

'He slep wit wood of Hodor's teachers,' Rihanna-Brogan goes. 'I know all abourrit, Rosser. Me ma let me listen to the voice message what got sent arowunt.'

I'm like, 'That was very nice of Shadden. I must remember to thank her the next time I see her.'

'And then he slep wit anutter wooban who was a friend of he's ma's – her nayum was eeder Dervilla or Deddlema.'

Helen goes, 'You don't mean Delma who has the interiors shop in Ranelagh?' and she says it in a definitely judgy way. 'I was in Holy Child Killiney with her – and that was neither today nor yesterday!'

'Well, she obviously likes them young,' Erika goes, 'because she's with JP now. Or *was* – until JP found out that Ross had been there before him.'

Yeah, no, I've tried apologizing to him too, except the dude won't take my calls.

Ri gallops off on the horse, then totally out of left field, Helen goes, 'It looks like the referendum is going to be carried.'

I'm like, 'Riiiggghhht,' not really knowing what the fock that even means. 'Carried? Jesus. *Carried?* That's a turn-up for the books alright.'

'It means that Ireland is going to be leaving the European Union,' Erika goes, seeing straight through my bluff. 'It means *he* got his way. It means the fire worked.'

'According to the news,' Helen goes, 'there's an angry mob surrounding the Belgian embassy in Ballsbridge.'

I'm like, 'Ballsbridge? Jesus Christ.'

'They're threatening to burn the place.'

'We need to do something,' Erika goes.

I'm like, 'In terms of?'

'We need to tell the world that it was him.'

Helen goes, 'Erika, what proof do you have?'

I'm there, 'And don't say Ronan. I don't want him dragged into this – not when he's storting a new life for himself in the States.'

Erika's there, 'What about Sorcha?'

'Like I said, I told her it was the old man who was behind it and she was having none of it.'

'So we get Sea-mon to tell her the truth.'

'See-mon?'

'No, Sea-mon – as in her Special Adviser?'

'Jesus, that's what I said.'

'I still remember all the stuff that Fionn found out about her.'

'You know, I was looking at her the night of the fire and she looked, I don't know, traumatized.'

'I saw that as well.'

'She was obviously regretting getting into bed with my old man.'

'She probably didn't think he'd go that far. She could be a weak link, then – I say we confront her.'

'Yeah, no, cool.'

Helen goes, 'You have to stop him – before they burn down that embassy.'

Erika's there, 'We have to stop him for the sake of the country. For the sake of democracy. For the sake of . . . Jesus Christ, Ross, are you checking out my mother's orse?'

And I'm like, 'Er, not really, no.'

The old man is full of himself tonight.

'Ross Kyle Gibson McBride O'Carroll-Kelly!' he goes in his block-capitals voice. 'An historic day! One for the ages!'

Yeah, no, like Helen said, it looks like the dude is going to get his way. We're in the RDS, where the counting of votes has finished and the result of the referendum is about to be declared. I've been wandering around looking for Erika, except she hasn't *arrived* yet?

The old man goes, 'I should have known that you – ardent constitutionalist that you are, Ross – would want to be here to witness the moment when Ireland takes back its sovereignty! By the way, Kicker, I received the strangest message from you – a recording, no less!'

I'm there, 'I know it was you,' quickly changing the subject. 'I know it was you who burned down the Dáil – you and your focking Russian mates.'

'Have you been drinking, Ross? Or is the historical gravity of the occasion making you feel a little heady? Understandable in the circumstances!'

'I'll never forgive you for what you did to Ronan.'

'Ronan?'

'You let him think he was going to go to jail – and it was just to stop him from going to the States. Well, Hennessy's probably told you that you failed. Because he's there right now.'

'I have literally no idea where any of this is coming from,' he tries to go, then he storts taking a sudden interest in something that's happening over my shoulder. 'Ah, there's our friend, Varadkar – the great European – trying to slip out of the room before the final tallies are announced! I'm going to go and offer him my commiserations! I'll try my best not to gloat!' and off he focks.

I feel an orm suddenly threaded through mine.

'You look so handsome tonight,' a voice goes, and my nostrils are suddenly filled with the unmistakable smell of denture fixative and sexual unfulfilment.

I'm there, 'Do I?' because I'm a sucker for a compliment, even from my old dear.

'I was looking at you across the floor of the count centre,' she goes, 'thinking, "Who is that man? He's positively ravishing!" Then I realized that it was my own son!'

I'm there, 'Yeah, no, don't make it creepy now – although I'm still accepting what you said. You look well too.'

She doesn't, by the way. She looks like –

Actually, I'm not going to say what she looks like. It would serve no purpose and I've decided to stop being mean about the woman.

'Thank you,' she goes, actually buying the line. 'Well, I have to look my best – now that I'm Ireland's First Lady. In the glamour stakes, you must remember that I'm now competing against the likes of Brigitte Macron and Sophie Grégoire Trudeau.'

Okay, I'm *going* to say it. She looks like someone took two hundred kilos of turkey mince, fashioned it into a life-sized model of Mickey Rourke from *The Wrestler*, then stuffed it into a mini-dress made for someone in their twenties, before letting the crows get at it.

'So how are you?' I go – and I genuinely *mean* it?

She's there, 'Oh, I'm feeling *very* lucid at the moment.'

I remember the days when that used to be a complaint. I'm remembering the time when Molloy's Liquor Store in Leopardstown refused to sell me a bottle of Stoli on account of me being eight years old and she rang up and demanded to speak to the manager. I think those were her actual words: 'I'm feeling very *lucid* at the moment.'

I'm there, 'Yeah, no, that's good. Have you mentioned it to *him* yet?'

'Mentioned what?' she has the actual nerve to go.

I'm like, 'What is it with this family and being in denial? Er, about the fact that your, like, *mind* is going?'

'I've tried to tell him, Ross, but he just fobs it off. Says we're bound to forget things at our age. Anyway, I don't want to upset him. He's waited a long time for this moment. All those letters he used to write to the *Irish Times*, calling for Ireland to pull out of the EEC, as it was in those days. You know they used to laugh at him in Doheny & Nesbitt's?'

'I can well believe it.'

Suddenly, a woman steps onto the stage and a hush falls over the Simmonscourt Pavilion.

'The votes in all of the constituencies have now been tallied,' she goes. 'And we have a final result. On the proposal to repeal the Third Amendment to the Constitution, the result is Yes 61 per cent, No 38 per cent.'

There's, like, a humungous cheer in the hall.

'Ireland,' the woman – not great, in case you're wondering – goes, 'has voted to repeal the Third Amendment to the Constitution.'

And that gets an even *bigger* cheer?

The old man bustles his way through the crowd – all his mates slapping his back and telling him he's great – and he makes his way up onto the stage. He takes the microphone in his hand, but it's a good, like, two minutes before he's allowed to speak.

'Let no man –' he tries to go. 'Let no man –' before the crowd finally settles down and he goes, 'Let no man ever underestimate the courage of the Irish people!'

And that sets them off again. Cheers and roars. The dude ends up having to shout.

He's there, 'Because yesterday, they chose to do something truly brave – to walk away from a failed bureaucratic project that, for fifty years, has treated our country as a vassal state! I know a lot of you sitting at home will be worried tonight! Many of the 38 per cent of voters whom we didn't manage to persuade may see this as the end of the world! But I can assure you that tomorrow morning, the sun *will* rise – and it will rise on a truly independent Ireland!'

The room goes absolutely ballistic.

The old man waits for the clamour to die down, then he goes, 'Like our great friends across the water, we have chosen to leave Ursula von der Leyen's Prison of Nations! We have chosen to free ourselves of the shackles of the 2008 – quote-unquote – bailout, which imposed on Ireland a burden more onerous than anything the world has seen since the Treaty of Versailles!

'I said at the time that *that* was our moment to walk away! Just as I'd been saying it for forty years! Ad nauseum! Even the *Irish Times* stopped publishing my famous letters on the subject! *Correspondence on this matter has now closed*, indeed! They laughed at me in Doheny & Nesbitt's! Well, they're not laughing now!

'Along with my Government colleagues, I will now begin the process of extricating our country from its unhappy relationship with the European *über Staat*! It won't be easy, and they will no doubt go to even greater lengths to try to subvert the will of the Irish people! We saw in their response to the Nice and Lisbon treaties votes what they think of our democracy! We saw in the arson attack on our national porliament this week what they think of our sovereignty!'

Some randomer in the crowd shouts, 'The Belgian embassy is on fire!' and I watch as a definite smile crosses the old man's face.

'I'm very sorry to hear that,' he tries to go. 'And I would appeal to the crowds gathering outside the other embassies and consulates across the city to please show restraint. During the period of negotiations that lie ahead, there will be further attempts to bribe us, to intimidate us and to belittle us into changing our minds! But at the end of it, I can assure you of this – we will be leaving the European Union and embarking on a happier future for our country!'

There ends up being, like, mayhem in the hall then – we're talking clapping, cheering and whatever else is going. I watch Hennessy and a few of the old man's wanker mates from Portmornock lift him up onto their shoulders and stort carrying him around the RDS.

Erika suddenly appears beside me.

I'm like, 'Where the fock have you been?'

She goes, 'All the roads around Ballsbridge are closed. The Belgian embassy is on fire.'

'Yeah, no – so I heard. Any sign of See-mon?'

'You mean Sea-mon? She's over here.'

I follow Erika over to the far side of the hall, where Sorcha is being interviewed by Gavan Reilly off Virgin Media News. The famous Simone – however you pronounce her name – is standing just over her left shoulder.

Sorcha is going, 'Well, of course I condemn the orson attack on the Belgian embassy. There is no place in our democracy for acts of vigilantism like this, be it on Elgin Road or anywhere else.'

I can see that Simone is sweating.

Gavan's there, 'I'm not sure if you've heard, but in the last few minutes, Raoul Trappaniers – Belgium's Minister for European Affairs and Federal Cultural Institutions – has accused the Taoiseach of burning the Oireachtas himself to drum up anti-EU feeling on the eve of the referendum. How do you respond to that?'

'By reminding all elected representatives that we have a responsibility to think very carefully about the weight of our words,' Sorcha goes, 'especially at a time of heightened tensions like this.'

'Does that include the Taoiseach? Do you believe his claim that this was – in his words – an *act of terror* by the European Union?'

Simone notices me and Erika staring at her. She suddenly doesn't know *where* to look?

'I'm saying let's wait until the investigators have completed their work,' Sorcha goes, 'and we know more about the cause of the fire. In the meantime –'

Gavan's like, 'Minister, do you believe that the EU was responsible for burning down our national –'

But Sorcha's there, '*In* the meantime – *as* Ireland's Climate Action Minister – I want to get on with the job of helping Ireland to achieve corbon neutrality, not in the medium term, in accordance with the EU's very limited torgets, but in the short term.'

'So you're pushing ahead with the plan to castrate all of Ireland's male sheep and cows?'

'If you're asking me if I'm pushing ahead with my radical programme to eradicate ruminant animals from our national herd, the answer is that work will begin in the coming days.'

The interview ends. Sorcha goes off to do a second interview with RTÉ, while Erika gives Simone the I-want-a-focking-word-with-you eyes – which I've always found quite sexy, although that could be just a personal thing.

We pull her to one side.

She goes, 'What's this about? The Minister needs me –'

'We know who you're working for,' Erika goes. 'Who you're *really* working for.'

'I don't have time for this,' she tries to go.

But Erika's there, 'My dad hired you. My dad and Hennessy. You were port of their plan. Although they didn't tell you the bit about burning down the Dáil, did they?'

Honest to fock, you can actually see the colour suddenly drain from the girl's face.

I'm there, 'We know everything about you,' because – yeah, no – Fionn spent a whole evening Googling the girl and going through her social media accounts.

Erika does that thing that you see in action movies, where one character storts speaking another character's CV to them. She goes, 'You studied Marine Biology in Trinity College – graduated first in your class. You did a Master's in Environmental and Natural Resources Law. Your research thesis was on the likely environmental benefits that would come from the extinction of cows and sheep.'

I'm thinking, I must rewatch all the *Jason Bourne* movies.

Simone's like, 'So?'

'But somewhere along the way – maybe in the Smurfit Business School – you were radicalized,' Erika goes. 'You got involved in the Shell to Sea protest and you were arrested, what was it, sixteen times? Then you hooked up with Extinction Rebellion. You took port in sit-in protests against fast fashion and you are banned under a High Court order from ever setting foot in Penneys again. A year later, you were convicted of a public order offence after attempting to disrupt a livestock sale in County Kildare. In the course of defending yourself, you attempted to read out your manifesto – which was essentially your Master's thesis. How am I doing?'

Simone goes, 'Sorcha knows all of that stuff about me. It's all in the public domain.'

'What's *not* in the public domain,' Erika goes, 'is what happened next. Because the girl who described herself in her Instagram bio as an Eco Terrorist suddenly went respectable.'

'Except she didn't stort *dressing* respectable,' I make sure to go, because she's wearing – I shit you not – a canary yellow, chunky sweater, black leggings and then Converse runner boots, odd ones, we're talking one red and one black. She has some focking nerve preaching to anyone about fashion – fast or otherwise.

'Let me guess what happened,' Erika goes. 'After you appeared in court, you got a call, probably from Hennessy Coghlan-O'Hara, who wanted to read your manifesto. Then he introduced you to the Taoiseach, who told you that he was interested in getting rid of sheep and cows too. Not only cows and sheep, but all agricultural activity. Which is something you agreed with. He told you to write a letter to Sorcha, as a fellow concerned environmentalist, suggesting what her policy priorities should be as Minister for Climate Action. He knew she was looking for a Special Adviser – and she was impressed by you.'

I'm there, 'She was actually in awe of her. Still is, by the way – as in, she won't hear a word said against her.'

'You gave her the idea of an outright ban on cows and sheep – and you reported everything back to the Taoiseach, through Hennessy. And you were more than happy to treat Sorcha as a useful idiot – until they torched the Dáil.'

Something random happens then. I notice Simone's eyes suddenly fill with tears.

Erika goes, 'Ross and I could both see it that night. You weren't expecting that. It was a step further than even you would have gone. I mean, this wasn't opening a paddock to free a herd of cattle at a livestock sale. This wasn't handcuffing yourself to a rail of tie-dye t-shirts in Penneys, O'Connell Street. This was burning down porliament. I mean, that's like treason, isn't it?'

Simone suddenly bursts into tears.

'I didn't know they were going to do it,' she tries to go. 'I swear.'

I'm there, 'Well, you can tell that to the Feds – right, Erika?'

'You have to believe me,' Simone goes – and she's seriously sobbing now. 'I had nothing to do with it.'

Erika's like, 'Here's what you're going to do, Sea-mon. You're going to tell Sorcha the truth.'

She's there, 'I can't.'

Erika goes, 'They're burning embassies out there, Sea-mon. You're going to tell Sorcha what they've been doing. And Sorcha is going to tell the world.'

'Okay,' she goes. 'Just give me a few days, will you?'

I'm like, 'A few days? Why do you need a few days?'

She goes, 'Because I'm going to need to make arrangements to get out of the country. I have a friend in Sweden. I can stay with him.'

I'm there, 'Why do you need to get out of the country?'

'Jesus Christ,' she goes, 'if they'd burn down Leinster House, do you think they'd think twice about getting rid of me?'

I suddenly feel a chill go down my spine. Erika must feel the same thing because we end up exchanging a look, as if to say – yeah, no, that's our old man she's talking about.

I haven't seen Fionn look this excited since Ciara Casaubon with the glasses and the hairy neck wart took his virginity on the night of his twenty-fourth birthday. I say it to him as well – as I'm pouring the boys their cereal.

I'm there, 'I haven't seen you this excited since, well, the mid-2000s.'

He goes, 'I feel like I've been waiting for this moment all my life.'

It was the same with Ciara Casaubon. He must have thought he was going to die without getting his V cord stamped.

I'm there, 'Fair – like I said – focks, Dude.'

Yeah, no, Castlerock reopens today with Fionn as Principal, and you can see that the dude is buzzing as he feeds little Hillary his mashed-up banana or whatever shit it is that he has the kid eating.

He goes, 'I want to bring in so many changes to the way the school is run. For instance, I'm going to set aside twenty per cent of places for non-fee-paying students from disadvantaged communities.'

I'm like, 'Jesus Christ!'

'What?'

'Twenty per cent? That sounds like a lot.'

'It is a lot. You know how serious I am about the idea of education for all.'

'And when you say disadvantaged communities, how disadvantaged are we talking? Do you mean, like, Cornelscourt and the likes?'

'No, I'm talking about *real* disadvantage, Ross.'

'Jesus, you're a better man than me, Dude. I think you could be letting yourself in for serious trouble. Leo, eat your focking Coco Pops, will you?'

Fionn goes, 'You didn't hear the news this morning, did you?'

I'm there, 'Dude, I never listen to the news. I make a point of it.'

'It's just they've discovered that the fire that destroyed the Oireachtas was storted deliberately.'

'I know that. I know who focking storted it.'

'Your old man is calling it an act of war. Jesus, Ross, how can Sorcha work for a man like that? No offence.'

'Don't worry, Dude, she's about to see the light. Me and Erika had a word with See-mon.'

'You mean Sea-mon?'

'I'm going to have to get my focking ears syringed, because it sounds like you're saying exactly the same thing as me.'

'So, what happened?'

'She admitted everything. She's going to tell Sorcha what the old man and Hennessy have been up to.'

'Well, they got their own way, didn't they? It looks like we're leaving the European Union. Which is going to be a disaster for this country, by the way.'

I'll have to take his word for it. For me, the EU was a bit like Heineken 0.0, in that I never saw the point of it in the first place.

My phone beeps. Muireann O'Connell has texted me to say that she got *the* most random voice message from me the other day – which she's just *listened* to? – and she's wondering how things were left with Delma and could I get her a discount on the Lincoln green lamp with the peacock-print shade in the window of her shop in Ranelagh.

The focking nerve of the girl. I reply and tell her I'll ask, though, because I've got a bit of a thing for her.

Fionn goes, 'Still, what can we do except teach the next generation to do better? Which is what I'm hoping to do. I just hope the Board of Management like my ideas.'

I'm like, 'Disadvantaged kids, though? Good luck with that.'

'It's not just disadvantaged kids. I also want to reduce the focus on preparing students for careers in Business and Law and offer more encouragement to those who are interested in the orts.'

I'm there, 'I don't hear much talk about rugby coming from your mouth, Dude. Are you going to enter a team into the Leinster Schools Senior Cup this year? It's a yes or no question.'

He smiles at me and pushes his glasses up on his nose with his finger.

He's there, 'Yes, I'm entering a team, Ross.'

I end up punching the air.

I'm like, 'Focking yes! And presumably you'll be wanting me to coach them?'

He's like, 'Er . . .' and I straight away pick up on, let's just say, a *vibe*?

I'm there, 'Dude, what the fock?'

He goes, 'I was thinking of maybe coaching them myself.'

I'm like, 'You?'

'Er, yeah.'

'And not me?'

'Well, no.'

'Even though I led Pres Bray to their first Leinster Schools Senior Cup win in nearly a hundred years? With you as my *Assistant* Coach, can I just remind you?'

'That's the thing, Ross, I got a real appetite for coaching from that time. Hey, I could use a good assistant.'

'Yeah, you're focking dreaming if you think I'm going to work under you.'

'Suit yourself. To be honest, I thought you'd be setting your sights higher anyway.'

'In terms of?'

'I'm just saying, you know, another Schools Cup team would be a sideways move, wouldn't it?'

'Well, in case you haven't noticed, Fionn, Leo Cullen isn't exactly knocking my focking door down.'

Honor walks into the kitchen then and storts fixing her breakfast.

Fionn goes, 'Well, what about the Ireland job? You know it's vacant at the moment?'

I end up nearly having a prolapse on the spot.

I'm like, 'What the *fock*? Has Joe Schmidt gone?'

He actually laughs.

'No,' he goes – and this is, like, word for word – 'I'm talking about the Ireland women's team.'

I'm there, 'The *women's* team?'

'Yeah,' he goes, 'they haven't been doing well the last two or three years. They could use someone with your knowledge and experience. Plus, it'd be a step up for you, Ross.'

I'm like, 'Yeah, I hordly focking think so. Dude, I actually laugh when I see them trying to play rugby. As a matter of fact, I sometimes watch clips of them on YouTube and I put the *Benny Hill* theme tune on at the same time.'

Suddenly, I notice that Honor is just, like, glowering at me. She's like, '*I* played rugby – remember?'

'And you were very good at it,' I try to go. 'As a matter of fact, you were every bit as good as the boys.'

'Yeah, you're a focking misogynist orsehole. *Iss ihre Coco Pops, boys. Machen sie ihren für die Schule fertig.*' Then she focks off upstairs.

Fionn shrugs his shoulders at me, picks up Hillary and says he's going to his sister's. Yeah, no, the famous Eleanor – been there more than once – is going to be minding him while Fionn is at work.

On his way out the door, he goes, 'You know, maybe you *should* apply for the job, Ross. It might teach you humility. It might even be a way of winning back your daughter's respect.'

And I'm like, 'What, by teaching women how to play rugby? Yeah, not a focking chance.'

I get a text message from – yeah, no – Oisinn, telling me that we're all meeting up in The Bridge 1859 tonight. He says he's not taking no for an answer because him and Magnus have news. I text him back to tell him I'll see him there, and he reminds me not to go to Kielys by accident.

I tip down the windy staircase, then I push the door into the study and I end up getting the fright of my actual life. Because Sorcha's old man is sitting there with his feet up on the desk and a big smile on his face.

He's like, 'How are you finding your new . . . *accommodation?*'

'The fock are you doing in my house?' I go.

Except he just ignores the question.

He goes, 'I put a gun to your head in this room – do you remember that?'

I'm there, 'It's not the kind of thing you forget in a hurry.'

'You did a shit – in your trousers.'

'That's because I thought you were going to pull the trigger.'

'Oh, there have been many, many times when I wish I did. What was that, fourteen, fifteen years ago? I'd be getting out of prison soon. Sorcha's mother always told me not to worry, that our daughter would one day see sense. And I'm happy that it's finally happened. I listened to your voice message.'

'It wasn't a voice message. It was a private conversation that got leaked.'

'Disgusting behaviour – but then, no worse than what we've come to expect of you.'

'There's worse than me out there. Ask your daughter about Josh Peasley.'

'What?'

'He played loosehead for King's Hos. Ask her specifically about what he used to do to his wife's shoes.'

'I didn't come here to listen to your wittering.'

'So why *did* you come – presumably, to gloat?'

'Yes, I did. Childish of me, isn't it? Naturally, my wife begged me not to, but I reminded her that I've waited a long time for this. I said, "I shall have my moment!"'

'Well, I hope it was worth the journey out here – now fock off.'

'It's a rather perverse twist to the fairytale, isn't it? That the tower in which Sorcha sat waiting for her prince to come should end up being the prison to which she banished him!'

'Well, just to let you know, I'm hoping to worm my way back in there. I've done it in the past.'

'Not this time, I'm delighted to say. She told her mother that whatever she once felt for you . . . is gone.'

'She's said that before.'

'Oh, this time she means it. She's getting on with her life. She has the political career that she always wanted.'

'Doing my old man's dirty work. Is that genuinely the future you wanted for her?'

'She's making her mork on the world – doing her bit to save the planet.'

'If you think her working for my old man is a good thing, then you're no kind of father.'

He laughs – except he does it in, like, a *sneering* way?

He's there, 'I did a darned sight better job raising my daughter than you did yours.'

I'm like, 'Daught-*ers*.'

'I beg your pardon?'

'You have two of them.'

Yeah, no, the other one – whatever she's called – is in Australia. A lesbian now, according to Sorcha, who hordly ever talks about her, and shacked up with some tattoo ortist called Rochelle.

It's obvious that he hates to be reminded.

'I'll go further,' he goes. 'I did a darned sight better job raising *both* my daughters than you did yours.'

I'm there, 'What's wrong with the way Honor turned out?'

He laughs again. It's very annoying.

'The girl is a sociopath,' he goes. 'She's completely lacking in human empathy and the most self-centred little bitch it's ever been my misfortune to know.'

In that moment, I end up suddenly snapping. I reach across the desk and I grab him by his lapels. He can see from my eyes that I've lost it and I can see from his that he's scared. I drag him across the desk towards me, then I swing him around and I slam him up against the oak-panelled wall.

I'm there, 'Don't you ever, EVER speak about my daughter like that again.'

He's there, 'Take your hands off me or I shall call the Gords!'

'Honor is worth ten of you,' I go. 'She's kind and thoughtful and sensitive and – yes, she *can* be a bitch at times – but if I ever, EVER hear you speak about her in that way again, I will focking kill you. And – unlike you – I would happily go to jail for the rest of my –'

Shit. I suddenly realize I have him down on the floor and my hands are around his throat. I'm pushing my two thumbs into his Adam's apple and he has a look of absolute terror on his face that I've never seen before.

I'm thinking, fock – am I really going to do this?

He's, like, choking. He's going, 'Stghtogh . . . Stghtogh . . . Stghtogh . . .' and he's pulling at my wrists, trying to loosen my grip, except I'm too strong for the dude.

But then the red mist suddenly lifts and I let go and climb off him. I throw open the study door – only to discover that Honor is standing outside in the hallway with her mouth wide open.

I realize that my entire body is shaking. I step past her without saying a word, then I open the front door, get into my cor and drive away.

I end up being twenty minutes late for Oisinn's drinks.

He's like, 'You went to Kielys, didn't you?'

I'm there, 'We all knew I would, Dude. We all knew I would. And I'm telling you, it broke my focking hort to see it all boarded up like that.'

Magnus goes, 'The shtory ish that the new ownersh are going to turn it into communal living apartmentsh.'

I'm like, 'Stop, Magnus. I can't even think about that. I still can't believe we had a chance to buy the place and we focking blew it.'

'Er, *you* focking blew it,' Oisinn goes.

I'm there, 'Dude, it wasn't my fault that a private conversation of mine ended up being sent to everyone's phone and I'm blue in the face saying it. And, by the way, I thought JP totally overreacted to what was said. He actually decked me – outside Cinnamon in Ranelagh.'

'Ross,' he goes, 'you had sex with his girlfriend.'

'Er, that was *before* she was his girlfriend? It was when she was just a mate of my old dear's.'

'You still should have told him.'

'A gentleman doesn't go around bragging about shit like that.'

I give Jamie Heaslip the nod and I go, 'Three pints, Dude.'

And he says the most unbelievable thing in reply. He goes, 'Pints of what?'

He might be one of my all-time rugby heroes, but the dude has a hell of a lot to learn about running a bor.

'Focking Heineken,' I go. 'Fock's sake.'

Oisinn's there, 'Dude, cool it – you're going to get us borred.'

I tell Jamie that I'm sorry.

'I think I'm still grieving for Kielys,' I go. 'Don't take it personally.'

He's like, 'Any more trouble out of you and you're getting thrown out.'

Which is fair enough.

Fionn suddenly shows up then and he's full of concern.

He's like, 'Ross, what happened in the house tonight?'

I'm there, 'What are you talking about?'

'Sorcha said there was an incident – between you and her father.'

Oh, fock – I don't know why I thought the focker wouldn't tell her.

I'm there, 'I'm racking my brains here, Fionn, as to what that might be about.'

He goes, 'She said you tried to strangle him.'

'What?' Oisinn goes.

I'm there, 'Yeah, no, he was dissing my daughter and I ended up just losing my shit. Let's be honest, it's been building up for years. Anyway, how was your first day in Castlerock?'

Fionn's face lights up – the proverbial dog with six mickeys.

'Brilliant,' he goes, pushing his glasses up on his nose. 'I actually had a meeting with the Board of Management this afternoon and I made my presentation to them about setting aside twenty per cent of school places for children from disadvantaged areas.'

'Twenty per cent?' Oisinn goes. 'Does that not sound like a lot?'

I'm like, 'That's exactly what I said – word for word.'

'It *is* a lot,' Fionn goes. 'My philosophy has always been that social disadvantage shouldn't be a barrier to receiving a good education.'

Father Fehily would be spinning in his grave to hear him talk like this. As usual, I decide to say nothing, though.

'How disadvantaged are we talking?' Oisinn goes.

And I'm like, 'Very – right, Fionn?'

'Yes, very,' he agrees.

It's at that exact point that Christian and JP decide to show their faces – focking miserable faces as well. You'd never know from looking at them that they're richer than the Collison brothers.

I turn to Jamie and I go, 'Pint for Fionn, pint for JP and a Diet focking Coke for Christian there.'

JP – without even looking at me – goes, 'No, thanks, we'll get our own.'

I'm there, 'Dude, I'm prepared to let bygones be bygones if you are – and I'm saying that even though you left me in a heap outside Cinnamon.'

He goes, 'Me and Delma had something special.'

I'm like, 'Hey, you knew she had a past. She's in her focking sixties. Divorced for *how* many years? *And* no stranger to Vanilla on Morehampton Road, by the way. You need to put it behind you.'

'Yeah, that's not why we broke up, Ross. It was you opening your mouth about her Hermès scorf.'

Yeah, no, he's talking about the one he stole from the coat-stand in our hallway when we were, like, *sixteen*? The one he brought to Irish college that summer. The one that smelled of her perfume. The one he used to stuff into his mouth every night before pulling himself blind in the bunk below mine.

Yeah, no, I may have mentioned all of this in my famous conversation with Fionn.

I'm there, 'Dude, all I can do is keep repeating that it was a private chat between me and Fionn – and Delma wasn't supposed to hear it. And, by the way, if you're talking to her, Muireann O'Connell is very interested in a lamp she's got in her window – although she won't pay the full mork-up price for it.'

'I'm not likely to be talking to her,' he goes, 'given that she thinks I'm a focking pervert.'

'In fairness, you kind of *were*, Dude. You used to be saying her name in your sleep.'

'Fock you, Ross.'

I turn to Christian and I'm there, 'And what's *your* problem with me?'

'What you said about Lychee,' he goes – as in, Lychee, his twenty-two-year-old influencer girlfriend.

I'm like, 'What did I say about Lychee?'

'You said she was an airhead,' he goes.

I'm there, 'She *is* a focking airhead. Take it from me. One airhead knows another.'

Magnus tries to take the heat out of the situation then by changing the subject.

'Sho, guysh,' he goes, 'you are posshibly wondering why we ashked to meet you here tonight.'

I'm like, 'Yeah, no, what's the story?'

He looks at Oisinn then. He's there, 'Do you want to tell them or will I?'

Oisinn ends up just blurting it out. He's there, 'We're hoping to have a baby!'

I'm like, 'Er, you *what* now?'

'A baby,' Magnus goes. 'I'm shorry, I cannot shtop shmiling every time I shay it.'

Fionn's there, 'Are you talking about going the foreign adoption route?' because he's obviously a lot quicker on the uptake than me.

'Yeah,' Oisinn goes, 'we've made contact with an agency in El Salvador.'

I'm there, 'And that's an actual country, is it?'

'Yesh,' Magnus goes, 'it'sh an actual country, Rosh.'

I'm there, 'It's just it doesn't sound like one. I don't want to see you ripped off.'

'Thanks for your concern,' Oisinn goes, which is a nice thing for me to hear. 'Anyway, we're going over there before Christmas. And hopefully we're going to be coming back with a little baby.'

I'm there, 'Fair focks,' because they're the only two here who haven't done the whole fatherhood thing. 'I genuinely, genuinely mean that,' and there ends up being high-fives, bear hugs and – I'm not going to lie – chest-bumps.

So that, basically, should be that. We're settling in for the night – three pints down the freeway to Monged Out, Minnesota – when all of a sudden who shows up in *my* new local only K . . . K . . . K . . . Kennet with Shadden in tow.

She's the one who ends up doing most of the talking.

She's like, 'C'mere to me, you!'

Yeah, no, that's her ice-breaker.

I'm like, 'Alright, Shadden? What's the story?'

She goes, 'What's the stordee? The stordee is my husband is arthur abandodden me – and you bleaten encoudaged him.'

I'm there, 'He's hordly abandoned you, Shadden. He's gone to New York to take up the internship of a lifetime – and he wants you to, like, join him over there,' and I somehow resist the temptation to go, 'God knows focking why!'

She goes, 'I doatunt want to lib in bleaten New York!' and of course *he* decides to stick his ample hooter into the conversation then.

He's like, 'You c . . . c . . . c . . . caddent moowuv to M . . . M . . . M . . . Medica, Shadden. You'd lose all yisser b . . . b . . . b . . . b . . . b . . . bedefits.'

Seriously, how the fock did my son get mixed up with these people?

Shadden sticks her finger practically in my face then and goes,

'You teddle that fooker from me that if he dudn't come howum, eer maddidge is oaber.'

I'm like, 'Tell him your focking self.'

'What koyunt of a madden turdens he's back on he's famidy,' she goes, 'and leabs them wirrout a peddy to their nayum?'

'For fock's sake,' I go, 'you're living in my old pair's gaff in Foxrock – rent-focking-free, by the way.'

'Shadden's m . . . m . . . m . . . m . . . miserdobble,' Kennet goes. 'You hab to remember, Rosser, that F . . . F . . . F . . . F . . . Foxrock is veddy far away from F . . . F . . . F . . . F . . . Finglas.'

'Yeah,' I go, 'that was the idea of putting it where they did.'

Shadden's there, 'And Ine woodied about pooer Ri. I see the diffordence in her evoddy day. Her accent's arthur turdening all posh, so it has – especiaddy hagging out with that fooken sister of yooers, the one has the snoppy accent.'

I end up instantly losing it with her. I'm there, 'I have no idea why Ronan would want you over there with him. But don't worry – give him another couple of weeks and he'll be riding all around him. Guaranteed.'

'You fooken ted him,' she goes, her finger in my face again, 'eeder he comes howum or eer maddidge is oaber.'

The bouncers arrive and they tell Shadden and Kennet that they're going to have to leave.

'D . . . D . . . D . . . Doatunt woody,' Kennet goes, 'we're leabon,' and then off the two of them fock.

And that's when Jamie Heaslip is like, 'I'm sorry, Ross, I'm going to have to ask you to leave as well.'

I'm there, 'Me? The fock did I do?'

'I don't know what sort of stuff you got away with in Kielys –'

'All sorts, Dude.'

'– but it's not going to be happening here.'

'You're genuinely focking us out?'

'No, Ross, just you.'

'What, even though I'm on the record as saying that you were the best Irish number eight of the past thirty years and one of the ten players I would most liked to have played alongside?'

'Yes, Ross, even though all of that.'

I'm like, 'Cool, so – come on, goys, let's see will Crowes take our money.'

But Christian and JP again don't stir.

I'm like, 'Goys, what the fock?'

JP's there, 'I'm happy here, Ross.'

I look at Oisinn and Magnus.

Oisinn goes, 'We're actually going to head off pretty soon. We're ringing Magnus's parents in the morning to tell them the news.'

I look at Fionn. He goes to give me his excuse, but I go, 'Do you know what? Don't even bother.'

I hail a taxi and I go back to Honalee. On the way there, I get a text from George Hook to say that he got a strange message from me the other day and I should check that my phone hasn't been hacked.

I let myself into the gaff. Sorcha is waiting for me in the hallway.

She goes, 'Oh my God, Ross! What? The? FOCK?'

I'm there, 'In reference to specifically what?' because I want to make sure I don't apologize for something she doesn't know about yet.

'You tried to strangle my dad!' she goes.

And I'm there, 'Oh – that,' like it's not a major deal.

'He has finger morks on his neck,' she goes.

I'm there, 'Hey, he said some shit about Honor and I will not listen to anyone speak about her like that.'

Sorcha doesn't even bother asking me what the dude said. She just goes, 'He wanted to press chorges, Ross. The only reason he didn't phone the Gords was because I told him the scandal would overshadow the EU withdrawal negotiations.'

I'm there, 'Oh, right – good luck with that, by the way.'

'What's that supposed to mean?'

'Yeah, no, nothing. Have you spoken to See-mon lately?'

'Sea-mon? No, she's phoned in sick the last few days. You know, I don't think Level 5 Veganism suits her.'

The girl is obviously getting ready to flee the country.

I'm there, 'Just tell your old man that if I ever hear him talk about Honor like that again, I *will* finish the focking job.'

With that, I turn my back on her. Ten seconds later, I'm making my way back up the cold, winding stairwell to the top of the tower.

But when I reach my new bedroom, I discover that something has changed. There's, like, a Dyson blow-heater in there and three or four humane mousetraps. I stand there just, like, staring at them for a good, like, thirty seconds and then – being honest – a tear suddenly slips from my eye.

I make my way over to the window and I look out. I stare down at Honor's bedroom and she suddenly appears in the window.

I mouth the words, 'Thank you,' to her.

And she just smiles at me, then she turns her back on me and goes to presumably bed.

2.

Moo Romance

'Yeah, no, thanks,' I go – this is over, like, breakfast the next *morning*?

Honor just shrugs.

She's like, 'Whatever.'

And I'm there, 'There's no whatever about it, Honor, so don't even try to, like, shrug it off. It was really, like, *thoughtful* and shit? I was so cosy in my sleeping bag last night. And, hey, look!' I hold up the humane trap with the little mouse inside. 'Caught the little focker.'

'Ich will die Maus zu morden!' Leo goes, making a grab for it with a seriously vicious face on him. *'Ich will die focking Maus morden!'*

I probably should insist on them speaking English in the house, but there's a port of me that's happy not to know the shit that comes out of their mouths half the time.

'Nein,' Honor goes, in a voice obviously intended to calm him down, *'morden die Maus nicht. Sie ist eine schöne Maus!'*

I'm there, 'Is that what I think it's about?'

She goes, 'He wants to eat it.'

See what I mean? I know this sounds possibly bad, but I'm happy to let Honor parent them from here on in and use the language barrier as an excuse for staying the fock out of it.

I'm there, 'Yeah, no, I got the gist of that from his tone. Anyway, I just want you to know that I really appreciated it, Honor. The Dyson heater. The mousetraps.'

She's like, 'You stood up for me – to that focking arsehole.'

'Ficken Arschloch!' Brian goes. *'Ficken, ficken Arschloch!'*

'When you walked out of the room,' Honor goes, 'I honestly hoped you'd killed him.'

I'm there, 'Came very close, Honor – came *very* focking close.'

She goes, 'I would have helped you dig a hole in the gorden to bury him.'

See, that's how *sweet* she can sometimes be?

I'm there, 'I was wondering, do you think me and you could go back to being friends again?'

She stares at me for a long time, then she shrugs again and goes, 'Maybe.'

I'm like, 'Maybe?' and my hort literally leaps in my chest. 'I'll take that maybe, Honor.'

'*Ich will die Maus zu morden!*' Leo goes, making another grab for the thing.

I'm there, 'I'd better release this little goy in the gorden before this bloodthirsty fockwit kills him.'

'Er, just before you do,' Honor goes, reaching into her schoolbag, 'this came for Mom yesterday,' and she whips out a brown envelope, which she hands to me.

I notice straight away that it's already been opened.

I'm there, 'What is it? Do I even *want* to know?'

'It's a notice to say that she's been banned from driving,' she goes. 'She hasn't seen it yet. I covered for you.'

I'm like, 'Oh, thank you, Honor!' hearing the relief in my voice. 'Thank you! Thank you! Thank you!' and then about ten seconds later, I go, 'Hang on, what do you mean, you covered for *me*?'

She's there, 'Er, because you were the one driving her cor when she *got* the penalty points?'

I'm like, 'Oh, fock! When *was* this?'

'About a month ago,' she goes. 'In Kilmacanogue. You were driving at 138 kilometres per hour in a sixty zone.'

'Yeah, no, that sounds like me alright. I'll have to ring them and tell them that it was me, not Sorcha, driving the cor that day.'

'Er, you *can't*?'

'Why not?'

'Because *you're* already *on* nine points? It would mean that *you'd* lose *your* licence.'

'But I *can't* lose my licence. I need the cor to drive you and these three fockwits to school.'

'*Ficken Arschloch!*' Brian goes. '*Ficken, focking Arschloch!*'

Honor's there, 'That's why I hid it from her.'

'Yeah, no, fair focks,' I go, 'but I can't *not* tell her that she's banned from driving.'

'Why not? She doesn't use her cor any more. She has, like, a *chauffeur*, remember?'

'Kennet – of course! How could I f . . . f . . . f . . . f . . . f . . . forget!'

'*Ficken ficken fick fick!*' Leo goes.

'So say nothing,' she goes. 'In twelve months, she'll get her licence back and she'll never know she lost it.'

I'm there, 'Honor, you're an absolute genius!' and it feels so good to have her back on my side again.

All of a sudden, Sorcha steps into the kitchen and I quickly stuff the letter into my pocket.

She's like, 'What are you two acting all conspiratorial about?'

I'm there, 'Er, nothing.'

Honor goes, 'Dad caught a mouse. I'm just going to take him out to the gorden and let him go.'

Sorcha's there, 'After that, go upstairs and get ready for school.'

Honor's like, 'Come on, boys,' and she takes the trap off me and leads Brian, Johnny and Leo out into the hallway. 'No, Brian, we're not going to eat him. We're going to let him go.'

I'm about to ask Sorcha what she's doing today when Honor suddenly shouts back into the gaff, 'Mom, Sea-mon is outside!'

'Sea-mon?' Sorcha goes. 'Oh my God, tell her to come in!'

Yeah, no, five seconds later, she walks into the kitchen. She looks in bits – and for once I'm not talking about the way she's dressed, although I will say that I've already got a focking headache looking at the girl.

Sorcha's there, 'Oh my God, what a lovely surprise!' but then she picks up on the fact that something is wrong. 'Sea-mon, you look awful. I really admire you for your commitment to veganism, but sometimes I wish you'd eat something that's even, like, animal-*derived*?'

'I've come to give you my resignation,' the girl goes.

Sorcha's like, 'Your resignation? Sea-mon, this is like, Oh! My God!'

'And to tell you something – something that you might not want to hear.'

'Sea-mon, you're frightening me now.'

'The EU didn't burn down the Dáil, Sorcha. Hennessy did it – and he did it on the Taoiseach's instructions.'

Sorcha's face turns instantly white. For a second, I think she's about to faint, then she reaches for one of the breakfast stools and manages to pork her orse on it.

Simone goes, 'Raoul Trappaniers was right. He did it to influence the outcome of the referendum.'

I'm there, 'In fairness, I said it before Raoul whatever-the-fock.'

There's, like, silence for a good, I don't know, thirty seconds, then Sorcha goes, 'Sea-mon, why are you saying this – and just as we're about to embork on my programme to achieve corbon neutrality by reducing the national herd to zero?'

Simone's there, 'It's not *your* programme, Sorcha. It never was.'

'*Excuse* me?'

'I'm just making the point that *I* came to *you* with the idea of getting rid of sheep and cows.'

'I'm sorry to disappoint you, Sea-mon, but I actually said it during the course of a debate hosted by the UCD Law Society – oh my God, twenty *years* ago? Ross, you were there.'

'Sorcha, I put the idea in your head.'

'Er, no, you didn't. Okay, I'm going to find out did someone record the debate.'

I'm like, 'Goys, I think we're getting off the point here. Sorcha, are you listening to what See-mon is saying?'

But Sorcha goes, 'Yes, but I'm more interested in *why* she's saying it?'

I'm there, 'What are you talking about?'

Sorcha's like, 'Well, I know you and Erika have your reasons for being angry with Chorles. But I'm wondering what Sea-mon's motivation is. Perhaps it's jealousy?'

'Jealousy?' Simone goes.

'Yes, jealousy. That I'm the Minister for Climate Action and you're just . . . an adviser.'

'That's bullshit.'

'Is it? You're not the teeniest bit envious that *I'm* the one who's being credited with – oh my God – *the* most radical plan ever undertaken to try to reduce greenhouse gases?'

'You're being used, Sorcha. I used you. They're using you. You're just a useful idiot.'

Sorcha goes, 'Get out of my house.'

I'm like, 'Sorcha, please, just listen to the girl.'

But then Sorcha just roars it. She's like, 'I SAID GET OUT!'

Simone sort of, like, shit-smiles her.

'Oh, I'm getting out,' she goes. 'I'm getting out of the country. That's how scared I am of these people.'

Sea-mon turns and heads for the door. She looks at me and goes, 'Hey, I tried.'

Sorcha goes, 'And I don't accept your resignation – because you're actually *fired*?'

Off the girl focks.

Sorcha goes, 'Jealous bitch.'

I'm there, 'Sorcha –'

'You put her up to it, didn't you? You told her to come here.'

'We just wanted you to hear it from –'

'*We?* You mean you and Erika?'

'Yes, me and Erika. Sorcha, my old man burned the focking building down. You've heard it from Ronan, from me, from Erika – and now from See-mon.'

'Do you really hate me having a career that much, Ross?'

'Sorcha, you're in denial.'

'You're the one who's in denial. It's like my dad said to me the night you tried to strangle him – you just hate that it's not about you any more.'

'Sorcha –'

'I've found something, Ross, that I was – oh my God – born to do. And all you want to do is take it away from me.'

'Sorcha –'

'Well, it's not going to happen.'

I end up just giving up. I'm there, 'Fine,' and I turn to walk out of the room.

'What's that sticking out of your back pocket?' she goes.

And I'm like, 'Nothing,' because if she's not in the mood to hear the truth about my old man, she's definitely not in the mood to hear that I've managed to get her banned from driving.

So I've dropped the kids off at school and I'm driving home the long way through Ranelagh when Erika decides to finally return my call.

I'm like, 'Hey, Babes – how the hell are you?'

She goes, 'What do you want, Ross?'

'I thought you might like to know that See-mon – or however you say it – called into the gaff this morning to see Sorcha.'

'Why didn't you focking tell me?'

'Er, I've tried to phone you, like, three times.'

'And did she tell her?'

'She tried. But Sorcha didn't want to hear it.'

'What?'

'She accused her of being jealous of her – because Sorcha was getting all the kudos for the whole banning cows and sheep thing.'

'Jesus Christ.'

'Then she accused *me* of being jealous because she has a career. I think the whole power thing has gone to her head, Erika.'

'Have you listened to the news today?'

'What is everyone's obsession with me listening to the news?'

'Rute Sobrinho–'

'Okay, I don't even know who that is.'

'She's the Portuguese Minister for Foreign Affairs. She wants an independent agency to carry out a forensic investigation into the fire.'

'I'm guessing the old man told her to fock off?'

'Words to that effect. We need to keep pushing this. I'm going to talk to her.'

'Who, Sorcha?'

'No, Sorcha's not going to listen. I'm going to try to persuade Sea-mon to go public.'

'Didn't she say she was going to move to, like, Sweden?'

'I'll have to get to her before she goes.'

Then she hangs up on me.

About sixty seconds later, it just so happens that I'm driving past Taste of Décor – in other words, Delma's interiors and soft furnishings shop – and I spot the woman herself in the window. Without indicating, I pull the wheel to the left and swing into a porking space opposite McSorley's. Some dude behind me in a Honda focking Brio gives me a beep and a filthy look as he passes.

Delma is just inside the door. She's bending down to fluff some cushions. Her short cordigan is riding up and there's a sliver of white knicker visible over the waistband of her trousers, which I do my best not to stare at, although it's obviously easier said than done.

'Delma,' I go, 'how the hell are you?'

She stands up. I've definitely stortled her, because she puts her hand to her chest.

'What do *you* want?' she goes – not happy with me.

She looks well. She has the usual sunnies on her head and she's had her hair cut in a bob that makes her look, I don't know, fifty-something.

I'm there, 'I was just passing and I thought I'd pop in and say hello – nice to be nice.'

She goes, 'I'm very busy,' giving me big-time hostile vibes.

I'm there, 'I also wanted to put in a word for JP.'

She laughs in a really, like, *bitter* way? The woman's already been through a pretty nasty divorce and her ex-husband – a prize prick of the highest order – is just about to become a father again at the age of seventy. It'd be a miracle if she *wasn't* cynical when it comes to men?

I'm there, 'He loves you, Delma.'

She's like, 'Love?' like even the idea of it is totally ridiculous. 'I'm just some twisted sexual fantasy he had as a teenager.'

'Look, he was just obsessed with you, Delma. Can I tell you something nice? He used to call to our gaff when he knew you were going to be there. He'd take your wine glass or your coffee cup out of the dishwasher and lick the rim where your mouth had been.'

'What?' she goes – it obviously didn't sound as romantic as it did in my head.

I'm there, 'I'm just saying that he was mad about you – even then.'

'He stole my Hermès scorf,' she goes, 'to do God knows *what* unspeakable things with it.'

I'm guessing she doesn't want a list.

'He was, like, fifteen years old,' I go. 'As someone who raised two kids, I thought you would have known about hormones.'

'He had a bag full of women's underwear. He wasn't fifteen years old when he collected those. Knickers and bras belonging to all his . . . *conquests.*'

'I wouldn't call them that. JP's standards were never that high – and that's no offence to you.'

'I feel sick to my stomach when I think about it.'

'Would you not maybe give him a second chance – to show you that he's, like, *changed* and shit?'

'No, I won't. If this episode has reminded me of anything, it's the age difference between us. It could never work – especially because his emotional age is still fifteen.'

I decide to put it all out there then.

I'm there, 'Delma, I've known JP for a long, long time. I've seen him with a lot of girls over the years – like I said, not many of them great in terms of looks. But I have never, *ever* seen him the way he's been since he got it on with you. The dude's in love – slash, lust.'

She sort of, like, huffs to herself, then opens the door wide and goes, 'If you don't mind, Ross, I have a business to run.'

I notice the Lincoln green lamp with the peacock-print shade that Muireann O'Connell has her eye one. Five hundred snots? It's no wonder she's looking for a few bob off it.

I'm there, 'Just think about what I said, Delma. Do you want your scorf back, by the way? I would definitely get it dry-cleaned if the answer is yes.'

And she's like, 'Get out!' while literally manhandling me through the door and out onto the street.

So – yeah, no – I'm walking back to the cor, my good deed done for the day, when all of a sudden my phone rings again. I'm expecting it to be Erika with news about possibly Simone, but it ends up being a man on the other end of the line.

He goes, 'Is this Ross O'Carroll-Kelly?'

And I'm like, 'That depends who's asking,' which is the answer Hennessy advised me to *always* give?

I'm a man with a colourful past.

'Verner Ryan,' he goes – he sounds like an old fort. 'I'm the IRFU Director of Excellence for Sevens and Women's Rugby.'

I'm like, 'Er, continue.'

He goes, 'I just wanted to confirm that we were very excited to receive your application for the post of Head Coach of the Ireland women's team. We'll be in touch in the next day or two about setting up an interview.'

Which is all well and good – except for the fact that I don't remember sending in an application.

So – yeah, no – mystery solved. It turns out that it was Honor who sent my CV to the IRFU. She tells me over the phone as I'm pulling into the driveway of the house.

She's there, 'It was me – so focking what?'

And I'm like, 'Honor, it was a very nice thing to do, but I'm not a hundred per cent sure I'd be suitable for the job.'

'Why not?' she goes.

I'm there, 'Because –'

'Because it's women?' she goes.

And I'm like, 'No.'

Meaning yes.

'You're such a focking orsehole,' she goes.

I'm there, 'Honor, I want to coach *actual* Ireland one day. This won't exactly enhance my CV.'

'Why not?'

'Because that's just the way the world works, Honor. I'd be better off looking for a job in the All Ireland League and using that to try to worm my way into the Leinster set-up.'

'It's just that they're doing really badly at the moment.'

'Who?'

'The women's team. I was reading about it. They haven't won a match in, like, three *years* or something?'

'And you want to wish that on me?'

'Well, you're the one who's always saying that you're this amazing, amazing rugby coach and you could turn any team into a team of winners.'

In the background, I hear a woman's voice go, 'Honor! O'Carroll! Kelly! What were you told about using your phone in class?'

Honor's there, 'Yeah, I'm trying to talk to my focking therapist here – or do you not *care* that I have mental health issues?'

I'm there, 'What class are you in?'

'Maths,' she goes. 'Miss Prenter. She's a stupid focker – like you.'

I'm like, 'Honor, please don't be like that.'

'You're a focking misogynist.'

'I'm hopefully not.'

'Well, you *actually* are. You think women are inferior. I'm hanging up on you now.'

'Honor, please don't. Okay, look, I'll go for the interview, okay?'

'Really?'

I'm there, 'Yeah, no, what's the horm? They're going to ring me with a time and a date. I'll sit the interview, okay?'

She's like, 'Okay, fine.'

In the background, I hear Miss Prenter go, 'Honor, hang up that phone this instant!'

And Honor goes, 'Yeah, swivel on this, you stupid focking cow,' and then she's like, 'Dad, I have to go,' and then – yeah, no – she hangs up.

Miss Prenter might not agree with me, but Honor is such an amazing kid. And it's nice that she believes in me to that degree, and I possibly owe it to her to at least sit the interview, even if I am going to fock it up on purpose.

As I'm getting out of the cor, I notice the old man's black stretch limo porked in front of the house with his driver sitting behind the wheel.

I let myself into the gaff and I can hear his big foghorn voice coming from the study. He's going, 'Don't let it upset you, Minister! You'll find another Special Adviser!'

Yeah, no, he's obviously talking to Sorcha.

'She said you were using me to try to destroy rural Ireland,' she goes. 'She said that you and Hennessy burned down the Dáil yourselves to try to – oh my God – influence the outcome of the referendum.'

'Oh, come on, Sorcha! How likely does any of that sound? No, she's just parroting what she's heard from our friend, the inestimable Monsieur Trappaniers! Bloody Belgium! We're all supposed to weep over their embassy when it's not even a proper country!'

'But why would she all of a sudden come out with this stuff?'

'Isn't it obvious? They've gotten to her!'

'Who?'

'The EU, of course! The same people who burned our national porliament to the ground! You don't think they're above placing *agents provocateurs* amongst us – pordon the French?'

'I thought it might have been just, like, *jealousy*?'

'Well, it could be that too!'

'She tried to say that reducing Ireland's national herd to zero was, like, *her* idea? I actually said it at a UCD Law Society debate when I was in, like, second year in college.'

'Minister, this Government is on the threshold of achieving something that no one thought possible! We are taking back our sovereignty and we are forming new trading relationships outside of the European Union! At the same time, Minister, *you* are demonstrating that it *is* possible to reduce our corbon footprint and reverse the effects of – quote-unquote – climate change!'

'I just can't believe she tried to say it was her idea.'

'You know, Sorcha, in all my conversations with other world leaders, it's your name that comes up time and time again!'

'Is it?'

'When I speak to the White House, the Kremlin, even our pals over

54

there in Red China, they all want to talk about this daughter-in-law of mine who is showing the rest of the world how we can save the planet!'

'That's, like, oh my God!'

'It's no wonder so many people want you to fail! They fear you, Sorcha!'

'Do they?'

He's there, 'Of course they do! That's why I want to formally ask if you would be port of the team that will negotiate the terms of Ireland's withdrawal from the European Union?'

'Oh my God!' she goes. 'Yes, Taoiseach! Oh my God, *so* yes!'

'Excellent! Hennessy and I shall enjoy working with you over the coming months as we extricate ourselves from this unholy political union!'

'And what about the fire, Chorles? Rute Sobrinho is calling for us to bring in independent investigators – possibly even the FBI – to find out who was behind it.'

'Well, I can't imagine the Portuguese police are much cop, but I for one have full confidence in the ability of An Gorda Síochána to investigate all of the circumstances surrounding the fire and bring those responsible to justice!'

So it's a few days later and I'm flirting with one of the girls in the Country Bake. Yeah, no, I'm doing my usual thing where I go to pay for my latte and my custard slice and then, when she goes to take the money from me, I quickly whip it away. And I don't do this once – I do it, like, six or *seven* times? They seem to get a kick out of it, even after all these years.

I'm finally handing over the money for real when my *phone* all of a sudden rings? It's, like, Tina – calling me for the tenth time this week. I decide to just answer the thing this time.

Big mistake. She storts screaming down the phone at me.

She's there, 'I AM GOING TO FOOKING MOORDER YOU!'

I'm like, 'Tina, will you cool the jets?' and I give the girl behind the counter a little wink as she hands me my change, then I drop a yoyo in the tip jor and I make sure she sees it as well.

'YOU KIDDLED THAT MADDEN!' Tina goes.

Jesus, between her and Shadden! I love my son very much, but there are days when I seriously regret not bagging it up before I had sex with this woman.

'Tina,' I go, 'I didn't kill anyone. The dude had a hort attack, which admittedly I may have caused.'

I've no idea what the customers in the Country Bake are making of this conversation, by the way, but I'd be shocked if it doesn't end up on the Dalkey Open Forum.

She goes, 'I WANT TO MEET YOU!'

I'm there, 'I'm not meeting you, Tina – not when you're in this kind of form.'

She goes, 'THEN I'LL HAB TO CUB LOOKING FOR YOU!'

And I'm like, 'Yeah, good luck with that,' and I hang up on her.

I give the girls the guns – then I blow on the tops of my fingers, because they seem to love that – and I step outside. I'm walking up Dalkey main street, in cracking form, when I'm greeted by a sight that stops me dead in my *literally* tracks? Sorcha is coming down the road in her Volvo XC40.

Oh, holy focking shit!

I end up quite literally throwing myself at her cor, waving my orms and going, 'Stop! Stop! Stop!'

She slams on the brake and she's like, 'Oh! My God! Ross, what the fock are you doing?'

I'm there, 'I could ask you the same thing,' talking to her through the front windscreen, my two hands resting on the bonnet. 'Er, why the fock are you driving your own cor?'

She goes, 'Kennet phoned in sick this morning. Well, hungover. The Dublin footballers were bringing the Sam Maguire Shield to the Broken Orms last night.'

'So, like, where are you driving to?'

'I have to be in Clonmellon for a photo call at eleven a.m.'

'Clonmellon? Where do they come up with these names? Where even is it?'

'It's in Westmeath. Ross, will you get out of the focking way?' she goes, then she presses down on the horn.

'Look,' I go, 'the thing is, Sorcha, well – you *can't* drive.'

56

She's like, 'Excuse me?'

'What I mean is – yeah, no – you're an *actual* Government minister. How's it going to look if you're driving yourself around the place?'

'Well, what choice do I have? The programme to sterilize ruminant animals is storting this morning – as the Minister for Climate Action, I'm expected to be there.'

I'm there, 'I'll drive you,' having one of my sudden brainwaves.

She's like, 'You?' and I can tell that she doesn't instantly *hate* the idea? 'Well, I do have my speech to think about. With Sea-mon gone, I have to write it myself.'

I'm like, 'There you are, then!' opening the driver's door for her and letting her out.

She goes, 'But I don't want you going on about your dad and the fire, okay?'

I'm like, 'I won't. I promise.'

So – yeah, no – she gets into the back of the cor and I hop in behind the wheel, then off we set – her with her nose in her laptop, hammering away at the keys.

After, like, twenty minutes, she looks up and goes, 'I want to emphasize to formers that the sterilization programme is entirely optional and we hope there'll be a big take-up of it before we have to make it compulsory.'

And I'm like, 'Er, cool,' even though I think she's actually talking to herself more than me. 'That definitely sounds like the way to go alright.'

We're on the M50, about to take the turn-off for Navan, when my phone rings again. I make sure that it's not Tina, then I answer on speaker phone.

I'm like, 'You've got Ross.'

It ends up being a woman from the IRFU telling me that my interview will be at ten o'clock on Monday morning.

I'm like, 'Er, yeah, no, that works. I'll see you then.'

I'm there, 'I don't know if you heard that, Sorcha, but the IRFU are pretty keen to talk to me about the job of Head Coach of the Ireland team, albeit women.'

There was a time when a line like that would have ruffled her truffles. She gives me nothing back, though. If me being involved in rugby again doesn't do it for her, then maybe our marriage really *is* over?

We eventually arrive in – I'm still laughing – Clonmellon.

Using the satnav on her phone, Sorcha directs me down a country lane, then up a boreen to a collection of what look – to these South Dublin eyes – like *cow* sheds? Of course, it could be someone's focking house for all I know about Westmeath and what the people get up to here.

There's, like, a little huddle of people waiting for us. The usual faces. I spot the famous Richard Chambers and then Samantha Libreri, who I have a major thing for, and I suspect the feeling is mutual because she always smiles at me for two or three seconds longer than someone who's just being friendly.

I get out of the cor and then – ever the pro – I open the back door for Sorcha. The questions stort the second she swings her trousered leg out of the cor.

'Minister,' Richard Chambers goes, 'what do you make of Rute Sobrinho's call for an independent body – possibly even the FBI – to investigate the arson attack on the Oireachtas?'

Sorcha smiles. She's like, 'Oh, I thought you came here today to find out about the important work the Government is doing to phase out ruminant animals, Richard, in line with our commitment to achieve corbon neutrality by 2025,' except she says it in, like, a *flirty* way?

Samantha Libreri goes, 'Does the Government have something to hide, Minister?'

Sorcha just shit-smiles her. She knows all about my fixation with the girl, bear in mind. She's there, 'The Taoiseach has made the Government's position clear. He has full confidence in the ability of An Gorda Síochána to investigate all of the circumstances surrounding the fire and bring those responsible to justice.'

Samantha goes, 'Minister, is it true that your Special Adviser has quit her post?'

Sorcha's there, 'I'm not here to discuss private staffing matters with you, Samantha. I'm here to demonstrate how, with just one simple act, our country can lead the way when it comes to reversing *climate* change?'

All of a sudden, some tall dude in a suit and glasses tips over to us.

'Sean Urch,' he goes, introducing himself. 'I'm the local vet,' and then he points at some old dude standing beside him, wearing – I shit you not – a jumper with Christmas trees and snowflakes on it, even though it's only September. Oh – yeah, no – he also has *the* worst attempt at a combover that I've ever seen. 'And this is Jerome. This is his farm.'

Sorcha extends her hand to him like Meghan focking Morkle meeting the in-laws for the first time.

'Pleased to meet you,' she goes, totally overdoing it on the false-ness front.

This Jerome dude grabs her hand and pulls her towards him like he's helping her off a rocking boat.

He's there, 'Come here to me, you. I'm a big fan of your father-in-law.'

'Oh, I'm glad to hear it,' Sorcha tries to go. 'I really do believe he's a sincere politician who genuinely wants the *best* for our country?'

He's there, 'I fooken love the way he hates the people of Cork. The people of Cork is fooken pricks – fooken pricks of the highest echelons. Am I right or am I right?'

She's there, 'Well, I'm not really sure if that's the porty's *actual* position.'

'And women drivers,' he goes – and I'm thinking, whoa, you're sailing close to the wind there, Dude. 'I'd no more get into a car with a woman intending to drive than I'd marry a fooken crow from the fields. A law unto themselves and a fooken danger to every other fooker on the road. Am I right or am I right?'

Sorcha decides it's time to possibly move along.

'Okay,' she goes, fake-smiling him, 'where's this famous bull?'

Jerome and the vet lead us all into this, like, shed, where the bull – obviously heavily sedated – is lying on its side, spitting zeds. He's a humungous animal, in fairness to the dude, and I notice his balls lying there between his legs like two honeydew melons in a tote bag.

'Smile please, Minister!' one of the photographers goes.

The air is suddenly filled with the click-click-click of, like, *cameras* going off? Sorcha seems to have no qualms whatsoever about posing for photographs next to a bull with a mickey that would confirm any suspicions you ever had about Peperami.

'Could you hold it in your hand?' another photographer asks – and, believe it or not, she actually *does* it? She grabs it without even hesitating and smiles for the cameras.

Her old man was right about one thing. The girl was made for politics.

Richard Chambers goes, 'How do you actually castrate a bull?' which is actually a good question. I'm suddenly imagining someone trying to cut a burned sausage with a blunt scissors and I find myself mentally crossing my legs.

Sorcha turns and looks at this Sean Urch dude – the mickey still in her hand, by the way.

'Well, there are several different ways,' the dude goes. 'There's surgical castration, where we use a knife or scalpel to make an incision in the scrotum –'

Jesus Christ, I feel suddenly sick.

He goes, '– to expose the testicles and then we sever the spermatic cords.'

I put my hand over mouth because I genuinely think I'm going to hurl.

'However, this comes with an obvious risk of haemorrhaging and infection,' the dude goes. 'Which is why many animal vets prefer to use a method called banding, in which specially designed elastic bands are placed around the neck of the scrotum, eventually leading the testicles to atrophy.'

The dude suddenly produces what looks very much to my eyes like a giant monkey wrench.

'I like to use this method,' the dude goes. 'This instrument here is called a Burdizzo. It's a pincer device that we use to cut off the blood supply to the testicles, causing them to shrivel up and die.'

Holy focking shit sticks, I actually feel faint.

The dude hands the device to Sorcha and he goes, 'Now, do you want to do it, Minister?' and he grabs hold of the bull's – I'm not sure if this is an actual veterinary phrase – but *ball*sack?

Sorcha wields the Burdizzo – honestly – like she's clipping her roses with a secateurs. Again, the cameras stort to click and there's, like, flashes going off.

'Now,' the vet dude goes, 'you're basically looking to crush the spermatic cords while ensuring that the skin of the scrotum remains intact. So I'm going to ask you to clamp the cord just here, Minister,' and he points to a spot on the bull's – again – ballsack.

Suddenly, I notice the look on Sorcha's face, we're talking half excitement and half determination – it reminds me of the time she queued outside Brown Thomas overnight for the first release of the Victoria Beckham x Estée Lauder collection.

Sorcha moves in for the kill, going snip, snip, snip with the clamping device – and maybe I'm being paranoid, but I stort to genuinely think that she's imagining herself going at *my* nuts?

'That's it,' the dude goes, 'catch it between the two jaws. And now squeeze for ten seconds. Don't be afraid to apply pressure.'

I haven't felt my hort beating this fast since I scratched the side of Jack McGrath's Nissan X-Trail in the VIP cor pork of the 3Arena after a Bruno Mors gig and drove away without telling him.

'Six, seven, eight, nine, ten,' Sorcha goes.

The dude is like, 'Excellent. Now repeat the trick just about an inch lower. That's it. Just there. Harder, Minister. Squeeze harder. That's it. Remember, we want those testicles to shrivel up and die.'

'Oh, Jesus!' I go, because I can suddenly feel all of the blood in my body rushing to my head. And that's when it happens. The cold, concrete floor of the cow shed suddenly rises up and smacks me full in the face.

I hear a scream – I would flatter myself to say it's Libreri – and then I hear Richard Chambers go, 'I think he just fainted.'

Someone rolls me over onto my back. My vision is – yeah, no – hazy, but I can make out the outline of Sorcha standing over me.

And through gritted teeth, I hear her go, 'I can't believe you're *still* focking embarrassing me.'

★

By eight o'clock that night, everyone has seen it. At least everyone in The Bridge 1859. Yeah, no, I try to slip through the door unnoticed – I don't know if I'm borred, bear in mind – but it's Dave Kearney who cops me.

'The sight proved too much for the Minister's husband,' Dave goes, doing a pretty good Richard Chambers impersonation, 'who fainted at the sight of his wife administering the death squeeze to the bull's testicles. Richard Chambers, TV3 News, Clonmellon.'

The entire pub laughs – including Jamie Heaslip, I'm relieved to see.

He's like, 'No trouble tonight, Ross.'

I'm there, 'Yeah, no, there hopefully won't be.'

He goes, 'We're operating a two-strikes policy, okay? You're on your last warning.'

I spot Christian, JP and Fionn standing together in a little huddle.

I tip over to them and I'm like, 'Hey, goys, how the hell *are* you?'

They look at me and they all grin at me. They've obviously seen the clip.

'What the fock?' JP goes – but at least he's laughing. 'What the *actual* fock?'

I'm like, 'Dude, you're not married. You wouldn't understand what it feels like to watch your wife take a monkey wrench to an animal's bangers.'

Christian goes, 'What were you even doing there?'

I'm like, 'Yeah, no, I gave Sorcha a lift. Long story, but K . . . K . . . K . . . Kennet was still presumably pissed from the night before and Sorcha was about to drive herself. And – yeah, no – she's sort of, like, *banned* from driving at the moment?'

Fionn's like, 'What?' because they usually tell each other everything.

'Except she doesn't *know*,' I go, 'so don't you go opening your mouth to her. Yeah, no, basically I was driving her cor and I was doing, I don't know, whatever speed going through Kilmacanogue.'

I whip the notice out of my pocket and I show it to Christian, who gives it a quick left to right.

I'm there, 'So I got three points put on her licence. Sixty is a ridiculous speed limit for that stretch of the road, by the way.'

'Why don't you just tell them that it was you who was driving?' Christian goes, handing the notice back to me.

I'm there, 'Because then *I'd* be banned. I'm on nine points as well. I actually *need* my cor? She has a full-time driver – albeit one who's a total pisshead.'

Fionn changes the subject then. He's like, 'Exciting news, by the way – I took the Fifth and Sixth years for rugby training today.'

'Whoa!' we all go.

He's there, 'And I've asked the IRFU to include Castlerock College in the draw for the Leinster Schools Senior Cup this year.'

'Yes!' Christian goes, punching the air, because it's, like, six or seven years since – I don't want to speak ill of the dead – but Tom McGahy, the thundering fock-clown, pulled the school out of the competition.

JP catches Dave Kearney's eye and goes, 'Can we get a bottle of champagne? Make it a good one!' Like a man from Dundalk would know the focking difference.

Christian's there, 'I presume there's a role for you, is there, Ross?' and suddenly there's just, like, silence. It's, like, *awks* much?

I'm there, 'Yeah, no, as Fionn pointed out, coaching another school team would be too much of a sideways step for me. By the way, the IRFU seem pretty keen to talk to me about the Ireland job – albeit women.'

I only say it to, like, test the water with the goys. I notice JP and Christian exchange a smile.

I'm like, 'What's so funny?'

'It's just the idea of you,' JP goes, 'coaching women's rugby. After all the things you've said over the years. Remember when they won the Grand Slam?'

'Hey,' I go, 'I just made the point that it wasn't the same as the men winning it – and I stand by that statement.'

'You asked them to turn off the TV in Kielys.'

I'm there, 'Look, I've agreed to go for an interview, but only to prove to Honor that I'm not a – what's the word, Fionn?'

'Misogynist,' Fionn goes.

And I'm like, 'Exactly.'

Dave Kearney arrives with the champagne then. A bottle of Pierre Darcys Brut Non-Vintage. What did I focking tell you?

I pick it up and I peel off the foil. I twist the metal cap and I whip it off.

'Just the three glasses,' I tell Dave Kearney, 'what with Christian here being –'

'An alcoholic,' Christian goes – owning it, in fairness to him.

I'm there, 'I still say you could have the odd pint. But you know your body best.'

I pop the cork. We all, like, cheer.

I pour three glasses and I go, 'Here's to you, Fionn! And Castle-rock College winning the 2019 Leinster Schools Senior Cup!'

The goys raise their glasses for the toast.

'By the way,' I turn around to JP and go, 'I bumped into your ex the other day.'

He's like, 'What?'

'Yeah, no, I was driving through Ranelagh and I popped into the shop to see her. She got her hair cut short.'

He looks away – suddenly sore.

He goes, 'What did she say? Actually, I'm not interested,' and he's suddenly on the big-time defensive.

I'm there, 'Dude, I would recommend that you go and tell her how you feel about her. She needs to hear from you that you love her.'

'I don't love her.'

'You've changed your tune.'

'Dude, she called me a sicko. And I've been thinking – who the fock is *she* to judge *me* anyway? Jesus, she had sex with *you*.'

'Okay, I'm going to let that go, Dude, because the whole break-up thing is clearly still raw.'

'And then she moved onto me – again, another dude who's basic-ally half her age. There's a name for women like that.'

'It's definitely cougar behaviour.'

'That's not the word I was thinking of.'

'Dude, can I just remind you,' I go, because I just think it's time I hit him with one or two hord truths, 'that you're not exactly a child yourself. You're nearly focking forty. You're a multi-millionaire with a thriving business and a gaff staring out at the Aviva. But I'm sorry to tell you this – your life is empty.'

'Ross, that's horsh,' Fionn tries to go. 'He's got Isa.'

I'm there, 'Yeah, no, a kid he had with a girl he didn't love – out of, like, pure convenience. Other than that, what have you got to show for your nearly forty years, JP?'

He doesn't answer me – he *has* no answers.

I'm there, 'I hate to sound horsh, but there's a woman in an interiors and soft furnishings shop in Ranelagh who – *I* think – loves you. And I think you love her too.'

Suddenly, from out of nowhere, Christian goes, 'Ross, show me that penalty points notice again.'

Which I do. I whip it out of my pocket and I hand it to him and he gives it the once-over a second time.

'The fourth of August,' he goes. 'That was the day we said goodbye to Cooper.'

Yeah, no, Lauren – his ex – had an actual funeral service for the family labradoodle that died and we were all shamed into going along.

I'm like, 'Yeah, no, sorry again for accidentally knocking over the ashes and then trying to clear them up without telling you. I had no idea they'd block up the hoover like that.'

He's there, 'Do you not get what I'm saying, Ross? You and Sorcha were both in Booterstown. You couldn't have been driving through Kilmacanogue at, what, three o'clock in the afternoon?'

'This happened to a friend of Eleanor's,' Fionn goes. 'Sometimes the camera can get an incorrect read on a licence plate – especially if the cor is swerving a bit on the road. You have to appeal it.'

I'm there, 'Dude, I am straight on the case,' obviously meaning I'm going ask the old man to do it. I hate the focker's guts at the moment, but he's still a man of influence. If he can burn down the focking Dáil, he can sort this shit-show out for me.

All of a sudden, from out of nowhere, I hear a woman's voice go, 'You doorty fooken . . . BASTOOORD!'

Oh, for fock's sake.

I turn around and standing there, looking as mad as a rat under a bucket, is Tina.

'YOU KIDDLED HIM!' she goes. 'YOU FOOKEN KIDDLED TOM MCGAHY!'

Of course, every conversation in the pub ends up stopping.

I'm there, 'That's actually libellous, Tina – and there are witnesses present. How did you even find me, by the way?'

'YOU DOORTY, MOORDOORDEN BASTARD!' the woman goes.

And then – I swear to fock – she picks up an empty Bulmers bottle off the next table and goes to smash it over my head.

Christian is the first to react. He catches her by the wrist a split-second before the bottle ends up embedded in my skull.

Tina storts roaring at me then, going, 'YOU GEB HIM A HEERT ATTACK, YOU DOORTY FOOKEN DOORT-BOORD!' and it takes JP, Christian *and* Fionn to hold her off me.

I'm there, 'I hordly *gave* him a hort attack, Tina,' suddenly acting the big man now that the goys have her orms pinned. 'There was just something about me that always sent the dude's blood pressure through the roof. He should have listened to his body.'

Unfortunately, though, they only have, like, Tina's *orms* pinned? She swings her foot like Sexton putting one over the bor from fifty yords in the Stade de France and manages to catch me – holy fock! – full in the nangberries.

I drop to my knees, going, 'Jesus Chr–' because I'm winded, and I suddenly know how that bull in Clonmellon felt. My eyes are shut, my face is screwed up in agony and my town halls are throbbing like a toad's throat.

Suddenly, Jamie Heaslip is standing over me, going, 'Second strike. I'm sorry, Ross – but you're borred.'

Honor sends me a text message. It's like, 'Good luck, Dad!!!' followed by a girl emoji, then a rugby ball emoji, then a shamrock emoji, then a fingers crossed emoji, then a kissy face emoji.

It's so sweet of her that I actually feel bad that I'm about to deliberately fock this interview up.

The door opens and there's a dude standing there. He's, like, an older, fatter and more unwell-looking version of my old man.

He's like, 'Ross O'Carroll-Kelly, is it?'

And I'm there, 'Er – *yeah*?' surprised – and a little bit hurt – that someone who *supposably* works in the IRFU has to even ask.

'Verner Ryan,' he goes, offering me a warm and sweaty hand to shake. 'Director of Excellence for Sevens and Women's Rugby.'

I'm like, 'Yeah, no, we spoke on the phone.'

He goes, 'We certainly did. We certainly did indeed.'

He leads me into a room. There's a woman – we're talking early thirties – sitting behind a table. Her face is weirdly familiar.

'Obviously you know Sive Keenan,' he goes, except the name means fock-all to me.

I'm there, 'Sive who?'

'She's the captain of the Ireland women's team,' he goes. 'Our number eight.'

I'm like, 'Oh, right – *that* Sive Keenan.'

I offer her my hand, but she leaves me hanging. I'm thinking this couldn't have got off to a worse stort and I'm absolutely focking delighted.

'Sit down,' Verner goes. 'I thought it would be helpful to have her here. Get some input from the players on who their next Coach should be.'

I'm like, 'Yeah, no, I'm cool with that. More the merrier – eh, Sive?'

Sive is just, like, staring at me. She goes, 'I know you, don't I?'

And I'm there, 'If you have any knowledge of rugby, I'd certainly hope so. I've been involved in the game as both a player and a coach for, like, twenty-something years – and that's not me trying to sound like a dick.'

Verner goes, 'I'm actually a friend of your old man's, Ross – for my sins!' and then he lets out a loud, guffawing laugh, whatever the fock that even means. 'He was the one who proposed me for membership of Portmornock – oh, many years ago now. And that solicitor of his seconded me.'

Fock it, I'm thinking, this is the last thing I need.

He's there, 'I used to meet them regularly in the famous Horse-shoe Bor! And if you'd told me back then that one of them would one day be the leader of the country and the other the Attorney General, well, I would have asked you what you were drinking. And ordered a round of them for everyone!'

There's more, like, guffaws out of him. There isn't even a smile out of *her*, though. She doesn't look like *much* would amuse her, in fairness.

She goes, 'Can I remind you that this is supposed to be a job interview?' clearly not a fan of the whole all-boys-together thing.

I'm there, 'Hey, I'm as keen to crack on with this as you are. I've only paid for twenty minutes' porking.'

I haven't even taken my baseball cap off, by the way.

'You said you've been involved in rugby all your life,' she goes. 'So how do you explain the long gaps in your employment record?'

I'm there, 'That's a very good question.'

'Thank you,' she goes. 'Now, can you answer it for me, please? Because you served as the national Coach of Andorra in 2006, but – according to your CV – you didn't hold another coaching position until you were hired by Pres Bray in 2017.'

I'm there, 'I also worked with the Facebook tag rugby team somewhere in between. Even though I didn't think it was worth putting down. They were shit and the only match I coached them for ended in a riot.'

She's like, 'So what were you doing during those, what, eleven years?'

'Mostly chilling,' I go.

She's like, 'Chilling?'

And I'm there, 'Yeah, no, chilling.'

Verner smiles and nods along like a dashboard doggy.

'Very impressive references,' he goes, then he chuckles, 'including the Taoiseach! Jamie Heaslip! And – oh! – Fiona Coghlan, I see!'

I'm like, 'Yeah, no, maybe don't ring Fiona. I'm not sure if she's still talking to me.'

'Yes, of course,' he goes.

'And maybe hold off on ringing Jamie Heaslip as well. He focked me out of his pub the other night because I had a massive drunken row with the mother of one of my kids. Yeah, no, she accused me of killing her ex by giving him a hort attack.'

The two of them just stare at me with their mouths open. Yeah, no, I wouldn't say they'll hear shit like this from many other candidates.

Sive is suddenly down on top of me again like a millennial on free Wi-Fi.

'You mentioned on your CV that you won the Leinster Schools Senior Cup as a player,' she goes, 'but you didn't mention that you had your medal taken from you.'

I'm there, 'I didn't know if it was relevant.'

She goes, 'You didn't know if it was relevant that you have a history of performance-enhancing drug use?'

'Well, I'm not going to deny it,' I go. 'I was on the juice. It's what made me the player I was,' and then I go to stand up. 'Anyway, I hope you've enough information there to go on.'

'Sit down for a moment,' Verner goes. 'We haven't asked you for your thoughts on women's rugby yet. Are you a fan? I know your father isn't!'

I laugh along with him.

'I wouldn't be a major fan,' I go. 'For me, it's like pass the porcel. I'm on the record as saying that women should stick to the likes of basketball and hockey. That's port of the reason Fiona isn't talking to me.'

'Right,' Verner goes – the interview is going so badly and he's absolutely crushed for me.

I'm there, 'Sometimes I watch clips of women's rugby with the *Benny Hill* theme tune on in the background. It makes it even funnier.'

'You know that the Irish team hasn't really kicked on since winning the Grand Slam in 2013,' he goes, throwing me a bone. 'For the last few years, they've been going backwards. What is it now, Sive – three Wooden Spoons in a row?'

Sive goes, 'What Verner is asking is what, specifically, could you bring to the role to improve the standard of the women's team between now and the next Six Nations?'

I'm there, 'Very little would be my answer. It's a poison focking chalice.'

'I've just realized how I know you,' Sive suddenly goes, sounding delighted with herself. 'A couple of weeks ago I was on the Still-organ dual carriageway. I was trying to change lanes and you wouldn't let me.'

I suddenly recognize her – it's the woman in the white Ford Explorer.

There's, like, ten seconds of silence then. It's majorly awkward.

'So, em, I think that's everything covered,' Verner goes, his hort broken for me.

I get to my feet and I'm there, 'So, er, what's the next step? When are we going to talk salary and exes? Because I'm warning you in advance, I don't come cheap.'

Poor Verner goes, 'It's, em, probably a little premature to be thinking in those terms just yet.'

I'm there, 'Will I hear from you?'

Sive – grinning like a constipated chimp – goes, 'I wouldn't wait in by the phone, Ross.'

I give her a big wink, then I walk out of there, absolutely delighted with my morning's work.

My phone rings. I can see that it's, like, Erika, so I answer, even though I'm supposed to be hanging out with my old dear here.

I'm like, 'Hey, Gorgeous.'

There's, like, silence on the other end of the line.

I'm like, 'Sorry, what's up?'

She goes, 'I spoke to Sea-mon.'

'Where is she?'

'She's in Sweden.'

'Holy fock – how did you find her?'

'I just messaged her on Facebook.'

'Oh, right. I thought it was going to be a bit more *Mission Impossible* than that.'

'She's agreed to come home. She's going to go public – with everything she knows about *him*.'

'Fock.'

72

'About the fire. About Irexit. About the plot to destroy rural Ireland and allow the Russians to use the Midlands as a dumping ground for their waste.'

I laugh. I'm like, 'Focking good enough for him.'

She goes, 'I've arranged everything. I've briefed RTÉ on what she knows. She's going to be doing a major interview on *Prime Time*.'

'This will be his final comeuppance,' I go. 'The dickhead.'

She's like, 'What's that noise in the background, by the way?'

I'm there, 'It's my old dear.'

Yeah, no, she's singing to the children, the way she used to sing to me when I was a baby, especially when she had a few on her.

Erika's like, 'What song is it supposed to be?' because – yeah, no – she sounds like a focked fanbelt.

I'm there, ' "The Zoological Gordens". She used to sing it to me as a kid, but I'm only just realizing now how absolutely filthy the words are.'

The children are all staring at the old dear, totally mesmerized by her voice. I'm holding little Cassiopeia, who's attempting to – yeah, no – sing along, although she has no actual words yet, so she's just going, 'Wa! Wa! Wa! Wa! Wa! Wa! Wa!' and making a better fist of the song than the old dear, certainly to the ears of this critic.

Erika's there, 'Anyway, I have to go, Ross,' and she hangs up on me.

The old dear suddenly stops singing and looks at me with a look of, like, *confusion* on her face?

She's like, 'What's next, Ross? I can't remember what comes next?'

I straight away look at Astrid, the children's German nanny.

'Now, you can stop that this minute,' the old dear goes. 'It's got nothing to do with my mind going. I've just forgotten the next verse. You remember me singing it to you, Ross, don't you?'

I'm there, 'Yeah, no, I said I did. It's a bit – I don't know – edgy for children, isn't it?'

Honestly, it's a wonder that Social Services didn't take more of an interest in my upbringing.

She goes, 'He loved it, Astrid. Sometimes, I'd come home from golf or lunch with the girls and he'd be absolutely hysterical at having been left on his own for the afternoon. Of course, he'd have dirtied his nappy – again! I'd lift him out of his cot and sing that song to him and he'd calm down instantly.'

I'm there, 'I'd say the fumes off your breath had quite a lot to do with that. Wasn't there a time when I was, like, knocked out for three days?'

'Oh, yes,' she goes, 'that was the time I got your dosage wrong.'

I'm like, 'What dosage?'

'Oh, come on, Ross, everyone gave children sleeping tablets in those days. I raised you without a nanny, don't forget. How would I have got anything done otherwise?'

Jesus Christ.

I'm there, 'I can't believe you focking roofied me so you could go and play golf.'

Cassiopeia's like, 'Wa! Wa! Wa! Wa! Wa! Wa! Wa!'

'I think Cassie is going to be the singer,' the old dear goes. 'Aren't you, Dorling? Will you have a drink, Ross?'

It's, like, half nine in the morning, by the way.

I'm there, 'Make it a small one, seeing as I'm driving.'

She goes, 'Of course, you don't want to lose your licence,' and I suddenly remember.

I'm there, 'Is the old man around?'

'He's in his office with Hennessy,' the old dear goes. 'I'll have a Whiskey Sour for you when you come down.'

So anyway – yeah, no – upstairs to the office I trot. I walk in, but neither of them notices me – they're, like, too busy plotting away.

'Micheál Martin just made a statement,' Hennessy goes.

The old man's like, 'What's he said now?'

'He said he doesn't want to speculate on who may or may not have been responsible for the burning of Leinster House as it's the subject of a Garda investigation.'

'Sensible man!'

'But he said that the failure to announce a date for the resumption of normal Dáil business poses major questions about this Government's commitment to democracy.'

'Where in the name of Hades are we supposed to meet? The building's been gutted!'

'Speaking of which,' Hennessy goes, reading something off his phone, 'someone's just thrown a petrol bomb through the window of the Portuguese embassy on Leeson Street.'

'Well, that'll teach Mrs Sobrinho to keep her nose out of Irish affairs!'

I go, 'Ahem!'

Poor Hennessy nearly has a focking hort attack.

'You better not have heard any of that,' he goes.

I'm there, 'Relax – I know what you two are up to.'

I spot the giant model of Malingrad. And the framed silk tie that once belonged to Chorlie Haughey and that the old man paid seventy Ks for at an auction for the Irish Hospice Foundation. And his favourite photograph in the world – him in his famous camel-hair coat with his orms around Ginger McLoughlin, who had just scored the try that won the 1982 Triple Crown, even though Ginger McLoughlin is clearly telling him to get the fock off the pitch.

I'm there, 'I see you managed to get all of your shit out of the building before the fire – fair focks.'

'Hennessy and I are rather busy!' the old man has the actual balls to go. 'We are about the business of Government! What can I do for you, Kicker?'

I'm there, 'Yeah, no, Sorcha's been banned from driving. She doesn't know yet, so maybe don't mention it to her. Except I'm pretty sure it's a case of mistaken identity, because neither of us was on the N11 that day.' I turn to Hennessy. 'We were actually in your daughter's gaff – at the famous funeral for the labradoodle.'

'Well,' the old man goes, 'the first step would be to request a copy of the photograph! Hennessy does it all the time – don't you, Old Scout? If the image is in any way hazy, you can raise a doubt in a judge's mind! Hennessy, you'll look into it, won't you?'

Hennessy just, like, glowers at me. He obviously doesn't want to do shit for me after the whole Ronan business – but then he doesn't want to say no to my old man either.

So he goes, 'Leave it with me. Now, fuck off.'

★

It's been, like, a week since I sat the interview and it's just, like, radio silence from the IRFU. Which is fine by me. No news is good news – although even better news would be that some other mug has been given the job. Gerry Thornley had a piece in the *Times* yesterday saying that the frontrunner for the job was Benedetta Bonansea, a woman from – apparently – Italy. According to Mr T, she won, like, a hundred obviously *women's* caps for her country and she's spent the last two years working as the Assistant Backs Coach to the Italian men's team.

She's focking welcome to it, I say, although I can only imagine the damage it will do to my reputation in rugby circles if I end up being passed over for – *not* sexist – but a *woman*?

I get out of my sleeping bag and I throw on my clothes. And that's when my *phone* ends up ringing? I check the screen. It's, like, JP.

I answer by going, 'Dude, how the hell are you?' in a really upbeat voice because – yeah, no – I'm worried that I may have been a bit hord on him in The Bridge that night.

'I need to see you,' he goes, his voice sounding a bit – I suppose – wobbly. 'Ross, I'm about to do something drastic – but I don't want you to try to talk me out of it.'

I'm there, 'As in what? Dude, where the fock are you?'

And he goes, 'I'm standing next to the canal.'

I'm like, 'Dude, don't you dare do it! Don't you dare do it, Dude!'

'It's what I want,' he goes.

I'm like, 'Where are you? Exact location – right now!'

He's there, 'I'm going to drop you a pin. You're going to have to be quick, Ross.'

I'm like, 'JP, promise me you won't do anything stupid until I get there.'

So I hop into the cor and I follow his directions to – it turns out – Clanwilliam Place. I spot him pretty much straight away, standing on the bank of the canal, staring into the water. I throw the cor into a porking space – two wheels up on the kerb – then I get out and race over to him.

'J-Town,' I go, grabbing him in, like, a bear hug, 'don't do this thing. Please don't do this thing.'

He's there, 'It's what I want.'

'How could *this* be what anyone wants? You're not in your right mind.'

'I was thinking about what you said –'

'Don't listen to me. Trust me, Dude, she's not worth it.'

'Ross –'

'Jesus Christ, she's not even that nice in terms of looks. I know you've got some kind of weird fixation with older women. Hazel Reeny said you blurted out the word 'Mom' while you were riding her around the back of The Millhouse at Eilish Hallinan's Going Away to Malawi porty. I've resisted the temptation to mention it for years and I'm only saying it now to try to bring you to your senses.'

'Ross, I love her.'

'You couldn't possibly. Dude, old bints like Delma are ten-a-focking-penny. I'll tell you what, why don't we hit the old Hampton Hotel tonight and I'll show you – if it's definitely a cougar you want.'

'Ross –'

'She's soiled goods, Dude. Bear in mind, her husband gave her the flick for a younger woman. He's obviously seen something that we've all missed. And, while probably neither of us had any complaints in terms of the quality of the sex, you've got to ask yourself was it always going to be that good? The woman is staring down the barrel of seventy – it won't be long before it's missionary-only with painkillers and handfuls of lubricant and 'Go easy! Watch my hip!' Jesus, I wonder has she even got long to live.'

'I can't believe you're saying this.'

'Dude, I'm just trying to get you to see that she's not worth killing yourself over.'

He gives me a look of total disgust – like I'm a toenail that he's just picked from his lobster bisque.

'Killing myself?' he goes. 'Who said anything about killing myself?'

I'm there, 'Er, you said you were about to do something *drastic*?'

He goes, 'I'm getting married, Ross.'

I'm like, 'Married? Who the fock are you marrying?'

'He's marrying me,' a voice behind me goes.

I spin around. Yeah, no, Delma is sitting on a pork bench about ten feet away. And sitting next to her – oh, fock a duck – is her son.

Tom McGahy – Lord have mercy on the absolute cock-goblin – used to say that if I ever left my brain to medical science, then medical science would contest the will.

I'm like, 'What's the crack, Bingley?' which is his name – yeah, no, it's random. The dude just stares straight through me. The two of them obviously heard every word I said.

JP's there, 'I wanted you here because I want you to be my best man.'

'In that case,' I go, desperately trying to row back, 'you're a lucky, lucky goy.'

Delma goes, 'Maybe *don't* let him say anything in the registry office,' and – yeah, no – on balance, that's probably a good call.

JP's there, 'What you said to me that night in The Bridge got me thinking. No one has ever made me happy like this.'

'Dude, I was thinking in terms of you two hopefully getting back together. Marriage isn't something you should enter into lightly.'

I know how focking ridiculous that sounds coming from me.

'I went to see her the next morning,' JP goes, 'and laid my cords out on the table. I told her I loved her and I didn't want to spend another minute aport from her.'

I notice that the two of them are, like, lost in each other's eyes.

'He got down on one knee,' Delma goes, 'and proposed to me – there in Taste of Décor.'

I'm there, 'Muireann O'Connell is interested in the lamp in the window, by the way – as in, Muireann O'Connell off *The Six O'Clock Show*. Not that I'm trying to ruin an obviously romantic moment.'

It's at that exact point that Delma's daughter, Belle, comes walking up the canal towards us. She doesn't look happy – not that she *ever* does?

She goes, 'What kind of a focking message is that to send me? *Meet me at Macquay's Bridge at 11 a.m. – I'm getting married today?*'

Delma goes, 'We wanted to do it without all the fuss. Without people telling us that we were making a mistake. So it's just fifteen minutes in the registry office followed by lunch in Dobbins.'

Dobbins? Jesus, you'd be seriously worried about the age difference.

Belle looks at JP and then at me. I'm wondering does she know that I had a scene with her old dear.

She goes, 'So which one is it, then? Which one of your focking rugger-bugger lovers have you decided to marry? Or have you even made your mind up yet?'

She knows alright. I'm thinking, yeah, no, she would have definitely heard the famous voice message because she's in my contacts book from the time I asked her to give me Physics and Chemistry grinds when I was going through a phase of liking girls who were cold and withholding.

She's there, 'Maybe they're going to wrestle for you, are they?'

'I'm marrying JP,' Delma goes. 'And I'm not looking for your approval, Dulcibella.'

Dulcibella! I actually laugh out loud. I forgot that's what Belle is short for. Where the fock was Delma going with the names? My old dear always said it was, like, post-natal depression.

Belle goes, 'This is to get back at Dad, isn't it?'

Delma's there, 'This has nothing to do with Breffni. This is about *my* happiness – to which I'm fully entitled.'

Belle's like, 'You're making the biggest mistake of your life.'

'No,' Delma goes, 'that was marrying your father.'

It's a good comeback, in fairness to the woman, but Belle is having none of it. She just turns on her heel and storms off, back up the canal, in the direction of presumably Leeson Street, where she teaches in the Institute.

'Two witnesses is all we need,' JP goes, then he takes Delma by the hand and helps her to her feet. 'Will we do this thing?'

They kiss each other on the lips – yeah, no, it's a definite moment – then we cross over the road and head for the registry office on, like, Grand Canal Street, with JP and Delma walking – yeah, no – hand in hand.

I turn around to Bingley – nice to be nice – and I go, 'So how's business, Bingley?'

But he's like, 'How focking dare you speak about my mother like that?'

He's a hedge fund manager apparently.

Into the – like I said – registry office we trot. And it all happens very quickly after that. We're taken into a room and we all sign the necessary paperwork before the actual gig itself.

Then JP reads something from the Bible. He's obviously still a fan of what he calls the good book. Delma reads a poem by some dude called – talk about random names – Wordsworth! And I'm sure it's fine – if you're into that kind of thing.

Then they exchange their vows, which they haven't even prepared beforehand, by the way. Yeah, no, they just say them off the top of their heads, which must prove *something*, I suppose?

JP – who's always had a nice turn of phrase – tells her that he loves her in word and deed, and he promises to laugh with her, and cry with her, and to be her kin, and her portner, on all of life's adventures, and to give himself to her unstintingly – the good, the bad and the yet to come.

Then Delma tells JP that he is her world, and that he completes her in ways that she never imagined possible, and she promises to listen to him, and learn from him, and support him, and accept his support, and celebrate his successes, and mourn his losses as if they were her own, and she will do this for all of her days, however many that ends up being.

The dude who's, like, marrying them, asks me if I have the rings. Yeah, no, JP slipped them to me on the way in. I hand them over and they put them on each other, then the dude goes, 'I now pronounce you husband and wife. Congratulations – you may kiss each other.'

Which they then do – they end up pretty much wearing the face off each other, in fact.

I'm there, 'Look away, Bingley!' just trying to break the tension.

'Fock you,' he goes, under his breath.

And, just like that, JP Conroy – a dude I've known since we were basically kids – is a suddenly married man.

It's at that exact point that my *phone* suddenly rings? I'm there, 'Sorry, everyone,' thinking it could be important, 'I've just got to take this,' and I step outside and answer it.

I go, 'You've got Ross!' because – again – people seem to enjoy it.

'Is that Ross O'Carroll-Kelly?' a man's voice goes.

I'm there, 'Depends who's asking.'

He's like, 'This is Verner Ryan – from the IRFU. I'm just ringing you with some news.'

I'm there, 'It's going to be the Italian bird, is it? Yeah, no, Gerry Thornley had the story yesterday. Good luck to her is what I say.'

But he goes, 'No, Ross, we would like to offer *you* the job – as Head Coach of the Ireland women's rugby team.'

3.

The Hateful Number Eight

The news comes on the radio while I'm in the cor on my way to the press conference in Donnybrook Stadium. It's after something about, I don't know, Shamrock focking Rangers and then some other bullshit about horse racing.

It's like, 'Ross O'Carroll-Kelly, the son of Taoiseach Charles O'Carroll-Kelly, is the surprise appointment as the new Head Coach of the Ireland women's rugby team . . .'

I'm there, 'The son of? The *son* of? Like, what the *actual* fock?'

But then it ends up getting worse.

The dude goes, 'Little is known about the 38-year-old Dublin native, who last year led Presentation College Bray to their first Leinster Schools Senior Cup title in almost ninety years.'

Little is known about me? Has this dude just woken up from a forty-year coma?

He goes, 'The highly regarded Italian coach Benedetta Bonansea had been considered the favourite for the job, although it's understood that members of the panel charged with filling the vacancy cooled on her appointment in recent days.'

Don't get me wrong, I'm still not exactly gone on the idea of coaching the Ireland women's team. As a matter of fact, I tried to price myself out of the job – we're talking three hundred Ks, plus exes – but Verner said yes straight away, which I definitely wasn't expecting. And now this focking joker on the radio is making me feel like I have something to possibly prove.

My phone rings and – yeah, no – I answer it. It ends up being Erika.

I'm there, 'I presume you just heard it.'

She's like, 'Heard what?' – she literally says that.

I'm there, 'The dude reading the sports headlines on Newstalk said little was known about me. There was fock-all about me coaching Andorra against Ireland A back in the day. There was fock-all about me captaining Castlerock College to victory in the Leinster Schools Senior Cup in 1999. There was fock-all about me nailing the last-minute kick that stopped Seapoint Rugby Club from being relegated from Division 2B to Division 2C of the All Ireland League a few years back.'

This seems to mean little or nothing to her. There's no reason why it should, of course. She was never really into rugby dudes.

She just sighs and goes, 'I spoke to Sea-mon last night. She's coming home from Sweden next week.'

I'm like, 'Whoa! And when's she going on TV?'

'RTÉ need to debrief her first – find out what she knows and what she's prepared to say on camera. They have to know that they can trust her. I mean, what she's accusing him of is serious.'

'Yeah, no,' I go, 'I know.'

She's there, 'He could end up spending the rest of his life in prison,' and she sounds definitely *delighted* about it? 'I'll keep you in the loop.' Then she hangs up just as I swing the wheel right, then drive through the big gates into the famous Energia Pork.

More than a few memories come flooding back to me. This is going to sound possibly random, especially given that I didn't really want the job in the first place, but I stort to feel actually positive about it. There's, like, a gaggle of photographers standing outside the clubhouse and they stort snapping away as they watch me arrive.

Little is known? Fock *his* shit.

I go, 'Hey, goys and girls!' as I breeze past them.

I love being papped – always did. And that goes all the way back to the time I crashed the 2005 VIP Style Awards by following Glenda Gilson up the red corpet and trying to make it look like I was actually with her. The papers the next day were full of stories about Glenda's new mystery man, which caused quite a stir, especially in our gaff, seeing as I was married at the time. Me and Glenda have been friends ever since.

'Can we get a picture of you standing in front of the goalposts?' one of the photographer dudes goes.

And I'm there, 'Maybe later – I've got a lot of work to do first.'

I walk into the clubhouse, whip off my sunnies and put them on top of my head.

The famous Sive Keenan is, unfortunately, the first person I see. She goes, 'You're half-an-hour late,' and I can tell that she hasn't exactly been won over by the idea of me being the man to lead her and her teammates to Six Nations glory.

I'm there, 'Good things come to those who wait, Sive!' and I give her a wink and I step past her into the room where the actual press conference is happening.

There's a bit of a buzz in the room, although no round of applause when I walk in. I make my way to the top table, where Verner Ryan is already sitting. He stands up and shakes my hand – a classy touch – and he goes, 'You're very welcome, Ross!' and again it's more cameras clicking and blah, blah, blah.

I'm not going to lie. I find myself getting suddenly into it.

I sit down at the table and I look out into the sea of people, recognizing one or two familiar faces, including the great Gerry Thornley and the legendary Tony Ward.

Sive pulls out the chair beside me and sits down, then Verner goes, 'I'd like to formally introduce you all to Ross O'Carroll-Kelly, a man with whom some of you will already be familiar. For those of you who aren't, he coached Andorra for several months back in 2006 and then last year he led Pres Bray to the Leinster Schools Senior Cup title. So if anyone has any questions –'

Gerry Thornley is the first man with his hand in the air. He goes, 'Ross, how do you feel?' and it's a nice easy one to put the ball into play.

I'm there, 'Yeah, no, I feel great. I have to say that I got a major buzz driving through those gates today. As you know, Gerry, this stadium holds a lot of happy memories for me. Including giving the famous middle finger to the Blackrock fans when they were on my back and I'd just silenced them by scoring a match-winning try.'

If I'm expecting a burst of laughter followed by a round of applause, I end up disappointed, because there *isn't* one? And that's when I stort to pick up on the vibe that I'm not exactly a popular choice for the role.

'You've taken on the job,' Sinéad Kissane from Virgin Media goes – and she says it like it's an *accusation*? 'How do you think you can improve the team?'

I'm there, 'Every team – no matter how good they are – can improve, Sinéad.'

'Well,' she goes, 'can you name any specific areas that could do with improving?'

Jesus, I know Eddie O'Sullivan had trouble with her back in the day.

I try to spoof my way out of it.

I'm there, 'Firstly, strength. And secondly, fitness. Those are two areas I'm planning to focus on in the short term. I've watched this team a lot over the last two or three years and I think they could definitely be stronger and definitely be fitter.'

She definitely doesn't buy it. Sinéad knows her rugby. She also knows bullshit when she smells it. She's from Kerry.

She goes, 'Are there any players in particular who've impressed you during your – what did you say? – two or three years watching this team?'

Oh, fock.

I'm like, 'What, you're asking me to name *specific* players?'

'Yes,' Sinéad goes, 'that's exactly what I'm asking you to do.'

I'm there, 'How many do you want me to name?' and I suddenly feel like I'm back in school, pretending to root through my bag for Geography homework that everyone knows I haven't done. 'Do you want to give me a figure?'

'Well, *one* would be a start,' she goes.

Verner, obviously remembering my performance during the interview, goes, 'Come on, Sinéad, it's not a table quiz. Does anyone else have any questions?'

Wardy – a fan of mine, bear in mind – goes, 'I have a question for Sive. Would it be accurate to say that Ross wasn't a unanimous choice for the job?'

Sive is just about to answer when Verner cuts across her. He goes, 'Ross O'Carroll-Kelly was the choice of the panel that was charged with finding a new Head Coach for the Ireland women's team. I don't think it's helpful to go into the specifics of who said what during our deliberations – which, by the way, are confidential.'

Sinéad Kissane isn't done yet, though. She goes, 'Can I ask you about Benedetta Bonansea, a woman with a great deal of international experience, as both a player and a coach, who was widely believed to be the favourite for the job? As a matter of fact, she was in Dublin last week looking at rental accommodation, with the clear impression that she had the job in the bag.'

'Well, clearly she *didn't* have the job in the bag!' Verner snaps at her – proper focking order as well. 'And if she believed she did, then she was mistaken in that belief.'

There's, like, silence, so I just decide, fock it, I'm going to make a statement here.

'Some of you know me of old,' I go. 'Although you wouldn't think that from the way you've been treating me since I walked through that door. I'm picking up on the vibe that I'm maybe not the coach you were expecting and you're all a little disappointed. I get that. Look, I'm not everyone's cup of tea. What I am, though, is a born winner.

'When I was hired by Pres Bray, I told the Principal that I would win them the Leinster Schools Senior Cup. Which I did. And today I'm making another prediction – that Ireland, under me, will win the Six Nations next year. And not only the Six Nations, but the Grand Slam as well. End of press conference.'

It's a genuine mic drop moment. I've actually just talked myself into wanting the job. I stand up and I walk straight out of there.

The first person I bump into when I step outside ends up being Hennessy. Yeah, no, he's standing there in his pinstriped suit with a humungous grin on his face and a cigor like a bull's mickey clamped between his lips.

'Appointing you as the Women's Coach,' he goes. 'I'm predicting a busy time ahead for the IRFU's HR department.'

There's someone with him, an absolute giant of a dude, we're talking maybe six-foot-seven with – yeah, no – a Conor McGregor beard and haircut and an identical suit to Hennessy's. He sort of, like, laughs along with the joke, even though it's obvious that he doesn't actually *get* it?

I go, 'Who the fock is this dude?'

And Hennessy's there, 'This is Peadar. He's the grandson of a good friend of mine.'

I can see that Peadar, for some reason, is itching to throw a punch at me.

I'm there, 'What are you, some kind of, like, cage-fighter?'

'I am,' he goes. 'And Ine thoorty and O.'

I'm like, 'You're what?'

'Thoorty and O.'

'Again?'

'Thoorty and O.'

'Still not getting it.'

'It's his fucking fight record,' Hennessy goes. 'Means he's had thirty fights and no losses.'

I laugh then, because the penny suddenly drops.

I'm there, 'So you're the new Ronan, huh?'

Peadar goes, 'Who?' and I can tell straight away that he's not the shorpest crayon in the drawer.

I'm there, 'Yeah, no, he's not a patch on the original, Hennessy – that's all I can say.'

Hennessy just smiles at me. He goes, 'You haven't even asked me what I'm doing here.'

I'm there, 'I just presumed you came to hear about my plans for the Ireland team – albeit women.'

'I'm the Attorney General,' he tries to go. 'You think I've got nothing better to do than to watch you take your first steps towards a class action for sexual harassment?'

He holds up a lorge brown envelope.

He goes, 'I got that photo for you.'

I'm like, 'Oh, the penalty points one?'

'Yeah,' he goes – seeming strangely pleased with himself. 'I had it blown up for you too.'

I'm like, 'And? Is it Sorcha's cor?'

'Oh, it's Sorcha's car alright.'

'And can you see who's driving?'

'Oh, yes – it's a very clear image.'

'Is it Sorcha?'

'No, it's not Sorcha.'

'Is it me?'

'Just look at the fucking picture,' he goes.

So I put my hand into the envelope and I pull the thing out. And when I do, I just go into, like, *shock*?

Because sitting behind the wheel of Sorcha's cor, raising an angry middle finger to the driver she's in the process of overtaking, is my thirteen-year-old daughter.

Hennessy laughs – we're talking insane, Bond villain laughter. And Peadar, the focking idiot, copies him.

I'm like, 'What the fock, Honor? What the actual *fock*?'

I'm like, 'What the fock, Honor?' because – yeah, no – I'm still saying it nearly four hours later. 'What . . . the *actual* . . . fock?'

She hands me back the photo and goes, 'I don't know why you're making such a big deal of it. I focking *hate* my hair in that picture, by the way.'

I'm there, 'Honor, you're driving a cor! On an actual motorway! At thirteen years of age! I wouldn't be any kind of father if I didn't ask – and I know I'm repeating myself at this stage – but, what the *actual* fock?'

We're having this orgument while standing in the cor pork of Mount Anville, by the way.

'I wanted to go to Greystones,' she goes – as casual as that, 'for a Battle of the Bands.'

I'm like, 'What the fock is a Battle of the Bands?' like there's a world in which the answer to that question might be in some way relevant.

She goes, 'What does it sound like? It's a competition between, like, bands. A boy I know – he goes to, like, Newpork – is in a band called Silmarillion.'

'What's his name?'

'His name is Adam.'

'And is he a friend, a boyfriend, or what?'

'Dad, I don't want to tell you how to parent me, but isn't the issue here that your thirteen-year-old daughter took her mother's cor and drove it to Greystones?'

'Yes, very good point. So what the fock were you thinking, Honor?'

'You and her were both out – at that dog's funeral.'

'So, what, you just decided that *you'd* drive?'

'Er, the cor is *automatic*, Dad? It practically drives itself. It's a bit like yours.'

'Please tell me that you haven't been driving mine. Because I was kind of hoping that this was a one-off.'

She goes, 'Yeah, right,' and she laughs – actually *laughs*? 'Dad, I've been driving your cors for, like, years.'

I'm like, 'Jesus Christ. This is like a bad dream.'

Honor notices Grainne Power – as in, like, Conwenna Power's old dear – standing a few feet away, pretending that she's rearranging her boot while earwigging the entire conversation.

Honor shouts, 'Why don't you mind your focking business? The focking bang of gin off you – and your husband's a bankrupt prick.'

I'm like, 'Honor, get in the cor,' and I swear to fock – I'm not making this up – she goes to open the *driver's* door?

I'm like, 'Yeah, wrong side, Honor.'

'Sorry,' she goes, 'force of habit.'

She's a focking comedian as well. We get into the cor.

The boys are like, '*Guten Tag, Honor!*'

She's there, '*Guten Tag, Jungen. Habt ihr hunger?*'

They're all, '*Ja! Wir haben hunger!*'

She goes, '*Wollt ihr zu Eddie Rocket's gehen?*'

But I'm there, 'Never mind your *wollt ihr zu Eddie Rocket's gehen*. You've got some serious explaining to do.'

She's like, 'Yeah, just to let you know, Dad, you're being *very* uncool about all of this?'

I'm there, 'How long has it been going on – as in, like, how long *exactly*?'

'I don't know,' she goes. 'I want to say, like, two years?'

I'm there, 'Two years?' in actual shock here. 'What, since you were, like, eleven?'

'Yeah, no, the first time was, like, one Saturday afternoon when we were in Dundrum. There was a jacket I liked in H&M – except they didn't have it in my *size*? But the woman said they had it in Liffey Valley.'

'And where was I when all of this was happening?'

'You were in Winter's, or whatever that pub is called, watching the rugby. I offered to mind your cor keys in case you lost them and you – like a focking dope – said yes.'

'*Oh, ficken Scheisse!*' Leo goes.

And I'm there, 'You took the words out of my *ficken* mouth, son.'

Honor's like, 'So I just decided to drive to Liffey Valley myself.'

'And?'

'Well, they had my size, but I didn't like the colour. It kind of washed me out.'

'I'm not talking about the focking *jacket*, Honor! Are you saying you got behind the wheel of a cor for the first time and you drove on an actual motorway?'

'Of course I did! What did you think I was going to do – take the back roads through Drimnagh?'

'Jesus Christ.'

'Then it just became a thing I did. If you and her were out, I'd drive to Dundrum, or Monkstown. One time, I drove to Cork.'

I just put my head in my hands.

She goes, 'I don't know why you're being such a drama queen about it. I'm a better driver than you – *and* her.'

I'm like, 'Yeah, your record would suggest otherwise, Honor. Those twelve points on Sorcha's licence – how many of them are yours?'

She's there, '*All* of them?'

'Yeah, I thought so. And what's going on in that photo? Why are you giving this dude the finger?'

'He was doing, like, fifty Ks per hour while hogging the fast lane.'

'Yeah, no, I hate that as well, in fairness to you.'

'There's a lot of fockwits on the road, Dad.'

'Says the girl with twelve points on her driving licence.'

'Er, I don't *have* a driving licence? I'm thirteen years old. You're being ridiculous now.'

'It's not funny, Honor. Your old dear is going to go absolutely batshit crazy when she finds out.'

'She won't find out. She has, like, a chauffeur. I told you, she'll get her licence back in twelve months and she'll never know she lost it.'

I end up just shaking my head.

I'm there, 'It's no wonder you were so quick to let me back into your good books. I'm just thinking, the mousetrap and the Dyson heater – you didn't mean any of that.'

'What are you shitting on about?'

'I thought you gave them to me because I tried to wring Sorcha's old man's neck for you. Now I find out that it's because you felt guilty.'

'Dad, I don't feel guilty – about anything – ever.'

'Oh, right – yeah, no, I forgot that. Although I *am* possibly going to have to tell your old dear – about you driving our *cors*?'

'You're not going to tell her.'

'Er, I'm *not*?'

'If you do, I'll just say that, oh my God, Daddy left me all alone standing outside the pub – eleven years old, bear in mind – while he watched the rugby inside. I ended up having an anxiety attack. Then, in a total panic, I got into the cor and just drove.'

I end up just sighing. I'm there, 'It sounds like I've no choice but to accept it, then.'

'Eddie Rocket's!' Johnny goes. *'Ich will zu Eddie Rocket's gehen!'*

I'm there, 'Fine, let's go to Eddie Rocket's.'

I stort the cor and I back out of my porking space.

'Check your mirrors,' Honor goes.

I end up *having* to laugh? It's impossible to stay angry with the girl for long.

'So this Adam dude,' I go, 'do you want to tell me a little bit about him?'

'As in?'

'Well, for storters, what does he *do* in this supposed band?'

'He sings and plays bass.'

'Sings and plays bass,' I go, turning this information over in my head. 'Sings *and* plays bass,' until I realize that I couldn't give a focking shit one way or the other. I'm just hoping this means she's finally over Reese.

I'm there, 'And does he –'

And she goes, 'No, Dad, he doesn't play rugby.'

'I was going to say. Newpork – I'd be very surprised if he did.'

'He has literally zero interest in the game.'

'I never thought I'd hear myself say this, but it's probably for the best. So when do I get to meet the dude?'

She goes, 'He's just a friend, Dad,' but there's a definite hint of *something* in her voice when she says it? And when I turn my head and look at her, I notice that she's, like, *blushing*?

I'm like, 'Sure he is, Honor.'

She goes, 'We're not putting labels on it. I haven't been with him.'

And I'm there, 'Well, hopefully you will be. I'm just glad it's not another little rugby wanker. Sings *and* plays bass. Fair focks to him. I'm putting it out there.'

Honor goes, 'Oh my God, how did the press conference go?' because she can be so thoughtful when she wants to be.

I'm there, 'I would say a bit like your driving, Honor – not focking great.'

She loves that one because – yeah, no – she laughs and goes, 'Good one, Dad!'

That's one in the eye for those who say you can't be a parent *and* a friend to your kids.

I'm there, 'Just make me a promise, Honor – that you won't drive either of our cors again. Not until you're, I don't know, whatever age you have to be to drive.'

But she just goes, 'Dad, I don't want to disappoint you by making promises that I might not end up keeping.'

The girls are already out on the pitch. The backs are flinging the old Gilbert around, while the forwards are pushing the scrummaging machine up and down. One or two of them stop what they're doing when they see the Rossmeister standing there on the sideline, watching them.

I spot Sive out there. She's built like Cian Healy, in fairness to her, with biceps like Galia melons.

She's like, 'Keep going, everyone,' and I'm getting the definite hint of a Galway accent for the first time. 'Stay focused on what you're doing and ignore *him*!'

It's lucky I'm not sensitive – otherwise, I could very easily take offence.

I stand there for fifteen, maybe twenty minutes – mostly just assessing their individual *skill* sets? – then I clap my hands together and I go, 'Okay, ladies!' at the top of my voice. 'Ladies! Ladies? Gather round!'

They all stop what they're doing, but they don't move. They stand where they are, just, like, staring at me – having obviously decided to give me a hord time.

'Fine,' I go, 'I'll come to you, then,' and I make my way to the centre of the pitch.

'Just to introduce myself,' I go, 'for those of you who haven't had the pleasure, I'm Ross O'Carroll-Kelly. And, like it or not, I'm your new Coach. Those of you who know your rugby will already know who I am and you'll know what I'm about. I'm about winning – something this team has forgotten how to do. And I'm going to change all of that.'

I make a point of staring at Sive. Always go in hord on the alpha. I read that this morning in my famous Rugby Tactics Book, although I don't remember where I first heard it, just that I like the idea of establishing my authority early on by taking down the top dog. Not that I'm calling Sive a dog – if anything, she's average in terms of looks.

I go, 'Some of you will like the way I do things. Some of you won't. The ones who don't will be gone long before the Six Nations comes around. You're going to do things my way – or you're out.'

I can see them all looking at me, obviously thinking, The rumours about this dude are true. He takes no shit – that's probably why he gets the results that he does.

I look at this girl with, like, red hair, who I saw practising her kicks earlier on. I'm there, 'What's your name?'

She goes, 'Me?'

I'm there, 'I'm focking looking at you, aren't I?'

She's like, 'Em, Joanne Wassell.'

I'm there, 'Well, Em Joanne Wassell, you've got one or two glitches in your kicking technique, which explains why you couldn't hit Kim Kordashian's orse with a focking griddle pan. They'll need to be ironed out – or I'll be looking for another kicker.'

I love the way my voice sounds right now.

I pick another girl out – the smallest there. I fix her with a look and I'm like, 'What's your name?'

'Grainne,' she goes – at the same time looking confused. 'Grainne *Hutton*?'

I'm there, 'And what position do you play, Grainne Hutton?'

And she's like, 'Er, scrum-half?' like I should somehow know this.

I'm there, 'I don't think you have the hands to play scrum-half. I don't think you have the hands to play international rugby, full stop. It's up to you to prove me wrong.'

All of a sudden, out of nowhere, a ball comes spinning through the air towards me. I don't actually *see* who throws it, but I react quickly – my reflexes are as good now as they were twenty years ago – and I catch it and take it into my midriff in a way I would *have* to describe as *textbook*?

What I don't see coming, though, is Sive. Obviously, my peripheral vision isn't what it famously was back in the old days, because she launches herself at me and I'm not even aware of her until she hits me hord around the waist and tackles me to the ground.

I honestly haven't been hit that hord by a member of the opposite sex since the day Munster lost the Heineken Cup semi-final to Toulon and I stood on a table and flashed my orse to the punters in the Thomond Bor in Cork.

All of the other ladies just, like, cheer – which they didn't in the Thomond Bor, by the way. Sive climbs to her feet, but I'm, like, winded and I can't actually *move*? For a few seconds, I wonder has she broken my back because I literally can't feel my legs.

I open my eyes and Sive is standing over me, staring down at me with a big, angry face on her.

She goes, 'Let's get one thing straight here – you only got the job because of who your daddy is.'

I'm like, 'Excuse me?' because I genuinely have no idea what she's talking about.

'You got the job,' she goes, 'because your old man rang Verner Ryan – his old drinking buddy, who didn't want to appoint Benedetta Bonansea anyway because he couldn't bear the idea that the best person for the job was a woman.'

I'm like, 'My old man . . . rang him? Is that true?'

She's there, 'How else do you think you got the job?'

And I'm like, 'On my . . . hopefully own . . . individual *merit*?'

They all laugh at that. They all laugh like literally lunatics.

Sive points her finger at me and goes, 'Don't you *ever* show up here again and try to throw your weight around like that! Don't you *ever* show up here again without knowing every single one of our names! And don't you *ever*, EVER call us ladies again!'

I can hear the old man's voice from the time I reach the top of the stairs. He's, like, ranting and raving, going, 'Who *are* you? I mean, yes, I know your names! You're Matisse! And you're Ingrid! And you're . . . someone else! Because it says so! On your little name tags! But who *are* you! Because I've never heard of any of you! And yet here you are!'

He sounds like – yeah, no – a schoolteacher, ripping into a classroom full of students, non-rugby-playing obviously.

'I mean, take a look at yourselves!' he's going. 'You, Sir, are like an accountant dreamt up by Dickens! This one looks like an undertaker who hasn't been well! And you, Madame, are like a yawn in human form! Collectively, you have the personality of a flat tyre and the charisma of a block of wood!'

Yeah, no, Sorcha mentioned this morning that the first round of the Irexit withdrawal negotiations was storting today. I push the door and I stick my head around it. On one side of this, like, boardroom table sits my wife and then two of the old man's mates from Portmornock – one of them is the Minister for Something and the other one is the Minister for Something Else. Opposite them are

95

two women and four men – and, yeah, no, in fairness to my old man, they don't look like much of a porty crowd.

The old man is, like, pacing the room, his jacket off, his shirt sleeves rolled up and his chest thrust out in front of him, sometimes pointing and sometimes throwing his orms in the air.

'So I'll ask you again!' he goes. 'Who in Hades *are* you? Who voted for you? I certainly didn't! And neither did anyone else in this country!'

I sort of, like, clear my throat to get the attention of the room. Everyone looks at me in pretty much shock. I'm there, 'Is this an important meeting?'

Sorcha goes, 'Er, we're *trying* to negotiate the terms on which Ireland will leave the European Union, Ross.'

I'm there, 'I just wanted a quick word with the old man.'

Except *he's* not even aware of me. He's, like, mid-rant. He's giving it, 'This isn't 2008 any more! This isn't your pals from the quote-unquote Troika, with their laptop bags and their designer glasses, swanning into Government Buildings and laying down the law to a weak and terrified Taoiseach! This isn't you and your political masters imposing poverty on Ireland just like you laid economic waste to Greece and the rest of the Mediterranean! Things! Have! Changed! The will of the people has been expressed! And that will says we don't want to be governed by you people any more!'

There's suddenly a dull thud as something hits the window. Yeah, no, I find out afterwards that it's, like, a bull's testicle. It sticks to the glass, then it slides down the window, leaving a slug trail of blood. A few seconds later, another one hits the window, then another, then another.

'Yes,' some German-sounding dude on the other side of the table goes, 'it is clear that your policies are very, very popular with the Irish people.'

Sorcha takes this as, like, a *personal* insult?

She goes, 'We are on course to achieve corbon neutrality within the next three years.'

'Yes, by exterminating all of the cows and sheep!' the same dude goes. 'And where will you get your meat from? Argentina, perhaps?

And how will you get it here? By using ships that pump CO_2 into the atmosphere.'

Another testicle hits the window.

The old man goes, 'Don't listen to him, Minister! Him *or* his subvention-loving fans outside! We are no longer a port of your failing political *über Staat*, Herr – actually, I'm not even going to bother learning your name because we're not going to know each other for very long! Like our good friends in Britain, we have taken back our fishing waters! We have taken back our natural resources! We have taken back our borders! And we have taken back our sovereignty!'

By the way, I'm being totally *ignored* during all of this.

He goes, 'It's goodbye and good riddance to the bureaucratic – inverted commas – elite who reduced this once-great country to the status of a protectorate! It's goodbye to the cosy cortels who –'

One of the women – it might be the one he called Ingrid – suddenly goes, 'I'm sorry, *who* is this person?' meaning obviously me. 'Since you are asking who we are and what right we have to be here?'

The old man looks at me.

'Oh,' he goes, suddenly copping me for the first time, 'this is my son, Ross! A long-time and strident critic of your so-called European project! What is it, Ross?'

I'm there, 'Did you ring your mate – as in, like, Verner Ryan?'

'He's just been appointed as the Coach of the Ireland women's rugby team, if you can believe such a thing exists! Political correctness gone mad and so forth!'

I end up having to raise my voice to him. I'm there, 'Did I only get the job because you called in a favour from one of your dick-head mates?'

He goes, 'You put my name down as a referee! And, as such, I extolled your virtues to the extent that they decided you were the man best qualified for the job! Although why you'd want it is quite another matter!'

The German dude who was giving Sorcha a hord time earlier goes, 'You talk to us about cosy elites and this is how *you* do business?'

Another testicle hits the window.

I'm there, 'The dude agreed to pay me three hundred Ks. Plus exes. He'd have gone higher as well.'

The old man goes, 'You've got a rugby brain, Ross. I've always said it. I'm sure what they've offered you is simply a reflection of how much they value you as a coach.'

It's at that exact moment that I feel a hand on my shoulder. I turn around and – yeah, no – the famous Peadar is looming over me with the big Conor McGregor head on him. Hennessy is standing next to him.

'How the hell did you get in here?' Hennessy goes.

I'm there, 'I flashed the old Blockbuster video cord at Ronan 2.0 here and the genius just let me in.'

He shoots Peadar an absolute filthy. It's obvious that he's not working out.

'You let him just morch into the centre of Government during the most highly sensitive negotiations this country has been involved in since the Treaty?' Hennessy goes. 'Get him the fock out of here.'

Peadar grips my shoulder – nearly tearing the muscle from the bone.

I'm like, 'Jesus Christ!'

You can tell that the EU heads are loving this.

'Will I throw him down the stairs?' Peadar goes.

And Hennessy actually thinks about it for a few seconds, before going, 'No, just show him to the door. Next time, break his legs, though.'

'Ross,' Fionn goes, 'you can't just turn up at the school like this.'

I'm there, 'Who says so?' sitting down opposite him and throwing the old Dubes up on his desk.

'*I* say so,' he goes, standing up, then sweeping my feet off.

The whole headmaster thing wasn't slow in going to his head. I say it to him as well.

I'm there, 'The whole headmaster thing wasn't slow in going to your head, was it?'

He goes, 'Ross, I have a lot of work to do today.'

'In terms of?'

'Ross –'

'Dude, I'm genuinely interested. I know how much this job means to you.'

He sits back down again – obviously realizing that he's being a bit of a dick.

He's there, 'I have a meeting with the Board of Management this afternoon,' and it's great to see him so in his element. 'There's been some, let's just say, pushback against the idea of twenty per cent of places going to children from disadvantaged areas.'

'I'm not surprised,' I go. 'Presumably these disadvantaged kids wouldn't be paying full fees?'

'They wouldn't be paying fees at all, Ross. That's the whole point of the exercise.'

'Excuse my ignorance, but who the fock is going to pay to teach them?'

'The plan would be to increase the fees for the students whose parents can afford to pay a little bit more.'

'Jesus, does that sound fair?'

'Well, it does to me. But it doesn't to some members of the board. They're pushing for five per cent instead of twenty.'

'Sounds like you're already making enemies, Dude.'

'Well, I'm sticking to my guns,' he goes. 'I also have to fill in this,' and he holds up a big sheaf of pages.

I'm like, 'What the fock is that?'

'Well, because I'm coaching the school team this year, I've got to go through the whole Gorda vetting thing.'

'Shit one.'

'The amount of information they need – including every single address I've ever lived at.'

'All means to an end, Dude. It's been too long since there was rugby in this school. Anyway, I wanted to talk to you about something this morning but you left the gaff early. You just mentioned the word pushback. I'm getting a bit of that myself. I had my first training session with the Ireland team – albeit women – the other day and let's just say they haven't exactly taken to me.'

'*Quelle surprise.*'

'I was thinking last night about the time I coached Pres Bray with you as my assistant. They were very Scooby Dubious about me at the stort, weren't they? I was trying to remember how I won them over.'

'Well, it would probably help if you stopped being an orsehole.'

'Whoa! Where's that coming from, Dude?'

'I'm sorry, I just think this is something you need to hear.'

'Okay, tough love – go on, Fionn, give it to me.'

'Why do you keep saying *"albeit* women"?'

'Er, because they *are* women?'

'But you talk about the job as if it's, I don't know, somehow beneath you.'

'Jesus Christ, Dude, it *is* beneath me. If there was any justice, I'd be doing what Joe Schmidt is doing.'

'You see, none of this sounds like the Ross O'Carroll-Kelly that I used to know.'

'Doesn't it?'

'The Ross O'Carroll-Kelly I knew believed he could coach anyone to play rugby.'

'Jesus, I love the way you're talking to me, Fionn. Say more things.'

'Look what you did in Bray –'

'You mean what *we* did – although it *was* mostly me. Continue.'

'No one gave Pres a chance. Including themselves. You walked into that dressing-room and you told them that they would win the Leinster Schools Senior Cup.'

'I believed it.'

'But your greatest achievement was getting *them* to believe it.'

'Dude, I'm nearly in tears here. I'm just warning you.'

'Give yourself some credit, Ross.'

'I should. More often.'

Fionn smiles and nods. 'Hey,' he goes, 'you'll never guess what I found when I was clearing out Tom's office?'

I'm there, 'Jesus, it wasn't a mannequin dressed as his mother, was it?'

'Why was *that* your first thought?'

'I've no idea. It's just where my mind *went* for some reason?'

'No,' he goes, 'what I found are these,' and that's when I notice, on the desk in front of him, a pile of – believe it or not – *records*?

I'm like, 'Holy shit, are they what I *think* they are?'

He sort of, like, smiles fondly.

'Father Fehily's old 45s,' he goes, 'of Hitler's most famous speeches.'

I'm like, 'Fock, that brings me back.'

'Munich 1929,' he goes. 'Nuremberg 1935. The Reichstag speech of 1939.'

I'm there, 'Great, great memories. So what are you going to do with them?'

'All I know is that I can't keep them here. I'd be cancelled in a second if I was found with them.'

'Er, *why*?'

'They're just not the kind of thing that kids should be listening to nowadays – or in *our* day, for that matter. Hey, I also found those.'

He points to about thirty lorge picture frames that are leaning against the wall behind me.

'What are *they*?' I go, standing up to check them out.

He's like, 'Just old photos. I thought Tom threw them out.'

And – yeah, no – it turns out that they're pictures of some of the great rugby teams and players who brought glory to the school over the years, which McGahy had taken down and replaced with photographs of the Castlerock College All Ireland-winning choristers and other focking dorks who brought the school nothing but shame.

I stort looking through the photos and I find the one of the so-called one-in-a-row team of 1999. I'm sitting on The Big O's shoulders and I'm holding the famous tinware.

I'm there, 'I know what I'm going to do with this!' and I head for the door, telling him over my shoulder, 'Bring a few more with you, Dude.'

I step outside into the corridor and I find the exact spot where Father Fehily hung this photograph all those years ago. In its place – I shit you not – is a photograph of Fionn and some randomer whose name I can't even remember winning a prize in the Young Scientist of the Year Contest in the RDS.

I whip it off the wall with one hand – Fionn goes, 'No, Ross, don't!' – and I fock it over my shoulder. The glass smashes all over the floor. Then I hang the photograph of me and the goys on the nail and I straighten it and smile.

'Was it necessary to break it?' he goes.

I'm there, 'I'm storting to think the only reason I ever got the job was because of who my old man is. Him and the dude who hired me know each other from the Shelbourne.'

He goes, 'Well, there's only one way to prove it's not true – and that's by being successful.'

I shit you not, there's a picture on the wall of McGahy and a bunch of Transition Year kids holding the humungous marrow that earned the school – this is, like, word for word what it says in the caption – a focking distinction in the 2016 Irish Schools Morket Gorden Awards.

That comes off the wall and goes over my shoulder as well. It shatters on the ground in about a thousand pieces.

'For God's sake,' Fionn goes, 'will you stop throwing them?'

I'm there, 'So talk to me, Dude – is this Ireland team any good?'

'What?'

'Hey, you're the one who goes to all their matches. I used to laugh at you for it.'

'So you've never actually seen them play?'

'Just clips. On YouTube. And, yeah, no, the captain – Sive Keenan is her name – was a bit put out that I didn't know all the players' names.'

'She was right to be. I can't believe you would turn up at training and not know anyone's name.'

'I kind of preferred it when you were bulling me up.'

'Look, Ross, all I'm going to say to you is this. There are musical geniuses in the world. You know the kind of people I'm talking about. Give them an instrument – any instrument – and they'll get a tune from it. Well, I've always thought that was like you with rugby.'

'Jesus, Dude. Focking goosebumps.'

I take another picture out of Fionn's hand. It's a black-and-white one of the Castlerock College team that reached the semi-finals of the Leinster Schools Senior Cup in 1929 but had a winning try disallowed in the last minute by a referee who just so happened to be a past pupil of Blackrock College. It's not for nothing that I always refer to it as 'a school for focking dicks' whenever I run into the likes of Shane Byrne with drink on me.

'Either way,' he goes, 'if you're going to take the money from the IRFU, you could pay players like Sive the courtesy of taking them as seriously as they take themselves.'

I'm there, 'Fair enough.'

I take down a framed photograph of the Castlerock College Players after they finished – hilariously – *third* in the Ten-Minute Play Contest in Stratford-upon-Avon in 2017. McGahy really dragged the school's reputation into the dirt – even though Tina wouldn't thank me for saying it.

I throw the frame over my shoulder and it lands with another explosion of glass, then I restore The Dispossessed to their rightful place on the wall of fame.

Fionn goes, 'Ross, please, get the fock out of here before I lose my job.'

And I'm there, 'Yeah, no, I'm out of here,' because already there's a plan forming in my head. 'Thanks for the pep talk.'

Honor holds up the first cord, which has a photograph on it of a girl with, like, short hair and shoulders like Taniela Tupou.

'Hannah Fox,' I go, quick as a flash.

She goes, 'Position?'

I'm like, 'Hooker – obviously.'

'Club?'

'University of Limerick Bohemians.'

'Province?'

'Munster.'

She holds up the next one.

I'm like, 'Megan Barrett. Full-back. Old Belvedere. Leinster. Next?'

She holds up the next one.

I'm like, 'Rachel Skeldon.'

She goes, 'Wrong!'

'Tara Murphy?'

'Wrong!'

'Oh, no, it's Lisa McGuin.'

'Position?'

'Left-wing. Her club is Tullamore and her province is – yeah, no – Connacht.'

She's like, 'You're doing really well, Dad.'

Yeah, no, the actual flashcords were *my* idea? But she was the one who printed off the photographs of every player in the Ireland squad, cut them out, stuck each one to a filing cord using Pritt Stick and then wrote their details on the back.

She's an amazing daughter – I don't care if she can't drive for shit.

She flashes another one at me. This one is tall with, like, brown hair.

'Emer Godsil,' I go. 'Tighthead.'

She's like, 'Wrong!'

'Loosehead, then.'

'Club?'

'Railway Union.'

'Province?'

'Ulster.'

My phone rings. It's Erika.

I'm like, 'Hey, Sis, how the hell *are* you?'

She's there, 'I've just collected Sea-mon from the airport.'

'Whoa!' I go. 'Holy fock! So this thing is, like, definitely happening?'

'I just dropped her to RTÉ. They're going to put her up in the Clayton in Ballsbridge while the *Prime Time* team pre-interview her.'

'Er, cool. This shit is suddenly getting real.'

'It's already real. Jesus Christ, Ross, our father burned the Dáil to the ground.'

'Yeah, no, I'm just saying that the shit is about to hit the fan – and in a big-time, big-time way.'

'There's still time to stop this thing and make sure that Ireland remains in the European Union.'

I'm like, 'That's, er, great news,' pretending that I give a fock one way or the other.

She's there, 'According to the news, the Irexit negotiations haven't been going well.'

I'm like, 'Yeah, no, I stuck my head around the door the other day and that was definitely the impression I got.'

'RTÉ are hoping to broadcast the interview next week.'

'And, em, you definitely think we're doing the right thing here, do you?'

'What do you mean?'

'In terms of, like, destroying the old man?'

'He's a focking danger to the world, Ross.'

'Yeah, no, I just wanted to, em, check.'

'If this thing plays out like I hope it will, he'll be forced to resign as soon as the interview goes out. Whoever replaces him as Taoiseach will have to accept that the referendum result is tornished and the country will be asked to vote again – around about the time *he* storts a thirty-year prison sentence . . . for treason.'

I've never been too proud to admit when I'm in the wrong – it's one of the things I love about myself – and right now is no exception.

'I'm sorry,' I go, 'if some of you got offended by one or two things I said the last day.'

'You're sorry *if* we got offended?' Sive goes – and I'm storting to wonder is it that she just hates men? 'Don't you mean you're sorry for turning up here and not showing us the respect we deserve as rugby players?'

I'm like, 'Yeah, no, that's *kind* of what I meant?'

'Focking say that, then,' she goes.

We're standing on the sideline in Donnybrook Stadium and the players are all gathered around me, waiting to hear what I have to say for myself.

I'm there, 'I'm *saying* sorry – to you, Sive Keenan,' and then – this is a real moment – I point at each of them individually and I go, 'And to you, Emer Godsil . . . and to you, Lisa McGuin . . . and to you, Megan Barrett . . . and to you, Rachel Skeldon . . . and to you, Joanne Wassell . . . and to you, Hannah Fox . . . and to you, Grainne Hutton . . .'

From the looks on their faces, they're obviously thinking, Whoa! What kind of Jedi mind shit is this?

'I'm not Rachel Skeldon,' one of them goes. 'I'm Louise.'

Yeah, no, they're identical twins. But the point is that they know I'm suddenly making an effort here.

'What, are we supposed to be impressed that you bothered to learn our names?' Sive goes – like I said, she's a tough audience.

I'm there, 'I didn't just learn your names, Sive. I also watched some of your matches.'

Well, I watched one or two of their matches, if I'm being one *hundred* per cent honest?

'Wow!' she goes, giving me a presumably sorcastic round of applause – and I can tell from the way the other, I don't know, ladies, girls, women, whatever you want to call them, are looking at her that they've got massive, massive respect for her. 'And what did you learn from these matches?'

'Well,' I go, 'I learned that, in the last Six Nations, you blew a sixteen-point lead against Scotland. And I learned that you were better than Wales in every single deportment, yet still managed to somehow lose.'

'Is that right?'

'Yes – and that if you'd tackled Aurora Bergamaschi with the intensity you showed when you tackled me the last day, then you might have beaten Italy.'

Oh, she doesn't like that – she doesn't like that one little bit.

I'm there, 'Look, today is the twelfth of October–'

'It's the tenth of October,' one of the Skeldon twins goes.

I'm like, 'Either way, the Six Nations Championship storts in ten weeks–'

'Sixteen weeks,' Lisa McGuin goes.

Seriously, it's like being married to twenty-five women at the same time.

I'm there, 'My point is, are we going to stand around just talking shite to each other, or are we going to come up with a plan to beat England on the first of February?'

'France,' Joanne Wassell goes. 'Our first match is against France.'

I'm there, 'Look, I meant what I said at the press conference the other day. I genuinely believe this team is capable of winning a Grand Slam. If any of you disagree with me, well, I honestly don't know what you're doing here and you'd be better off leaving now. Go on – get the fock out of here.'

No one moves. I suddenly have them eating out of my hand.

I'm there, 'As a group of players, I think you've got massive, massive potential. But you need to be stronger and you need to be fitter. That's why I'm planning to bring in weight sessions and roadwork – that's in addition to what we do here on the pitch. I want each and every one of you running ten Ks three times a week and I want to see you working hord in the gym to build up muscle mass.'

I watch a few of them – including Sive – roll their eyes.

I'm there, 'Like I said, you don't have to play for me if you don't want to. Okay, let's train.'

Which is what we then do.

I'm going to put my hand on my hort now and say that I end up being pleasantly surprised by what I see in terms of their basic skills. I put them through a few drills, the kind of things I did with the goys in Pres and – yeah, no, without wishing to come across as, like, patronizing – they're well able for them.

I'm making sure to dish out the compliments as well, because if I've learned one thing in my thirty-eight years on this planet that we call, I don't know, Earth, it's how much women enjoy hearing nice shit being said about them.

So I'm going, 'Excellent hands, Megan Barrett . . . that's it, Grainne Hutton! All of the great out-halves in history have had one thing in common – fast ball coming at them from a top scrum-half . . . superb stuff, Hannah – I'd nearly say you did that as well as any man . . .'

Anyway, they end up putting in a good, like, two-hour shift, at the end of which they're out on their feet.

Again, I make the effort with Sive as we're walking back towards the dressing-rooms. There's just, like, something in me that makes me believe I'm capable of chorming any woman.

'Did you enjoy that?' I go – a big stupid grin on my face.

She's like, 'What, having rugby mansplained to me by someone who never won an international cap in his life?'

'There were reasons for that,' I go, 'which I won't go into. Warren focking Gatland is all I'm prepared to say on the subject. And Declan Kidney. And Eddie O'Sullivan.'

She's there, 'Unlike you, I've actually represented my country – fifty-seven times, by the way!'

And I'm like, 'Yeah, no, but it's not –'

I suddenly stop myself.

She goes, 'Go on, say it.'

I'm there, 'I wasn't going to say anything.'

She's like, 'You were going to say that playing for the Ireland women's team isn't the same as playing for the Ireland men's team.'

Jesus Christ, this woman can read me like the instructions on an airplane sick bag.

I'm there, 'That's not what I was going to –'

But she disappears into the dressing-room then. And that's when I hear a woman's voice – loud and shrill – going, 'Anton! Anton!'

I turn around and I can't believe what I end up seeing. The old dear is walking across the cor pork wearing – I swear to fock – just her nightdress.

I'm like, 'What the fock?'

'Anton,' she goes, 'you'll have to be quick. I've got a taxi waiting.'

I look over her shoulder. Yeah, no, there's a taxi there alright.

'The fock are you talking about?' I go. 'Who's Anton?'

She's there, 'Just a wash and set, Anton. I've got the Lady Captain's Lunch in an hour.'

I'm like, 'It's nine o'clock at night,' and I notice that the top three buttons of her nightdress are open and I can see her bips.

I'm there, 'Jesus, cover yourself up,' and I do up her buttons for her.

She goes, 'And don't use that shampoo that you used the last time. My scalp was like a bloody croissant.'

I'm there, 'I'm not your focking hairdresser, okay?'

I just happen to look around and – yeah, no – the entire Ireland women's team is staring in our direction.

I'm there, 'Come on. We need to get you home.'

I stort walking her towards the taxi, but then all of a sudden a black Merc screeches to a stop beside us. The back door flies open and the old man jumps out.

He goes, 'I've got it from here, Kicker!'

Then he storts talking to the old dear in, like, a soothing voice, going, 'It's okay, Fionnuala – it's just those tablets of yours making you feel confused again.'

She goes, 'Chorles!'

And he's like, 'That's right! It's me, Dorling.'

'Where am I?'

'Oh, it doesn't matter. We'll have you home in an instant.'

He puts his orm around her shoulder and he sort of, like, slow-walks her to the limo and helps her into the back seat.

I'm like, 'What the fock?'

But he goes, 'She's fine, Kicker. Everything is going to be fine.'

Simone looks wrecked – like she hasn't slept. Which she probably *hasn't*, by the way? And I won't even tell you what she's wearing. It's enough to say that she looks like someone switched off the lights in a charity shop, then told her to take seven random items and throw them on her.

She's shaking like a literally leaf as well.

Erika goes, 'Drink some water.'

But Simone's like, 'I *can't* drink any more water. I'll need the toilet again.'

Yeah, no, we're in RTÉ, sitting in a sort of, like, green room area, although I'm disappointed to see there's no booze. They probably don't put it out in the mornings.

I'm there, 'Maybe just try to relax,' and she shoots me an absolute filthy.

She goes, 'That's easy for you to say. You don't know what these people are capable of.'

I'm like, 'Yeah, no, I sort of *do*?'

And she's there, 'No, Ross – you *definitely* don't.'

The famous David McCullagh walks in then. Sorcha has a

massive, massive crush on him. I remember she went through a period of saying his name in her sleep when she was on hormonal tablets for her back acne.

He goes, 'Hi, Sea-mon – right, let's get you upstairs to hair and make-up.'

But Simone is there, 'No.'

David is like, 'What?' and you wouldn't blame him – she looks a focking state.

'I don't wear make-up,' she goes.

She never brushes her hair either.

Erika's there, 'It's presumably just for the cameras, Sea-mon.'

'That's right,' David goes. 'The studio lights can make you like look pale and washed out.'

Simone's there, 'I think people will be far more interested in what I have to say than in how I look.'

The girl has a hell of a lot to learn about the world.

David just nods, then tells us to follow him, which we do, into the actual TV studio where the interview is going to happen. There's, like, two hord chairs there and four cameras – two pointing at each chair from different angles. David tells Simone to sit down, then they mic her up.

He goes, 'There'll be an introduction at the top, which I'll record later on. We'll just go straight into the interview, if that's okay with you?'

Simone gives him a tight little nod, takes one final sip of water, then looks at Erika, who gives her a smile of – I want to say – *encouragement*?

'Sea-mon,' David goes, 'can you tell us how you first became involved *with* Charles O'Carroll-Kelly?'

She takes a deep breath, swallows hord, then goes, 'The initial contact was actually with Hennessy Coghlan-O'Hara.'

'The Attorney General?'

'Yes, the Attorney General.'

'And how did that come about?'

She takes another deep breath.

'I was in court,' she goes, 'which wasn't unusual for me. I've been involved in environmental activism for twenty years. I've been arrested over a hundred times – mostly for public order offences. Anyway, I went to a livestock auction in Monasterevin and I opened a gate and let about seventy cows and fifty sheep loose on the Main Street.'

'You're a vegetarian.'

'A vegan – but I'm also against the exploitation of animals generally. So I was charged with that. Pleaded not guilty because I didn't want the case dealt with in the district court. I wanted a full jury trial. Wanted an audience. Didn't care if I got jail. I decided to defend myself and spent three days in court essentially just talking about intensive farming and the damage that it's doing to the planet.'

'Was this to waste the court's time?'

'No, I really wanted to make people aware of what was going on. There are four million sheep in Ireland and one and a half million cows. We have more sheep and cows than we have people. These animals weren't meant to be bred in those kinds of numbers. And because they're ruminant animals – which means they produce gases that harm the environment – they have been the single biggest contributor to the depletion of the ozone layer and the overheating of our planet.'

I turn to Erika. I'm there, 'It's gone a bit boring, hasn't it?'

She shushes me.

David goes, 'So you were in favour of getting rid of Ireland's entire sheep and cow population?'

Simone's there, 'Well, that's a slight oversimplification. My point was that we shouldn't have had a cow and sheep population in the first place – certainly not one that was equivalent to our human population. But, yes, I did mention in court that I wanted to see the national herd reduced to zero.'

'And then, what, you had a call from Hennessy Coghlan-O'Hara?'

'No, he actually came to court. Said he'd been following the case in the papers. I didn't even know who he was. Then he told me that he was the Attorney General.'

David laughs – presumably at the idea of Hennessy being the Attorney General.

Simone goes, 'He said that the Taoiseach wanted to meet me. He said we had a lot of similar ideas, which he'd love to discuss. I said I was in the middle of a trial in case he hadn't noticed. He just laughed. And that afternoon, the judge declared a mistrial because of something that one of the jurors had been overheard saying.'

'Do you know what that was?' David goes.

'No, just that the trial was suddenly over and that was the last I ever heard about it. So then a car arrived at my house the next morning and I was taken to meet – yeah, no – the Taoiseach.'

'In Government Buildings?'

'No, in Áras an Uachtaráin. He was still in his dressing-gown at ten o'clock in the morning. I remember it kept opening.'

I look at Erika. I'm there, 'The man is a focking disgrace.'

Simone goes, 'He told me that he loved the things I'd said in court about the need to get rid of sheep and cows.'

David's there, 'The Taoiseach is a vegetarian?' presumably ripping the piss.

'No,' she goes, 'he just hates farmers. He kept saying what a waste of land it was and how he'd made it a priority of his to smash the Political-Agricultural Complex.'

'The Political-Agricultural Complex?'

'That's what he called it. The one thing he hates more than farmers, he said, was politicians from farming backgrounds. He said Ireland was a backward, peasant country with an unhealthy attachment to the land and we'd learned absolutely nothing since the Potato Famine. He said wiping out all of Ireland's cows and sheep was consistent with his vision of a post-agricultural Ireland.'

'So he used you?'

'I would say we were using each other. At that stage we were two people who wanted the same thing. He said he'd just appointed his daughter-in-law as the Minister for Climate Action.'

'Senator Sorcha Lalor.'

'That's right. At the time, she was looking to hire a Special Adviser and he suggested that I write to her, to introduce myself, and to tell her what her policy priorities should be for her first one hundred days in office. Two days later, she rang me, said she'd read my letter and she said it was oh my God. I remember those were her exact words, in fact. She said, "I read your letter. It was, like, oh my God. It was, like, oh! my God!" '

'And what do you think she meant by that?'

'I took it to mean that she was impressed.'

'Right.'

'Because then she offered me the job as her Special Adviser.'

'What did the role involve?'

'Writing speeches. Offering her guidance on matters relating to the environment. But what she didn't know was that I was reporting to the Taoiseach. The Taoiseach and the Attorney General.'

'On a daily basis?'

Simone laughs. She's like, 'Sometimes hourly.'

David goes, 'And what was the nature of those conversations?'

'They wanted me to steer her in the direction of the ban on sheep and cow breeding, but they wanted her to think that it was her idea. So that's what I did. Then, as the weeks went by, they asked me to write more and more speeches for her that were full of – I suppose you'd call it, inflammatory language. They wanted to put her into conflict with other European leaders.'

'What was the reason for that?'

'Well, the Taoiseach knew she was the only member of the Cabinet who was against his plan to pull out of the European Union. He thought if he could get her to change her mind – and do it in a very public way – it would sway a lot of, I suppose, moderates, although *he* called them wishy-washy types.'

'How did you feel, leading this double life?'

'Look, I'm not going to pretend that it bothered me. Reducing the national herd to zero, withdrawing from the EU – these were all things that I was in favour of politically, so I'd be lying if I said it made me feel in any way uncomfortable. But that was because I didn't realize that, well, I was being used as much as Sorcha Lalor.'

'Describe for me the circumstances in which you discovered that.'

She goes, 'Well,' and then she takes a big gulp of air – for a second, I think she's about to burst into tears – 'I was in the Taoiseach's office one day – not in the Áras, this was on Merrion Street – and

I overheard a conversation between the Taoiseach, the Attorney General and a man named Fyodor, who's a Russian businessman with links to Vladimir Putin.'

'The Russian President.'

'Yes. And that was when I discovered that this secret War on Rural Ireland, as the Taoiseach and the Attorney General called it, was really a plan to depopulate the Midlands.'

'Why did they want to depopulate the Midlands?'

'The Taoiseach has been selling off Ireland's natural resources to Fyodor and other Russian business interests – our oil, our gas, our forests, our turf. It was all part of the deal that helped him get elected using Russian cyber-terrorism. Once the Midlands have been depopulated, the Russians are going to lease the land to build nuclear power stations and dump their rubbish.'

'You do realize that these are explosive allegations you are making?'

'Yes, I do.'

'And what else did you hear at that meeting?'

She goes, 'I heard –'

And that's when the tears really *do* come?

David's there, 'Take your time, Sea-mon.'

Me and Erika look at each other.

'This is it,' Erika whispers.

Simone takes a second or two to, like, compose herself, then she goes, 'I heard the Taoiseach tell the Attorney General . . . to burn the Dáil.'

'Can you please repeat that?' David goes. 'You heard the Taoiseach of this country tell the Attorney General –'

'He said that if the opinion polls were in any way close leading up to the referendum vote, then Hennessy should go ahead with the plan to burn the Dáil, as previously discussed, and blame it on the European Union.'

'You heard that?'

'Yes, I did.'

'You're absolutely sure?'

'Yes, I am.'

'A lot of people watching this interview would ask why you didn't do anything about it at the time? Why didn't you alert the Gardaí?'

'I don't know is the honest answer. Maybe I didn't take it seriously until it actually –'

And it's at that exact moment that I hear – yeah, no – a kerfuffle going on behind me. I hear, like, raised voices saying, 'You can't go in there!' and then other voices going, 'Step aside or I'll arrest you for harbouring a criminal and obstructing a Garda in the course of his duties.'

Me and Erika both look at each other.

She's like, 'What the fock?' and she says it before I get there myself.

The studio is suddenly full of people, we're talking, like, nine or ten Gords in uniform, then two or three presumably plainclothes detectives, all dudes.

David McCullagh is like, 'What's going on?'

Simone looks suddenly terrified.

'See-mon Donne?' one of the Gords goes, whipping out a pair of handcuffs.

She's like, 'It's Sea-mon,' obviously out of pure habit.

'No!' Erika shouts. 'No!'

But the dude goes, 'See-mon Donne, I am arresting you on suspicion of arson.'

4

Man Go On Chained

'What the fock?' Erika goes. 'What the focking *fock*?'

This is, like, two days later and the girl still hasn't calmed down. If anything, she's, like, *worse*?

She's there, 'How the fock did they know?'

I'm like, 'Know? In terms of?'

She goes, 'How did they know that Sea-mon was talking to RTÉ?'

'I don't know,' I go. 'Do you think maybe –'

She's like, 'What?'

I'm there, 'Do you think maybe our *phones* are possibly tapped?'

She suddenly stares into space, as if considering this possibility for the first time.

'The focker,' she goes. 'The focking –' and she's suddenly in such a rage that I'm wondering has she been having any conversations recently that she wouldn't want the old man or Hennessy hearing. Sex conversations, in other words. 'He tapped my focking phone – my own father.'

Yeah, no, we're in the kitchen in the gaff, by the way.

I'm there, 'Have you spoken to her?'

She's like, 'Who?'

'Er, See-mon?'

'She's being questioned about a plot to burn down the focking Dáil, Ross. I don't think they're going to be letting visitors in and out.'

'So, er, do you think RTÉ will show the interview?'

She shakes her head like she can't believe that even *I* could be so thick?

I'm there, 'I'll take that as a no, then.'

She's like, 'Of course they're not going to focking show it. She's being questioned about a serious crime.'

'Which she didn't do – *we* know that for a fact.'

'The reason they arrested her was to destroy her credibility. I would say that's job focking done, wouldn't you?'

'Well, hopefully the Feds will find out that she had fock-all to do with it and just let her go.'

She laughs.

She's there, 'They can't let her go. Not now. She's too dangerous.'

I'm like, 'So what are they *going* to do?'

'They're going to fit her up, of course.'

'You're shitting me.'

'It's already happening. Have you *seen* the newspapers this morning?'

'I don't know if that's a serious question or not.'

'They're already talking about her arrest record. There's photographs of her at the Shell to Sea protest, with her head shaved, looking like a crazy person. There's photographs of her being led out of Penneys in handcuffs. One of the tabloids is calling her Girl Fawkes.'

'Jesus,' I go, even though I don't really *get* the reference? 'But there's no actual evidence against her – as in, there *can't* be?'

All of a sudden, I hear the front door slam, then I hear Sorcha in the hallway, going, 'Erika? ERIKA?'

She steps into the kitchen then and I don't think either me or Erika is ready for what we end up seeing. Sorcha is covered in blood.

She goes, 'I saw your cor outside! How are you?'

I'm like, 'What the fock?'

Even Erika goes, 'What happened? Were you in, like, a cor crash?'

Sorcha's just like, 'Oh, it's not *my* blood,' as casual as you like. 'I got pelted with bulls' testicles leaving the withdrawal negotiations today.'

Politics is definitely hordening her.

I'm there, 'Are you okay?'

And she goes, 'I'm fine. It was nothing compared to the shock of finding out about Sea-mon. I don't know if you heard the news, but she's just been chorged with Orson and Conspiracy to Usurp the

Functions of Government. They're saying the second chorge might even be upgraded to Sedition or even, like, Treason.'

Shit the bed.

I'm there, 'Sorcha, the girl is innocent – and I'm saying that as someone who was never her number one fan.'

She goes, 'It turns out there were a lot of things I didn't know about Sea-mon. You see, when I read her letter telling me what my policy priorities should be, I was like, "Oh my God!" I was *literally* like, "Oh! My God!" I should have done a proper background check on her.'

Erika goes, 'What's in the newspapers this morning, Sorcha, is all bullshit.'

'Well, it's hordly bullshit,' Sorcha goes. 'She told me about her arrests. I didn't know about the other stuff.'

'What other stuff?'

'She's been receiving regular payments from a charitable organization with links to a senior official in the European Commission. Ten thousand euros per month.'

Erika gets suddenly upset. She's there, 'Sorcha, you have to listen to me. Sea-mon had nothing to do with the fire. She's being set up.'

'Oh my God,' Sorcha goes, the blood still dripping off her, 'not this again, Erika.'

She goes, 'My dad burned the Dáil. Sea-mon was going to go public. When she was arrested, she was in the middle of doing a big interview with *Prime Time*.'

'With David McCullagh,' I go.

She's like, 'David?' and I watch her eyes definitely sporkle.

Erika's there, 'I arranged the whole thing. Except Dad found out about it – because he has my mobile phone tapped.'

'Oh my God,' Sorcha goes, 'do you know how *actually* paranoid you sound right now?'

Erika goes, 'Sorcha, you and I have been friends since we were, like, *how* old?'

'I don't know. Since we storted in Mount Anville – as in, like, the *junior* school?'

'You have to trust me, Sorcha.'

'Erika, I know you *mean* well? And I'm really sad that your relationship with your dad has deteriorated to the extent that you would think him capable of *doing* something like this? But you really have to let this thing go – you *both* do?'

'Open your focking eyes, Sorcha! He's an evil dictator and you can't even see it.'

'Well, for your information, Erika, this afternoon he put out a statement saying he's decided to become a vegan in support of my efforts to help Ireland achieve corbon neutrality in the short term.'

I'm suddenly smiling at the idea of my old man going to Shanahan's and ordering, I don't know, the roasted aubergine curry.

Sorcha's there, 'He said it was important that he – *as* the elected leader of the country – sets an example when it comes to switching to a more environmentally sustainable diet. Does that sound like the action of an evil dictator to you?'

Erika goes, 'He's taking you for a fool. Sea-mon was right – you're just another one of his useful idiots.'

Sorcha's there, 'This is the kind of stuff you were saying about Chorles four or five years ago. That he was a Moscow agent and whatever else. I'm not being a bitch, Erika, but you had a nervous breakdown. You focked off to Australia, then you came back and – oh my God – it looks like *nothing* has changed.'

I'm there, 'Sorcha, you have to believe us.'

'Er, no, I don't,' she goes. 'Look, I'm sorry if my having a political career inconveniences you, Ross, but you're going to have to get used to the fact that things have changed.'

'See-mon didn't do it. She's an innocent woman.'

'Well, maybe you can explain to the jury at her trial why her Google search history is full of references to orson. Now, if you don't mind, I'm going upstairs to take a shower.'

I feel shit for Simone. I mean, how could I *not*? But over the next few weeks, I stort to think – yeah, no – hopefully the truth will come out during her trial, which according to Erika is going to be held in front of a thing called the Special Criminal Court.

If anyone is going to get to the bottom of what really happened, it sounds like they're the crowd to do it.

While we're all waiting for that to happen, I decide to throw myself fully into my coaching job. As October turns into November, and the evenings get shorter, my competitive juices stort to genuinely flow. I've actually storted to look forward to these nights, training under the lights in Donnybrook Stadium.

Anyway, I arrive there while the ladies – sorry, *women* – are getting changed. As they stort to drift out of the dressing-room in their dribs and drabs, I tell them to go back inside and change out of their boots and into their runners.

Yeah, no, I've got something a little different planned for tonight.

They do what they're told. They're picking up on the vibe that all of the misunderstandings of the past few weeks are behind us and now it's time to get down to business – and when I say business, I mean the business of winning the Six Nations Championship.

All except for Sive, who stares at me like I've turned up at her old dear's funeral in a focking clown suit.

'Our runners?' she goes. 'Why are we putting on our runners?'

Honestly, it's like talking to my children.

I'm there, 'We're putting on our runners because we're going running. Although you can stay here if you want – maybe lift some weights?'

All of the other players arrive out in their runners and she disappears inside – pissing and moaning – to get hers.

'Where are we running to?' Grainne Hutton – scrum-half, Horlequins, Munster – goes.

I love her little sing-song voice.

I'm there, 'We're running to Herbert Pork and back.'

Megan Barrett – full-back, Old Belvedere and Leinster – goes, 'Why can't we just do laps of the pitch?'

I'm there, 'Because I want you out there – on the streets of actual Donnybrook.'

'Why?'

'How many people out there know that Ireland even *has* a women's rugby team?'

'I would say everybody,' Heather Hobson – tighthead, Railway Union and Ulster – goes.

I'm there, 'Is that so? Well, it certainly doesn't translate into ticket sales. You didn't fill Donnybrook Stadium for any of your Six Nations matches last year – or the year before.'

'This is bullshit,' Sive goes, arriving out again.

I'm there, 'I want to create a buzz around this team. I want people to see you out and about on Anglesea Road, Eglinton Road, Beaver Row, and ask, "Who *are* these goys?" '

Sive rolls her eyes and goes, 'Come on, lads, let's just do it.'

I love the way she says that. Whenever I'm in Galway, I always make a point of going to the big Supermacs in Eyre Square, not to eat the food, just to hear women refer to each other as 'lads'.

So they set off – no more complaints – out onto Donnybrook Road and across Anglesea Bridge, then they hang a shorp left onto Anglesea Road. By then, they're, like, spread out, as you would expect them to be – the backs way out front and the forwards lagging a good fifty metres behind them.

At first, I manage to keep pace with the backs, including Joanne Wassell – out-half, Leinster, Clontorf – who's an absolute flier. But by the time we get a third of the way down Anglesea Road – just outside Ollie Campbell Pork, in fact – I stort to slip back and pretty soon I find myself running alongside Sive at the very back of the field.

There's this, like, uncomfortable silence between us. I'm actually kind of relieved when I hear my phone ring in the pocket of my tracksuit bottoms. I whip it out. It ends up being Honor.

I'm there, 'I might need to take this. It's, like, my daughter.'

Sive doesn't respond. Doesn't give a fock one way or the other.

I answer anyway. I'm like, 'Honor, how the hell are you?'

She goes, 'Dad, Adam's playing a gig.'

I'm like, 'Er, right,' wondering where this conversation is heading.

'You remember Adam – the goy I told you about, who was in, like, the Battle of the Bands? He goes to, like, Newpork?'

'Yeah, no – in other words, *not* a rugby school – I remember.'

'He's playing, like, a solo gig in Whelan's this Friday.'

'Whelan's? Whelan's on –'

'Wexford Street.'

'Yeah, no, I was going to *say* Wexford Street. Fair focks was going to be my follow-up to that. A solo gig – he's obviously doing well.'

'So I was wondering can I go?'

'What? To Whelan's? Are we talking, like, on your own?'

'Of course I'm talking about on my own.'

'Er, I don't think that's going to happen, Honor.'

'Why the fock not?'

'Well, I don't know if this is me being overprotective, but my instinct tells me that this is another one of those things that you're probably too young to do.'

'But I told Adam that you'd been cool with it because you're, like, an amazing dad.'

'Right – that's good for me to hear from, like, a *confidence* point of view? It's just I'm not sure I'd feel comfortable letting you go to a pub on your own at – let's be honest – thirteen years old. Especially after you got shit-faced the last two or three times we let you out.'

'I won't drink. I was thinking that I might actually drive.'

'You're not driving.'

Sive just looks at me, presumably shocked at the thought of a thirteen-year-old girl driving a cor – even though they're all up on tractors at the age of eight over her side of the country.

'You're a focking wanker,' she goes – this is Honor, by the way, not Sive.

I'm like, 'Honor, just wait. What if I told you that you *could* go?'

There's, like, five seconds of silence on the other end of the line, then she goes, 'Keep talking. There's a focking catch, isn't there?'

I'm like, 'It's not exactly a catch. You can go to Whelan's – but I'll have to come with you.'

She's there, 'How is that not a catch?'

'I'll let you do your thing. Jumping around in the mosh pit or whatever the equivalent is these days. And I'll keep an eye on you from the other side of the bor.'

'Er, *creepy* much?'

'That's what's on offer, Honor. You can take it or leave it.'

She sort of, like, huffs to herself.

'Fine,' she just goes.

I'm like, 'Hey, you'll have to excuse your old man if you find I'm holding on a little bit too tight. It's just you're growing up so fast – going to see boys in bands and drinking vodka and getting banned from driving. It seems like only two years ago that you were making your Confirmation,' and I give Sive a little wink.

Honor goes, 'Er, it *is* only two years ago that I made my Confirmation?' and then she hangs up on me.

'Teenagers,' I go, shaking my head, but Sive doesn't take the conversational bait.

Whatever other qualities she might have as a player, I can see that her fitness wouldn't be great, by the way. She's already out of breath.

She goes, 'What . . . the fock . . . is this . . . supposed to be . . . even proving?'

I'm there, 'Like I told you, Sive, I want people to see you.'

'No one can see us,' she goes. 'It's focking dork out.'

I'm there, 'I'm going to ask the IRFU to give us any fluorescent bibs that the men aren't using.'

She suddenly stops running.

She's like, 'Do you know what? Fock this!'

I carry on running, though. Literally five seconds later, I hear the screech of brakes and then a loud bump, followed by a noise that sounds like the screams of an animal caught in a trap. I turn around just in time to see a bus pulling to a sudden halt and Sive lying on the road, on the flat of her back, clutching her shoulder and – like I said – making the most horrible noises.

She's going, 'NNNGGGHHH!!!! NNNGGGHHH!!!! NNNGGGHHH!!!!'

I'm the first to reach her. I'm like, 'What happened? What the fock?'

But she can't even talk. She's like, 'NNNGGGHHH!!!! NNNGGGHHH!!!! NNNGGGHHH!!!!'

I peg it over there, going, 'What happened? What happened?'

Suddenly, there's a bus driver standing there and he's like, 'She just stepped off the road in front of me.'

It's obvious straight away that she's badly hurt. And then I notice that her orm is, like, literally hanging out of its socket and I end up having to turn away at the sight of it.

At the same time, I'm there, 'You're going to be okay, Sive.'

But then the other players, who've heard the commotion, have storted drifting back towards us and their faces tell the tale. Hannah Fox – hooker, UL Bohemians, Munster – takes one look at her and puts her hand over her mouth, looking like she might be about to *vom*?

'It's her shoulder,' Lisa McGuin – left-wing, Tullamore, Connacht – goes. 'She's dislocated it.'

I'm there, 'Okay, do *not* panic!' and maybe it's the sound of my voice, but Sive – her face, I don't know, grimacing – manages to get herself up into a sitting position. And that's when the most unbeliev-able thing happens. Sive grips the top of her orm really hord and – I shit you not – pushes the thing *back* into its socket!

'NNNGGGHHH!!!' she goes – except even *louder* this time? 'NNNNNNGGGGGGHHHHHH!!!!!!'

I've never seen anything like it in my life, except maybe the time that JP dislocated his thumb falling face-first out of a rickshaw the night Ryle Nugent was made Head of Sport in RTÉ. He pushed the thing back in himself as well, but he had, like, sixteen pints and seven or eight vodka and Red Bulls on him – Ryle is his cousin, in fairness – and it was only, like, a thumb. This is, like, an actual shoulder.

'NNNNNNGGGGGGHHHHHH!!!!!!' she carries on going.

I whip out my phone and I'm there, 'I'd better call you an ambu-lance. Are you with the VHI or is that a ridiculous question?'

She doesn't answer me, because the initial pain of the injury is storting to give way to something else – the thought of what it's going to mean for her Six Nations campaign.

'FOCK!' Sive shouts, furious with herself. 'FOCK! FOCK! FOCK! FOCK! FOCK!'

I'm there, 'It's a dislocated shoulder, Sive. It doesn't necessarily mean –'

She goes, 'What are you, a doctor?'

I'm like, 'No, I'm not a doctor – are you?'

'Yes, I am,' she goes. 'Well, nearly – I'm in my final year of Medicine in Trinity.'

I have to say, this *does* surprise me? Usually people who are doing Medicine in Trinity find a way to drop it into the conversation before they've said hello.

She goes, 'That's me out of the Six Nations, lads.'

Honor asks me what's wrong with Erika.

I'm there, 'In terms of what, Honor?'

This is us standing in the queue for, like, *Whelan's*, by the way?

She goes, 'She just seems really, I don't know, *sad* at the moment?'

I'm there, 'It's grown-up stuff, Honor. You wouldn't understand.'

'Is it because Grandad and Hennessy burned down the Dáil and now they're trying to blame it on Mom's friend with the dreadlocks and the shit clothes?'

Okay, it turns out she *does* understand.

I'm there, 'Yeah, no, that's pretty much it in a nutshell – well done.'

She goes, 'She's still coming to New York with us, isn't she?'

And I'm like, 'Yeah, no, the flights are booked. The tenth of December. We're talking me, we're talking you, we're talking Erika, we're talking Rihanna-Brogan.'

While I'm doing all this talking, I'm looking over my shoulder at some of the people queuing behind us and I suddenly feel like some, I don't know, middle-aged dude, which I suppose is what I *am*?

We eventually reach the top of the queue. Honor walks up to the dude in the booth and goes, 'Hi, I'm on, like, the *guest* list?'

The dude is a sort of, like, Emo dude, with about ten rings in his nose and the same number in his bottom lip.

He goes, 'What's your name?'

She's like, 'Honor? As in, like, Honor O'Carroll-Kelly?'

'And what about him?' he goes, nodding in my general postcode.

Honor – I swear to fock – goes, 'No, he's not with me.'

I'm there, 'What, so there's no free ticket for me?'

She goes, 'I told you – I don't want people to know we're together.'

I walk up to the dude in the booth.

I'm like, 'One, please.'

He goes, 'You're not going to keep bothering that girl, are you?'

'That *girl* – as you call her – happens to be my daughter. How much?'

'Twenty-seven euros and fifty cent.'

'Yeah, no, I'm just looking for *one* ticket?'

'That's what it costs. Twenty-seven euros and fifty cent.'

Jesus. You wouldn't focking blame them. I pay the chorge, then I follow Honor inside the actual venue.

I go, 'That skirt is way too short, by the way. I was trying to avoid saying anything, but, after handing over twenty-seven fifty, I feel like I'm entitled.'

She's like, 'I need a hundred euro,' holding out her hand.

'And am I allowed to ask what it's even for?'

'It's for focking drink, Dad.'

Seriously, she should be doing stand-up.

I'm there, 'You won't be drinking, Honor. And, by the way, if you're thinking of having a sneaky one – a Crouching Cider, Hidden Naggin, as we used to call it back in the day – I definitely *wouldn't*, if I was you? Because if I catch even one whiff of alcohol off your breath tonight, I will storm that stage, grab the microphone from your boyfriend and sing 'Walking on Sunshine'. And I will dedicate it – I shit you not, Honor – to my daughter, who's standing over there wearing a focking facecloth for a skirt.'

Let's just say the message gets through. She just, like, stares me out of it. But she knows I'm not bluffing.

I'm there, 'Have a good night, Honor,' and off she jolly well focks.

The evening ends up being, I'm going to be honest with you, one of *the* most boring of my life – until an incident that happens close to the end.

I should put on the record that I actually hate the whole, I don't know, live music scene. It's full of try-hord fockers like Garret from Greystones of all places, who have facial hair and zero interest in rugby and who say hello by nodding at each other or muttering under their breath instead of high-fiving or chest-bumping like *normal* human beings?

This is just, like, general shit that goes through my mind while keeping an eye on Honor, who's, like, staring at the stage, waiting for the famous Adam to come on. Although I actually think I'm more keen to get eyes on Adam than even Honor is – just to suss him out. And – yeah, no – it's, like, after ten o'clock when he finally shows his face. And, Jesus, what a face. The dude is basically a fifteen-year-old version of Ed Sheeran, to the point where you know he's actually *modelling* himself on him? He's got, like, the red hair, the bum-fluff beard, the nerdy glasses. And that's not me being a dick. I'm saying that this is someone who's very much *in* my daughter's league – as in, she'd never be worried about some other bird running off with him.

He steps up to the mic and he goes, 'Hello, Whelan's!' and I'm thinking, he's got a lot of confidence, especially for someone with so little going for him in terms of looks.

The crowd goes absolutely ballistic. They're obviously easily pleased. I'm imagining what they'd have done if they'd seen me in my rugby prime. Probably shat themselves.

The dude storts tuning his guitor, then he goes, 'This is a song called 'Planet You'!' and he's suddenly straight into his first number.

It's, like, a catchy song and the dude has a pretty good voice. I'm standing there watching, portly admiring his confidence, and portly visualizing myself smashing that guitor over his focking head and fracturing his skull.

I'm no different to any overly protective father.

Honor is just, like, staring at him, totally mesmerized, and I'm, like, staring at her, totally mesmerized by her being mesmerized by him.

After six or seven numbers – if that's what we're agreeing to call them – he goes, 'Thank you all for coming,' like he's addressing an audience of thousands rather than a couple of hundred. 'I wrote this song about a girl called Honor. And I'm so glad that she's here tonight to hear me perform it for the very first time.'

I notice Honor mouthing the words, 'Oh! My God!' like it's a definite surprise to her.

The dude storts strumming his guitar and singing in this sort of, like, girly voice. He's going:

They say there's someone for everyone,
And I found mine today.
A girl who made this heathen heart
Look to the sky to pray.

Jesus, it's heavy shit. As the dude sings, him and Honor are just, like, smiling at each other, all gooey-eyed. Not putting labels on it, my focking hoop.

Hand in hand on a beach,
The give and take of the sea,
One flash of her smile makes me
Want to be the best man I can be.

I'm actually on the point of vomming when he gets to the chorus and then his voice became suddenly growly and – I shit you not – he goes:

She's so fucking hot!
She's so fucking hot!
She's so fucking hot!
Fuck! Ing! Hot! Bitch!

I turn around and I look at Honor, who's obviously loving it, judging from the smile on her face. I honestly don't know where to look, or even how to respond. And, to my great shame, I end up just, like, nodding my head along to the music, as a fifteen-year-old boy, who looks like Ed Sheeran, sings about my beautiful, innocent daughter in, like, *the* most sexist way.

She's so fucking hot!
She's so fucking hot!
She's so fucking hot!
Fuck! Ing! Hot! Bitch!

When the song is thankfully over, I tip up to the bor and order a

Coke, because I've obviously got the cor with me, although, after listening to that song, I'm half tempted to have a few pints and let Honor drive me home.

'Hi,' a voice beside me goes.

I turn my head and it ends up being a woman of roughly my age. At first glance, I decide that she's a ringer for Hannah Jeter, except a bit chunkier and without the sticky-out ears.

She's like, 'So do you feel as old as I do?'

I laugh. I'm there, 'Yeah, no, it's a very young crowd alright.'

She goes, 'Are you a fan of Adam's?'

'I was keeping an open mind until that last song. So what's your name?'

She's like, 'Norma.'

'Norma?' I go. 'That's a gorgeous name.'

It's not. It's the name of a lollipop woman.

I'm there, 'I'm Ross, by the way.'

She's like, 'It's nice to meet you, Ross. What are doing here, then? You don't look like the Whelan's kind to me.'

I'm there, 'Don't I? What kind do I look like to you?'

She cocks her head to the side, looks me up and down, then smiles. 'I don't know,' she goes. 'Maybe I haven't seen enough of you yet.'

Holy shitting fockbiscuits. I do believe this woman is flirting with me.

Quick as a flash, I'm straight back with, 'How much of me do you *want* to see?'

She goes, 'That's a very good question,' and she sucks on her Mint Julep in a way that makes me wish I was that straw. 'That's a very, *very* good question.'

I'm like, 'Hey, I can take a compliment,' and I'm absolutely on fire with the old return serve tonight.

She goes, 'You're wishing you were this straw, aren't you?'

I laugh.

I'm there, 'What are you, a mind-reader?' and I actually mean that.

'Well, you're making it pretty obvious from the way you're looking at me,' she goes, 'as I'm *sucking* on it.'

Jesus.

'So,' she goes, 'do you want to come to the ladies' with me?'

I'm like, 'Excuse me?'

'Or are you one of those men who enjoys just *talking* dirty?'

I'm just there, 'Errrrrr,' because I haven't been propositioned like this since the night of Ronan's eighteenth birthday in the Broken Orms pub in Finglas, when a woman with a limp who used to collect debts for Buckets of Blood invited me around the back of the pub for a hand job, then beat me up and stole four hundred quid from me, plus my Dubes.

'Well?' the woman – Norma – goes.

'Look,' I go, having a sudden flashback, 'if this ends up being what I think it is, just don't hurt my face, okay?'

But she grabs me by the waistband of my chinos – going, 'Come on, you focking wuss!' – and literally pulls me in the direction of the ladies' toilets.

Once we're in there, it *all* kicks off. She sort of, like, hustles me into Trap One, then she pulls down my trousers, pushes me back onto the bowl and closes the door behind her.

'Wait'll I flush the toilet,' I go – because yeah, no, there's a synchronized swimmer in there – but I don't get the chance to, because she hoiks up her knee-length skirt and sits – I want to say – *astride* me?

She takes her top off over her head and unhooks her bra.

I go, 'Whoa, *someone* drank her school milk!' and I don't even know what I mean by that. It's just a line that comes to me in the moment, but she seems to definitely appreciate it because she goes, 'Oh, I did!' in a breathless whisper. 'I was *always* first in the queue!'

I've no idea why, but it's hot.

She gets our various bits and pieces out and manoeuvres them into position, then she takes my hands and places them on her chest. Her face is flushed red and her nipples are hord like Iced Gems.

And there – I'm sorry – but I'm going to pull the curtain on the proceedings out of respect for the woman's privacy and my own reputation as a gentleman who doesn't tell. All I will say is that the whole transaction takes no more than a couple of minutes, during

which time she bounces up and down on me like she's riding a carousel horse and trying to make it go faster. And all the time, she's
giving me instructions to touch her here, and to bite her there, and
to kiss this bit of her, and to lick that bit of her, while I'm watching
her patticakes bob up and down like Phil and Grant Mitchell running from a focking bank job.

The whole sweaty business comes to a close with me effing, blinding and blaspheming at the flickering fluorescent light overhead and
Norma sitting on me with her eyes lightly closed and her mouth
forming a perfectly round O like she's testing the heat of a bath
with her toe.

'That was, em, quick,' she goes as she dismounts.

And I'm like, 'Take it as a compliment,' as I stand up and put
everything back in its original place. 'I'm actually a little bit relieved
that you didn't steal my money and my shoes.'

We tip back outside to the bor and I notice that – yeah, no – the
music has stopped. Adam has finished his, I don't know, set and
everyone is just standing around, skulling mostly pints. I'm thinking, I might even buy the woman a drink. Her Mint Julep has been
cleared away and we've both built up one hell of a thirst with our
carry-on.

Suddenly, I hear Honor's voice behind me, going, 'I don't want
you to meet him! He's a focking embarrassment!'

I turn around and – yeah, no – there's my daughter, holding
hands with this focking Ed Sheeran sap.

'Hey,' the dude goes, 'you're Honor's dad, yeah?'

I focking hate that nerdy kids have confidence these days.

He goes, 'I'm Adam. It's nice to meet you.'

The dude is trying to see around me, obviously looking for an
introduction to the woman I'm with, except I'm obviously pretending not to *know* her?

'Hi,' he goes, smiling at Norma over my shoulder and it suddenly
feels more awkward *not* to introduce them?

So I go, 'Yeah, no, this is Norma.'

The dude goes, 'Hi, Norma, how are you?'

She's like, 'I'm fine, thanks. Great set, by the way.'

The fourteen-year-old in me sniggers.

He's like, 'Yeah, no, thanks.'

All of a sudden, some random *older* dude arrives over? He's, like, well built with blond hair that is sort of, like, *thinning*?

'Ross,' he goes, 'I'm Steve. I'm Adam's dad.'

I'm like, 'Yeah, no, hi, Steve.'

'Hey, Steve,' Adam goes.

Allowing your children to refer to you by your first name is very much a Newpork thing – like raising them not to believe in God and letting them leave school at the age of sixteen to try to make it as a documentary film-maker.

He's like, 'Hey, Steve, you'd better watch Honor's dad. I'm pretty sure I saw him flirting with Norma just now.'

Norma laughs and goes, 'Oh, stop it, Adam! You're terrible!' and I'm suddenly confused.

In that moment, I can feel Norma's hand on my orse, squeezing my left buttock like she's testing a peach for firmness.

I'm there, 'Wait a minute – do you two actually know each other?'

'You could say that,' Adam goes. 'Norma, this is Honor. And Honor, this is Norma – in other words, my mom.'

'The fock do *you* want?'

Yeah, no, I'm standing at the door of – believe it or not – Sive's aportment building, next to what used to be the Burlington Hotel, but she's making me feel about as welcome as an Elastoplast floating around in a hot tub.

I go, 'I came to see how you were.'

But she just laughs.

I'm there, 'As in, like, how's the shoulder doing?' because it's been over a week since the accident.

There's, like, a long silence, then through the intercom speaker she goes, 'You've got five minutes,' and – yeah, no – she buzzes me in.

Two minutes later, she's opening the door of her actual aportment to me. Her entire shoulder is strapped up.

I'm there, 'I, er, got you these,' and I go to hand her the bunch of hydrangeas that cost me nearly forty snots.

She's like, 'Flowers? Are you *actually* serious?'

I'm there, 'I got them in Donnybrook Fair. They weren't cheap.'

But she clearly doesn't want them. I don't mind. They won't go to waste. There's at least three exes of mine who have birthdays in November. Forty snots is forty snots.

She turns her back on me and I follow her into the gaff, which is as sporsely decorated as you'd *expect* a medical student's aportment to be?

'Just to let you know,' I go, 'a mate of mine, namely Oisinn, had the exact same injury as you and he was back in full contact training within –'

But she just goes, 'What the fock are you doing here?'

I'm there, 'I wanted to apologize because I feel – yeah, no – portly responsible for what happened.'

'There's no *portly* about it – you *were* responsible, full stop.'

I'm like, 'I wasn't the one driving the bus, Sive,' pointing out the obvious to her. 'And I wasn't the one who stepped out onto the road without looking.'

She goes, 'Just get out of here.'

And that's when I end up suddenly losing it with her.

I'm like, 'Why are you giving me such a hord time?'

She goes, 'Look at my shoulder. I might never play rugby again.'

'I'm talking about before this even happened. You were on my case from, like, minute one.'

'That's because from the very first second you walked into that interview, I could see what you were.'

'And what am I, Sive – in *your* view?'

'You're a complete and utter wanker.'

'Fair enough,' I go. 'I get that a lot.'

She's there, 'I've met hundreds of men like you over the years. Condescending pricks who'll tell you that women's rugby should be treated with the same seriousness as the men's game – except they don't really believe it.'

'You don't think I'm serious about Ireland winning the Six Nations next year?'

'I think you're using the job as a stepping-stone to something else. And the only reason you got the job – apart from your father – is because of the cultural bias that says that an average man is better than a great woman.'

'I suppose *you* could do a better job than me, could you?'

'I've no *doubt* I could.'

'And what would you do? I'm talking about if you were in chorge?'

'Well, for storters, I wouldn't have us running laps. Or lifting weights.'

'Oh, so you don't think strength and conditioning are important in modern rugby? That's interesting.'

'I can name you four things that are *more* important.'

I'm there, 'Go ahead. I'm sure this'll be fascinating to hear.'

And she goes, 'The ball. The ball. The ball. The ball.'

Holy focking fock. I end up just, like, staring her. Because that was one of Father Fehily's sayings – word for *literally* word?

'Have you ever watched women play rugby,' she goes, 'and wondered why they handle the ball like it's a hot casserole dish?'

I'm like, 'Er, no – hand on hort, I've always been a fan.'

'It's because they're frightened of it. How old were you when you held your first rugby ball?'

'Jesus – too young to remember is all I know. My old man put one in the bassinet with me when I was, like, a day old – to familiarize me with the shape, or so *he* claimed.'

'And I bet that thing was never out of your hands as a kid?'

'The hilarious thing is that I never owned a single teddy bear. I was told if I wanted a hug, I was to hug Old Gilbert – as my old man called it.'

She goes, 'That might explain a thing or two.'

I'm like, 'No offence taken.'

It's at that exact moment that I spot something out of the corner of my eye and suddenly I'm only half listening to her.

I'm like, 'What the fock is that? Over there?'

She follows my eyes to the coffee table. On it, there's a sort of, like, ledger, with Post-it notes and bits of paper sticking out of it. It has a red cover with the word 'Rugby' written on it in, like, Tipp-Ex.

She shrugs and goes, 'It's just a book that I use to write down my thoughts about rugby.'

I'm there, 'So it's what . . . like, a rugby *tactics* book?'

She's like, 'I don't have an actual name for it. I watch matches and I take notes – that's all. Things I would have done differently if I'd been the coach. Ideas that I have for moves. Then, if I hear a motivational quote that I like, I scribble it down.'

I'm just, like, staring at her, my hort pounding, my breathing all over the place, like a focking fort in a colander. I'm thinking, this is what people must feel when they fall in love for the first time.

'The fock is wrong with *you*?' Sive goes. 'Why are you suddenly sweating?'

It's possibly because I've had an idea – and it's one of my best ones ever.

I'm there, 'Sive, will you be my Assistant Coach?'

She's like, 'Get out of here,' and she storts steering me towards the door.

I'm there, 'I'm being serious, Sive. It's, like, a serious offer. That shit you were saying about the ball, the ball, the ball, the ball – it gave me genuine goosebumps.'

'I don't *need* validation from you.'

'Sive, I know it's a shit state of affairs that – certainly to an outsider – it looks like I got the job because of the old boys' network.'

'You *did* get the job because of the old boys' network.'

'Fine – but I'm offering *you* a job now. I need an Assistant Coach. And it needs to be someone who thinks about rugby as deeply as hopefully I do.'

'There's never a time when I'm *not* thinking about rugby.'

'Jesus Christ, it's like you're a female version of me – and I don't mean that as an insult to you. Sive, what do you say?'

'I say I'll think about it,' she goes, sort of, like, shepherding me towards the door.

I'm there, 'Cool – you have my number.'

She's like, 'Are you not going to leave the flowers?'

I'm there, 'You said you didn't *want* the flowers.'

'Give me the flowers.'

I give her the flowers.

'I'll ring you,' she goes.

I'm like, 'When?'

And she just goes, 'Whenever.'

It's, like, the best port of a week before I feel ready to mention the incident in Whelan's to Honor. I bring it up in, like, a *subtle* way? I can't just blurt out that her boyfriend's old dear is a nymphomaniac, a fun fact I discovered while she was bouncing me around one of the toilet stalls in Whelan's.

So – yeah, no – instead I go, 'So, em, how are things going with you and the famous Adam?'

She's there, 'Er, *fine*?' on the big-time defensive.

'So are you, like, boyfriend-girlfriend now?' I go.

She rolls her eyes – this is in my room in the famous tower, by the way. She goes, 'Dad, it's not the 1990s any more.'

'I know teenagers these days don't like to put labels on things, but that song –'

'It's called "Fuck! Ing! Hot! Bitch!"'

'Yeah, no, I thought it might be – well, it sounds like he's pretty into you.'

'We like each other.'

'And, em, Adam's old dear seems nice,' I go.

Honor's like, 'Nice in what way?' because she obviously knows my form.

'I just think she seems like a really cool person,' I go.

She's there, 'Norma's lovely.'

I let a couple of seconds pass, then I'm like, 'And, em, what's the story with Adam's old man? When did he and Norma break up?'

She looks at me like she thinks I'm off my meds.

She's like, 'Er, Norma and Steve are *not* broken up?'

'Oh,' I go, trying to hide my surprise. 'I just assumed –'

'Oh my God!' she goes, suddenly staring past me.

I'm there, 'Honor, let me explain what happened.'

'Oh! My! God!' she goes, except even louder this time. 'Is this some kind of record?'

I'm tempted to point out that this is the first time I've ever ridden the mother of one of her friends. I don't actually count Roz Matthews because Honor hates Sincerity's guts.

I'm there, 'She was the one who –'

'It *is* a record,' she goes. 'Oh! My God!'

I follow her line of vision and I'm relieved to discover that she's talking about one of the Hitler 45s, which is sitting on the chair that I'm using as a bedside table. I suddenly remember Hennessy's famous advice that you should never admit or deny anything until you've been actually accused – and then, of course, you should deny it, and go on denying it, even after no one in the world believes you.

She picks it up, holding it like a steering wheel.

She goes, 'Adam has – oh my God – *loads* of these.'

I'm there, 'Yeah, no, there's a pile of them over there in the corner.'

She's like, 'They were originally Steve's. He has, like, Nick Drake, Joni Mitchell, the Velvet Underground –'

I'm there, 'Fair focks,' even though I've never heard of any of them.

'He has, like, everything Jimi Hendrix ever did,' she goes. 'And a very first pressing of "Sorgeant Pepper's Lonely Horts Club Band".'

I'm there, 'You keep naming bands and I'm going to go on saying fair focks.'

She's like, 'So who's on this record?'

'Hitler,' I go.

She's there, 'Hitler? As in, like, *Adolf* Hitler?'

I'm like, 'Could be. Rings a bell.'

She laughs. She's there, 'Was he in, like, a band when he was younger or something?'

I go, 'I know little or nothing about the dude, Honor, except that these are all his, like, *speeches* and shit?'

She storts looking through the ones in the corner.

She's like, 'Nuremberg! Weimar! Danzig! Oh my God, why do you have these?'

I'm there, 'Father Fehily used to play them to us before we went out onto the rugby pitch to get us riled up.'

'Löwenbräukeller! Stuttgart! Berchtesgaden!'

'Yeah, no, Fionn found them when he was clearing out his office. He says he can't have them in the school. Apparently, you can't say the kind of shit that's on them these days. Mind you, you can't say anything these days, can you?'

'Dad, can I have these?'

'Er, yeah, no, I don't see why not.'

'It's just that we're learning all about Hitler in History and we have to do a project on, like, the Second World *War*?'

'Is that when he was knocking around, yeah? For the second one?'

'Yes,' she goes, 'he was the Chancellor of Germany from 1933 to 1945.'

I'm going to stort reading a lot more. Okay, that's ridiculous. I'm not going to stort reading a lot more. But I'd love to just *know* shit?

I'm like, 'Yeah, no, take them. I don't even have a record-player.'

And that's when my phone all of a sudden rings. I look at the screen.

I'm there, 'It's Ronan.'

'Oh my God, I was just talking to Erika,' Honor goes. 'Tell him she's booked our hotel in New York.'

I answer the phone. I'm there, 'Ro, how the hell are you?'

He's like, 'Howiya, Rosser?'

I go, 'Where are you?' because it's kind of, like, *noisy* in the background?

He's there, 'Ine at JFK, Rosser.'

I'm like, 'JFK? As in, like, the airport?' and Honor's eyes go wide.

She's there, 'What's he saying?'

'Ine cubben howum,' he goes, then he suddenly bursts into tears. 'I caddent take it addy mower, Rosser. Ine missing Ri and Ine missing Shadden.'

I'm there, 'Ro, Honor was just talking to Erika. You're going to be seeing us in, like, two weeks. The flights are booked – right, Honor?'

Honor nods.

Ronan goes, 'Ri woatunt be cubben, Rosser.'

I'm like, 'What do you mean? Erika's booked her ticket.'

'Shadden's decided not to lerror go.'

That's cold. That's as cold as a mother-in-law's tit.

I'm there, 'She can't do that.'

'Appadently, she cadden,' he goes. 'Ine arthur getting a lethor from her solicitodder.'

'Saying?'

'Saying that I walked out on them.'

'What?'

'And if thee let Ri go to Amedica, thee think I woatunt lerror go back to Aerlunt arthurwards. The lethor also said I was to hab no foorther contact with Ri – me own thaughter, Rosser.'

Honor's like, 'What the fock is going on?'

I'm there, 'Shadden's solicitor has told her not to let Ri go to America slash the States. Hang on, isn't Hennessy her solicitor?'

'He's wooden, Rosser – he's wooden the war. Ine joost godda hab to accept that Ine beaten and go howum wit me tayul between me legs.'

'Don't you focking dare get on that flight.'

'I hab no choice.'

'Ro, go back to the hotel, will you? I'm going to go and see her now. I'll sort this out.'

So I'm passing Dunnes Stores in Cornelscourt when my phone rings. I check the screen and – yeah, no – it's Sive.

I'm like, 'Sive, how the hell are you?'

And she just goes, 'I'll do it.'

I'm there, 'Do it? In terms of?'

She goes, 'Stop being an asshole, Ross. I'm saying I'll take the job.'

'As my number two?'

'No, as your Assistant Coach.'

'Right. And just to point out, Sive, there's no actual money involved. For you, I mean.'

'That is just so typical.'

I'm there, 'I'm only mentioning it to avoid any awkwardness down the line. Look, let's meet up and talk rugby. How does Eddie

Rocket's in Donnybrook sound – let's say after training on Thursday night?'

She's like, 'Fine.'

I hang up, then I take the left turn onto Westminster Road. Two minutes later, I'm pulling up outside the old pair's former gaff – and I can't actually believe what I end up seeing. The gorden is a scene of chaos – and I *mean* chaos?

Shadden has had my old dear's good Eggersmann kitchen ripped out and she's just – yeah, no – dumped all the old bits in the gorden. We're talking the sink, we're talking the wine cooler, we're talking the AGA range cooker – all just focked outside and left to rust in the rain.

I'm looking through the front gate at Moxy, Rihanna-Brogan's poor pony, wandering around, trying to find a patch of uneaten grass in between all the discorded domestic appliances.

'What was your mother thinking?' I hear a voice go.

It ends up being Sasha Cormichael, one of the old dear's mates – a typical Foxrock Fanny – from across the road.

I'm there, 'Yeah, no, the girl wasn't long making shit of the gaff.'

'I mean to say,' Sasha goes, 'what was the point of all those campaigns we fought – to stop the Luas coming to Foxrock, to stop them building affordable housing on Leopardstown Racecourse, to stop Thomas selling National Lottery scratchcords – if your mother was just going to give her beautiful home away to, let's call a spade a spade here, the lowest of the low.'

I'm like, 'Careful, Sasha – that's my granddaughter and my daughter-in-law you're talking about. Although I do get where you're coming from.'

'She has her friends over every Friday night for karaoke,' Sasha goes. 'And you can hear them from the other end of Brighton Road. And the accents! It's dis, dat, dees and dose. What *was* Finny *thinking*? Or perhaps she wasn't – was that it?'

'What are you shitting on about?'

'Oh, come on, Ross – everyone knows your mother is losing her morbles. Jenny Birtles said she played nine holes with her last week and Finny thought she was talking to Miriam O'Callaghan.'

I'm there, 'She was probably just off her tits,' actually defending the woman. 'Drinking on her meds again.'

I push the gate open and I step into the gorden.

'You just tell that daughter-in-law of yours,' Sasha shouts after me, 'that we wear outdoor clothes when we leave the house around here. And, while she might consider pyjamas with *The Bitch Is Sleeping* written on them to be appropriate daywear, they are *not* something I wish to look at while I'm enjoying coffee and carrot cake in The Gables.'

I walk up and I knock on the front door – as in, I literally knock on the door, because she's had the doorbell disconnected. There ends up being no answer, so I tip around the back of the house, where I find the kitchen door is unlocked. I let myself in.

Shadden is in the kitchen, pouring herself a glass of wine and listening to – talk about a blast from the past – the All Saints on, like, full volume. And she's singing along – practising her karaoke – giving it:

Nebbor, ebbor hab I ebbor feddelt so low,
When you godda take me ourra this black howult,
Nebbor, ebbor hab I ebbor feddelt so sad,
The way Ine feeden, yeah, you got me feeden reedy bad.

I'm there, 'I see you're ingratiating yourself with the neighbours.'

She gets such a fright that she screams and drops her glass. I'm not even sure that ingratiating is a word, by the way.

She goes, 'What the bleaten heddle are you doing hee-or?'

I'm there, 'Er, this is my childhood *home*, remember?'

'Well, it's not addy mower – gerrout!'

'I'll go when I'm good and ready to go. Where's Rihanna-Brogan?'

'She's not hee-or. She's staying in her Nanny Tuite's toneet. I think it's impowarant for her to stay in touch wirrer roots.'

Jesus.

I'm there, 'Good – because I don't want her to hear what I have to say to you.'

She's like, 'Would you ebber fook off?'

'You have no focking right to stop Ronan seeing his daughter.'

'Rosser –'

'*No* focking right. He loves that girl. And she loves him.'

'Rosser –'

'She's been looking forward to going to the States for weeks. He has all sorts of shit planned for them. We're talking Christmas shopping in Macy's. We're talking seeing Central Pork in a horse and cort –'

'Rosser –'

'And now you're going to deny her all of that. You know what, Shadden? I rue the focking day he ever met you. I rue the focking day he ever got involved with you and the rest of your scumbag family, especially your stuttering p . . . p . . . p . . . p . . . prick of a father –'

'Rosser, I said she could go.'

'Excuse me?'

'Hodor rag me about twedenty midutes ago. She said I was being unfeer to Ro, so I chayunged me moyunt and said she could go arthur all.'

Jesus, she could have focking told me she was going to ring.

'Er, cool,' I go. 'Obviously, I take back everything. I just –'

Suddenly, I hear footsteps on the stairs.

I'm there, 'I thought you said Rihanna-Brogan wasn't here?'

Then I hear a voice – a dude's voice – saying he heard shouting and asking is everything okay.

Shadden shouts, 'Doatunt cub in hee-or!' obviously not wanting me to see whoever it is that she's, let's just say, *entertaining*?

But he pushes the door and he walks into the kitchen, ducking his head to get under the door frame.

I'm like, 'What the –'

Because standing there in front of me, as plain as the tattoos on his neck, is Peadar.

He's like, 'Ah, it's you,' instantly recognizing me. 'Are you wanton me to thrun him out, Shadden?'

She goes, 'Yeah, thrun him out on he's fooken head.'

I'm there, 'Are you, like, with each other now – as in, like, *with* with?'

The dude is wearing a dressing-gown designed for a much smaller man and I'm guessing it must be Ronan's. He walks up to me, grabs me by the scruff of my shirt and drags me to the front door, with Shadden following us, going, 'Yeah, he's me new fedda. And you can teddle that Ronan fooker when you see him – he's a bethor lubber than *he'll* ebber be.'

And with that, the dude opens the door with one hand and, with the other, focks me out into the gorden like I'm, well, a brand-new, ten-thousand-yoyo Winterhalter undercounter glasswasher.

'Like I says to you,' Shadden goes, 'make shurden teddle the bastoord.'

Ronan is as giddy as a goose on rollerblades.

He's there, 'Thanks, Rosser. Wouldn't hab happened if it wadn't for you.'

I'm there, 'That's not *technically* true, Ro? It was actually Honor who talked her round.'

He goes, 'I caddent belieb Ine godda see me thaughter next week. I oatently wish –'

'What?'

'I oatenly wish Shadden was cubbing with yous.'

'Shadden?'

'Shadden, Rosser!'

'Yeah, no, I know who you're talking about – are you still not over her?'

'Oaber her? She's me bleaten wife, Rosser.'

'One way of looking at it, I suppose.'

'Hee-or, she's not with some wooden else, is she?'

'In terms of?'

'Ine asking has she gorra new fedda, Rosser?'

I can't lie to him.

I'm like, 'Of course she hasn't.'

Okay, once again, I'm proven wrong.

I go, 'I'm just making the point that you should be riding all around you. There's some unbelievable-looking women in the States. You must be walking around with your focking eyes closed over there.'

All of a sudden, I notice Sive walk through the door of Eddie Rocket's. I give her a wave and she tips over.

I'm there, 'Ro, I have to go. I'll see you next week.'

Sive sits down opposite me. Her shoulder is still heavily strapped and her orm is still in a sling.

I'm there, 'Hey, how the hell are you?'

She shrugs one shoulder.

I'm there, 'I meant what I said. I don't think you should go ruling yourself out of the Six Nations just yet.'

She goes, 'The ligaments will take at least six weeks to heal. Which means it's going to be the middle of January before I can go into full contact training again. I'll never be ready in time.'

'Never say never,' I go. 'The body is a mysterious thing. You should know that if you're going to be a – hopefully, one day – doctor.'

'Are we going to talk about rugby or are we going to talk about other subjects you know absolutely nothing about?'

She has no time for my horseshit, but I can't help but like the girl.

I'm there, 'Okay, let's talk rugby. I'd be interested in hearing your thoughts on –'

'You're wasting our time.'

'Er – in terms of?'

'The running and lifting weights, Ross. What's that all about? We've got players in that dressing-room who could win body-building competitions – but when you throw the ball to them, they act like it's a live grenade.'

'So we're back to this thing you said about the ball, the ball, the ball? Which I loved, by the way. It was one of Father Fehily's sayings.'

'I don't know who that person is.'

'He was a priest who had a major, major influence on me in terms of –'

'What I mean is, I don't need you to validate everything I say by telling me that a man said it before me.'

'Fair enough.'

'My point is that we're unfamiliar with the ball – because most of *us* never handled a rugby ball until we were in our late teens or early twenties.'

'Are you serious?'

'There's no rugby for girls at schools level. We were playing hockey and basketball while you were training, what, five days a week?'

'Yeah, no, sometimes seven.'

'One or two of us have brothers who played rugby. But most of the players you're working with held a rugby ball for the first time when they started playing it in college. Or when they discovered tag rugby in work.'

'Jesus.'

'So it doesn't matter how fit they are, or how strong they are, if they're scared of the ball.'

'I like that take.'

'Ross, if I'm going to do this, I'm not going to be some token woman sitting next to you in the stand just to make you look good. I want input.'

'I'm interested in your input. As a matter of fact, I wouldn't mind having a flick through that rugby tactics book of yours – that's if you have it with you.'

'I'm not showing you my rugby tactics book.'

'Why not?'

'What, so you can steal all my thoughts on the game and pass them off as your own? And, anyway, I'm not sure you could handle it all at once.'

I pick up the menu and I sort of, like, smile to myself.

I'm there, 'So I was wondering would you take training next week?' and I say it like it's not a major deal.

She's like, 'What?' and she's in genuine shock.

I'm there, 'Yeah, no, I'm going to New York for the week to see my son. I'll need you to take training on Tuesday and Thursday night and again on Saturday morning. Are you going to have something to eat, by the way? I was thinking of getting my usual Classic with bacon and cheese fries.'

'What's the catch?'

'Sorry?'

'I'm *supervising* training, am I? And presumably you're going to give me a programme to follow?'

'I'm not giving you shit, Sive. You know this set of players. You know the things they need to work on. So do it.'

I've had women look at me in amazement before, but Sive's expression in that moment is a new one on me.

I'm there, 'So what are you going to have?' handing her a menu.

She gives the thing the old left to right. Then she looks up and goes, 'Was that your mother who turned up at training that night?'

I'm there, 'Er, yeah, no, it was.'

'I'm sorry,' she goes. 'I didn't mean to be –'

'Hey, it's cool.'

'So what's wrong with her?'

'I don't know – dementia and blah, blah, blah.'

'That must be very stressful for you.'

I just nod. Shit, I can suddenly feel my eyes filling up.

I'm there, 'I'm just going to, em –' and I can hear my voice coming out all wobbly.

I stand up.

'I'm sorry,' she goes, 'I shouldn't have –'

I'm there, 'Yeah, no, I'm just going to go for a hit and miss – in other words, a piss.'

I head for the jacks. I stand in front of the mirror and I notice that I've got, like, tears streaming down my face. Jesus, I'm thinking, what is focking wrong with me?

I turn on the tap and splash cold water on my face. Then I take a deep breath. And that's when my phone all of a sudden rings.

It's, like, a withheld number, but I answer it anyway.

I'm like, 'You've got Ross.'

'Hi, Ross,' a woman's voice on the other end goes. 'This is Norma.'

Holy focking shit.

I'm like, 'Er, hi, Norma, how did you –'

'How did I get your number?' she goes. 'I asked Adam to get it from Honor. I told him I found a leather glove on the floor in Whelan's and I wanted to check was it yours?'

'No, it's not mine, Norma. The only gloves I ever owned was a pair of green fingerless ones that Brian O'Driscoll wore against Australia at the 2003 World Cup and which my old man bought at an auction in Riverview to raise money for trigeminal neuralgia.'

'I probably owe you an explanation,' she goes, 'for what happened that night. Look, I honestly didn't know that you were Honor's dad.'

I'm there, 'Is that *all* you have to say?'

'Well, what else is there?'

'Er, you're *married*?'

'So are you.'

'I know, but –'

'But I'm a woman?'

'Maybe. I don't know. Does that make me a hypocrite?'

'Look, me and Steve don't have what you might call a conventional marriage. Do you know what I mean when I say that?'

'Yeah, no, I'm in a very similar boat myself.'

'Oh, really?'

'Yeah, no, big time.'

'Because Steve asked me.'

'He what?'

'After we . . . you know –'

'Are you saying Steve knows about us?'

'Of course! He saw us going into the toilets together!'

'Jesus.'

'It's fine.'

'You're saying he's cool with it?'

'Yes, he's cool with it. I just told you, we don't have a conventional marriage.'

'Right.'

'But you don't either?'

'No.'

'I'm glad to hear it. So, em –'

'What?'

'I don't know, do you want to call here one night and, well, check is this your glove?'

'I didn't think there *was* a glove.'

'There isn't a glove.'

'So why am I – Oh, it's code for . . . right, I get it now. Yeah, no, I wouldn't mind another shot at the . . . well, I wouldn't mind seeing you again. That's possibly a nice way of putting it. When would suit?'

'Adam's going to be away on Sunday,' she goes.

That's the night before we head to the States.

I'm like, 'Er, cool.'

She's there, 'He's going to London to check out this documentary film-making course. Steve and I are thinking of letting him do it instead of Transition Year.'

I'm such a great reader of people.

I'm like, 'Fair focks. I'm saying it.'

'We're on Carysfort Avenue,' she goes.

I'm like, 'There's some gaffs on that road. I sold one or two of them in my Hook, Lyon and Sinker days.'

Jesus, I hope they weren't one of the people I ripped off.

She's there, 'I'll send you a pin. See you about eight o'clock?'

And I go, 'Yeah, no, eight works for me.'

Sorcha's in the kitchen – on the phone to my old man.

She's going, 'It says *what* in the *Irish Independent* tomorrow? Oh my God . . . Oh. My. God . . . Oh. *My*. God . . . Well, of course I believe you, Taoiseach . . . exactly . . . your enemies are trying to blacken your name because you're threatening to walk away from the withdrawal talks without a deal and to renege on the terms of the 2010 so-called bailout.'

She's such a suck-up, it's unbelievable.

After she's hung up, I'm like, 'What's going on?'

She goes, 'There's going to be a report in tomorrow's paper saying that your dad was seen eating meat in Shanahan's on the Green two nights ago. A T-bone steak. Have you ever heard such nonsense?'

I actually laugh out loud.

I'm there, 'You're a fool for him, Sorcha.'

But she goes, 'When the Taoiseach says he had the vegetarian jambalaya, I trust him.'

Yeah, no, trusting the O'Carroll-Kelly men has always been her Achilles heel.

I'm there, 'I have to head out. I think I lost a glove in Whelan's and I'm going to see if –'

'I've never seen you wear gloves,' she goes.

'Er, yeah, no, I've *storted* wearing them?'

'Well, you don't have to explain yourself to me, Ross. Like I said – Bill and Hillary.'

'Cool.'

'Although don't forget, you do have to be up early for your flight tomorrow.'

'Yeah, no, I shouldn't be long. I'll be in and out in no time.'

On the way out the door, I end up running into Fionn. He's got, like, a big smile on his face.

I'm there, 'What's up?'

He goes, 'You didn't hear the draw for the first round of the Leinster Schools Senior Cup?'

And I'm like, 'Er, no, who did you get?'

He laughs.

He's there, 'Blackrock College.'

And then *I* laugh.

I'm there, 'Focking brilliant. What a way to celebrate Castlerock College's return to rugby – by putting those fockers in their place. Dude, I have to head out, okay?'

He's like, 'Where are you going?'

'I'm, er, pretty sure I dropped a glove in Whelan's.'

He goes, 'I didn't know you wore gloves. The only gloves I ever saw you with were those Brian O'Driscoll ones that your old man –'

I'm like, 'Long story. Later, Dude.'

I hop into the old A8 and point it in the direction of Blackrock. Twenty minutes later, I'm porking the cor in front of the house.

The front door is wide open. Yeah, no, I'm standing on the door-step and I hear Norma's voice coming from upstairs.

She's like, 'It's open. Just come up,' and I climb those stairs like a squirrel going up a tree.

She's standing at the door of her bedroom wearing what would have to be described as a tight leather – I want to say – *bodice* and literally fock-all else. She looks incredible. I think I mentioned Hannah Jeter and I'm sticking by that assessment.

I walk up to her and without saying a word I throw the lips on her. She grabs me by the front of my green IRFU Eco Poly Tee and she pulls me into the bedroom.

She goes, 'Have something to drink first,' and she pours me a glass of Moët.

I'm there, 'I possibly shouldn't. I'm technically driving.'

She goes, 'Oh, you won't be going *anywhere* for hours!'

I smile at her. It's a nice idea in theory, but I am going to disappoint this woman like I've never disappointed a woman before.

We both sip our champagne.

'So,' she goes, 'have you ever *been* with a nymphomaniac – before me, I mean?'

I'm there, 'Er, my wife would say I probably *am* one?'

'Good,' she goes, smiling at me, then she puts her hand on my chest and storts tracing the outline of my pecs and – not being bigheaded here – but abs with her thumb. I'm sweating buckets and I'm grateful for the Eco Poly Tee's breathable fabric and revolutionary Vapo-Dri+ technology, which, according to the website, wicks away moisture and provides dynamic cooling.

I kiss her again and we both put down our drinks and move over to the bed. She pushes me down on it and takes off my Dubes and then my chinos and boxers together, then I reach behind her and try to open the lace on her bodice with my trembling fingers. I finally manage to get the thing open and then off her. I have a quick go of her Dublin's Fair City's while she goes to work below stairs, working the old bicycle pump like she's trying to force air into a focked tyre.

'Whoa, slow down,' she goes, 'you're about to come.'

And I'm there, 'There's no higher praise than that, Norma.'

'Well, if you do,' she goes, 'I know *someone* who definitely won't be happy.'

I think nothing more of this statement until, like, sixty seconds later, when, totally out of the blue, in the dork of the bedroom, I hear a man's voice go, 'I can't believe you've started without me!'

I'm like, 'What? In the name? *Of* fock?'

'Yet again!' he goes.

Norma's there, 'Don't be such a baby, Steve. I can't help it if you take forty minutes to get dressed for bed.'

I open my eyes and – holy focking aioli – Adam's old man is standing over me, wearing a white, it has to be said, *negligee*, as well as a full face of make-up, and he's sizing me up like I'm his focking Christmas dinner and he doesn't know what bit to eat first.

I sit propped up on my elbows. I'm like, 'What the fock? As in, what the *focking* fock?'

He goes, 'Is something wrong?'

'Yes,' Norma goes, 'he's losing his erection.'

I'm there, 'I thought you said we'd have the place to ourselves?'

Steve goes, 'We do have the place to ourselves. Adam is in London, checking out this documentary film-making course that Norma and I are thinking of letting him do instead of Transition Year.'

Jesus, no wonder the dude was cool with me riding his wife in the toilets of Whelan's – they're focking swingers.

'Check out his abs,' Norma goes. 'Remember I told you about them?'

The dude pulls up my IRFU Eco Poly Tee and goes, 'Whoa! *How* did you get a six-pack like that?'

I'm there, 'Mostly sit-ups,' because, even in a focked-up situation like this, I'm a sucker for a compliment. 'A hell of a lot of sit-ups – we're talking two or three hundred a –'

The dude suddenly storts kissing me. Now, I'm a pretty open-minded goy when it comes to most matters sexual. I went to see *Fifty Shades of Grey* in Dundrum and the only reason I walked out was because (a) it was shite and (b) Anna Nolan and Bláthnaid Ní Chofaigh were sitting behind me, honking with laughter for the whole thing. But even I have to admit to being shocked by this. I'm not homophobic – one of my best friends is gay and so is his

husband – but I should probably explain that there's been a major, major crossing of wires here.

And that's when the dude – totally randomly – goes, 'I like this top. What fabric is that?' and I find myself going, 'It's a polyester blend that was actually created by Canterbury. Its advanced wicking properties accelerate sweat evaporation and allow it to dry almost instantly.'

'He's getting hard again,' Norma goes – and then she suddenly climbs up on me and that's the moment when I decide – yeah, no – to just, like, *go* with it?

The next three minutes end up being *the* weirdest three minutes of my life. I've got Norma bouncing up and down on me like she's stretching her glutes on her Pilates ball while her husband is licking my nipples and saying that he knows synthetic, petroleum-based materials get a bad press but what *never* seems to get mentioned is that polyester is wrinkle-resistant, long-lasting *and* wonderfully versatile.

Norma is making formyord noises, going, 'Maah! Maah! Maah! Maah! Maah!' and I'm thinking this is the most focked-up feeling I've ever known. From the waist up, I'm thinking, I need to get the fock out of here now – but from the waist down, I'm thinking, Dude, what's your focking hurry?

Again, it's not homophobic – no one could have been happier for Oisinn and Magnus the day they got hitched and I bought them a set of dessert forks, we're talking genuine Newbridge Silver, to prove it – but I'm having to use one or two visualization techniques from my kicking days to blank out Steve, who's now kissing my face, and to focus instead on Norma, who's hopping up and down on me like she's riding me to Aga Khan glory.

It's – believe it or not – working fine until I suddenly hear the rattle of metal and I open my eyes to discover that Steve is holding a pair of handcuffs.

He goes, 'You don't mind if I cuff you to the headboard, do you?'

And that ends up being the moment when I decide that the fun is over – at least for Steve.

I'm there, 'I'll tell you what, Dude, why don't *I* cuff *you* to the headboard?'

He smiles. He's like, 'Yeah, I'd actually like that.'

So that's what I end up doing. I push Norma off me, then I snap one bracelet on him and the other on the iron headboard. Then I take Norma over to the dressing-table to resume hostilities.

And there I'm going to bring the story to a close – in the interests of decency, if nothing else. My last word on the subject is that the whole affair comes to a loud and sweary finish with me staring at my ugly, lipstick-smeared mouth in the vanity mirror; Norma, with her legs wrapped around my waist, telling me to take my time, we've got all night; and Steve, watching from the other side of the room with his plumb in his hand, telling me that the reason he was asking about my jersey is because he's actually *in* the textiles business himself – import *and* export.

'Don't tell me that's it,' Norma goes when the deed is done.

I'm there, 'That's how turned on I was,' as I stort picking my clothes up off the floor. 'Take it from me, it's a good thing.'

'Well,' she goes, a look of confusion on her face, 'when will you be good to go again?'

And I'm like, 'I don't know – maybe when I get back from New York?'

5.

Yankee Brown

We've landed in New York – we're talking me, Erika, Honor, Amelie, Rihanna-Brogan and enough luggage for a six-week Lions tour to New Zealand. Yeah, no, we're standing at the carousel and I'm lifting off suitcase after suitcase.

'That wooden's moyen as weddle,' Rihanna-Brogan goes.

I'm like, 'Which one are we talking?'

And she goes, 'The wooden with the leopard skin.'

I should have recognized it. It was a wedding present to Ronan and Shadden from Nudger and Buckets of Blood.

I lift it off the conveyor belt – it feels like it's got breeze blocks in it – and Ri wheels it over to where Honor and little Amelie are standing with our literally *three* baggage corts.

Out of the corner of my mouth, I go, 'So what am I going to say to Ronan?'

'What are you talking about?' Erika – standing beside me – goes.

I'm like, 'Er, his wife is having an affair with a six-foot-fifteen cage-fighter, Erika.'

'What do you mean, what are you going to say to him? You're going to tell him the truth.'

'And what if he decides to then come home to try to fix his marriage? I think that's why Kennet introduced her to Peadar. It's what he wants – it's what Hennessy and my old man want as well.'

'Ross, you can't keep something like that from your son. If you don't tell him, then I will. Grab Amelie's suitcase there.'

Which is what I do. It's, like, the last one we're waiting on. A minute or two later, we're walking through the Arrivals gate – Rihanna-Brogan is practically sprinting ahead of us – and we're looking out for Ronan's face in the crowd.

All of a sudden, I see him, in a beautifully fitted navy suit, with a red tie loosened and the top button of his white shirt open. He comes pegging it towards us – there's, like, *already* tears in his eyes? – and he scoops Rihanna-Brogan up in his orms and spins her around, the two of them just bawling.

He's going, 'Ine arthur been missiden you so bleaten mooch,' and she's going, 'Ine arthur been missiden you as weddle, Daddy,' and it's like something from a movie, albeit one requiring subtitles.

'Hodor,' Ronan goes, 'cub hee-or,' and gives her a huge hug.

She's crying – and Honor, like, *never* cries? We took her to a consultant in the Eye and Ear Hospital when she was nine because Sorcha thought she had underactive lacrimal glands, but it turned out, much to our relief, that she just didn't give a fock about anything.

He's like, 'Are you behaving yisser self?'

Honor smiles and goes, 'Not really, no.'

And he's there, 'Ine glad to heerd it,' and he gives her a wink.

Next in line is Erika. She throws her orms around him and she's like, 'Hi, Ronan.'

He goes, 'Howiya, Edika?' then he sort of, like, holds her at orm's length, looks her up and down and goes, 'Moy, Jaysus – you're eeben mower gorgeous-looking than the last toyum I seen you. You're like a bleaten model, so you are.'

Which she seems to think is perfectly normal, even though when I said something similar on the flight – I told her that I loved her natural smell and that she had a neck that I would never grow tired of kissing if we weren't technically related – she insisted that I go and sit in economy class.

'And Amelie!' Ronan goes, giving her a hug and a kiss. 'Look at the soyuz of you – you're arthur getting huge, so you are.'

She hands him the little teddy bear in the leather flying jacket that she bought from the duty-free cort.

'Is that for me?' he goes.

And she nods her little head. It's very cute.

He turns to me then and I could never put into words the look that passes between us – we're talking, like, pure love.

157

'Rosser, you bleaten flute,' he goes, throwing his orms around me. I'm there, 'It's great to see you, Ro.'

And he just whispers in my ear, 'Thanks, Rosser – you're the best fadder addy wooden could hab asked fower,' which makes me feel like I possibly have to tell him the truth about Shadden.

He looks at our three trolleys full of luggage. 'Moy Jaysus, are yiz shewer yous packed enough? Mon, Ine arthur booking us a seben-seathor.'

He leads us through JFK and outside. Half an hour later, we're all squeezed into this – like he said – seven-seater taxi, driving through a freezing cold Queens, when the Manhattan skyline comes into view. The cor is filled with, I don't know, excited chatter as we all bring each other up to speed on what's happening in our lives.

Rihanna-Brogan tells Ronan about her showjumping, and Honor tells him about Adam and how 'Fock! Ing! Hot! Bitch!' is now available on iTunes, and Ronan talks about some of the work he's been doing for Shlomo, Bitton and Black – Civil Rights Attorneys – and Erika tells us that she's thinking of becoming an actual horse-breeder, and I talk about some of the work I've been doing with the Ireland women's rugby team and how they're not nearly as shit as I *thought* they were going to be?

And all the time, I'm just, like, stealing little sideways glances at Ronan sitting beside me. I know he's only been here for, like, a few months but he seems, I don't know, *years* older, especially in the suit. It's like he's suddenly become a man.

I'm there, 'The States obviously suits you. He's a bit like you, Erika. Do you remember that summer you spent working as a maître d' in Newport, Rhode Island, and you came back with an unbelievable tan? I actually couldn't stop looking at your legs.'

'Ross,' she goes, 'you need cognitive behavioural therapy.'

Ronan's there, 'Either that or a bucket of iced wather oaber he's head!'

Everyone in the cor laughs.

A few minutes later, we take the Queens–Midtown tunnel into actual Manhattan and that's when the buzz *really* storts to kick in? It's, like, five o'clock in the day and it's dork outside and we're driving slowly through crowded streets that are lit up in, like, neon. It's, like, three weeks before Christmas and there's decorations everywhere and it feels genuinely cold enough to snow.

Erika goes, 'How would you like to go ice-skating, Ri?'

Rihanna-Brogan's face is suddenly lit up like Times Square.

'Cad we reedy?' she goes.

And Erika smiles at her and she's there, 'Of course – there's a rink at Rockefeller Plaza, right under the tree. We'll go tomorrow.'

Ronan's like, 'I'd say you caddent wait to hit the shops, Hodor, wha'? Saks. Bloomendayults. Beergdorf Goodmadden.'

'Oh my God,' she goes, 'what I'd *really* love to do is see *Hamilton*,' and her face is full of, like, *wonder*?

'It's supposed to be amazing,' Erika goes.

'All I know is that Sincerity Matthews is going to see it in London in the New Year,' Honor goes, 'and I want to be able to tell her that I saw the original production on Broadway – just to see the look on the stupid bitch's face.'

'Right,' Erika goes. 'The only problem is that it's nearly impossible to get tickets. It's apparently booked up for, like, years in advance.'

Honor's there, 'I just focking hate that she's going to be the first girl in Mount Anville to see it. I hope her focking plane crashes on the way to London and she dies.'

No one says shit in response to that – there's, like, nothing *to* say?

Pretty soon, we're pulling up outside the Hotel Pierre on East 61st Street, overlooking – yeah, no – Central Pork. It's where Ronan's been living since he arrived in the famous City of Love and where we're going to be staying for the next, like, week.

Erika takes Honor, Rihanna-Brogan and Amelie inside to check us in while me and Ro help the valet dudes to take our luggage out of the taxi.

'Hee-or,' Ronan goes, suddenly remembering something, 'how's Shadden?'

I'm like, 'I've no idea,' maybe a little bit too eagerly. 'I haven't seen her or been anywhere near the house.'

He just, like, stares at me. I'm pretty sure he knows I'm lying.

He's like, 'Is evoddy thing alreeet, Rosser?'

I'm there, 'Yeah, no, why do you ask?'

'It's joost you seem a bit shifty,' he goes, 'alls of a sududden.'

And I'm like, 'Yeah, no, definitely nothing to report. Nothing at all.'

And with that, I stick a C-note in the driver's hand and I follow our luggage into the hotel.

'It's SNOWING!'

It's, like, nine o'clock in the morning or some other ludicrous hour and Rihanna-Brogan is banging on the door of my suite.

'GRANDDAD!' she goes. 'I MEAN, ROSSER – IT'S SNOW-ING OUTSOYUT!'

I get out of bed and make my way over to the window. She ends up being right. It's really coming down out there. I look out over Central Pork and it looks like an actual Christmas cord.

I'm like, 'Yeah, no, that's great, Ri. Maybe go back to bed for a few more hours, though.'

But then I hear little Amelie's voice as well, going, 'Uncle Ross! Uncle Ross! It's snowing! It's snowing! It's snowing!' and I realize there's no chance of me enjoying a lie-in this morning.

The phone beside my bed rings and it ends up being Erika. She's like, 'Get dressed – we're going ice-skating,' and she hangs up, making it pretty clear that I've no actual *choice* in the matter?

So I throw on my chinos, my Leinster jersey, my Dubes and my Henri Lloyd and I join the rest of them downstairs in the hotel lobby.

Honor is helping Amelie to put her little mittens on and Ronan is zipping up Rihanna-Brogan's coat.

'Come on,' Erika goes, 'let's get there while it still looks magical.'

We set off down Fifth Avenue as far as the Rockefeller Plaza. The famous Christmas tree looks spectacular all lit up with the snow falling on it. I'm holding Amelie in my orms and her mouth is wide open just staring at it in wonder.

Erika goes, 'Isn't it beautiful, Amelie?'

Some old lady who happens to be standing beside us – yeah, no, a real New Yorker – tells us that we have a beautiful family.

I'm there, 'Thanks – we're very lucky.'

But then Erika storts going to great pains to explain that we're not an actual couple.

'He's my brother,' she goes. 'Honor and Ronan are *his* children and Amelie is mine. Rihanna-Brogan belongs to Ronan.'

I'm there, 'Okay, Erika, the woman doesn't want your life story. Would it not be easier all round if we just let people think we were a married couple?'

'You are *so* weird, Ross.'

'I'm not talking about walking around holding hands. I'm just saying it might save time if we didn't have to explain to everyone we meet our actual relationship to each other.'

'Okay, I'm ignoring you now. Let's join the queue.'

So that's what we do. It ends up being pretty long and it takes us nearly an hour to reach the top. Honor isn't happy at having to wait.

She keeps going, at the top of her voice, 'Why the fock do we have to stand in line with all these ordinary people?'

I blame Sorcha for that. Yeah, no, we Fast Passed our way around Disneyland Paris when Honor was, like, five years old and it may have created an expectation in her that her entire *life* was going to be like that?

Still, the last time she set foot in this city, she stood up in front of the United Nations and called her old dear a bitch in front of Michelle Obama, so the disapproving looks and mutters of, 'Who the hell does she think she is?' are water off a duck's back to the girl.

We eventually get to the top of the queue and the bird behind the counter asks us what size ice skates we want.

I'm there, 'Yeah, no, I don't need any. I'm not going to be skating.'

But Honor and Rihanna-Brogan are like, 'You *have* to!' keen for the Rossmeister to be fully involved in the day.

I'm there, 'I've never actually skated before. Plus, I'd have to actually read my IRFU contract to find out if I'm even *allowed* to?'

But they're not going to take no for an answer. Erika asks for a pair of skates in my size, then Honor and Ronan drag me to the seating area, where they insist I put them on. Which I do.

Then we hit the ice. I walk out onto it on the fronts of my blades with Rihanna-Brogan holding my hand and telling me, 'Doatunt be skeered, Rosser.'

It's easy for her to say. It's one of the great mysteries of life – and it used to occur to me every time I took Ronan to the Premiere Rink on the North Road in Finglas on one of our unsupervised access days together – how people from that side of the city are able to skate expertly pretty much from birth.

As if to prove the point, Ronan takes off at full pelt and storts skating backwards and performing turns and – I don't know – pirouettes. In fairness, though, Erika and Honor are pretty handy too, as is Amelie, who has absolutely no fear, but then neither does she have a contract with the IRFU that she hasn't bothered her hole reading to find out if she's covered insurance-wise in the case of an accident.

I'm there, 'I'll tell you what, Ri, just walk me over to the side here,' which is what she does, with me clinging to her orm and shuffling along beside her like I'm her grandfather, which technically, of course, I *am*?

I cling onto the wooden hoarding at the side of the rink and I watch Ronan, Erika and the kids skate circuits of the rink, laughing and having the most unbelievable fun, while Kelly Clorkson sings 'Underneath the Tree' and Leona Lewis sings 'One More Sleep'.

Eventually, Erika skates over to me and goes, 'What are you doing?' I'm like, 'It's an insurance issue, Erika.'

But she grabs me by the hand and goes, 'Come on, don't be a coward – you were never a coward on the rugby pitch.'

And being an absolute sap for a pat on the back – especially from her – I let her drag me out into the middle of the ice. With one orm around my waist and one hand gripping my elbow, she shows me how to push off with one skate and how to position my legs when I'm actually in motion so that I maintain my balance.

Ronan and Honor both cheer when they see the Rossmeister skating past them, a bit wobbly on his feet, but at least upright. And that's how I stay for the next, I don't know, ten minutes or so, proving to my critics once again what an unbelievable competitor I am when it comes to sport of any kind, except obviously soccer, which can fock off.

I'm actually storting to get a bit cocky, laughing and joking with Honor and Rihanna-Brogan, when all of a sudden I hear my phone ring. And – like I said – filled with confidence, I actually whip the thing out of my pocket and answer it.

I'm like, 'You've got Ross,' sounding – as usual – totally full of myself.

There's, like, a man's voice on the other end of the line. He's sort of, like, mumbling to himself and he sounds possibly *drunk*?

He's going, 'Never expected . . . happen . . . not to me . . .'

I'm like, 'Hello? Who the fock is this?'

'It's me,' he goes. 'Ross, it's . . . me.'

I'm like, 'Who's me?'

'It's Steve,' he goes. 'Adam's dad.'

Honor overtakes me and smiles at me as she passes. I wait until she's well out of earshot, then I go, 'What the fock do you want?'

He goes, 'To talk to . . . to talk . . . to you.'

I'm like, 'Dude, are you banjoed?'

'I've been drinking . . . all night.'

'Er, so why are you ringing me?'

'To tell you something . . . something that I wouldn't have the nerve . . . the nerve to tell you if I was . . . if I was . . . sober.'

I'm like, 'What?' storting to lose the rag with him now. 'What do you want to tell me?'

And – I shit you not – he goes, 'I think I've fallen in love with you.'

In that moment, you could knock me over with a feather. Actually, it doesn't even take a feather. I suddenly lose my footing and – all orms and legs – I end up crashing to the ground, my phone falling out of my hand and skidding across the ice, and I'm listening to Adam's old man going, 'I love you, Ross! I don't mind saying it! I'm in love with you!' until I suddenly can't hear him any more.

So – yeah, no – I'm with Ronan and we're crossing Pork Avenue when I suddenly get a text message from Steve, apologizing for the phone call yesterday – end-of-year, boozy lunch, can't even remember what he said, obviously didn't mean a word of it, and blahdy focking blah-blah. It's such a gutless, chicken-shit way to deal with a

call you wish you hadn't made – and I should know because it's what I do all the time.

'Who's texting you?' Ronan goes.

I'm like, 'You don't want to know, Ro. You do *not* want to know.'

He laughs, in fairness to him.

'Although, seeing as you're asking,' I go, 'I was involved in a threesome just before I came away.'

He's there, 'What koyunt?'

'Yeah, no, it was a devil's threesome.'

'Two horns?'

'Two horns – unfortunately. Although the dude was there mostly in a *watching* capacity? But – yeah, no – he rang me yesterday morning, totally shit-faced, and told me that he was in love with me.'

'Rosser,' he goes, 'hab you ebber thought of mebbe simplifoying yisser life?'

But I laugh and I'm like, 'Where would the fun be in that?'

We're heading for the offices of Shlomo, Bitton and Black – Civil Rights Attorneys. Erika has taken the rest of the crew shopping this morning and Ronan wants me to see his, like, work set-up.

It storts literally the second we walk into the building.

'Hey, Roh-*nan*!' the dude sitting behind the security desk goes.

And Ro's like, 'Howiya, Deontay – how's she cutten?'

'She's cutting just fine, my friend.'

'This is Rosser – me auld fedda. He's oaber for the week with me thaughter and me niece and me addenty and *her* thaughter.'

'Hey, that's great – nice to meet you, Rosser.'

I'm like, 'Yeah, no, you too.'

Ronan swipes us in. Twenty seconds later, we're in the lift slash elevator and we hear a woman's voice go, 'Hold the doors!'

Like most normal people, I usually just pretend I'm deaf in those situations, but Ro actually puts his hand over the sensor to stop the doors from closing, then a woman appears – I'm guessing late fifties and nothing to email home about in terms of looks. But she smiles and goes, 'Hey, Ronan – *stooorrrdddeee*?' and she says it in a fake Irish accent, which – while obviously terrible – is slightly more convincing than Saoirse Ronan's real Irish accent.

'Stooorrrdddeee?' Ro goes, playing along. 'How's it going, Becka? Addy woord on the Baychester Six case?'

The woman's there, 'The judge has set a date for the appeal. The first of March. And we are going to win!'

'Ah, feer fooks,' Ronan goes. 'Hee-or, Becka, I waddant you to meet me auld fedda – this is Rosser.'

She's like, 'Hi, Rosser – it's so lovely to meet you!'

And I'm there, 'Becka, how the hell *are* you?' really trowelling on the chorm.

We reach our floor and we get out of the lift slash elevator and there ends up being more of it.

It's all, 'Hey, Ronan!' or else it's 'Hi, Ro!' or else it's 'Ronan, how *are* you?' and it's coming from, like, all angles. It reminds me of – dare I say it? – *me* walking into Club 92 back in the day.

We make our way to the office of his boss – we're talking Hazel Rochford. She's obviously delighted to see me because she goes, 'Ross! Oh my God, you are *so* welcome!' and it's a nice touch that she remembered my name. 'Ronan told us that his family was coming to visit. So are you guys having fun?'

And I'm like, 'Yeah, no, time of our lives, Hazel. Time of our literally lives.'

Ronan points to a photograph on the wall of Hazel with a woman who's – I'm just going to come out and say it here – *black*?

'That's a pitcher of Hazel,' he goes, 'with Kamada Haddis, Rosser.'

I just nod like I know who the fock he's talking about.

'Yes, Kamala and I go way, way back,' Hazel goes. 'Matter of fact, I worked on her campaign when she ran for the District Attorney's job in San Francisco.'

'Interesting,' I go, which is a sort of stock line I use when I find myself involved in a conversation that isn't in some way about me. 'Very, very interesting.'

Ronan points at another framed photo, this one on Hazel's desk.

'And that's Hazel with Keddy Washingtodden,' he goes.

I'm like, 'Ah, Chenille Reynolds from *Save the Last Dance*! Yeah, no, I had a major thing for Julia Stiles back in the day. Jesus, I watched that movie a lot – probably *too* much?'

No one says shit to this. It's just me riffing.

'So what's the stordee with the Dearborden Robbedy case?' Ronan goes.

Hazel's there, 'Hey, aren't you supposed to be on leave this week?'

But he's like, 'Are thee thropping the cheerges or what?'

She smiles and she's there, 'Go and talk to Murad. He may have some news.'

Ro goes, 'I'll be back in a midute, Rosser,' and off he focks, full of the joys.

Hazel watches him go, then she goes, 'He's amazing.'

And I'm like, 'Yeah, no, he is – definitely.'

'No, I mean *really* amazing.'

'So he's getting on well here, is he?'

'He sits in on all of our case conferences. He has this extraordinary eye – he sees things that we don't see. Like this Dearborn case, for instance. He said, "Why would anyone rob a jewellery store and make their getaway along that road? It doesn't make any sense." And we're all like, "Oh my God, he's totally right!" You see, we all think like lawyers. Ronan thinks like a criminal.'

I'm like, 'Tell me about it. The first time I ever met him, he was sandpapering the tips of his fingers to try to remove his prints.'

She goes, 'He was what?'

And I'm there, 'It was, em, just a joke, Hazel.'

Which it wasn't, by the way – his left thumb and index finger are as smooth as Ryan Gosling.

She's like, 'So what are you going to do while you're here in town? Please tell me you're going to see *Hamilton*!'

'Yeah, no,' I go, 'my daughter's been banging on about it alright.'

'Oh my God! It! Is! Sublime!'

'Right.'

'And *so* uplifting.'

'Thanks for the recommend.'

'It's one of those musicals that manages to be both timely *and* timeless?'

'Although it's pretty hord to get tickets – from what I'm hearing.'

'You need tickets?'

'Er . . .'

'How many of you are there?'

'We're talking, like, *six*?'

Shit. I should have said five, because I focking hate the theatre almost as much as I hate books. But then I don't want to come across as a dick.

'I will arrange that for you,' she goes. 'So when do you want to go – tomorrow night?'

I'm there, 'Er, yeah – are you serious, by the way?'

'Absolutely. We have tickets reserved for every performance – for special clients.'

'I mean, if it turned out that you could only get five, I'd still say thanks to you.'

'There'll be six tickets waiting for you at the box office.'

'And – again – if it ends up being just the five, that's totally cool. I mean, it'd kill me to miss out, but I'm sure I'd find something else to do.'

Like drink myself brainless.

Hazel goes, 'Can you do something for me – in return?'

I'm there, 'Er, in terms of?' not wanting to commit myself one way or the other, because, at the end of the day, it's just a few theatre tickets.

'Look, I know it's a lot to ask,' she goes, 'but we'd really like Ronan to stay.'

I'm like, 'Stay?'

'Well, as you probably know, his internship is due to end next summer,' she goes. 'But we've already told him that we see a big future for him at this firm.'

'Whoa!'

'We'd like to send him to Harvard Law School, then have him take the bar.'

'He never mentioned any of this to me.'

'We know he has a wife back in Ireland –'

'Fock *her*.'

'Excuse me?'

'Yeah, no, I was just saying, em – *poor* her.'

'Of course – it must be so tough for her.'

I'm there, 'She was bearing up alright the last time I saw her.'

'I know Ronan is really missing her,' Hazel goes, '*and* his daughter. Do you think there's any possibility they might be persuaded to relocate here?'

I'm there, 'Very little, I would say.'

'We would provide really nice accommodation for them,' she goes.

'It'd be wasted on them – feeding truffles to a moose.'

'I beg your pardon?'

'I'm just saying that I don't think the States would be Shadden's scene. My old pair put her in their gaff in Foxrock and she got home-sick crossing the East Link Bridge.'

'Oh, that's such a shame.'

'I wonder why Ronan never told me – about Horvord and all the rest of it.'

'Perhaps he doesn't want you to know that he turned it down flat. I probably shouldn't have said anything.'

'No, you did the right thing telling me, Hazel. Leave it to me. I'll have a word.'

'The fock are we going?' Honor goes.

And I'm there, 'It's a surprise,' leading the entire porty through a crowded Times Square until we're suddenly standing in front of the theatre.

I'm there, 'Ta-dah!'

Erika, Ronan and Honor all look at me, going, 'What?'

And I'm there, 'We're going to see, I don't know, whatever the fock it's called.'

'*Hamilton?*' Honor goes.

And I'm like, 'Exactly – got it in one.'

Erika's there, 'But it's impossible to get tickets.'

'Not if you know the right people,' I go, then I point to myself with my two thumbs. 'And, luckily, you goys know the right people!'

170

'Oh! My God!' Honor goes, holding her two hands up to her face. 'Oh! My! *Actual!* God!'

Erika goes, 'Ross? This isn't a joke, is it?'

'No, it's not a joke, Erika.'

'How did you get them?'

I probably should tell them that Ronan's boss gave them to us. But it's a long time since anyone looked at me with this kind of awe, so I decide to – yeah, no – grab the kudos for myself.

I'm there, 'Let's just say I have ways and means.'

Ronan goes, 'Ah, feer fooks to you, Rosser.'

I'm like, 'It's not a thing. I don't want you all making a major deal out of it, even though – as you say – they *are* nearly impossible to get.'

Erika is just, like, lost for words – she ends up just kissing me on the cheek.

I laugh and go, 'I probably won't wash my face now for a week! Obviously, I'm joking.'

I'm not joking. I'm not even nearly joking.

The loveliest thing of all, though, is seeing the excitement on Honor's face.

'Oh my God,' she goes, handing Rihanna-Brogan her phone, 'will you take a photo of me standing next to the poster.'

Then she sticks up her two middle fingers and goes, 'Focking swivel on that, Sincerity Matthews,' while Ri takes the shot.

It's hord not to be excited as we shuffle into the theatre with the rest of the crowd. Erika tips up to Will Call and returns with our tickets, going, 'Oh my God, you actually *did* get them. Ross, I'm sorry I ever doubted you.'

I'm there, 'Hey, it's cool – is there five or six?'

'There's six,' she goes, opening them out.

And I'm like, 'Fock!' because that's my night focking ruined.

'Oh, well,' I go. 'It looks like I've no choice in the matter.'

So we head into the actual theatre and we find our seats. I end up sitting with, like, Ronan on one side of me and Honor on the other.

I'm there, 'What's this supposed *musical* even about, Honor?'

And she goes, 'It's about Alexander Hamilton – he's, like, one of the founding fathers of the United States.'

'Spare me,' I go, rolling my eyes. 'And what actually happens in it?'

Ronan's there, 'Hee-or, you don't wanth her spoiding it for you, Rosser.'

And I go, 'The only way anyone could spoil a night at the theatre for me is by waking me up.'

But Honor doesn't get the chance to explain the whole point of the exercise to me, because suddenly the theatre goes dork, a hush falls over the audience and the curtain comes up.

They get straight into it, in fairness to them. The actors are all dressed like it's the olden days – as in, like, the olden, *olden* days? – but they're singing hip-hop songs.

I go, 'It's like everyone went rummaging in the wrong costume box,' and I end up getting shushed by the dude sitting in front of me.

I'm like, 'Yeah, shush yourself, you total knob-end.'

Anyway, predictably enough, I can make neither head nor tail of what's going on – Honor had to explain *Paddington 2* to me three or four times, bear in mind – and my brain, unable to cope with things I find boring, ends up just powering down. I sleep for pretty much the entire first half.

The only reason I wake up at half-time – slash, the interval – is because Ronan gives me a shove and shows me his phone screen.

He goes, 'You're some can of bleaten piss, Rosser.'

I'm there, 'What are you talking about? Is it over? Thanks be to God!'

'A text message from Hazel,' he goes, 'saying she hopes we're enjoying *Hamiltodden*. Hee-or, Edika, it wadn't eeben Rosser what geb us the tickets – it was me boss!'

Erika shoots me an absolute filthy.

'Why are you taking the focking credit for it?' she goes.

I'm there, 'I never said I bought them. You just assumed and I decided to go with it.'

She just shakes her head.

Honor, I notice, has bought up pretty much every piece of merchandise in the place as gifts for people back home – we're talking t-shirts, we're talking tote bags, we're talking programmes – her plan being, in *her* words, to flood the school with *Hamilton* paraphernalia, so that by the time Sincerity goes to see it in London, it will be, like, *so* last year.

She's not someone you'd make an enemy out of lightly.

The second half kicks off and it becomes obvious very early on that it's going to be more of the same. Again, typical me, I nod off and sleep the sleep of the just until I'm awoken again, not by a nudge this time, but by the uneasy sense that I'm being stared at by fifty or sixty people.

It turns out that I *am* being stared at by fifty or sixty people. And the reason is that I was apparently snoring – and not *just* snoring, but snoring like a focking rhinoceros.

It's like someone's forted at a funeral. People are literally turned around in their seats, trying to put a face on whoever's ruining this experience for them. Jesus, even one or two of the actors are staring in my general postcode, their concentration broken.

On either side of me, Honor and Ronan both have their hands over their eyes, while Erika is just, like, shaking her head and even Rihanna-Brogan describes herself as 'scarleh'.

I'm there, 'I'm focking jetlagged, goys!' but I end up being shushed again – by quite a few people this time.

Anyway, well and truly awake now, I manage to catch the last ten minutes of the show, including the closing number, although I have no idea what they're making – literally – a song and dance about.

When it's over, the audience is immediately on its feet, including Ronan, Erika, Honor, Rihanna-Brogan and Amelie. And Honor has actual tears rolling down her cheeks. I'm being serious. She's sobbing her hort out like I did when Ian Madigan moved to Bordeaux.

Everyone's, like, clapping and roaring as the cast take their bow. I'm watching all the actors standing there, stretched out across the stage, when all of a sudden I spot a face among them that I'm pretty sure I recognize.

I'm there, 'Honor, give me one of your programmes.'

She goes, 'Why aren't you clapping?'

And I'm like, 'Just give me a programme, will you?'

She hands one to me, then goes back to clapping and cheering, while I flick through it, quickly finding the page with the names of all the *cast* on it?

'Jaelin Sauerbrunns,' I say to myself.

Ronan's like, 'What was that?'

I'm there, 'Jaelin Sauerbrunns,' and this time I say it out of the corner of my mouth. 'I know her.'

'How?'

'She's the Rockette I rode on my Jier back in the day.'

'Are you shewer?'

'Ro, how many Jaelin Sauerbrunns do you think there are working in the world of New York theatre?'

'Which wood is she?'

'The third one from the left.'

He doesn't comment on her one way or the other.

I'm there, 'Dude, imagine what she was like seventeen or eighteen years ago. I have to meet her.'

He's like, 'Are you off your bleaten rocker?'

'Ro, I have to – just for old time's sake. Nice to be nice and blah, blah, blah.'

We get outside to the lobby. Honor and Erika – I'm surprised at *her* – are still wiping away tears.

'That was sublime,' Honor goes.

And Erika's like, 'So, so uplifting.'

Rihanna-Brogan's there, 'Edika, cadden we get hotdogs?'

And quick as a flash, I'm like, 'You goys go and do that. I'm just going to go for a dump.'

Ronan goes, 'Yeah, I need the jacks as weddle – we'll foddy yous on out.'

Seriously, I have literally no idea how they understand him over here.

'Here,' Honor goes, handing us two ginormous bags, 'will you carry my merchandise? I couldn't be bothered.'

So – yeah, no – I take it from her, then me and Ronan wait at the stage door at the side of the theatre in the freezing focking cold with, like, two hundred other fans, all of them still buzzing from the performance.

'It's *such* an uplifting show,' I hear a – believe it or not – *dude* go.

And then a woman standing next to him goes, 'How can a show be *that* timely – but at the same time totally timeless?'

It's a focking headscratcher alright.

Eventually, the stage door opens and the actors stort coming out in ones and twos. One of them ends up being mobbed – as in, he literally disappears under a pile of screaming fans. And it's while this is happening that the famous Jaelin steps out into the cold night.

I call her name. I'm like, 'Jaelin! Jaelin Sauerbrunns!'

She turns around, looking surprised – yeah, no, she's obviously not used to being stopped like this. She used to look like Sarah Michelle Gellar, by the way, and that was back in the day when *Buffy* was huge. The kindest thing I can say about her now is that she doesn't look like Sarah Michelle Gellar any more.

I'm like, 'Jaelin – how the hell are you?'

She looks down and she sees the bags of merchandise at our feet.

She goes, 'You're not going to ask me to sign all of that, are you?'

I'm like, 'No, we're not mental like this lot. Jaelin, it's me – it's Ross O'Carroll-Kelly!'

She looks straight at me and – I'm not making this up – goes, 'Who?'

I'm like, 'Er, Ross O'Carroll-*Kelly*? I met you back in, like, 2000 or 2001. I was on a J1er.'

She's like, 'What's a J1er?' and I'm thinking, has this girl had a head injury or something?

I'm there, 'It's a visa scheme for Irish students who . . . actually, the ins and outs of it don't matter. I'm just saying I met you all those years ago.'

'I'm sorry,' she goes, 'I'm actually struggling to understand your accent.'

Ronan's there, 'He's saying he was oaber hee-or woorking twedenty-odd years ago. You were peert of the Rockettes.'

She's like, 'I was a Rockette, yes.'

I'm there, 'Seriously? You can understand him, but you can't understand me?'

She goes, 'So did we, like, meet or something?'

I'm like, 'Yes!'

And I swear to fock, she sticks out her bottom lip, shakes her head slowly and goes, 'I'm sorry. I just can't place you.'

And with that, she just walks off.

Ronan laughs and goes, 'Rode a Rockette – you bleaten spoofer, Rosser! It was all in yisser Jaysusing head.'

I'm like, 'Ro, I swear to fock.'

He's there, 'How logg are you dining out on that stordee, Rosser? It was all fooken med up.'

I'm like, 'It wasn't made up, Ro – it actually happened.'

He goes, 'You're a bleaten tin-roofer, Rosser,' and he crosses the road to where Erika, Honor, Rihanna-Brogan and Amelie are standing next to a hot dog van.

And I'm left standing there, thinking, what the fock? What the *actual* fock?

And that's when I suddenly hear a woman's voice go, 'You asshole!'

I spin around and – yeah, no – it ends up being Jaelin.

She goes, 'You ASSHOLE!'

I'm there, 'You've remembered me?' and I feel my mouth twist into a smile.

'Yes, I remember you. We hooked up.'

'We certainly did.'

'Then after we hooked up, you tried to hit on my flatmate, Roniesh.'

I'm like, 'Ronan!' shouting to him across the road, except he can't hear me. 'Ronan!'

She goes, 'You asked her for her number while you were still getting dressed.'

I'm like, 'Yeah, no, that sounds like my M.O., in fairness to you,' and then I'm like, 'Ro! Ro!'

'You, like, vomited all over the carpet – Bacardi and blackcurrant.'

'It's all coming back to you now, Jaelin.'

'The landlord made us pay for it. Two thousand dollars. I phoned you, like, twenty times and left messages.'

'Yeah, no, that's because I would have given you a fake number – we're talking ten random digits off the top of my head.'

'You're a piece of shit.'

'Sorry, would you mind telling my son all of that? He's over there at that hot dog van with my sister – the hot one – and my –'

Then suddenly, out of nowhere, she slaps me hord across the face, turns on her heel and walks off again into the night.

I cross the road to the hot dog van.

'Here he is,' Ronan goes, 'Hans Christian Rosserson – writer of feery tayuls.'

I'm there, 'Ro, did you not hear me calling you? She came back and confirmed everything. I got sick on her corpet.'

'Go on ourra that, you bleaten spoofer. Are you habbon a hot dog or what?'

We're on top of the world. Or at least that's what it feels like, because – yeah, no – we're on, like, the eighty-sixth floor of the Empire State Building and the kids are just in, like, awe of how the world looks from up here.

I hear Erika tell Honor and Amelie and Rihanna-Brogan that if you dropped a quarter from this height, it could kill someone standing on the street below.

'Whoa!' I hear Honor go, then a few seconds later she sidles up to me and goes, 'Dad, have you got a quarter?'

I'm there, 'Er, yeah, but I'm not a hundred per cent sure if I should *give* it to you, Honor?'

She goes, 'It's to put into the view-finder – I want to see the Chrysler Building up close.'

I'm there, 'I'm going to be honest with you, Honor, I'm having a hord time believing that.'

She goes, 'You're no focking fun,' and she walks off in a huff.

I find Ronan. He's on, like, the eastern side of the observation deck, staring out at whatever the sea is called between the States and Ireland. It's not difficult to guess what's on his mind.

I'm there, 'I was thinking of hitting the town tonight – if you're interested. I was going to text Davy "Two Mickeys" Fraser and Johnny "Wanker" Byrne, two Clongowes heads from back in the day who are living here and working on, like, Wall Street.'

He goes, 'It's veddy good of you to ast me, Rosser, but I wanna spend as mooch time wit me thaughter as possible.'

It's funny because that's the exact opposite of how I feel?

I'm there, 'Horses for courses, Dude. What have you got planned?'

'Belieb it or not,' he goes, 'Ine taken her to Radio City to see the Rockettes – her and Hodor. And Erika and Amelie if they're wanton to come.'

I'm there, 'Why didn't you tell me, Ro?'

He's like 'Teddle you what?'

'Tell me that you'd been offered an actual job. Hazel said they want to send you to, like, Horvord.'

'I toordened it dowun.'

'Why?'

'Why do you think, Rosser? I waddant to go back to Arelunt.'

I actually laugh at that.

I'm there, 'What the fock is in Ireland for you?'

He goes, 'Shadden for steerters.'

He must see something in my face – some little tell that I'm not aware of. Knowing the way I feel about Shadden and the rest of the Tuites, it was probably about as subtle as a kick in the mebs.

He goes, 'What?'

I'm there, 'What do you mean by what?'

'You rowult yisser eyes when I mentioned Shadden's nayum joost theer.'

'I'm not sure I did, Ro.'

'You bleaten did, Rosser.'

Suddenly, I hear Honor go, 'Ronan, can I borrow a quarter?'

He reaches into his pocket and before I can say anything, he hands one over. I decide not to make an issue of it. Honor focks off and Ronan goes, 'Is she seeing some wooden, Rosser?'

I'm there, 'What? Who are you talking about?' playing for time – running down the clock. 'I have literally no idea who you're –'

He goes, 'Ine thalken about Shadden, Rosser – you know some-tin, doatunt you? Has she got anutter fedda?'

I take, like, a deep breath, then I go, 'I'm sorry, Ro, but yeah.'

He's like, 'Who is he, Rosser?'

'He's no one, Ro.'

'What's his name, but?'

'His name is Peadar something. He's, like, a mixed mortial orts fighter.'

'Nebber hoord of him.'

'He's working for Hennessy. Doing your old job. Except he wouldn't be the brightest bulb in the box.'

'How logg is it arthur been going on?'

'A few weeks, as far as I know. From what I hear, Kennet asked the dude to pop out to the gaff to fix a security light and that was when they first got it on.'

'Does Ri know?'

'No, Shadden sends her to Finglas at the weekends. She pre-tends it's about keeping her connected to her roots – but it's only so Peadar can come around and, well, I don't want to paint a pic-ture. He's a pretty big dude, so I can only imagine the stuff he does to her.'

He doesn't say anything, just stares off sadly in the direction of the, I don't know, but I'm going to take a punt and say *Pacific*?

And that's when I suddenly notice Erika giving me the come-over-here eyes and I don't mean in that way. There's nothing sexual about it.

I'm there, 'Back in a second, Ro,' and I tip over to her.

She goes, 'Did you get a text message?'

I'm like, 'No – from who?'

She's there, 'From *him*,' and I know straight away that she's talk-ing about the old man.

I'm there, 'No, did you?'

She doesn't give me a straight answer. She just goes, 'He's here. In New York.'

I'm like, 'What? Er, *why*?'

'Government business,' she goes, 'whatever the hell that means.

I saw on CNN that he was in Washington yesterday – meeting his good friend, the President of the United States.'

'Is that still Trump?'

'Yes, Ross, it's still Trump. Who, by the way, is fully backing his claim that the EU burned down the Oireachtas. He said this is what happens when people try to take back their countries.'

'What a dick. There's a pair of them in it. So what did the text say?'

'He wants to meet me.'

'The old man, I'm guessing, not the other dude?'

'Tonight. For dinner.'

'Where? Why?'

'Says he wants to clear the air between us.'

'And you told him to presumably, what, fock off?'

'No, I'm going to meet him.'

'You're shitting me.'

'I'm not ashamed of what I did, Ross. I'm just sorry that I got Seamon fitted up for a crime she didn't commit.'

'Yeah, no, that was a bummer alright.'

'I'm going to ask him to have her released.'

'I, er, might come with you actually.'

'I thought you were meeting your Clongowes friends – Penis Breath and Wanker?'

'It's Two Mickeys and Wanker. Penis Breath went to Cistercian.'

'Whatever.'

'I'll hopefully see them when they're home for Christmas. The thing is, Erika, I don't want you meeting him on your own. We don't know what he's capable of doing – or saying.'

The old man is standing outside Gallaghers Steakhouse on West 52nd Street, staring through the window of the restaurant's famous meat locker, with all these animal corcasses hanging from the ceiling. The man is pretty much drooling. Yeah, no, he's a focking vegan alright.

We walk up to him and I'm like, 'Alright, Dick Features?' and four dudes in black suits suddenly appear out of nowhere with – I shit you not – guns drawn and pointed at us.

The old man goes, 'It's quite alright, chaps – this is my son and daughter!'

One of the dudes goes, 'Are you sure?' his gun still trained on me. 'This one sounded hostile.'

'Oh, that's just Ross!' the old man goes. 'That would be typical of the back and forth between us. One will say one thing, and then the other will come back with something else. Hello, Kicker! Hello, Erika!'

I'm like, 'Whatever,' as the dudes lower their guns and back off.

Erika doesn't say shit to him, except, 'Is this where we're eating?' and then she walks straight into the place without even looking at the dude.

We follow her inside.

I'm there, 'Sorcha said you'd given up meat.'

He goes, 'What happens beyond Tearaght Island *stays* beyond Tearaght Island – as your godfather used to say in his sailing days!' and he seems to find this for some reason hilarious.

We're shown to a table in the corner of the restaurant and we all sit down. The old man opens up his napkin and tries to make small talk. He says that Donald Trump told him that the United States would pay the bill for rebuilding Leinster House.

He goes, 'Your friend, Vladimir Putin, promised the same thing, Ross! Although a little bit of me is tempted to never rebuild the thing! You know Varadkar said last week that my ongoing refusal to announce a date for the resumption of the Dáil suggests I'm a leader who prefers to rule by fiat – like my good pal in the Kremlin! I said to Hennessy, he's not bloody wrong! The amount of work you can get through as a Government without the need to keep turning up at the place every second day to explain yourself to the likes of him and Mortin and Mary Lou what's-it!'

'What do you want?' Erika goes – straight down to business.

He's there, 'A civil conversation with my daughter and my son! That's all! How's the trip going? How's everyone enjoying New York?'

I'm like, 'Yeah, no, fine. Ronan's taken Rihanna-Brogan, Honor and Amelie to see the Rockettes tonight.'

'Oh, that's wonderful! And how's he getting on in that – inverted commas – *job* of his?'

'He's loving it.'

'What is it he's doing again – civil rights, wasn't it? Each to his own, I suppose! I'm hearing wonderful things about the work you're doing with those rugby-playing ladies!'

I'm there, 'What do you mean?' because I'm a sucker for a compliment and he knows it. 'As in, what specific things have you heard?'

He goes, 'Verner says there's a real buzz around Donnybrook – a sense that this could be their year.'

I'm wondering did Verner also mention that the team captain got hit by a bus when I sent her out running in the dork. If he did, the old man doesn't bring it up.

A waiter storts making his way across the floor to our table. Without looking at him, the old man goes, 'Dom Perignon! Rosé Vintage Coffret Gold 2000!' and the dude does an instant U-ey and heads back to the kitchen.

I open my menu. There's, like, a moment of awkward silence, then the old man looks at Erika and goes, 'How's Helen?'

She's there, 'You don't give a fock how my mom is,' and then, after a ten-second silence, she goes, 'She can't wait to be divorced from you – that's how she is.'

'Well, as it happens,' he goes, 'a divorce might not be required! Hennessy thinks there's a very good orgument to be made for an annulment! In which case she could be free to wed again within weeks – if that's her desire, of course!'

'Am I supposed to say thank you or something?'

There's, like, more silence. It's big-time awks.

'And how's the lovely Amelie?' the old man tries to go.

Erika's there, 'I would say that's none of your focking business.'

'I know things aren't good between us, Erika, but I'd like to see her from time to time!'

'I don't want you in my daughter's life. I don't want you corrupting her like you corrupt everyone and everything you come into contact with.'

The waiter dude arrives back with the bottle and three glasses.

He pops the cork, then he pours. The old man raises his glass for a toast.

'To family!' he goes.

I lift mine as well – although I say fock-all – but I end up feeling like a spare prick then, because Erika doesn't even touch hers.

The old man turns suddenly serious. He goes, 'So why did you do it, Erika?' and it suddenly feels like this is the reason we're here.

She goes, 'Do what?'

'You put that poor, delusional girl in contact with *Prime Time*.'

'She's not delusional. She was telling the truth.'

'So you weren't aware that she's a self-confessed anarchist?'

'Anarchist or not – you know she's innocent.'

'Oh, don't worry, she will have an opportunity to state her case before the Special Criminal Court!'

'Yeah, she'll be given some half-horted defence by some barrister mate of Hennessy's who'll be rewarded within three years with a judgeship. She'll get, what, thirty years? That's if you don't have her declared insane before she stands trial.'

'And what was the alternative, Erika? For *me* to go to jail?'

'You focking belong in jail. You burned down the Dáil.'

'You were happy for that interview to go out? For those things that she alleged about me to be made public? For me to be forced out of office in disgrace? Then to be locked away for the rest of my life, with no one to look after Fionnuala and our beautiful children?'

'It's what you deserve.'

'Be that as it may, it was never going to happen!'

I'm there, 'Does everyone know what they're having yet?' trying to lighten the mood. 'I like the sound of the salmon tortor followed by the bone-in New York sirloin with hopefully peppercorn sauce.'

Erika goes, 'Sea-mon is innocent. You have to let her go.'

The old man's there, 'Enormous changes are about to happen in the world, Erika! There is going to be a great geopolitical shift that will change the way our planet is governed for centuries to come! I am making sure that our country is on the right side of history when it happens! And no one is going to stop me! Not Sea-mon!

Not even you – my own flesh and blood, who would have happily sent me to prison for treason!'

'Don't talk to me about flesh and blood as though it means something to you. You've been listening to my phone calls.'

'Listening to your phone calls?'

'My phone has been bugged. How else could you have known about the interview?'

He goes, 'I knew because –' and then he pauses for a good, like, twenty seconds before going, 'because it's my business to know! Look, I know you feel responsible for what happened to this girl, Erika, but you'd be best advised to forget she ever existed!'

Erika suddenly stands up, the legs of her chair scratching across the floor.

She's like, 'Come on, Ross, let's go. We still have time to make it to Radio City.'

I'm there, 'Are you not going to order something?'

'What, you're happy to sit and eat with the devil, are you?'

'I don't know, maybe – what if we skipped the storter and just had a main?'

She goes, 'I'm leaving – now.'

And – yeah, no – I've no choice but to stand up and follow her out of the restaurant.

The old man shouts after us, 'Enjoy the rest of your trip!'

'Theer she is!' Ronan goes. 'The Statue of Libertoddy!'

Yeah, no, we're on a night-time cruise of the horbour – and it has to be said, it's a pretty spectacular sight when it's all lit *up* like this?

Ro's like, 'What do you think, Ri?'

'I lub it,' Rihanna-Brogan goes. 'Daddy, will you take a pitcher of me in fruddent ob it?'

I'm sitting down on a bench on the upper deck of the ferry. Erika comes over and sits down beside me.

She's there, 'He's really going to miss her when we go back.'

I'm there, 'I know – it's going to kill him.'

'It's only for another six months.'

'It's hopefully not.'

184

'What do you mean?'

'They've offered him a permanent job, Erika – as in, they want to send him to, like, Horvard and then they want him to take the American bor exams.'

'Are you serious?'

'His boss told me that herself.'

'And what? Please don't tell me he's thinking of turning it down.'

'He is. Wants to go home and try to patch things up with Shadden.'

'Did you tell him she's seeing someone?'

'Yeah, no, I wasn't going to, but then he asked me straight out if she had another fella – anutter fedda. And you know me, I can't lie.'

'What did he say?'

'Not much. Nothing in fact.'

'It was obviously a shock to him.'

'Big time. Hey, I'm sorry the old man was such a dick to you.'

'I can't believe he's going to let Sea-mon go to prison for something she didn't do.'

'I'll say it again – he's a dick.'

'I can't let it happen, Ross. I feel responsible.'

'Responsible? In terms of?'

'I was the one who persuaded her to come back to Ireland to tell the truth.'

'Yeah, no, I know.'

'I'd just love to know how they found out.'

'About?'

'About the interview.'

'Like you said, they probably have people listening to our phone calls. Let's be honest, Erika, if he'd burn down the Dáil, he'd do anything.'

I notice that Honor is holding Amelie and she's teaching her how to spit over the side of the ferry.

I'm there, 'It's nice to see our children bonding, isn't it?'

She goes, 'I love the idea that they'll always have these memories to treasure – even long after we're gone.'

I'm like, 'Yeah, no, that's a nice thought alright.'

Some old lady walks over to Honor and tells her that what they're doing is disgusting.

'Keep your focking nose out of other people's business,' Honor goes, 'you stupid focker.'

And Amelie's like, 'Fock off, you focker!'

Me and Erika burst out laughing – what else can we do?

'So what about you?' she suddenly goes. 'What are you going to do?'

I'm like, 'In terms of?'

'Oh, come on, Ross, you're not going to spend the next ten years of your life sleeping on a mattress in that freezing cold tower, are you?'

'I don't know. I haven't thought about it long term. I'm still hoping to weasel my way back into Sorcha's bed.'

'It's not going to happen, Ross. She told me it's over.'

'Yeah, no, she's said that loads of times in the past. I rode her sister, bear in mind. I always think, if I turned things around after riding her sister, there has to be hope for me.'

'I'm sorry to tell you this, Ross, but I think you're wrong. When she says she's finished with you, she means it this time.'

'Do you genuinely think?'

'She has her political career now. You don't really fit into her life any more.'

'I want to be around for my kids – even though the boys have turned out to be a pain in the hole.'

'Ross, I'm saying this as your sister rather than as Sorcha's friend –'

'Half-sister – but continue.'

'It suits Sorcha to have you there as a full-time nanny. But make sure it's also what *you* want. You're entitled to a life, Ross –'

She can be great, Erika.

'– even though you should be focking chemically castrated for what you did,' she adds.

I'm like, 'Thanks, Erika.'

She stands up and she tips over to where Honor and Amelie are spitting over the rail.

I hear Amelie go, 'Mommy, I spitted on a seagull!' and I smile to myself.

I walk over to Ronan and Rihanna-Brogan. We're, like, heading home tomorrow night and I can already sense the sadness in them. He's holding her hand and he's giving her – yeah, no – advice like, 'Make shurden you do yizzer homewoork' and 'Altwees do what yisser mammy teddles you.'

She gets embarrassed when she sees me standing there and goes, 'Ine godda go and foyunt Hodor.'

Off she focks.

I stand next to Ronan, the two of us leaning over the rail, as the ferry heads back to Battery Pork.

I'm there, 'I can never remember whether it's the Atlantic or the Pacific.'

He goes, 'It's the Atlantic, Rosser.'

'Are you sure?'

'Yeah.'

There's, like, silence between us then. After about thirty seconds, he goes, 'I reng Hazel this morden, Rosser.'

I'm there, 'Hazel? As in your boss?'

'I toawult her –'

'What did you tell her?'

'Ine godda take the job.'

I laugh out loud. I'm there, 'Ro, I'm delighted.'

He goes, 'Me and Shadden is fidished. I know that now.'

'It's for the best, Ro.'

'Ine lubben the woork Ine doing. Hazel says thee'll get me an apeertment to lib in. Ine hoping Ri can cub oaber at Easter and for the subber hoddidays. Then, in Septembor, I'll be moobin to Boston.'

'Is that where Horvard is?'

'Yeah.'

'Fair focks, Ro. Fair focking focks.'

The boat is just about to dock when I suddenly feel a shadow thrown over us. Ronan looks around and goes, 'Ah, howiya, Edika?'

But Erika doesn't say shit to him. She just goes, 'It was *you*!' and without even looking around, I automatically know that she's talking to me.

I'm there, 'What was me?' and I turn my head to look at her.

She looks mad enough to kill me right here.

She goes, 'You tipped him off. About the interview.'

I'm like, 'No, I didn't.'

'I was wondering why he was so angry with me and not you. He kept saying that *I* was prepared to send him to prison for the rest of his life – but he never said anything to you.'

'Yeah, no, you've lost me, Erika.'

'And that's why you didn't want me to meet him on my own that night. You were scared that he might let something slip.'

'Ro, have you any idea what she's talking about?'

'You were the one who told him that Sea-mon was back in the country. You were the one who told him that she was going to tell David McCullagh everything.'

'Erika, I don't know what you're banging on about.'

But then she roars at me. She's like, 'DON'T FOCKING LIE TO ME!'

And then I end up spilling everything – as per usual.

I'm there, 'Erika, please don't hate me. I just didn't want to see him go down. I mean, I *thought* I did? But then the old dear turned up at Energia Pork in her nightdress after training one night and she thought I was the dude who does her hair. And it suddenly made the whole thing – I don't know – *real*? I just thought, fock, who'll look after the old dear if the old man ends up banged up for the rest of his life? And what'll happen to the children they brought into the world? So – yeah, no – I rang him, just to tip him off, but I didn't think he'd end up fitting See-mon up for the fire.'

Erika just stares hord at me and goes, 'You and I are finished, Ross.'

I'm there, 'You've said that before.'

She's like, 'This time, I mean it. I am never, *ever* going to speak to you again.'

'Dude,' I go, 'you understand why I did it, don't you?'

And Ronan's there, 'I do, Rosser. I doatunt waddant to see Cheer-lie go to jayult eeder. I hated it when he was in theer befower.'

I sometimes forget that Ronan first got to know his granddad through an inch of bulletproof glass.

I'm there, 'I wish Erika saw it that way.'

He goes, 'Edika's angry wirrem, Rosser – and it's not because he burdened Doddle Airdint. It's because of the way he treated her ma. She waddants to hoort him.'

Yeah, no, we're in the very fine toilets of the Plaza Hotel on Central Pork, by the way, where we're having afternoon tea in the Palm Court – the last item on Honor's wish list – before we head for the airport.

I'm there, 'The old dear's losing it, Ro. I mean, one minute, she has her shit together – she's talking about things that happened forty or fifty years ago. The next minute, she doesn't know where she is – or even who she is. I know I sound like I'm describing an average afternoon in The Gables for her, but I'm not. If he gets sent down, she'll end up in a home and God knows what'd happen to the kids.'

'You doatunt hab to explayun it to me, Rosser. I wontherstand what you're saying – a hondoord per cent.'

We go back to the table. Erika is making a big point of blanking me. Honor is spreading jam, then dolloping clotted cream onto, like, a scone.

I'm there, 'So did you buy a present for the famous Adam?' because that's what she went out to do this morning.

She's there, 'Yeah, I bought him, like, a book?'

'A book?' I go. 'I thought you and I agreed that a book was a shit present at any time.'

'It's a book about the Apollo Theater,' she tries to go. 'It's this, like, really famous *music* venue?'

A book about a theatre. I'm giving it until Christmas.

My phone all of a sudden beeps. It's a text message from, like, Sive.

It's like, 'Are you thinking about rugby?' and I end up just laughing out loud.

I text her back. I'm like, 'Always and at all times, Sive.'

She goes, 'Good – me too. I've had an idea. I'll tell you about it when you get back.'

I'm actually looking forward to getting back to work with the team. I text her a thumbs-up emoji, then Erika stands up and goes, 'We should stort making our way to the airport.'

I'm like, 'Good idea, Sis!'

But she's there, 'Fock off, Ross.'

We've got a taxi waiting outside with all our luggage in it and the meter running for the last, like, hour.

So we all head outside and it's there, in front of the Plaza, that we all say our goodbyes to Ronan. It ends up being a really, like, tearful scene as well. Rihanna-Brogan is basically inconsolable. She's, like, bawling her eyes out, going, 'I waddant you to come howum, Daddy!' holding on to him as tightly as she can. 'Why caddent you joost come howum?'

He's there, 'I'll be howum in anutter few weeks, Ri. I've a week off in Meerch, so I have.'

Honor goes, 'Do you promise?' wiping away a few tears of her own.

He pulls her close to him as well.

'I probbis,' he goes.

I'm there, 'We better get in the taxi. There's already about two hundred snots on the meter.'

Ronan gives Erika a hug then. He goes, 'Thanks, Edika. I love you, so I do.'

And Erika goes, 'I love you too, Ronan.'

Then it's, like, *my* turn?

'Rosser,' he goes – and he's crying too now, 'you're arthur gibbon me the best week of me life.'

I'm there, 'Hey, Ro, there's no need to thank me. We had the time of our lives as well.'

He throws his orms around me.

A few minutes later, we're pulling away in the Jo and we're waving our tearful goodbyes to Ronan through the window. Then a few minutes after that, we're crossing Madison, then Pork, then Lexington, then Third, on our way to the airport.

I'm like, 'Erika –'

But she goes, 'Don't even *try* to speak to me, Ross. When we get back home, I never want to lay eyes on you again.'

And that's when my phone rings. It ends up being – *weirdly?* – Fionn and I can straight away tell from his voice that something is wrong.

I'm like, 'Dude, what's up?'

'Ross,' he goes, 'I failed the Gorda background check.'

I'm there, 'What?'

'I told you I had to fill in a load of forms – it's part of the vetting procedures if you want to coach kids.'

'And?'

'I have a conviction for indecent exposure.'

I'm suddenly in, like, shock.

I'm there, 'You never told me about that before.'

'That's because I didn't know about it,' he goes. 'But, apparently, in 2014, I was arrested for exposing my orse in the Thomond Bor in Cork.'

My entire body turns cold. And that's the moment, I suppose, when I *should* tell him the truth? Except I don't.

I just go, 'Dude, we're about to go into a tunnel – I'm probably going to lose you.'

6.

From Ruck till Dawn

I've never seen Fionn so upset before – and that includes the time I booked four male strippers for his eighteenth-birthday dinner and his granny had a mini-stroke in Blakes in Stillorgan.

We arrive home from the airport to find him sitting at the kitchen table and just, like, staring into space, while Sorcha – with little Hillary in her orms – paces backwards and forwards, going, 'We will get to the bottom of it, Fionn – I can promise you that.'

I'm like, 'Hey, we're home from the States,' and Honor swans into the kitchen behind me, carrying her bags from Bloomingdale's, Saks and Bergdorf Goodman.

She's there, 'I spent fifty thousand euros on clothes!'

But Sorcha just goes, 'Yeah, Honor, that's nice – would you mind taking Hillary upstairs to play while we talk?'

And Honor's like, 'Er, whatever,' and she takes the little dude out of Sorcha's orms and goes, 'Come on, Hill, let's go and give the boys their presents! You are going to – oh my God – *love* what I got you!'

So off she focks, leaving me alone with Fionn and Sorcha.

I'm there, 'So, er, what's the craic – what happened?'

'Fionn is on the sex offenders register,' Sorcha goes. 'That's what happened.'

I'm there, 'What, for taking your orse out in a pub?'

He's like, 'I *didn't* take my orse out in a pub.'

'But even if you did,' I go, 'it would have been meant as a joke. Jesus, have these Gords nothing better to do?'

He's like, 'Ross, I've never even *been* to the Thomond Bor.'

And Sorcha goes, 'Like I said to you, Fionn, we are going to find out what really happened.'

What really happened? Yeah, no, what really happened was this.

One weekend, back in the day, I went on the big-time rip with Johnny 'Shagger' Sorenson and Robbie 'The Shit' Murphy – two random dudes I knew from the Sportsman Dip. course in UCD. We ended up in, like, Cork, where The Shit is originally from. It was the day that Toulon beat Munster in the semi-final of the Heineken Cup and we found ourselves watching the match in the Thomond Bor in the City Centre. Munster fans won't enjoy being reminded that Jonny Wilkinson was in the form of his life that day, nailing six of his seven kicks, not to mention a first-half drop goal. I cheered each and every one of them as they sailed between the old chop-sticks, which didn't exactly endear me to the local population. They were very much of the view that I should leave the bor, or, better still, 'Fuck off back up the N8, you Dublin fucking langball.'

The demand for this grew as it became clear that Munster were about to lose their second Heineken Cup semi-final in a row. There were chants of 'Out! Out! Out!' and I attempted to defuse matters by pointing out that I was a massive Simon Zebo fan – I was the one who said he should have been a storter for the Lions against Australia – and that Ian Keatley learned his kicking technique from watching videos of me on YouTube.

None of it helped. The chants of 'Out! Out! Out!' continued until the manager told me that I would have to leave, and I let them know what I thought of that by whipping down my chinos and mooning at them.

Anyway, some random girl decked me – it was a hell of a punch, which knocked me senseless – and the Gords arrived shortly after-wards and announced that they were arresting me – *me!* – for indecent exposure. It was total bullshit, of course, and I made sure to tell them that back at the station.

When they asked me for my name, though, I said, 'Fionn de Barra,' which is something I tended to automatically do whenever I was in trouble. They asked me for the phone number, so that they could confirm that I lived at the address I'd given them, and I said we didn't have a landline, but I could give them my old man's mobile. I ended up giving them Shagger Sorenson's. He was sitting in the waiting room, off his tits, shouting that he wanted to make a

statement, when his phone all of a sudden rang and some Gorda dude asked if he could vouch for the fact that Fionn de Barra lived at Rathcrogan, Carysfort Avenue, Blackrock. Shagger – who figured out what was going on – immediately went, 'Yes.'

Which is how I ended up appearing in court the following morning, chorged with indecent exposure – I mean, come on! – under Fionn's name. I – slash, he – was fined fifty snots and given the Probation Act on condition that I – slash, he – agreed to be placed on the sex offenders register – I mean, give me a break! – for ten years.

I possibly should mention this to him now. Except I don't, because I'm thinking that a conviction for indecent exposure would probably cost me my job as Head Coach of the Ireland women's team, regardless of who my old man knows in the IRFU.

So instead, I go, 'Are you sure it wasn't you, Fionn? As in, were you possibly too drunk to remember?'

Yeah, no, I hate myself for it.

He's like, 'Too drunk to remember appearing in court chorged with indecent exposure?'

I'm there, 'I've seen you in some states, Dude.'

'Trust me,' he goes, 'I would remember *that*.'

I'm there, 'How are we suddenly living in a world where mooning is no longer considered hilarious?'

And that's when I catch Sorcha staring hord at me.

She goes, 'Ross, it wasn't –'

I'm like, 'Wasn't what?'

'It wasn't . . . *you*, was it?'

'Excuse me?'

She's like, 'You didn't expose yourself and then pretend to be Fionn, did you?'

And I'm there, 'No, Sorcha, it wasn't me.'

Fionn – in fairness to him – goes, 'I don't think even Ross would stoop that low,' which is a nice thing for me to hear, even though it's total horseshit.

Sorcha's there, 'He pretended to be you the time RTÉ showed up at the school to interview students who got maximum points in the Leaving Cert. He put on a pair of glasses and everything.'

She really does hate me.

He goes, 'I think even this would be a step too far for Ross.'

And I'm like, 'Thanks for the support, Dude.'

Sorcha's there, 'So when did you say this supposedly happened – as in, like, what date?'

Fionn goes, 'The twenty-seventh of April 2014.'

'Okay,' Sorcha goes, 'so what you have to do is find out where you actually *were* that day?'

I'm like, 'That sounds like needle in a haystack stuff, Sorcha.'

But Fionn's there, 'I already know where I was that day. I pulled out my old diaries. I was with you, Sorcha – at the Feminist Climate Conference in Dublin.'

Focking spare me.

'Oh my God,' Sorcha goes, her hand to her forehead, 'the one exploring the role of women and non-binary persons in climate resilience and how the goal of saving the planet can only be achieved with a gender-inclusive perspective?'

He's like, 'In the Radisson St Helen's. You're my alibi, Sorcha.'

And Sorcha goes, 'Then it shouldn't be too hord to get your conviction overturned.'

I'm there, 'Is there an orgument to be made for leaving well enough alone?'

Fionn's like, 'What?' obviously not happy.

'Bear with me,' I go, 'I'm just spit-balling here. You were never going to beat Blackrock College anyway – and that's not a reflection on you as a coach, Fionn. They've got a seriously good team this year – we're talking four or five players who'll walk straight into the Leinster Academy.'

'This isn't *about* rugby,' Sorcha suddenly goes. 'This is about Fionn's future.'

'I've been suspended from my job –' Fionn goes.

'What, for taking your orse out in a pub?'

'– pending a disciplinary hearing in front of the Board of Management.'

I'm like, 'So who's going to coach the Senior Cup team?'

Sorcha goes, 'Oh my God, Ross – *why* is that important?'

If she doesn't know that by now, she never will.

'No one,' Fionn goes, his voice cracking with emotion. 'Molly Gordon, who's taken over as Acting Principal, has pulled the team out of the competition because there isn't another teacher in the school who knows anything about rugby.'

I'm like, 'That's Tom McGahy's legacy – and to think that people actually felt sorry for the dude for being, like, dead.'

'Well,' he goes, 'my career is going to be dead – unless I can prove that it wasn't me in Cork that day.'

I'm there, 'I know what this is really about. They want to get rid of you just because you wanted to open the doors to, let's be honest, poor people.'

Sorcha goes, 'They're not *going* to get rid of you, Fionn – because we are going to prove that you didn't do what you've been accused of doing. And we're going to find out who *actually* did?'

It wouldn't be an exaggeration to say that there's a genuine buzz around Donnybrook Stadium tonight. I have no idea what Sive said to them while I was in the States, but there's no doubt they seem like happier campers. Plus, they're, like, trying shit out.

Sive has got our two centres, Rachel and Louise Skeldon – they're from somewhere around Limerick direction, intense girls who never seem to smile or blink – practising this pretty slick wraparound move that they manage to pull off two out of every maybe *five* times they try it? But like I said, at least they're experimenting with things.

They all have massive, massive respect for Sive. As a matter of fact, when she says we'll finish up the session now with a game of Sevens, and I go, 'No, let's train for another twenty minutes,' it's Sive they end up listening to. Which is cool, because – yeah, no – they've trained hord tonight and it's our last training session before Christmas.

Heather Hobson – our tighthead from Belfast, who's built like a focking Portaloo – hands out Santa hats to everyone and the banter would actually remind you of me and the goys back in the day.

She insists that I put one on as well. She's like, 'Here, put that on your hod,' meaning, put that on your head. 'That's uf ut futs.'

When I pull the thing on, it ends up being a tight squeeze alright.

'Least ut'll keep your wee breen warm,' she goes, because – yeah, no – she's definitely the joker of the team, and all of the women laugh. I laugh as well – yeah, no, it's good for team bonding – even though I *could* point out that she'd be better off focusing on her handling skills, which simply aren't good enough in an era when a front-row player is expected to do more than just carry the ball.

We get on with the Sevens match. Even though it's, like, a warm-down exercise, Sive insists that everyone maintains the same intensity. She's standing next to me on the sideline, with her shoulder still strapped, giving out yords to Grainne Hutton, our scrum-half, who's from Cork. She's going, 'Deliver the ball, Grainne! What are you waiting for – nine reindeers to help you?'

I'm there going, 'Yeah, no, I was going to say something very similar. Quick ball, especially from the ruck, can be the difference between good teams and great teams at this level.'

She's there, 'Yeah, I've already told her.'

'Now that I'm back,' I go, 'I wonder would it be best for the players to hear just one voice – as in, if you've got shit to say to them, maybe you could say it *through* me? Does that work for you?'

'So, what, I'd be the ventriloquist and you'd be the dummy?'

'It was just a thought.'

When the Sevens game ends, I call everyone into a circle. I'm there, 'Gather round, everyone. I just wanted to say, you did very well today. Heather, I'm not singling you out, but when you're passing the ball, you tend to give away little cues as to your intentions. You need to be cleverer than that. Think Tadhg Furlong. Aport from that, well done, everyone.'

They turn around and stort drifting away, but I go, 'Wait a minute – I haven't given you your Christmas presents yet!'

They're all like, 'What? Did he just say Christmas presents?' because women love surprises, although not the kind I've sprung on Sorcha over the years.

I'm there, 'It's just a little something for each of you,' and I walk over to the sideline and pick up the canvas equipment bag in which I have them all stashed, wrapped in Christmas paper.

I reach in and I stort pulling them out, one by one, then – yeah, no – handing them to them. They all laugh. Because, from the shape, it's straight away obvious that my present to each of them is a rugby ball.

Megan Barrett, our full-back, rips the paper off hers, then goes, 'Okay, what am I, like, *missing* here?'

I'm there, 'It's a rugby ball, Megan.'

She gives me a shrug. She's like, 'I know what it is.'

And I'm there, 'I'm glad to hear it. You're all a bit underwhelmed, aren't you?'

They're all like, 'Errr . . .' wondering where this is going.

'Good,' I go. 'Now, I want you to pretend that those rugby balls were a present from, say, your favourite grandmother – and you don't want to hurt the woman's feelings!'

Heather looks around and goes, 'The fuck is he talking abite?'

And I'm there, 'I want you to carry them everywhere with you over Christmas – especially you, Heather.'

'What do you mean by everywhere?' Megan goes.

'I mean, if you meet your friends for a drink on, say, Christmas Eve, I want you to bring the ball with you.'

'But whay?' Heather goes – she's apparently a cop with the PSNI, by the way, and not used to taking shit from people.

I'm there, 'What are the four most important things in rugby, Sive?'

Sive goes, 'The ball. The ball. The ball. The ball.'

I'm like, 'Spot on. But too many of you play rugby like you've never actually seen one before. And that's not *your* fault? I've had a ball in my hands ever since I was a kid.'

'Focken *two* balls in your hawnds, *I'd* say,' Heather goes.

Again, everyone laughs. She's a character – there's no question.

I'm there, 'You're someone who could benefit from this, Heather, so maybe you should drop the comedy routine and just listen.'

She stares at me – doesn't like it one bit.

I'm there, 'I want you to bring the ball to bed with you at night. I want you to take it into the shower with you in the morning. I want you to have it on your lap when you're driving. I want you to get so used to handling it that it feels weird not to have it with you. Have a great Christmas – and I'll see you back here the day after Stephen Zuzz Day.'

They're all like, 'What?'

Grainne Hutton goes, 'Sure, *I'm* going to be in Cork, like?'

I'm there, 'If you want to play for Ireland in the Six Nations, you won't be.'

'But my sister's getting married the day after Christmas – I'm supposed to be doing bridesmaid, like.'

'Then you'd better lay off the sauce that night. Because you're going to have to be on the road early the following morning. We stort training at ten bells.'

It's a trick that worked on the goys in Pres Bray.

Grainne goes, 'I can't imagine Scotland and France will be training at ten o'clock in the morning two days after Christmas.'

And I'm like, 'Exactly, Grainne – that's why *we're* going to do it. And, by the way, I'll want to see your sister's wedding photos. And I expect to see you holding that rugby ball in them. Merry Christmas, goys.'

Off they fock with their balls under their orms – some of them happy, some of them not so much. Out of the corner of my eye, I can feel Sive just, like, staring at me, with – I can feel it – a grudging respect.

'The balls,' she goes. 'That was a nice touch.'

I'm there, 'I actually got the idea from the nuns in Mount Anville. They used to make the Transition Year girls carry an egg around with them for three months to terrify them out of ever getting pregnant. I just applied it to rugby.'

She smiles at me – first time.

'It's clever,' she goes. 'Provided they all do it. What do think of Joanne Wassell?'

I'm like, 'In *terms* of?'

'Well, I'm not asking if you fancy her. What do you think of her as a player? Number ten – that was your old position, right?'

'Yeah, no,' I go, 'she's, em, not bad.'

She just, like, stares at me.

She's there, 'Just because we're women, you don't have to pretend we're all great. Do you rate her? Be honest.'

'I think she's got a good tactical brain,' I go, 'in terms of calling the play. But she couldn't kick petals off a focking rose bush.'

'Agreed,' she goes. 'The last two years, we've been leaving a lot of points behind on the pitch because she's just not up to it with the boot. Remember I texted you when you were away and said I had an idea?

'It doesn't involve me dressing up as a woman, does it?'

'What?'

'I remember I dressed up as Britney Spears once for a Hallowe'en porty on Tubbermore Road and spent half the night drunkenly eyeing myself up in the hallway mirror. Okay, I'm guessing from your expression that's not the plan.'

'What are you doing on St Stephen's Day?'

'You mean Stephen Zuzz Day? Yeah, no, I usually go to Leopardstown with the goys?'

'Well, you're not this year.'

I'm there, 'Errr . . .' because she's a bigger ballbreaker than even me.

She goes, 'Me and you are going to a soccer match.'

I'm there, 'Sorry, Sive – for a second there, I thought you said we were going to a soccer match.'

And she's like, 'I did.'

'Why does *he* have to be here?' Sorcha's old man goes.

He is obviously me and *here* is the dining room in my own focking house. Yeah, no, the Lalors are having their traditional Christmas Eve family dinner and her old pair aren't happy that the Rossmeister has a seat at the table.

'He still focking lives here,' Honor goes, leaping to my defence. 'He's still my focking dad.'

Sorcha's old dear is like, 'He is no longer a member of this family,' talking about me like I'm not even there.

Johnny waves his little fork at the woman and goes, '*Halt's Maul, focking Zicke!*'

To which *she's* like, 'How *dare* you speak to me like that!' because it's pretty obvious from the way he bared his teeth at her that it wasn't a compliment.

'Focking *Hund*!' Brian goes. 'Focking *Zicke*!'

'Oh, *big* news,' Sorcha goes. 'I'm planning to bring a proposal before Cabinet in the New Year to place a cap on the number of flights that Irish nationals are allowed to take in a calendar year. It could help us achieve corbon neutrality a year sooner than forecasted.'

'Well,' her old man goes, 'if the big polluters, such as China, India and the United States, won't take the lead with safeguarding the future of the Earth, then it's up to small countries like Ireland to set the example and you're certainly ensuring we do that, Dorling.'

I'm there, 'Any word from Sea-mon, by the way? It's just nobody seems to be mentioning her any more.'

That kills the conversation dead for about thirty seconds.

'The story I'm hearing,' Sorcha eventually goes, 'is that she might never stand trial. According to Hennessy, they've moved her to the Central Mental Hospital in Dundrum.'

I instantly think of Erika, who hasn't been returning my calls since we got back from the States, except once to tell me to stop focking contacting her and once to tell me that she was blocking my number.

Sorcha's like, 'They're saying that she's, like, insane?'

Sorcha's old man goes, 'Well, the girl would *have* to be insane to burn down the Dáil, wouldn't she? She's obviously deeply unwell. It's just sad that someone in Brussels has clearly taken advantage of that.'

Her old dear's like, 'But we're so proud of *you*, Sorcha,' desperate to change the subject. 'What a year it's been for you!' She holds up her champagne glass for a toast. 'Our daughter! A member of Government!'

The three of them clink glasses. I don't bother my hole.

Honor's phone beeps. She's got, like, a text message. I've no idea who it's from, but I notice the sudden smile on her face.

I'm there, 'Who's that, Honor? Adam?'

Yeah, no, 'Fock! Ing! Hot! Bitch!' was the seventh most downloaded song in Ireland last week and Adam said on his Instagram account that the song was about Honor, his – not my word – but *girlfriend*?

Honor goes, 'No, it's Reese,' and I feel my shoulders instantly tighten.

I'm there, 'Reese? I thought he was off the scene – as in, like, permanently?'

'He texted me yesterday,' she goes. 'He wants us to be friends.'

I'm there, 'Friends? Is this because everyone's talking about the song?'

'I don't know.'

'Because that'd be focking textbook Michael's alright. If you want my advice, Honor, delete his number and never reply to him again.'

'*Geschenke!*' Leo goes. '*Gib mir meine Geschenke!*'

'Good idea,' Sorcha goes. 'Let's do presents.'

So – yeah, no – we all get up from the table and head over to the tree, where they're all piled up, waiting to be opened.

Sorcha goes, 'Ross, I didn't get anything for you – given, well, you know . . .'

I'm there, 'Yeah, no, it's cool, Sorcha. I didn't get anything for you either.'

Although in my case, I just forgot. Christmas is for the kids anyway and it's enough of a present for me to hear the ripping of wrapping paper and the boys going, '*Oh mein Gott!*' and Honor going, 'I focking hope you kept the gift receipt for this!'

Anyway, they're tearing things open at a rare old pace and I'm sort of, like, smiling to myself, the five cans of Heineken I knocked back before dinner giving me a happy, peaceful buzz. Which lasts until the moment I watch Johnny tear the wrapping paper off a sort of long present that at first I *think* is an umbrella but it turns out that it unfortunately *isn't*?

I'm like, 'What the fock is that?'

'What?' Sorcha's old dear goes, already on the big-time defensive.

I'm there, 'That thing in Johnny's hand.'

'It's a hockey stick,' she tries to go – like it's hurting no one.

I'm there, 'Who the fock bought my son a hockey stick?'

'*We* did,' Sorcha's old man goes. 'We bought one for each of the boys.'

I'm like, 'You've some focking balls – I'll give you that.'

Sorcha goes, 'What's the problem?' and that's when all hell breaks loose.

I'm there, 'We've been through this before. First it was soccer jerseys. Now it's hockey sticks. They're trying to derail their rugby careers.'

'What rugby careers?' *he* goes. 'They're children.'

I'm there, 'You're trying to turn them off it by interesting them in other sports. Focking hockey – the nerve of you people.'

Sorcha goes, 'Ross, they play hockey in school.'

I'm there, 'No, they don't.'

'Er, they *do*, Dad?' Honor goes.

I'm there, 'How come this is the first I'm hearing about it?'

Honor goes, 'Dad, they're always talking about it.'

I'm like, 'Yeah, in focking German obviously.'

Sorcha's old dear goes, 'I loved hockey when I went to St Kilian's. No one ever gets hurt playing it,' and she says it like it's somehow a good thing.

I'm there, 'I wouldn't have sent them to that school if I'd known they were going to end up playing hockey.'

'No other school in Ireland would take them,' Sorcha's old man goes. 'Their reputation – like that of their father – preceded them!'

I'm there, 'I shouldn't have let go of your throat that day,' all the anger at being made to feel like an intruder in my own home finally reaching boiling point. 'I should have wrung your scrawny chicken neck and taken my chances with a jury.'

'How *dare* you!' Sorcha's old dear goes.

And I'm like, 'No, how dare *you* – you focking hockey-loving focker!'

And it's at that exact moment that a voice goes, 'I see it's the usual happy Lalor Christmas, then.'

We all look around and we end up just staring in, like, stunned silence. Because standing there at the door is someone that none of us has laid eyes on for, I don't know, it must be like, five years?

It's Sorcha's sister.

'Oh! My God!' Sorcha goes.

Her old dear is like, 'What are *you* doing home?'

'Nice welcome,' the girl goes.

Her old man is there, 'I thought you were in Australia.'

I wish I could remember her name. It's not Estelle, although it could be something very like it. Or nothing like it at all.

'Yeah,' the girl goes, 'I *was* in Australia – and now I'm obviously not.'

'And you wouldn't have thought to tell us you were coming home?' her old dear goes.

She's like, 'I thought I'd surprise you.'

'Well, you've definitely done that,' Sorcha goes. 'How long are you home for?'

'I haven't decided yet.'

'And what about . . . what's her name?'

'Rochelle? My lesbian lover?'

Her old pair both tut and shake their heads. They're those kind of people – all for equality but can't bear the thought of a child of theirs being gay.

'I don't know,' she goes. 'I'm not even sure if I'm into chicks any more.'

Honor laughs. She's like, 'Mom, can she stay with us?'

But Sorcha – obviously sniffing trouble – goes, 'No, Honor, we don't have the room.'

Honor's there, 'Yes, we do – we have, like, *loads* of spare rooms.'

The sister looks at me then – looks me up and down in fact, pushing her cheek out with her tongue, drinking me in like chocolate milk.

She goes, 'Hi, Ross.'

And I'm like, 'Hi, em – *you*.'

She goes, 'You look amazing. You obviously still work out.'

And I'm like, 'Yeah, no, press-ups and sit-ups specifically,' and I very subtly drop my napkin onto my lap to cover the enormous boner in my chinos.

Of course, *she* ends up noticing. She smiles at me.

She goes, 'Yes, don't forget your napkin, Ross. You need to be careful you don't spill something in your lap.'

*

Honor's there, 'Who's Jules?' examining Sorcha's sister's – yeah, no – Max Cady-style tattoo sleeve.

It's, like, Christmas morning and we're sitting in the kitchen, drinking coffee and listening to, like, carols being sung on the radio – we're talking 'Away in a Manger' and all the rest of it.

'Jules is an ex of mine,' Sorcha's sister goes. 'From before I met Rochelle.'

She's got, like, a tattoo of a girl's face on her upper orm – if I had to say she looked like anyone, it'd be Jamie Chung.

Honor's there, 'You must have really liked her.'

'Zir,' Sorcha's sister goes.

Honor's like, 'Excuse me?'

'I must have really liked *zir*,' the sister goes. 'Ze is gender neutral.'

Honor's there, 'That is, like, *so* cool.'

Sorcha walks into the kitchen and sees her sister sitting at the island in just a flimsy camisole and me – if I'm being one hundred per cent honest – trying to look down the thing.

'And this one here,' the sister goes, 'is a quote from 'Nothing Else Matters'. I went through a whole Metallica phase after I had my abortion.'

'Would you mind putting some clothes on?' Sorcha goes, with a serious scowl on her face.

The sister is like, 'And a Merry Christmas to you too, Sis.'

'I don't know how they do things in Sydney,' Sorcha goes, 'but as long as you're living under my roof, you will wear clothes – especially on Christmas Day.'

The sister goes, 'Fine – whatever.'

Honor's there, 'Mom, can I get a tattoo?'

'No,' Sorcha goes, 'you can't get a tattoo. Is anyone coming to Mass with me?'

It ends up being a genuine tumbleweed moment.

Sorcha goes, 'Honor?'

But Honor's like, 'I'm an atheist. And, anyway, Adam's going to be calling in this morning to give me my present.'

Sorcha turns to her sister then and goes, 'What about you?'

I'm thinking, okay, someone *please* say her *focking* name!

'I think I'm beyond God's redemption,' the sister goes, 'don't you?'

Sorcha picks her cor keys up off the kitchen counter and goes, 'Fine, I'll go by myself.'

Oh, shit.

I end up just blurting it out – I'm like, 'Er, you can't drive!'

She's there, 'Excuse me?'

I'm like, 'What I mean is – yeah, no – you had quite a bit to drink last night. You're probably still over the legal limit.'

'Ross,' she goes, 'I had two glasses of wine with dinner.'

'They were, like, big glasses, though – so it was more like four. *And* you'd a Baileys afterwards.'

Fionn walks into the kitchen with Hillary then and he ends up saving the day.

He goes, 'I'll drive you if you want,' because he was at his old pair's last night and he wasn't drinking. 'I was going to take Hillary anyway.'

Sorcha's there, 'That'd be amazing. Oh my God, it'll be lovely to bring him to his first Nativity Mass together.'

Fionn smiles sadly. I can barely even bring myself to look at him.

Sorcha goes, 'Don't worry, Fionn, we're going to get it cleared up in the New Year.'

He's like, 'I hope so, Sorcha.'

Off the two of them fock then, while Honor says she's going upstairs to wake the boys, leaving me alone with the sister.

'So what was all that about?' she goes.

I'm like, 'Sorcha's been banned from driving for a year – except she doesn't know about it. It was actually Honor who got the penalty points and I agreed to cover it up for her.'

The sister laughs. She's like, 'I was actually asking about *him*?'

I'm there, 'Who? Fionn?'

'What are they talking about getting cleared up in the New Year? What has she got – a urinary tract infection? Or is it *him*?'

It's, like, my turn to laugh then.

I'm there, 'Yeah, no, he's been suspended from his job as Principal of Castlerock College – for taking his orse out in a pub in Cork.'

She goes, 'Are you serious?'

'I know – I never thought I'd see the day when flashing your orse was a sackable offence.'

'No, I just mean he doesn't seem the type.'

'Yeah, no, the thing is, he's claiming it wasn't *actually* him? That someone – like I said – did a mooner in the Thomond Bor and, er, gave the Feds *his* actual name.'

'Oh my God,' the sister goes, putting her hand over her mouth, 'it was *you*!'

I'm like, 'It wasn't. I swear on my old dear's life – well, my old man's.'

She just laughs.

'Oh! My! God!' she goes. 'So why don't you just tell them the truth?'

I'm there, 'Because I'm still hoping to get back with your sister. Then also –'

'What?'

'Yeah, no, I don't know if it was covered in the Australian papers, but I'm coaching the Ireland women's team at the moment – as in, like, rugby? I'm just worried if it gets out that I took my orse out in a public place that *I* might be the one who ends up losing his job. I know that sounds possibly selfish – but people are being cancelled for way, way less these days.'

'Oh my God, I think it's going to be a lot of fun living here over the next few months.'

'I'm glad we entertain you.'

'No, I just mean *her*. Mom and Dad make out that she's this, like, perfect person who has this, like, perfect life. But it's all focking bogus.'

'Bogus in terms of?'

'She's a phoney, Ross. Look at her Twitter profile – it's, like, her in a Repeal jumper.'

'Yeah, no, she was port of that whole campaign.'

'And yet did you see her face when I mentioned my abortion?'

'It was possibly the fact that you said it in front of Honor, in fairness to her. She thinks you say shit just for the shock value – like the whole thing about you not being into chicks any more.'

'I mean, who is *she* to act all morally superior to us? She has you sleeping on a mattress in a tower – why, because you focked some friend of your mother's and Honor's teacher in Irish college?'

Yeah, no, she would have heard the recording because she's in my list of contacts – obviously under 'Sorcha's Sister'.

'And yet she gets pregnant by one of *your* friends,' she goes, 'and they're living under your roof – *with* the actual baby.'

I'm like, 'So *are* you still into chicks, just as a matter of interest – or is it dudes again?'

She doesn't give me an answer one way or the other.

'What a focking hypocrite,' she just goes. 'And then she's off to church this morning with the baby she mothered outside of her marriage and the father of the baby who isn't her husband. I wonder does she ever wear her Repeal jumper to Mass?'

Suddenly, Honor arrives downstairs with the boys, who are all worked up to ninety.

I'm there, 'Merry Christmas, goys!'

And Brian and Johnny are like, '*Frohe Weihnachten!*' and your guess is as good as mine.

Leo is going, '*Ich bin deutscher Nationalist, das heißt, ich bekenne mich offen zu meinem Volkstrum,*' while pointing his hockey stick at me. '*Alle meine Gedanken und Handlungen gehören dazu.*'

I'm like, 'What's that he's saying?'

Honor goes, 'It's from one of those Hitler records. I got them, like, digitalized – they listen to them all the time!'

I'm there, 'I knew I'd heard it somewhere before.'

'*Ich bin Sozialist,*' Johnny storts going then. '*Ich sehe vor mir keine Klasse und keinen Rang, sondern eine Geminschaft von Menschen, die blutsverwandt, durch die Sprache vereint und dem gleichen kollektiven Schicksal underworfen sind.*'

I laugh. Like I said, it brings me back.

There's, like, a ring on the doorbell then.

'That'll be Adam,' Honor goes. 'Dad, will you get that?'

Honor has made it a point of principle never to answer the front door on account of it being a job for – this is a direct quote – the house staff. Meaning me.

I'm like, 'No problem.'

So I open the front door and the dude is, like, standing there with what looks like two bags full of presents and the big, smiley, ginger Ed Sheeran head on him.

He goes, 'Merry Christmas, Ross.'

I think I'd still prefer if he called me Mr O'Carroll-Kelly, but I let it go because of the day that's in it.

He's like, 'Is Honor there? I have some unbelievable news for her!'

I'm there, 'Yeah, no,' stepping to one side, 'she's down in the kitchen – with her aunt,' and I'm thinking of following him, just to hear Sorcha's sister introduce herself to him.

But that's when I notice Adam's old man – the famous Steve – getting out of his black Volvo XC90.

He's like, 'Hello, Ross! Merry Christmas!' and you'd never guess from his casual manner that the last time he saw me I was knocking the Glory Be's out of his better half while he was manacled to the headboard.

I'm there, 'Yeah, no, greetings of the, er, season,' because *I'm* a little bit embarrassed even if *he* isn't? 'What's this unbelievable news he just mentioned?'

He goes, 'Oh, the song that Adam wrote for Honor is the most downloaded song on iTunes in Ireland this week.'

I'm there, 'The song about my thirteen-year-old daughter being hot is the Christmas number one? Yeah, no, that's just what every father wants.'

'I've a little surprise for you as well,' he goes, then he hands me – I shit you not – a little package, wrapped in – yeah, no – Christmas wrapping paper.

I'm there, 'Er, what the fock is this?'

He goes, 'A little present. A fun thing – silly, really.'

I'm like, 'Er, riiight,' because it probably goes without saying that I don't have anything for him.

He goes, 'Norma and I were wondering did you, em, fancy popping over one night, perhaps after Christmas?'

I'm like, 'I don't know about that, Dude.'

'It's just I thought we all had a jolly time the last night,' he goes, 'although I'd like to think I'd be less of a spectator next time.'

I'm like, 'Dude,' deciding to just level with him, 'I'm not into the whole two dicks in the room thing.'

'Oh,' he goes, clearly disappointed by this.

I'm there, 'And that's not me being homophobic. I'm into, like, women, full stop.'

'Well, you could have fooled me.'

'In terms of?'

'It's just when you kissed me –'

'Yeah, I'm pretty sure it was *you* who kissed *me*?'

'– you seemed to be really into it.'

'Yeah, no, I think your memory is possibly playing tricks on you, Steve.'

'No man who kisses another man like that could be completely straight.'

'Dude, did you not get the hint when I handcuffed you to the headboard and took the show across to the other side of the room?'

He just, like, stares at me – quietly devastated.

I'm there, 'Steve,' deciding to give it to him right between the eyes, 'I've no interest in you.'

I shit you not – his bottom lip storts, like, quivering then and I can see, like, tears forming in the corners of his eyes. I'm thinking, this is the focking weirdest Christmas morning I've ever had.

'Silly old sod,' he goes, wiping them away with his hand. 'We bring these men home and, well, the only rule we've ever had was that neither of us would fall in love.'

Jesus Christ.

Suddenly, Honor storts screaming at me from the kitchen, going, 'Dad! Dad! The song that Adam wrote for me is the Christmas number one!'

I'm there, 'Dude, what *is* this?' showing him the present, wondering do I even *want* to open it?

'Golden nipple clamps,' he goes. 'And I feel like such a fool now!'

Then he turns and makes his way tearfully back to his cor.

And I'm thinking, 'Focking Newpork!'

*

My phone beeps – this is while I'm sitting at the Christmas dinner table in the Áras. It's, like, a text message from Oisinn to all the goys in the Castlerock College Team of 1999 WhatsApp group and my hort ends up nearly skipping a beat when I open it.

It's a picture of, like, a new-born baby and the caption is, like: 'This is Paola. Born 16 December 2018. We can't wait to introduce you to the newest member of our family! Oisinn and Magnus x.'

I'm there, 'Oisinn and Magnus got a baby!'

'They what?' the old man goes.

I'm there, 'Yeah, no, they went to, I don't know, El Salvasso to adopt.'

I hand the phone across the table to Sorcha.

'Paola!' she goes. 'Oh my God, she's *so* cute!'

She hands the phone back to me. It beeps again. Christian says that he and Lychee can't wait to meet Paola. I just roll my eyes. Focking Lychee.

'Well, as the mother of five infant children,' the old dear goes, 'I can attest to the fact that the experience is very rewarding.'

'Six,' I go.

She's like, 'What's that, Ross?'

I'm there, 'You have six infant children. One, two, three, four, five, six,' and I am so tempted to add, 'The same as the number of gimlets you had before dinner, you focking soak,' but I manage to resist the temptation because of the day that's in it.

'Well, it's wonderful to have you all around the Christmas dinner table,' the old man goes, 'especially after the year that's been! It's turned out to be a good year for Ireland – the full-frontal attack on our democracy notwithstanding! Eh, Hennessy?'

Hennessy lifts his glass and goes, 'I'll drink to that!'

The old dear squints her eyes and looks at Shadden, who's helping herself to roast potatoes. She goes, 'What on earth is Roksolana doing here?'

We're all like, Roksolana? The fock is she talking about?

'If I've told you once,' she storts roaring at the girl, 'I've told you a thousand times, you are *not* permitted to just help yourself to our food. If you don't like it, you can fock off back to your own country

213

and take that little husband of yours with you – him and his gimpy leg!'

I'm there, 'Yeah, it's not your focking cleaner, Mom. It's Shadden – as in, like, *Ronan's* wife? – and their daughter, Rihanna-Brogan.'

Yeah, no, they've been invited for dinner, even in Ronan's absence.

The old man tries to pretend that the issue is with the old dear's eyesight rather than her mind.

He goes, 'I think we shall have to get your eyes tested, Dorling! It's Ross's daughter-in-law, Fionnuala, and our great-granddaughter! They're living in our house in Foxrock!'

'I *know* very well who it is!' the old dear tries to go, her head obviously clearing. 'Penny Rowley says they have the place looking like Syria! She says they've wiped half a million euros off the value of her house – and Christ knows how much off ours!'

Sorcha tries to change the subject.

She's there, 'Oh my God, this plant-based turkey substitute tastes just like the real thing, doesn't it?'

I watch the old man and Hennessy exchange a look.

'Yes,' the old man goes, 'it's extraordinary the things they can do these days!'

It's hilarious because Sorcha seems to be the only person at the table who doesn't realize that we're eating *actual* meat.

She goes, 'There's no even difference, is there? And the ham is the same!'

It's the old man's turn to change the subject then. He's there, 'Honor, tell us about this famous boyfriend of yours! The word I'm hearing is that he's written some sort of pop song about you!'

Honor goes, 'His name is Adam.'

'Adam! Quote-unquote! And am I permitted to ask the all-important question?'

'Newpork Comprehensive,' Honor goes. 'He's in, like, *third* year?'

Sorcha's there, 'He's *such* a lovely goy, isn't he, Ross?'

'He's a bit of a sap,' I go, 'but he's a definite improvement on focking Reese. *He* hasn't been in touch since, has he, Honor?'

She's there, 'He texted me this morning – just to wish me a Merry Christmas.'

'I hope you didn't text him back,' I go.

She's there, 'Dad, I told you, we're friends.'

'Good for you, Honor,' Sorcha goes. 'If anything, it'll help keep Adam on his toes.'

Mount Anville leaves its mork on all who cross its threshold.

I'm there, 'The dude is only back on the scene because the song has gone viral and Honor is suddenly hot.'

The old man's like, 'I would love to hear this song!'

Sorcha goes, 'It's the number one most downloaded song in Ireland this week.'

Hennessy's there, 'How does it go? Can you sing it for us?'

Sorcha's like, 'I'm not really sure it's a fitting song for the Christmas dinner table, Hennessy.'

But Honor looks at Brian, Johnny and Leo and goes, 'Okay, boys, do you want to sing the song with me?'

She counts them in, then they stort giving it:

She's so focking hot!
She's so focking hot!
She's so focking hot!
Fock! Ing! Hot! Bitch!

She's so focking hot!
She's so focking hot!
She's so focking hot!
Fock! Ing! Hot! Bitch!

'Good Lord!' the old man goes. 'Popular music has certainly changed since we were that age, eh, Fionnuala?'

And the old dear – randomly – goes, 'The woman is going to eat us out of house and home, Chorles! We should have had her deported the time she asked me for a raise to pay for her mother's lung transplant!'

All of a sudden, the door opens and into the room walks the famous Peadar. I haven't seen the dude since the night I walked in on him and Shadden doing God knows what and he threw me out of the gaff on my head.

He's there, 'Meddy Christmas, evoddy wooden,' pulling out a chair for himself. 'Ine soddy Ine late.'

I'm looking at the old man and then the old dear as if to say, 'What the fock is he doing here?'

Then I decide to just come straight out and say it.

I'm like, 'What the fock is *he* doing here?'

Hennessy goes, '*I* invited him.'

I'm there, 'Why? He's not port of this focking family.'

The old man's there, 'Peadar's parents have gone to Lanzarote for Christmas, Ross! He was going to be spending the day by himself! Help yourself to some of this, em, plant-based turkey substitute, Peadar!'

Sorcha's there, 'You're going to absolutely love it! It tastes just like the real thing!'

'Good stuff,' Peadar goes, helping himself to the meat. 'Ine in training for a fight in anutter few weeks. I need to keep me sthrength up – that reet, Shadden?' and then – I swear to God – he winks at her across the table.

I'm not sure who else notices, but I certainly do – and she turns red and then giggles like a focking schoolgirl.

The old man suddenly goes, 'Okay, since we are all here, gathered around this wonderful Christmas feast, I wish to say something! And don't worry, everyone, I *shall* be brief!'

'Thank fock for that,' I go.

He's there, 'As all of you – well, most of you – will no doubt know, Chorles O'Carroll-Kelly made the greatest mistake of his life a number of years ago when he allowed himself to become estranged from – indeed, divorced from – the great love of his life, the wonderful and delectable Fionnuala!'

I'm there, 'Some of us are still focking eating here!'

'I might be old,' the old man goes, 'but thankfully I'm still young enough to put that error right! Provided she permits me to do so, of course!'

The old man stands up from the table and – oh, holy shit – whips a little box out of his pocket. Then he drops to one knee right in front of the old dear.

Sorcha's like, 'Oh my God! Oh! My God! Oh my God!' because we pretty much all know what's coming.

'Fionnuala,' he goes, opening the box and showing off a diamond ring, big enough to choke a focking python, 'I want to ask you, on this Christmas Day, in the presence of our family, friends and, of course, Government colleagues – and pending the outcome of Hennessy's efforts to secure an annulment from my current wife – will you remarry me?'

The old dear stands up – she's got sprout leaves on her upper dentures – and goes, 'Yes, Chorles! I will! I will! I will!'

JP rings me and he asks me where the fock I am. Yeah, no, I totally forgot to ring him.

He goes, 'The first race is about to stort – at least tell me you're in the bor.'

And I'm there, 'Dude, don't hate me for this, but I'm not going to make it to Leopardstown this year.'

He's like, 'What? You never miss Leopardstown!'

I'm there, 'I know, I know – but I've got a good excuse.'

'Okay, let me hear it.'

'I'm at a soccer match.'

'Sorry, Dude, the reception here isn't great – I thought you said you were at a soccer match.'

'I did.'

He goes, 'What the fock are you doing at a soccer match?' obviously worried about me.

I'm there, 'To be honest with you, J-Town, I have literally no idea,' because Sive still hasn't shown her face yet and I'm standing in the middle of – I'm not even joking – Bushy Pork in Terenure, watching a bunch of women – *not* sexist – chase around after a soccer ball. 'I'm sorry I can't be there.'

He's like, 'Don't sweat it, Dude. I was coming anyway – anything to get out of having dinner with Delma and her kids.'

'Belle and Bingley,' I go. 'I'm still focking laughing at that, by the way.'

'Hey, you saw the picture Oisinn and Magnus sent, I presume?'

'Yeah, no, Paola – I'm delighted for them.'

'I was thinking, we should all hit the airport to, like, welcome them home.'

'When will that be?'

'Well, according to Magnus, they've got some paperwork to do, but they're hoping to be home on, like, New Year's Eve.'

'I'll be there, Dude – we're talking banners, we're talking balloons, we're talking everything.'

I suddenly spot Sive walking along the – I suppose – sideline, towards me.

I'm there, 'Dude, I have to go. Enjoy the racing – and tell Fionn and Christian I said the same.'

I hang up on him.

Sive goes, 'What score is the match?'

And I'm there, 'How the fock would I know? As a sport, it makes literally no sense to me.'

'What do you mean?'

'It's like I used to say when my son brought me to see his beloved Bohs – I honestly feel like they're making the rules up as they go along.'

Sive laughs, in fairness to her. I think she's genuinely storting to warm to me.

She goes, 'I want you to keep an eye on the number ten for the team in white.'

I'm there, 'Yeah, I've been watching both number tens, Sive. They're not doing any of the things I would expect a number ten to do. Why are we even here?'

'Okay,' she goes, 'why can't Joanne Wassell kick the ball? What's wrong with her technique?'

I'm like, 'She's going for, like, brute force.'

'Why?'

'Because she's worried that she can't get enough distance on the ball.'

'She's kicking the ball with the laces of her boot.'

'Same thing – you just put it differently.'

'What part of your foot do you strike the ball with?'

'Er, the base of my big toe obviously.'

'So do these women,' she goes, nodding at the pitch, where I notice number ten white launch a long, high ball from one side of the pitch to the other, the point of which totally escapes me, because she fails to find touch. 'You see, they learned to kick the ball when they were five or six years old.'

I'm there, 'So did I.'

'Well, Joanne didn't play rugby until she was, like, twenty. That's why she's never learned how to kick the ball properly.'

The referee – also a woman – blows her whistle for a penalty, even though in soccer it's called a free-kick, unless it's inside *their* equivalent of the twenty-two, when it *is* called a penalty. It's focking bizarre – the whole set-up.

The number ten in the white jersey steps up to take it.

'Now,' Sive goes, 'watch what she does with this.'

The woman takes five steps backwards, while the other team form a sort of, like, human wall, ten metres in front of her. It's very odd. Then she takes a run at the ball and strikes it, it has to be said, pretty well. The ball curls around the wall, past the goalkeeper, who doesn't even bother moving, hits the goalpost and ends up in the back of the net.

Sive cheers and then claps – as do the forty or so other people watching. I actually don't. I just find it random that it's classed as a score when you kick the ball *under* the crossbor.

Sive looks at me and goes, 'So what do you think?'

I'm there, 'She's got a pretty good technique, in fairness to her. So what are you saying – you think Joanne can learn how to kick the ball properly from, like, watching her?'

'No, it's too late for Joanne to learn,' Sive goes. 'We're playing France in four weeks.'

'So why am I watching this woman then?'

'She's a friend of mine. Her name is Nadine Delaney. And she's going to be our kicker.'

'You've *got* to be shitting me.'

'I'm *not* shitting you.'

The referee blows the final whistle. The white team seem to have won – insofar as *anyone* is a winner playing a sport like this. As the women are walking off the pitch, Sive calls the white number ten over.

She's like, 'Nadine!'

Yeah, no, Nadine trots over to us. She's, like, tall – we're talking six-foot-two, maybe six-foot-three, with short hair.

She goes, 'Hi, Sive. How was your Christmas? Were you in Galway?'

Sive's like, 'No, I didn't go home this year. This is Ross O'Carroll-Kelly – the lad I was telling you about.'

Nadine looks me up and down, then sort of, like, smiles to herself. I can only imagine the kind of shit that Sive has said to her.

Sive goes, 'Ross and I have a proposition for you?'

Nadine's like, 'Oh?'

Sive's there, 'How would you like to play rugby – for Ireland?'

I'm like, 'Whoa, steady on, Sive.'

Nadine laughs – even more than *I* did, in fairness.

She's like, 'You're joking, right? I haven't played rugby since second year in college.'

'That's only, like, two years ago,' Sive goes. 'We're training tomorrow morning. Donnybrook, at ten. Why don't you just come along, meet the rest of the team and see what you think?'

Nadine shrugs and goes, 'Okay, what have I got to lose?' then off she trots.

I'm there, 'Sive, are you trying to get me sacked?'

She goes, 'What do you mean?'

'What do I mean? Er, there's, like, just over a month to go before the stort of the Six Nations and you're suggesting we give the most important job on the pitch to a woman who hasn't played rugby for, like, two years?'

'She was a very good player, Ross. She played for Trinity.'

I'm there, 'And, what, we're going to turn this woman into an international rugby player in, like, four-and-a-little-bit weeks?'

'*We're* not,' she goes. '*You* are.'

★

Grainne Hutton sticks her phone in front of my face.

She goes, 'There!' in her sing-song Cork accent. 'Are you satisfied, boy?'

I look at the screen. On it, there's a photograph of a bride and groom, surrounded by their – yeah, no – wedding porty. And to the bride's immediate left stands Grainne, in a silky, green dress, holding a rugby ball where a bouquet would usually be.

I'm there, 'Er, wow!' because she really did take me literally.

She goes, 'There's also one of me on the dancefloor – dancing to the Frank and Walters – with the thing under my arm, like. And one of me sitting at the top table, with the ball on the plate where my bread should have been.'

'Technically,' I go, 'it shouldn't have been on the plate. It should have been on your lap – but I'm going to let it go.'

She's there, 'Oh, that's sound of you, like,' except she's got a big smile on her face when she says it. '*Fierce* sound.'

I'm standing on the side of the pitch in Donnybrook Stadium, with the players arranged in a horseshoe shape around me. It's, like, ten o'clock on the day after Stephen Zuzz Day and most of them look like they'd prefer to be still in bed.

Sive joins the group then. She's there, 'What about the rest of yee, lads? Did yee bring the ball with yee everywhere yee went?'

God, I love the Galway accent. I must ring Síle Seoige more often – that's going on the list of resolutions for 2019.

'Aye,' Heather Hobson goes. 'May suster hod a wee beebee boy on Christmas Eve. Ay'm gonnay spend may whole lafe explaining tee hum why, in the photos, Ay'm holding a rugbay bawl in one hawnd and hum in the other!'

Everyone laughs, including me, even though I haven't a focking breeze what she just said.

'I corved the turkey with the ball wedged between my thighs,' Megan Barrett, our full-back, who's actually *from* Donnybrook, goes. 'My mom thinks I've – oh my God – *totally* lost it.'

I'm there, 'I wonder will she think that when you're having that Six Nations winner's medal hung around your neck? Because this is it, people! It's what I like to call Get Focking Serious Time!'

All of a sudden, I spot the famous Nadine walking across the pitch towards us. She's late. Not a good stort for the girl. I can see the players looking at her and obviously wondering, who the fock is this? I make the introduction.

I'm like, 'Everyone, this is Nadine, em, something or other.'

'Delaney,' Nadine goes.

I'm there, 'That's right. Nadine Delaney. I've added her to the squad.'

I can see them all sizing her up – I think I mentioned that she's tall – and they're obviously wondering what position she's going to play.

'What position does she play?' one of the Skeldon twins – either Rachel or Louise – goes. I do love the way Limerick women can make even the most innocent question sound like a threat.

Nadine speaks up for herself. I like that about her. She goes, 'I played everywhere when I was in Trinity. Second row, full-back, on the wing. I also kicked.'

'You're a kicker?' Joanne Wassell goes. She's in the middle of tying back her scraggly ginger hair with a headband and she suddenly stops. She obviously knows what this means for her. 'Are you telling me that I'm –'

'Look,' I go, 'I want you as my ten. I want you to call the plays and do all the other things that an out-half should do. But we need a new kicker. That's been obvious for a long time.'

I can see from Joanne's face that she's not a happy bunny rabbit.

She's like, 'Fine, whatever.'

I can also see that her teammates are, like, crushed for her too.

I'm there, 'I'm sorry, Joanne, but in the last two Six Nations Championships, you missed four out of every five kicks. That's a lot of points we're leaving out there on the pitch.'

I turn to Sive, expecting her to back me up, except she doesn't say shit.

The other Skeldon sister stares at Nadine and goes, 'This is no offence to you, love, but who do you play for?'

Seriously, the two of them are focking terrifying. I can tell you now that I won't be dropping either of them, however shit they play.

'Bushy Park Rovers,' Nadine goes.

'Ay've navver hurd ay thum,' Heather Hobson goes. 'What league do they play rogbay un?'

I'm there, 'They're not a rugby team, Heather. They're, like, a *soccer* team?'

Whoa! It's like a focking drunk has just shambled into a crystal showroom. Everyone is just, like, looking at each other, going, 'Did he really just say soccer?'

I'm there, 'Anyway, are we going to train or are we going to stand around chatting?'

Everyone storts warming up and I tip over to Sive. I'm like, 'Yeah, thanks for the focking support.'

She goes, 'What do you mean?'

'I'm talking about Nadine. I mean, you've actually seen her play. You could have helped me sell her to the others.'

'I just don't think that was the kind of news Joanne should have been given in front of an audience. Could you not have pulled her to one side to tell her you were taking the kicking duties off her?'

'Hey, I'm not here to pander to people's feelings, Sive. I'm here to win the hopefully Six Nations Championship.'

'Well, *you're* the Head Coach,' she goes, 'not me. So how do you want to work this morning?'

I'm there, 'In terms of?'

She goes, 'Well, I was going to suggest that I take the backs and the forwards and work on a couple of issues I've identified with the ruck while you work with Nadine on her kicking.'

I'm like, 'Yeah, no, my forte – sounds good to me.'

So that's what ends up happening. I grab a bag of balls and tell Nadine to follow me to the twenty-two-metre line. I throw down a tee, then I get down on one knee and I stand the ball up in the thing.

I'm there, 'I'm just going to show you how it's done first and then you can have a crack at it yourself – is that good?'

She goes, 'I don't need you to mansplain to me how to kick a ball.'

I'm there, 'Well, a rugby ball behaves very differently from a soccer ball, Nadine. My old schools coach used to say it'd break your hort in more ways than any lover could. Although I don't know how the fock he knew, what with him being a priest and everything.'

She goes, 'Yeah, I've played rugby *before*, remember?'

'It's been a couple of years, though, so maybe just watch.'

I stand up and I take five steps backwards, then four to the side, then I rub my hand through my hair. All of the other players stop whatever it is they're doing and I can nearly hear them thinking to themselves what an honour it is to see an absolute master at work.

'Okay,' I go, 'now watch my technique and try to copy it.'

I look from the ball to the posts, then back to the ball again, then back to the posts again. Then I rub my hand through my hair one last time before running at the ball. I end up making the sweetest contact with it and I watch it trace a perfect orc through the air before splitting the sticks right down the middle.

So then – yeah, no – it's *her* turn? She stands the ball up in the tee, then takes four steps backwards.

'Five,' I remind her, but – yeah, no – she obviously has her own technique, because she totally blanks me.

I'm there, 'Now, four steps to the side.'

She takes three steps to the side.

I'm like, 'Yeah, no, each to their own. Now, do you remember what I did? I drew a straight line in my mind between the ball and the posts. Can you do that?'

She doesn't bother. She takes a run at the ball and she swings her foot at it. But instead of the sweet sound of leather on leather, I hear a sort of, like, dull slap and I watch in total shock as the ball leaves the tee and wobbles across the grass like my old dear when she was focked out of the Febvre Wine Wholesalers tent at Taste of Dublin three years ago.

I hear the literally gasps from the other players. I look at Sive, except she's making a point of looking the other way. But then Joanne Wassell catches my eye. I feel like nearly telling her that I've changed my mind – that she can go back to being our number one kicker. But she just, like, smiles to herself and turns her head away.

'Okay,' Nadine goes, 'so I'm a bit rusty.'

★

I'm there, 'I don't see it up on the board. I was the one who *said* it sounded made-up, wasn't I?'

Fionn goes, 'What exactly are you looking for, Ross?'

I'm there, 'Al Salfazzar. Il Solderosso – something like that.'

This is us standing at the Arrivals gate in Dublin Airport, by the way.

He's there, 'It's El Salvador, Ross,' because he's never *not* acting the focking teacher. 'And it won't *be* up on the board – their connecting flight is arriving from London.'

I'm holding a giant helium balloon that says, 'It's a Boy!' because – yeah, no – they didn't have one for a girl. Christian is holding a giant, cuddly polar bear that Ross Junior and Oliver bought with their pocket money, while JP and Fionn are holding a sign that says, 'Welcome, Paola!' which was apparently painted by Isa, JP's little goy.

'They've just landed,' Christian goes, squinting up at the board. 'There it is. It's the midday flight from Heathrow.'

Erika has brought flowers, which is a nice touch, although she's still not talking to me.

I'm there, 'You heard the old man proposed to my old dear, did you?' just trying to make conversation with the girl.

She goes, 'All I care about is that my mom is getting her annulment. After that, I don't give a shit about you or the rest of your family.'

I'm like, 'Yeah, no, good old Hennessy, huh?'

I notice Fionn taking a great deal of interest in this conversation. I'm there, 'You should think about using him for *your* case.'

Fionn goes, 'I probably would – if I was guilty. But I want to clear my name. I don't want people to think I got off because he pulled strings.'

Jesus, what country does he think *he's* living in?

I'm like, 'And you're definitely, *definitely* sure you didn't take your orse out in that pub?' at the same time hating myself for asking the question.

He's there, 'Yes, Ross, for the fiftieth focking time, I'm sure I didn't take my orse out in a pub in Cork.'

'There's no need to take that tone with me,' I go. 'I'm one

hundred per cent behind you, bear in mind – even though it sounds to me like none of your teacher mates believe you.'

He's there, 'There's a process that has to be followed, Ross, and I respect that.'

Erika goes, 'Don't you have an alibi to say you weren't in Cork that day?'

He's there, 'Yeah, I was actually with Sorcha at a conference on the role of women and non-binary persons in climate resilience and how saving the planet can only be achieved with a gender-inclusive perspective. I have a photograph of us with Erin Brockovich.'

'So can't you explain all of this to the Board of Management?' Erika goes.

Fionn's like, 'Unfortunately not. Rightly or wrongly, I've ended up on the sex offenders register. To get my name removed from it, I'm going to have to get my conviction overturned. Dad's solicitor said it could take months.'

I'm like, 'Blackrock College are the only real winners out of this – as per focking usual. God, they make me sick, even though I've massive respect for what they've achieved on the rugby pitch.'

'I spoke to the Gords in Cork,' he goes. 'They were very sympathetic. They said they've done vetting checks on men with multiple murder convictions and they've approved them as being fit to teach children boxing.'

'And here you are,' I go, 'banned for taking your orse out in a pub, which is as much a port of the colour and the camaraderie of the game as the focking haka.'

JP tries to stick his ample honker into the conversation then.

He goes, 'I keep thinking, who the fock would do something as low as that – to get themselves arrested and then try to hang it on someone else?'

I'm there, 'My guess would be someone from Pres – as in, like, Pres Cork?'

'What?' he goes. 'Why?'

I'm like, 'I'm remembering some of the epic matches we played against them over the years. Fionn, you always kept a little bit in reserve for those games. I'm not surprised to hear that you might have made an enemy or two down there. I rest my case.'

All of a sudden – I shit you not – Christian's girlfriend, the famous Lychee, shows her face.

I'm like, 'Fock's sake!' because I honestly can't hide the way I feel about the girl.

She walks over to where we're standing – blanks the rest of us, by the way – air-kisses Christian and goes, 'You got the house! Oh my God, I'm so excited!'

I'm like, 'House?' like any friend would. 'What house is this, Dude?'

Christian's there, 'I've, em, bought a house in Harold's Cross,' and he at least has the decency to look embarrassed about it. 'Lychee and her friends are going to use it as a collab house.'

I'm like, 'A collab house? Okay, what the fock is that?'

She rolls her eyes – focking millennials – and goes, 'It's a house where a bunch of influencers live and spend their days creating content for TikTok and other platforms.'

Christian goes, 'It's the quickest way for influencers like Lychee to really grow their social media presence,' like that's any kind of excuse, 'especially in the spheres of lifestyle, beauty and travel.'

I am *this* close to telling Christian that he's being taken for a focking mug.

'You bought her a gaff in Harold's Cross?' I go. 'You're being taken for a focking mug.'

Told you.

Lychee just looks me up and down and goes, 'Yeah, typical Gen X dream crusher,' and then she sees the polar bear and goes, 'Oh my God, *so* cute, Christian! Will you take a picture of me with it for my InstaStories?'

Christian hands over the bear and takes her phone from her.

'Focking young people today,' I go. 'They think the world revolves around them. I know that's rich coming from me.'

JP's like, 'Be nice, Ross.'

I'm there, 'I'm sorry, Dude. She *calls* herself an influencer. I just

don't want to see Christian being taken advantage of by a focking –
let's be honest here – freeloader.'

The girl looks at the picture that Christian took and she's like,
'Oh my God, *look* at the state of me!'

He's there, 'Yeah, no, I took a few there, Babes.'

But she's there, 'I don't like any of them,' handing him back the
phone. 'Go again. But hold the camera higher. You're making me
look like I've got four chins.'

The girl would want to have four tits for me to listen to that. But
that's me – I'm old-fashioned.

She's like, 'Also, make my orms look thin. And be thinking of
something I could do with the bear for TikTok.'

I'm there, 'I could think of something – but I'm too focking polite
to say it,' and JP laughs, in fairness to him.

'There's Magnus!' Fionn suddenly goes and he storts frantically
waving his orms like he's trying to direct a plane to land.

I see the dude coming through the electric doors. He cops us
standing there with the banner and the balloon and his face turns
suddenly pale. He doesn't look pleased to see us. He looks over his
shoulder for Oisinn, who comes through the doors just behind him,
pushing a trolley with all their luggage on it.

I'm looking around for – yeah, no – Paola. Except there's no sign
of any baby. I'm thinking, maybe she's in one of the suitcases, but
then I think, no, that's ridiculous.

'Oh, fock,' Erika goes. 'They said this sometimes happens.'

Fionn and JP drop the banner and we all rush over to them.

JP's like, 'Goys, what happened?'

'Red tape,' Oisinn goes – and he looks sadder than I've ever seen
him look. 'They said don't take anything for granted until you're
sitting on the actual –'

And then – I swear to fock – the big man just bursts into tears. He
puts his head on Erika's shoulder and storts sobbing his hort out
and Erika just holds the dude and goes, 'Oh, Oisinn, I'm so sorry.
I'm so, so sorry.'

I'm there going, 'Red tape? What the fock does that even mean?'

And Magnus goes, 'It meansh that Paola hash gone to shome

other lucky couple, Rosh,' and he's got, like, tears in his eyes when he says it.

I'm like, 'The focking nerve of these people,' although I don't know what I'm even talking about. 'I feel like decking someone.'

We walk slowly back to the cor pork, passing Christian, who's still trying to take the perfect picture of Lychee with the bear.

'I don't want to see my bottom teeth,' *she's* going. 'I focking hate my . . . Oh my God, where's the actual baby?'

All I can do is just roll my eyes. I said she was an airhead and I stand by that statement.

I catch up with Erika and I go, 'Puts everything into, I don't know, whatever the actual word is – doesn't it?'

She's like, 'Fock off, Ross.'

I'm there, 'Erika, I did what I thought was right at the time.'

She goes, 'You might like to know, Ross, that I saw her on Christmas Eve.'

I'm like, 'Who? See-mon?'

'No, Sea-mon. I went to visit her – in the Central Mental Hospital in Dundrum.'

'Yeah, no, Sorcha was saying there might not even be a trial.'

'*They* don't want her going on trial – because of what she might say on the stand.'

'Well, that's good news, isn't it?'

'Ross, she could spend the rest of her life in a mental institution.'

'Oh, right – that's a bit shit alright.'

'Because of you.'

'Hey, maybe I could help you try to, I don't know, break her out of there.'

She's like, 'Fock you, Ross – you chose your side.'

I go, 'Erika, I didn't want to see the dude sent down, especially with the old dear slowly losing her morbles.'

But she's there, 'Get the fock away from me. I meant what I said in New York. I don't have a brother any more. You are focking dead to me.'

7.

Reservoir Underdogs

The old dear asks Honor if she wants a Vodka Mortini and I say no, she one-hundred-per-cent doesn't.

'Why not?' Honor has the actual cheek to go.

I'm there, 'Because (a) it's one o'clock in the afternoon, (b) you're thirteen years old, and (c) I'm already worried that you have a possible drink problem.'

'Didn't do *you* any horm,' the old dear goes. 'When you were a baby I used to soak the teat of your bottle in Chorles's Courvoisier – you absolutely loved it. Of course, giving you alcohol was the only way I could discourage you from trying to get at my breasts. That went on until you were about eight years old.'

It's nice to see the woman back to her old self.

I'm there, 'You know, I watch *Succession* on TV and think, why can't *we* be a normal family like that?'

It's, like, a Saturday lunchtime – I've finished training for the morning – and we're sitting in the nursery in the Áras, spending time with the kids. All six of them are walking now, although they're a little bit unsteady on their feet – something they have in common with their mother.

Honor goes, 'Cassiopeia is *so* like you, Fionnuala!'

The old dear's like, 'Is she?'

And I'm there, 'I'm always saying that. Out of all of them, she's the one who's the absolute spit of you.'

The poor girl. She better have a good personality or she'll die a focking spinster.

'Fionnuala,' Honor goes, 'can I see your engagement ring again?'

And the old dear – loving it – goes, 'Of course!' and she holds out her hand like she's offering it to be kissed.

Honor's like, 'Oh my God! I have *never* seen a diamond that big!'

Brian, Johnny and Leo, by the way, are screaming their little heads off, going, '*Ich habe den Befehl gegeben, und ich lasse jeden, der nu rein Wort der Kritik äußert, von einem Erschießungskommando ausführen hass unset Kriegsziel nicht darin besteht, bestimmte Linien zu erreichen, sondern in des physischen Vernichtung de Feindes!*'

But none of us even acknowledges them.

The old dear's there, 'So how's your own romance going, Honor?'

Honor just shrugs.

She's like, 'Er, fine,' and I hear a note of definite doubt in her voice.

I'm there, 'What's going on? Don't tell me that Adam did the dirt. He seems like too much of a sap for that.'

'No, he didn't do the dirt. It's just –'

'Go on.'

She goes, 'It's Reese.'

I'm like, 'Reese?' and I feel the muscles in my jaw tightening.

She's there, 'He told me last night that he still has feelings for me.'

'That focker,' I go.

'He said breaking it off with me was the biggest mistake of his life.'

'You know he's only saying that because he sees that you're happy with someone else? It's a typical rugby wanker move. I should know because I pretty much invented it.'

'I'm just, like, so *confused* at the moment?'

'I'll sort that out for you now, Honor, by telling you that if I ever see that focker hanging around you, I will pull out his colon and feed it to him. And I mean that literally.'

All of a sudden, the old man steps into the room. He's like, 'Kicker! Honor! I thought I heard voices! How the hell are you?'

Honor's like, 'Fine, Granddad.'

The boys are still roaring, '*Ich habe den Befehl gegeben, und ich lasse jeden, der nu rein Wort der Kritik äußert, von einem Erschießungskommando ausführen hass unset Kriegsziel nicht darin besteht, bestimmte Linien zu erreichen, sondern in des physischen Vernichtung de Feindes!*'

The old man screws up his face. He's there, 'Isn't that –'

I'm like, 'Yeah, no, Hitler.'

'God, that brings me back to old Denis Fehily playing us his famous 45s in the dressing-room before matches!'

'That's because they *are* Fehily's 45s. Honor had them, like, digitalized – the boys seem to love them.'

'What a wonderful way to keep the old man's spirit alive! I'm talking about Denis, of course, rather than the other chap! How are the ladies doing, Ross?'

I'm like, 'They're women. And they're doing fine.'

I don't mention that I've handed the kicking duties to a woman who couldn't kick away a blind man's stick. I wouldn't give him the pleasure of saying I told you so.

'Well, just to let you know,' he goes, 'I shall be there in Donnybrook to see you take on France, notwithstanding everything I've said – and written – about ladies playing rugby!'

'I wouldn't bother – seriously.'

'By the way, Kicker, just a heads-up that there's some nasty stories about me in one of the newspapers this morning – isn't that right, Fionnuala?'

I'm like, 'There's nasty stories about you in the newspapers *every* morning. Did they find out that you burned down the Dáil?'

He ignores this dig at him and instead goes, 'Well, *these* stories are especially scurrilous! They're going to all sorts of lengths to try to prove that I *didn't* have the vegetarian jambalaya on that famous night in Shanahan's!'

I'm there, 'You didn't. You're no more a vegan than I am.'

'It seems someone has leaked the bill from that night to the newspapers! Miriam Lord has used the phrase "Vegetarian Jamba-liar"! I said to Hennessy, I'd sue that bloody woman if it wasn't such a great line! How *does* she come up with them, Kicker?'

'I've no idea.'

He goes, 'Anyway, as I said to your mother – or should I say, my *fiancée!*' and he smiles at her in a way that is frankly puke-making. 'I said, I just hope it doesn't overshadow next week's announcement about Malingrad! You're coming to Donegal next week, I hope! For the sod-turning!'

I'm there, 'If I go, it'll only be to support JP and Christian.'

Yeah, no, they got the contract to provide two hundred thousand Vampire Beds for, like, the project.

'Of course! It's a huge day for the chaps! If it wasn't for young JP's vision of a world in which everyone sleeps standing up, then Malingrad wouldn't be Malingrad! Which reminds me, I have a video conference with your friend Vladimir Putin shortly! I'll tell him you were asking for him, Ross!'

I'm there, 'Whatever.'

He goes, 'I know it'd mean a lot to him! He says he sees a lot of himself in you! Oh, Fionnuala, don't forget to ask Honor for her ideas!' and then off the dude focks.

I'm like, 'What ideas? What's he shitting on about?'

The old dear goes, 'We were thinking of having a *theme* wedding.'

I'm like, 'Okay, *that's* hilarious. You always said theme porties were C as M. Didn't you take out a High Court injunction to stop Lesley Morrison hosting a Masks and Mimosas porty on the morning of William and Kate's wedding?'

'Well, we can't very well have a *traditional* wedding,' the old dear goes. 'I'm in my sixties now. I'm hordly going to wear white.'

I'm there, 'Honor, will you check the floor there and see can you find the decade that your grandmother seems to have lost from her life?'

The old dear goes, 'Even though I *could* still carry off a white dress. No, Chorles and I decided that we'd do something fun. And we thought we'd ask you, Honor, if you had any ideas.'

'Oh my God,' Honor goes, 'what about *The Great Gatsby*?'

The old dear loves it.

She goes, 'What a wonderful idea!'

Honor's like, 'Flapper dresses! Feathered headbands!'

'Highballs. Gin Rickeys.'

'Bobbed hair. Cigarette-holders.'

'Sidecars. French 75s. Oh, I love it, Honor. And now I have something *else* that I want to ask the two of you.'

I'm there, 'Is it to fetch the Grey Goose to smorten up your Mortini?'

'No,' she goes, 'I'd like to ask you . . . to be my bridesmaids!'

Honor's like, 'Your *bridesmaids?*'

Oh, fock, I think, she's having another one of her turns.

I'm there, 'Yeah, you know you're talking to me? As in, your son? As in, an actual man?'

'I know very well who I'm talking to,' she goes. 'I saw it in *Irish Tatler*, Ross. Someone – I can't remember who – had her eldest son as her bridesmaid at her second wedding.'

Honor's like, 'Her *bridesman*. That's what they call them, Fionnuala.'

'Then *that's* what I want,' the old dear goes. 'You as my brides-maid, Honor – and you, Ross, as my brides*man.*'

I'm there, 'As long as I don't have to wear a focking dress.'

'And, of course, as my bridesmaid and bridesman,' she goes, 'I'll need you to help me plan every single detail of the wedding.'

Honor's like, 'Oh my God, this is *so* exciting!'

And I'm there, 'Focking spare me.'

Fionn says that today should have been the day.

I'm there, 'In terms of?' except I'm not really listening to the dude – because I'm the middle of, like, *training?*

'Our match,' he goes, pushing his glasses up on his nose. 'It was supposed to be this afternoon. Right now, as a matter of fact. This stadium should have been full of fans, singing and cheering for the red and black of one Rock and the blue and white of the other.'

Blackrock College were given a bye into the second round, proving once again that absolutely nothing happens in this world that isn't in some way good news for those fockers.

I'm there, 'Yeah, no, it's, em, a bummer alright,' and I can't bring myself to even look at him. Yeah, no, the dude is guilt-tripping me in a major way and – like I said – I'm trying to prepare my team for the match against France, which is in, like, less than two weeks' *time?*

Sive has taken the forwards and I'm working my usual magic with the backs. I've given them a simple exercise to get storted, tell-ing them all to stand in, like, a diagonal line – we're talking Grainne Hutton, Joanne Wassell, the Skeldon twins, Nadine Delaney, Lisa

McGuin and Megan Barrett – and to pass the ball along the line while sprinting from one side of the pitch to the other.

I'm just warming them up before I stort sharing one or two tricks with them from the Rossmeister's playbook. But I can see that they're looking at Fionn, wondering who the fock he is and why he's hanging around – with his focking glasses – bringing the general mood down.

I end up having to go, 'Dude, should you even be here?'

He's like, 'I had an hour to kill before I collected Hillary from my sister's and I just popped in to say hello.'

I'm there, 'Yeah, no, I mean are you *allowed* to be here?' and I feel like an absolute dick for asking him.

He goes, 'Jesus Christ, I'm not under house arrest, Ross.'

I'm there, 'I know that, Dude, but you're on – look, I hate saying it – but a *register*?'

He's like, 'By error, Ross – and you'll be happy to hear that my solicitor thinks I could clear my name within a matter of weeks.'

'Really?' I go, trying not to sound too disappointed. 'That's, em – yeah, no – *good* news, isn't it?' and then I shout, 'That pass was forward, Louise! Nadine, you keep running ahead of the play!'

Jesus, I've been working with her for, like, two weeks now and she still can't be told.

Fionn's there, 'The real flasher –'

I'm like, 'Flasher is maybe a bit strong. The dude probably just whipped it out in the spirit of things.'

'– the real flasher was fingerprinted when he was arrested. I'm going to Cork with my solicitor next week to have my own prints formally taken. When it's shown that the two sets don't match, the Guards will have to admit they got the wrong man. The case against me will be expunged from the court record and my name from the sex offenders register.'

Sive has noticed that I'm, like, yapping instead of working. She goes, 'Ross, what's going on?' as if *she's* suddenly the boss of, like, *me*?

I tell Fionn that I have to go back to work.

He's like, 'Do you mind if I stick around and watch?'

And I'm there, 'Like I said, as long as it's definitely, definitely legal.'

I gather the players around me and I'm like, 'Okay, good work, everyone – although I want to see faster hands from you, Grainne. You too, Joanne.'

Joanne just, like, glowers at me, while readjusting her hair in her headband. She's definitely not over me taking the kicking duties from her and giving them to a woman who couldn't kick shit if it fell on her foot. And redheads have never loved me anyway for some weird reason.

I'm like, 'Nadine, again, you're two metres in front of the ball when the pass is made – every single time.'

She goes, 'Like I said, it's been a few years. It'll click.'

And I'm there, 'Well, it better click soon, Nadine. We're playing France in, like, two weeks. We can't afford to give away penalties – they know how to kick them.'

'Is that a dig at me?'

'What?'

'You're saying I don't know how to kick them – is that right?'

No one knows where to look, even though they all agree with me.

I'm there, 'All I'm saying is that Sive vouched for you. She said you were a brilliant player in college. But I'm not seeing any *evidence* of that? And I'm storting to wonder has the soccer, I don't know, destroyed whatever talents you once had – just like it destroys every-thing eventually.'

I'm very much channelling Father Fehily now.

Nadine gets in a snot with me then and says she's going to go and practise her kicking.

I'm there, 'Yeah, no, you could definitely do with it,' and off she focks with a bag of balls.

I tell everyone to take five minutes and maybe do some stretches, then I tip over to Sive, who's leaning against the scrummaging machine and staring at a page in her Rugby Tactics Book.

I'm there, 'She can't stort against France.'

She's there, 'What are you talking about?'

'Er, I'm talking about your mate. Focking so-called Nadine.'

'What's wrong with her?'

'She keeps running ahead of the ball. And on the rare occasions

236

when she doesn't, she drops it, or she knocks it on. Are you definitely sure she's played rugby before?'

'Yes, she was the star of the Trinity College team. She's a great player, Ross. Be patient with her. It'll click.'

'Yeah, *she* keeps talking about it clicking. It's, like, two weeks now and I'm still waiting for that click. I'm nearly tempted to –'

'What?'

'– tell Joanne that I made a mistake and that I want her to be our kicker against France.'

'What, after the way you humiliated her in front of all her teammates? I think she'd tell you where to go, Ross. And anyway –'

'What?'

'It'd be a sign of weakness, wouldn't it? Admitting that you were wrong – about something you claim to know a lot about. I've heard you call it an art.'

'Kicking *is* an ort. And I was once described as a master of that ort. It was by – believe it or not – Sallie McOrdle when I did a skills segment on *The Grip* back in '98.'

'Believe me, Ross, you show these women any sign of weakness and they will rip you apart.'

She smiles at me then. And the thought occurs to me – a horrible, horrible thought – that I'm being stitched up here. And when I say stitched up, I mean in a major way.

I'm about to say it to her when, all of a sudden, a ball comes dropping out of the sky and hits me right in the back of the head.

I spin around and Nadine is holding up her hand in apology.

'I'm sorry,' she goes. 'Should have shouted *Fore!*'

And the worst thing isn't the sudden pain in my head or even the ringing noise in my ears. It's actually the realization that we're standing a good, like, thirty yords away from the posts and she still managed to somehow hit me. I'm just thinking, okay, we are focked – we are totally and utterly focked.

Oisinn and Magnus are in good form – especially considering what they've been through. And you'd have to say fair focks to them for coming. As a matter of fact, I *do* say it?

I'm like, 'Fair focks, goys. I'm sure JP and Christian would have totally understood if you'd, you know – blah, blah, blah.'

Oisinn goes, 'We weren't going to miss their big day – not for anything.'

I'm there, 'So how *are* you – in terms of . . . ?'

'Rosh,' Magnus goes, 'nobody hash died. There wash a beautiful baby and we thought that she wash going to be oursh. But she went to shomebody elshe. We are shad – but it ish okay.'

Yeah, no, we're standing in a field in the middle of Donegal, freezing our literally tits off while we wait for the old man to arrive. There's a decent turnout as well – we're talking a couple of hundred people, a lot of them press. I spot JP talking to Delma, then Christian – as per usual – taking photographs of Lychee, who isn't happy with any of them.

She's going, 'Oh my God, could you *make* me look any fatter?'

Oisinn's there, 'There's fifty years between their two girlfriends – wouldn't that just melt your head?'

I'm there, 'I still can't believe he bought a house for her and her mates. He's being taken for a ride – and in a big-time way.'

JP spots us then. Him and Delma tip over to us.

JP's like, 'Thanks for coming, goys.'

'Hey, ain't no thing but Anine Bing,' I go. 'Fionn sends his appologeys, by the way. The dude's in Cork today.'

'Oh, yeah,' JP goes, 'they're taking his fingerprints. Jesus, I hope that gets sorted out soon. It's shitty what happened to him.'

I'm there, 'It certainly is,' feeling like a piece of shit. 'It certainly, certainly, certainly is.'

Oisinn's there, 'I really hope they find the focker who gave the Feds his name. So how are things going with the women's team, Ross?'

'Yeah, no,' I go, 'don't ask.'

'Are they that bad?'

'I think Sive is trying to, like, fock me over.'

'As in?'

'Well, she persuaded me to give the kicking duties to this girl who hasn't played rugby for, like, two years. She's, like, a *soccer* player?'

'Jesus.'

'Sive says she's good, but I'm storting to wonder has she even played the game before.'

JP's there, 'So, what, you think this Sive is trying to make you look bad?'

I'm like, 'Yeah, no, I possibly do. She says the girl is just rusty and she'll come good. But we're running out of time. We're playing France next Friday night.'

JP's like, 'Fock.'

Delma smiles sadly and goes, 'So how *are* you both?' meaning obviously Oisinn and Magnus.

In other words, she's changing the subject.

Oisinn's there, 'We're good, Delma, thanks. Staying busy.'

Delma goes, 'Will you go back – to El Salvador?'

It's still such a random name for a country. Focking ridiculous carry-on.

The two goys exchange a look.

Oisinn's there, 'The, em, agency *wants* us to? But we were thinking about maybe exploring the surrogacy route.'

All of a sudden – before any of us has a chance to even ask what surrogacy is – there's the sound of a helicopter overhead. The old man is about to arrive. There's, like, a sudden buzz, especially among the press, who haven't a breeze what today is even *about* yet?

We watch the helicopter touch down on the other side of the field, then out they get – we're talking the old man, we're talking Hennessy, we're talking Peadar and we're talking Fyodor, surrounded by goons in suits, both Irish *and* Russian? Then, lastly, Sorcha gets out. I had no idea she was even going to *be* here today.

The old man walks up to the microphone, his hair slash wig blowing in the wind. He smoothes it down with his hand and goes, 'Hello and welcome, ladies and gentlemen – as well as my dear friends in the mainstream press! It's wonderful to be here today in County Donegal for the announcement of something that I hope will lift the spirit of a nation that is still sad in its hort because of the terrible, terrible orson attack on our national porliament!

239

'I have come here today, along with my Cabinet colleague, the Minister for Climate Action, Sorcha Lalor, to announce a major new initiative for the too-often-overlooked – quote-unquote – North-Western Region! As part of New Republic's vision for our country post-Irexit, I promised the Irish people that we would develop new relationships with countries outside of the European Union to deliver a brighter – *and* more prosperous – future for our country! And today, I am happy to say, is all about that!

'I am here in the – inverted commas – Forgotten County to turn the first sod of what will become, within five years, Ireland's second largest city! Or third if you count Cork, which I myself personally do not! As you are no doubt aware, licences have been issued to a number of Russian companies to drill for oil and gas off the North-Western coast! This is a huge undertaking that will involve tens of thousands of migrant workers, who will of course require some-where to live! And they, I am proud to tell you this afternoon, will be the first residents . . . of Malingrad!'

You can hear, like, mutters among the press people, all of them repeating the word, 'Malingrad?'

'Malingrad,' the old man goes, 'will be a synergy of Irish resources and Russian money and know-how! Not only will it serve as a home to the tens of thousands of migrant workers extracting the valuable energy sources from the seabed that will secure our country's eco-nomic future for centuries to come, it will provide the model for how we will all live in the future!

'Malingrad will bring the concept of aportment living to a new and spatially efficient level! I am very excited that two of Ireland's leading entrepreneurs, JP Conroy and Christian Forde, are here today! Their Vampire Bed – inverted commas – has helped bring about a reconceptualization of what constitutes a liveable space! Working in portnership with Éadbhard Ó Cuinneagáin, inventor of the Homedrobe – yet another Irish innovation – they have been contracted to supply sleeping quarters for two hundred thousand people, who will be the first to experience a new kind of living!

'As I said at the outset, Malingrad will provide the prototype for all future urban development in Ireland, where people will sleep standing up in more intelligently designed spaces and work for exciting, cutting-edge tech companies, who choose to avail of our low tax rate! And they will sleep not only vertically in those beds, but soundly, because they will be unencumbered by the worries of property ownership and mortgage debt!

'Like I said, the chaps are here to talk to you about how it will all work! They've tried to explain it to me and, well, it really is the stuff of science fiction! When you've retired to your cosy Homedrobe after work, you'll be able to – inverted commas – plug yourself in and find out vital data about how many steps you've taken that day, the number of calories you've consumed, whether you're suffi-ciently hydrated and the exact day you're likely to die! It's all very exciting indeed! Now, does anyone have any questions?'

'Taoiseach,' a dude from one of the papers goes, 'do you have any-thing to say about the most recent allegations that you ordered a steak –'

'*That's* what you wish to ask me about?' the old man goes. 'On the day that I announce an initiative that will involve hundreds of billions of euros being poured into a port of Ireland that was essen-tially abandoned by successive Governments?'

'Taoiseach, it's being alleged,' another reporter – a woman – goes, 'that you ate a T-bone steak –'

The old man's like, 'I dealt with this matter in my statement a week ago! I ordered the vegetarian jambalaya! The waiter – out of force of habit – brought me a steak! When the error was pointed out to him, he removed the steak from the table and brought the correct main course!'

'But according to the bill –' the original dude tries to go.

But the old man's like, 'The bill was not corrected in line with the order! I noticed this at the time, but because the two main courses were roughly the same price, I didn't ask for the bill to be altered and I paid it in full – along with my usual two-hundred-euro tip!'

'Taoiseach,' the woman again goes, 'a further allegation has emerged that you were seen in Restaurant Patrick Guilbaud last night eating a loin of Wicklow lamb with chartreuse and olive crust!'

The old man's like, 'Who is making this allegation?'

'It went up on *Independent* dot ie a few minutes ago.'

The old man goes, 'Let me check with my Attorney General! Hennessy, what did I have in Guilbaud's last night?'

Hennessy – standing next to him – goes, 'The croustillant of soft cheeses with heritage beetroots and honey citrus aigre-doux,' and it's obvious that he's lying.

The woman's like, 'Minister Lalor, do *you* believe the Taoiseach?'

And Sorcha goes, '*Excuse* me?' and it reminds me of the time she tried to return a white shirt to Reiss but the sales assistant pointed out that there were, like, deodorant morks on the ormpits.

The woman's there, 'Do you believe what the Taoiseach is claiming?'

'What I believe,' Sorcha tries to go, 'is that this Government is doing important work – negotiating the terms of Ireland's withdrawal from the European Union, announcing economic initiatives that are vital to our country's future post-Irexit and reducing our national herd to zero in line with my commitment to achieve corbon neutrality in the short term – and all you want to focus on is trivial matters such as who ate what and when!'

'That's hardly a ringing endorsement,' another voice shouts. 'Do you believe the Taoiseach is telling the truth?'

'Say yes!' the old man – out of the corner of his mouth – goes.

And Sorcha's like, 'Yes. I do believe him.'

The old man goes, 'Fyodor – hand me that shovel!'

And Fyodor suddenly appears on his shoulder, holding – yeah, no – a shovel, which he gives to the old man.

Some flunky in a suit points out a piece of ground just in front of him. The old man walks over to it, puts the head of the shovel against it, then tries to press down on it with his good John Lobbs. Hilariously, the ground is too hord to actually dig and all the old man succeeds in digging up is a sod of grass about one inch deep.

'Does that count?' the old man asks, looking around him.

Fyodor nods and goes, 'I think!'

And the old man's there, 'Then I would like to declare the city of Malingrad . . . open for business! Exclamation mork!'

There's, like, a *bit* of a round of applause? Then the old man turns and, with Sorcha at his side, storts heading back to the helicopter amid shouts of 'Taoiseach, is it true you had the carpaccio as a storter?'

A few minutes later, the helicopter is, like, taking off and that's when my *phone* all of a sudden rings? It's, like, a number I don't recognize and I make the mistake of answering it.

I'm there, 'HELLO?'

'Is that Ross?' the voice on the other end goes.

I'm like, 'WHO'S THIS? YOU'RE GOING TO HAVE TO SHOUT. THERE'S A HELICOPTER TAKING OFF HERE.'

'It's Adam.'

'SAY AGAIN?'

'IT'S ADAM!'

'ADAM? ADAM, AS IN –'

'ADAM, AS IN HONOR'S BOYFRIEND, ADAM!'

Shit, he sounds *upset* about something?

I'm there, 'IS HONOR OKAY? HAS SHE BEEN DRINKING? OR DRIVING? OR DRINKING *AND* DRIVING?'

And that's when he hits me with it from straight out of nowhere.

He goes, 'I KNOW YOU KISSED MY DAD.'

I'm like, 'EXCUSE ME?'

'I HEARD STEVE AND NORMA TALKING LAST NIGHT – IN THE KITCHEN. HE SAID HE'S IN LOVE WITH YOU.'

Jesus Christ, what I wouldn't do for just one day without any complications.

I'm there, 'DUDE, ARE YOU SURE HE WASN'T JUST SHIT-FACED?'

'HE SAID HE'S NEVER BEEN KISSED THE WAY YOU KISSED HIM,' he goes. 'HE SAID HE TOLD YOU HOW HE FELT ON CHRISTMAS DAY, BUT YOU REJECTED HIM.'

'YEAH, NO, THIS ISN'T RINGING ANY BELLS FOR ME, ADAM.'

'NORMA FOUND A RECEIPT IN HIS JEANS – FOR GOLDEN NIPPLE CLAMPS.'

Oh, for fock's sake.

He goes, 'I'M GOING TO TELL HONOR!'

I'm like, 'DUDE, DON'T SAY ANYTHING – I'M BEGGING YOU.'

'WHAT, SO YOU'RE ADMITTING THAT SOMETHING DID HAPPEN?'

I should just tell him the truth – that his old pair swing like a busted gate in the wind – but I don't want to hurt the dude's feelings. I am, and always have been, a *people* person? So, instead, I go, 'YES, FINE, I GOT OFF WITH YOUR DAD, OKAY? BUT IT WAS A ONCE-OFF EVENT.'

He's like, 'I FOCKING KNEW IT.'

I'm there, 'BUT YOU CAN'T TELL HONOR.'

'I'M TELLING HONOR.'

'DUDE, SHE DOESN'T KNOW THAT I'M GAY? AS IN, I HAVEN'T ACTUALLY COME OUT TO MY FAMILY YET. DO YOU NOT THINK I SHOULD BE ALLOWED TO TELL MY WIFE AND KIDS AT A TIME OF *MY* CHOOSING?'

Fock, I suddenly realize that the helicopter has gone, but I'm still shouting. Oisinn, Magnus, JP, Delma, Christian and – yeah, no – Lychee are all staring at me with their mouths open. I give them a little to wink to say, yeah, no, don't sweat it, it's just the Rossmeister up to his usual antics.

'WELL, YOU SHOULD TELL THEM,' Adam goes. 'ESPE-CIALLY IF YOU'RE GOING TO GO AROUND KISSING OTHER PEOPLE'S DADS AND LEADING THEM ON.'

'Dude, just, em, give me a few weeks – to tell her. I've got a big match coming up next week.'

The dude goes, 'YOU HAVE TWO WEEKS. AND IF YOU HAVEN'T TOLD HONOR BY THEN, I WILL!'

He hangs up on me and I'm left thinking, what a terrible focking shame. Honor genuinely, genuinely liked him. It's such a pity that I'm going to have to split them up.

'Now *don't* laugh!' the old dear goes from the other side of her dressing-room door. 'And *don't* say anything mean, Ross.'

I'm there, 'Hey, I'm not promising anything,' because she's trying on – I shit you not – the wedding dress that she wore when she married my old man forty-three years ago.

Honor looks at me – the two of us are sitting on the end of the old pair's bed – and goes, 'Dad, don't!' because she's always been very protective of my old dear, more so since her *mind* storted to go?

'Honor,' the woman goes, 'have some bubbles! There's a bottle of Cava on my bedside table.'

I'm like, 'Yeah, she's *still* only thirteen, you know?'

'Oh, it's only rosé,' the old dear goes. 'Chorles and I first had it on a golf trip to Valderrama to celebrate our twenty-fifth wedding anniversary. I thought we might give it to our wedding guests as they arrive.'

Honor pours herself a glass and knocks it back before I can say a word to her.

'Oh my God,' she goes, 'that is *so* nice, Fionnuala!'

I'm there, 'Let that one be your last, Honor,' except she immediately pours herself a second.

I'm there, 'Okay, let *that* one be your last,' putting my foot down firmly.

'Get ready!' the old dear goes. 'I'm coming out!' and she opens the dressing-room door and steps out into the bedroom.

She's focking bet into the dress. She looks like someone tried to force thirty super-king duvets into a phone box.

I laugh. Can't be avoided. Honor punches me hord in the orm. She's an aggressive drunk, in fairness to her.

'She said not to laugh,' she goes.

I'm there, 'Who did you say wore the same dress for their wedding?'

'Princess Anne,' the old dear goes.

And I'm like, 'Jesus!' because – yeah, no – she is spilling out of it like oil from a tanker run aground.

She's there, 'What about you, Honor? Do *you* think it still fits me?'

'It's actually not as bad as I *thought* it was going to be?' Honor goes – and I'm thinking she never tiptoes around *my* feelings like that?

I'm there, 'Bear in mind that she necked that first glass of Cava and she's already pissing her way through her second.'

And the old dear goes, 'I did have this crazy notion that I'd perhaps wear it again. But I think it's a *little* bit on the snug side.'

'Yeah,' I go, 'snug covers it about as well as the dress covers you – in other words, it doesn't.'

Honor goes, 'The thing is, Fionnuala, it doesn't really fit in with the flapper theme. You should, like, get a dress made. Something spectacular. There's this – oh my God – amazing dress designer in, like, Milltown called Tipper Tynan. I follow her on Instagram.'

She calls up her website on her phone and storts showing the old dear pictures of her shit.

'Oh,' the old dear goes, 'those look absolutely fabulous!'

Honor's like, 'Why don't we make an appointment to go and see her?'

'That's a wonderful idea!' the old dear goes. 'We could have lunch afterwards. The three of us could make it a real girls' day out!'

The old dear disappears into her walk-in wardrobe then and storts rummaging around. About a minute later, she steps out, holding a lorge, leather-bound book. It turns out to be the old pair's wedding album. She sits down on the bed beside us and there's suddenly the sound of, like, stitches bursting, which I decide to ignore for once.

'Oh, I wish you could have *seen* me on my wedding day,' she goes.

Honor's there, 'We will, Fionnuala – in, like, *April*?'

The old dear's like, 'I mean back then,' and she opens the album and drops it onto Honor's lap. 'I'm under no illusions, Honor. I might *look* fifty, but I definitely don't feel it.'

I'm letting an awful lot go here.

Honor's there, 'Oh! My God! Fionnuala, I've never *seen* photographs of you when you were young before!'

The old dear goes, 'People used to say I looked like Geneviève Bujold,' because all she's looking for is a sniff of a compliment and she'll run with it.

Like mother, like son, I suppose.

She goes, 'That's Chorles and me standing outside the church on Stephen's Green.'

'Oh my God,' Honor goes, 'you look absolutely stunning, Fionnuala!'

I'm there, 'Don't drink any more, Honor.'

Honor storts practically forcing the album on me then, going, 'Dad, look at her! She's gorgeous!'

And I have no choice *but* to throw my eyes over it.

I'm like, 'Yeah, no, she's nice.'

'Dad,' she goes, 'look at it properly!'

I'm there, 'Fine. No problem. Yes, she's nice. Nice-looking. Move on.'

The old dear goes, 'Your father's terribly repressed, Honor. I blame myself for making him massage my feet every night when he was five.'

I'm there, 'Seriously, has this family even *heard* of boundaries?'

Honor's there, 'Oh my God, look at Granddad in his suit!'

'He was so handsome!' the old dear goes. 'Even though everyone told him that I was way out of his league!'

Honor is, like, quiet then for a moment. It's like she has something on her mind.

I'm like, 'What's up, Honor?'

She goes, 'How do you know – if you're out of somebody's league, I mean?'

I laugh. I'm like, 'You're out of everyone's league, Honor – and that's me being biased.'

She's there, 'No, what I mean is, well, I think Adam has gone off me.'

I'm straight on it like stink on doodoo.

I'm there, 'Why do you think he's gone off you, Honor?'

She goes, 'He's being, like, *so* weird at the moment – as in, like, basically *ghosting* me? He says there's stuff going on at home – something to do with, like, Steve and Norma, but I think there might be someone else.'

I'm there, 'Kick him to the focking kerb, Honor – like Ronan O'Gara finding touch.'

She goes, 'I thought you liked him.'

'Yeah, no, I did – until he storted jerking you around. The big focking Ed Sheeran head on him.'

The old dear backs me up at least. She's there, 'You're far too

247

young and far too pretty to be committed to just one boy! Let me top you up there, Dorling.'

Honor holds out her glass and lets the old dear do the honours.

I'm there, 'What about Reese? Is he still sniffing around you?'

Honor's like, 'Reese? You said if you ever saw him again you'd rip out his colon and feed it to him.'

'Yeah, no, that was a possible overreaction on my port. I never asked you, is he playing rugby this year?'

'Yeah, he's on the Senior Cup panel in Michael's – even though he's only in, like, *Transition* Year?'

'Another Johnny Sexton in the making by the sounds of things. Johnny played Senior Cup for Mary's three years in a row and that was without even repeating.'

Honor and the old dear don't react to this. There's no reason why they should.

I'm there, 'What I'm saying is that it sounds to me like he maybe deserves another chance.'

Honor's like, 'But he only wants me because I'm with someone else – someone who likes me enough to write an actual song about me.'

I'm there, 'Well, if Reese gets any game time this year, he might even score a try for you. That's worth twenty songs. Ask your mother.'

The old dear's there, 'Your father had lots of romances when he was younger, Honor.'

Still does, I'm nearly tempted to say.

She goes, 'Of course, most of the girls he got involved with ended up crying to me at the kitchen table – including your mother, dozens of times.'

Honor cracks up laughing. She loves having the goods on her old dear. She's there, 'Oh my God, was she, like, a total sap for him?'

The old dear goes, 'Oh, it was "How can I make him like me as much as I like him, Fionnuala?" and "Why is he such a Chandler in terms of commitment?" She used to confide all sorts of things in me – including what they got up to in her mother's Peugeot 206.'

I'm there, 'Again, Mom – do you *have* to?'

'Or maybe it was a Peugeot 208?' she goes. 'Anyway, my advice to you, Honor, would be to follow your hort,' and then she looks down at the photograph of her and the old man outside the church on their wedding day. 'Just like I did.'

I excuse myself and I step out of the room. I tip down the stairs and outside into the gorden of the Áras. Then I whip out my phone and I dial the dude's number. To say he's surprised to hear from me would be the understatement of the century.

I'm like, 'Hey, Reese – how the hell *are* you?'

He goes, 'M . . . M . . . M . . . M . . . Mr O'Carroll-Kelly!' sounding like Ronan's father-in-law.

I'm there, 'What's all this I'm hearing about you making the Senior Cup team in Michael's?'

He's like, 'So, em, wh . . . wh . . . where did you get my number?'

I'm there, 'I got it from Honor's phone last year – when I was considering breaking your legs for dicking her around.'

He's like, 'I . . . I . . . I . . . I . . .' and all I can do is laugh at him.

I'm there, 'Calm down, Dude. It's all good. I hear you're back texting her.'

'Er, look, if you have an issue with it –'

'I don't. Like I said, I'm totally cool with it – especially if it makes Honor happy.'

'Does it? Make her happy, I mean?'

'What, having you sniffing around? Yeah, no, it seems to – she's always got a big smile on her face after you text.'

Honor never has a big smile on her face and I'm wondering for a minute if I've over-egged the pudding.

But then he goes, 'Are you serious?'

And I'm there, 'I'm deadly serious.'

'It's just, you know, she's sort of, like, seeing that dude from, like, Newpork?'

'But you have feelings for her, don't you?'

'Yeah, no, I do.'

'Or is it just because she happens to be with someone else?'

'I don't know – probably, yeah.'

'Excuse me?'

'I don't know – well, maybe no.'

'Okay, that's good to hear. So what are you waiting for? Make your move, kid.'

'She said you threatened to make me eat my own colon.'

'Er, *slight* exaggeration?'

'So do you think I'd have a chance with her?'

'I would say you've got every chance, Dude. This focking New-pork sap is hanging on by his fingernails.'

He goes, 'Okay, er, thanks for the information.'

I'm like, 'Don't blow it this time, kid. Do *not* focking blow it.'

So it's, like, Wednesday morning – we're talking two days before we play France – and the IRFU have arranged a press conference ahead of the match.

It's a long time since I've felt this nervous. I was awake for most of the night – up and down the tower stairs, shitting chocolate malt. I had Sorcha's sister tapping on the toilet door in the middle of the night, asking if I was having trouble sleeping and telling me she knew a great cure for insomnia.

I was like, 'Er – yeah, no – you're cool. I always get like this in the week of a big game.'

She actually tried the door – gave it a good old angry rattle – and I was relieved that I'd for some reason locked it.

She was like, 'It's just a technique I have for helping you relax,' trying to force it open with her shoulder.

I went, 'It's chemical focking warfare in here – you maybe don't *want* to step beyond the door.'

Anyway, the little room in Donnybrook Stadium, where I was first introduced as the Head Coach of the Ireland women's team, I don't know, three or four months ago, is absolutely rammers, everyone waiting to hear what I have to say. Except I'm nowhere near as full of myself as I was that day.

Verner Ryan – the IRFU Director of, I don't know, Women's Excellence – walks up to me.

'Ross,' he goes, offering me a big, sweaty hand to shake. 'How's it all going?'

I'm like, 'Er, not too bad, Verner,' deciding not to tell him about the kicker who can't actually kick. 'Can I just ask you, though, do you remember at the last press conference when I mentioned that I'd win the Six Nations with this team and possibly a Grand Slam as well?'

He's there, 'Not really, no.'

'That's good,' I go, as I watch Sive step into the room, her orm still in a sling. 'That's a definite relief for me to hear.'

He's there, 'I saw poor Chorles on the news again last night. They're really not letting this business go, are they? I was actually with him in Guilbaud's that night – for my sins!'

And I'm like, 'Yeah, no, whatever – are we going to get storted here?' because all of this hanging around is making me even *more* nervous?

He's like, 'Good idea,' and we head for the top table – as does Sive.

Verner goes, 'Ladies and gentlemen of the press – thank you for coming. At the outset, I just want to make it clear that the Head Coach is here to talk about rugby matters only. He will *not* be taking questions about the Taoiseach and whether he had the Wicklow lamb or the soft cheeses with heritage beetroots in Restaurant Patrick Guilbaud.'

I suddenly realize in that moment *why* the room is so packed – because literally half of the people there stand up and leave.

I end up being given a nice easy question to stort the ball rolling.

'Ross, how do you feel about tomorrow's match?' Gerry Thornley goes.

I'm there, 'Yeah, no, all good, Gerry. We've, em, prepared well. Worked on a lot of areas that I thought *required* work? And, em – yeah, no – I'm confident that people will see a definite performance from us on Friday night.'

'And a result?'

'Let's, em, get the performance right first and hopefully that will lead to a – yeah, no – result.'

'There was, er, one surprise name in the squad when it was

announced,' the famous Derek Foley from *The Stor* goes. I'm thinking, fock's sake, One F, you're supposed to be a fan of mine. 'Nadine Delaney, whose background, I think, is in soccer. What's the thinking behind that?'

I turn to Sive and I'm like, 'Do you want to take that one?'

And I swear to fock, she goes, 'No, you fire ahead, Ross,' hanging me out to dry.

I'm there, 'Er, yeah, no, that's a pretty decent question in fairness to you, One F. I think we all need to maybe open our minds a bit more in terms of what we can learn from other sports. For instance, I think we can learn a lot from soccer.'

We can learn nothing from soccer.

Sinéad Kissane goes, 'Could you be a bit more specific than that?'

And I'm like, 'I'm not sure I can, Sinéad, no.'

'What I mean is, what qualities did you see in Nadine that persuaded you that she could make the leap from soccer to rugby?'

I turn to Sive again.

I'm there, 'Are you sure you definitely don't want to take this one?'

But Sive goes, 'Absolutely sure.'

Fock's sake.

I'm there, 'Well, firstly, Sinéad, it would be wrong to describe Nadine as some kind of newbie in terms of rugby. She played for Trinity College back in the day – alongside her great mate Sive here. And she's bringing a lot to the table in terms of her – yeah, no – kicking ability.'

'Are you saying that she's taking over the kicking duties from Joanne Wassell?' Sinéad goes, putting me on the spot in a major way.

I'm like, 'Er, yeah, no, it looks like it.'

'How did Joanne take the news that she's being dropped?'

'She's not being dropped. She's still my number ten.'

Sinéad turns to Sive then and goes, 'Sive, how's the shoulder healing?'

'Slowly,' Sive goes.

'Do you think you'll be fit enough to play in maybe the later stages of the Championship?'

'I won't really know how well it's healed until I go back into full-contact training – and unfortunately, Sinéad, I'm still a few weeks away from that.'

'But you *are* playing a part *off* the field,' Sinéad reminds her. 'How are you enjoying the role of Assistant Head Coach?'

She's like, 'I'm enjoying it a lot. As you just heard there, Ross has a lot of innovative ideas in terms of his approach to the game and how we can learn from other sports. He's a real outside-the-box thinker and I'm learning a lot from just working with him.'

I'm thinking, what the fock?

One F is suddenly back on my case again. 'Ross, you said when you were appointed Coach that Ireland would win the Six Nations Championship,' he goes – again, a supposed *mate*? 'And the Grand Slam.'

I'm there, 'I'm not sure those were my exact words, One F.'

The dude storts flicking back through his notes to try to find what I said.

He goes, 'Yeah, it's right here. *Ireland, under me, will win the Six Nations next year. And not only the Six Nations, but the Grand Slam as well.* Do you stick by that assessment?'

I'm there, 'Well, I suppose that depends on your definition of win and whether you mean *literally* win?'

'I don't understand you.'

'Well, some people might say that if we did better than the last two or three years, then that would be a win.'

He's like, 'But the team hasn't won a match in, what, three years?'

'Exactly,' I go. 'So if we end up beating someone – *anyone* – then it's a win, am I right?'

'Are you trying to dampen down expectations?' Gerry Thornley goes.

And I'm there, 'One hundred per cent, Gerry – the damper the better, as far as I'm concerned!'

When the press conference finally ends, Sive stands up – as do I.

I'm just about to ask her what the fock she's playing at when my phone all of a sudden rings. I answer it and it ends up being Honor.

She goes, 'Oh! My God!'

I'm like, 'What's wrong?'

'Reese just rang.'

'Er, yeah, no, cool – what did he say?'

'He asked me if I wanted to go and watch him practising his kicking in Michael's this afternoon.'

I have to say, I love his style.

I'm there, 'Honor, I couldn't be happier for you.'

So it's, like, twenty-four hours before we play France and I'm sitting in – believe it or not – Insomnia in Donnybrook with Sive. My Rugby Tactics Book is open in front of me and there's a blank page waiting for me to write fifteen women's names on it.

I'm like, 'So what do you think?'

She goes, 'What do *I* think?'

'Yeah, no, who do you think I should stort with?'

'I don't know – you're the Coach.'

'Well, you're the Assistant Coach. And I pay you because I want to hear your opinion.'

'You don't pay me at all.'

'Figure of speech, Sive. Figure. Of. Speech.'

At the same time, I'm staring down at her Rugby Tactics Book, and I can't help but notice that she's got, like, way more Post-it notes sticking out of the pages of hers than I have sticking out of the pages of mine.

I'm like, 'Genuinely, Sive – who do I pick?'

She goes, 'I think the pack pretty much picks itself when everyone is fit.'

'Agreed.'

'I think you should make Heather Hobson your captain.'

'*Our* captain, you mean. Continue.'

'She's tough. Suppose you have to be to work in the PSNI. And the lads respect her.'

'What about the back line?'

'I'd go with Grainne Hutton at scrum-half and Joanne Wassell at out-half. The Skeldons at inside- and outside-centre. Nadine on one wing and Lisa McGuin on the other, then Megan Barrett at full-back.'

And I decide to just come out and say it – as in, like, what's been on my mind. I'm there, 'Are you gaming me, Sive?'

She's like, 'Gaming you?'

'Yeah, no, *playing* me – as in, like, playing me for a mug?'

'The hell are you talking about?'

'It's a straight question and I want a straight answer. You told me that Nadine was good enough to play rugby at this level. I'm going to be honest with you and say that I don't see it. Judging by the thickness of your Rugby Tactics Book and the number of Post-it notes sticking out of it, it's pretty obvious that you know your rugby. You know your rugby inside as well as out. Which makes me think the reason you suggested Nadine to me was because you're setting me up to fail.'

I know straight away from her expression that it hasn't gone down well at all.

She's like, 'Why would I do that?'

And I'm there, 'Well, I know I wasn't exactly your first choice as Coach.'

She ends up suddenly losing it with me. She slams her hand – the good one – down on the cover of her Rugby Tactics Book and goes, 'Screw you, Ross.'

I'm like, 'I'm just asking the question, that's all.'

'What, you think I'd do something so unprofessional just to try to get you the sack? I've played fifty-seven times for my country. Which is fifty-seven times more than you, by the way.'

'I fell out with three or four Ireland coaches, in fairness to me.'

'I've put my blood, sweat and tears into that green jersey – and, what, you think I want to see us collect another Wooden Spoon?'

'Okay, I'm sorry.'

'Screw you, Ross.'

'Hey, I apologized. Look, I'm putting her down on the teamsheet – on the right wing. There you are. Nadine Delaney.'

'*You* asked *me* to be your Assistant Coach – wasn't the other round.'

'Like I said, she's going to stort. We'll let her take all the kicks in the first half, then look at it again at half-time, depending obviously on how she's doing.'

I suddenly spot James Ryan – *the* James Ryan – walking in. The dude has to literally dip his head as he steps through the door. I give him a wave, except he doesn't see me.

'Do you know him?' Sive goes.

And I'm like, 'Yeah, no, we go way, way back. He's said in interviews that I was a big influence on his career. Watch this – bet he orders a macchiato.'

'Why do you say that?'

'Because I'm in here a lot. All of the Leinster goys drink macchiatos. It's, like, their *thing*?'

Of course, the dude ends up letting me down by ordering a double espresso ristretto. As he pays for it, he spots me and gives me a big wave, then he drops his change in the tip jor – 'That'd be typical of Cheese,' I go – and he wanders over to where we're sitting.

I'm like, 'Hey, Dude! How the hell are you?'

It turns out, of course, that it wasn't even *me* he was *waving* at?

He goes, 'Hey, Sive – how's the shoulder?'

Shit, they're obviously mates.

She's there, 'On the mend, James – you know yourself.'

He goes, 'Will you play at all this year?'

'Might be back for the last match. Not counting any chickens, though.'

'But you're *coaching* the team?'

'Yeah,' she goes, flicking her thumb at me, 'do you know Ross O'Carroll-Kelly?'

I swear to fock, he's like, 'Er, no, I don't. Hello, how are you?' talking to me like I'm some randomer who won a competition to meet him. I don't say anything back to him – wouldn't give him the focking pleasure – except to tell him that I'm a massive, massive fan and that if I was picking my Fantasy Lions team today, he'd be storting ahead of both Maro Itoje *and* Alun Wyn Jones. Then I stort flicking through my Tactics Book, looking for the page where I wrote down that exact thing on Christmas Day, but he doesn't have time to hang around.

He's like, 'Good luck tomorrow, Sive. I'll be watching it on TV,' and off he focks.

When he's gone, I'm there, 'Goys who went to Michael's always pretend not to know who I am. They do it to rip the piss. Goys who went to Blackrock also do it. And Gonzaga.'

But Sive just goes, 'Let's get one thing straight, Ross. I didn't take this job to fail. I'm a winner – more than you'll ever be.'

I arrive home from Donnybrook to find the entire Lalor clan gathered around our dinner table yet a-focking-gain. Honestly, they spend more time here now than they did when they actually lived here.

I say it to them as well.

I'm there, 'Are you ever *not* here these days?'

Out of the corner of my eye, I can sense the sister looking me up and down, doing all sorts of filthy shit to me in her mind.

Sorcha goes, 'I invited them, Ross. It's my mom's birthday. I cooked her favourite dinner – moussaka with a Mexican twist.'

I shrug just to let them know that this means diddly focking squat to me.

Her old dear goes, 'You don't have to justify yourself to him. We're just as entitled to be here as him – more so.'

'What, even though he owns the house?' Honor goes, ever the Daddy's girl. 'You focking fat-legged fock.'

'You see?' Sorcha's old man goes. 'All *he* has to do is walk into a room and the atmosphere immediately dorkens. You should have taken my advice, Sorcha, and made a clean break of it.'

I'm like, 'Thanks, Honor,' and I can't help but notice that she's wearing a sky blue and navy scorf – presumably a gift from, like, *Reese*? 'Nice, em – even though I hate that focking school.'

She smiles at me.

I'm like, 'How's Reese?'

Sorcha goes, 'Reese?' and I can hear the concern in her voice.

I'm there, 'Yeah, no, he invited Honor to watch him practise his kicking, didn't he?'

'Not just watch,' Honor goes. 'I stood behind the posts, collecting all the balls for him.'

I'm there, 'I'd say that brings back a few memories for you, Sorcha.'

From her old man's face, it's obvious that he wants to kill me.

Sorcha's sister goes, 'Ross, come and join us.'

But her old dear's like, 'We're having a family dinner – he can't just walk in here and expect to –'

But I just blank her out and sit down. I'm actually storving, but I also love pissing off her and her husband.

I'm there, 'By the way, Honor, I picked the team today for the match tomorrow night. The Six Nations and blah, blah, blah.'

Honor goes, 'Oh my God! Can I go?'

'I'd be hurt if you didn't.'

'And can I bring Reese?'

'I don't see why not. He might learn a thing or two from the tactical master that is your old man! Although, jokes aside, tell him not to expect miracles. If we lose by less than twenty points, I'll consider it a major plus.'

Sorcha's old man can't bear *not* being the centre of attention. He goes, 'Yes, we were in the middle of a conversation when *you* walked in. Sorcha, you were saying that the EU withdrawal negotiations aren't going well.'

Sorcha's there, 'Well, obviously, I'm restricted in what I'm allowed to say, but the Taoiseach made it clear to Jean-Claude Juncker today that we would rather leave with no deal than a bad deal. Monsieur Juncker was – oh my God – adamant that Ireland would abide by the terms of the 2010 bailout deal, but the Taoiseach was like, "Oh! My God!"'

'I wouldn't blame him.'

'He was like, "Er, *hello*?"'

'I said something very similar when the deal was agreed – a bloody well gun to our heads.'

And that's when Sorcha's sister – totally out of left field – goes, 'You might as well know, since you're all here, that I'm going to have a baby!'

Oh, it's a *genuine* conversation stopper.

'I *beg* your pordon?' her old man goes, because the girl has always been an attention-seeker.

I wish I could remember her name.

She's there, 'I'm having a baby. I've decided.'

'What are you saying?' her old dear goes. 'Please don't tell us you're pregnant *again*. I'm a Minister for the Eucharist!'

'Oh my God,' Honor goes, 'will you focking listen to yourself?' because her and the sister have definitely bonded.

I must ask Honor her name.

The girl's like, 'No, I'm not pregnant – but I hopefully will be *soon*?'

'What are you talking about?' Sorcha goes.

And the sister's there, 'I've agreed to carry a baby – for Ross's friend Oisinn and his husband.'

Holy focking shit. I actually laugh out loud – probably nerves. And they all look at *me* then – like this is somehow *my* doing?

'Hey, I'm sorry to disappoint you,' I go, 'but this is the first I'm hearing about it.'

The sister's there, 'I met them in the Queens in Dalkey last weekend. They were telling me about El Salvador and how they've decided to go down the surrogacy route.'

Ah, *surrogacy*, I think. That's that mystery cleared up.

I can see that Sorcha's face has turned red – but she's too furious to even talk.

Honor's there, 'So, like, how does it work?'

'Well,' the sister goes, 'in this case, Oisinn and – I don't know, what's his name, Magnusson? – they don't want to know which of them is going to be the actual father, so I'm going to have sperm from both of them injected into my uterus by intrauterine insemination.'

Okay, that's *my* appetite focked.

'No, you're not!' Sorcha suddenly roars. 'No, you are *focking* not!'

The sister's like, 'Yes, I focking am. And what business is it of yours anyway?'

'Because you're doing it for attention. Ross, she is *not* carrying a baby for your friends.'

'Sorcha,' I try to go, 'I can't stop it from happening.'

'Yes, you can – you can talk to Oisinn and Magnus and tell them that she'd probably agree to it and then refuse to hand over the baby at the end.'

The sister goes, 'You're such a focking bitch.'

But Sorcha's like, 'Ross, I want you to talk to them and tell them it's not happening.'

I'm there, 'Sorcha, I've a lot on my plate right now. I think I mentioned the Women's Six Nations storting tomorrow night?'

She goes, 'I don't give a shit about the Women's Six Nations!' even though she went to the homecoming when they won the Grand Slam in 2013 and for a while mentioned Fiona Coghlan in her roll-call of female role models.

Yeah, no, how quickly they forget.

She goes, 'She is *not* carrying that baby. And if you don't talk to Oisinn and Magnus, Ross, then I will.'

The conversation doesn't get to develop much further beyond that because there's all of a sudden a ring on the doorbell and Sorcha stands up and goes, 'Oh, this could be them – they might have come with their sperm in a focking sippy cup!'

Which is a cracking one-liner, in fairness to the girl.

She goes out to answer the door, then she returns about thirty seconds later along with – oh, holy fock – the famous Adam.

Honor looks up from her moussaka with a Mexican twist and goes, 'Oh! My God!'

The dude goes, 'You break it off with me with, like, a text message?'

I laugh. Can't help it. I like her style.

She goes, 'Er, you've been ghosting me for, like, two *weeks* now?'

He's there, 'I haven't been ghosting you. I told you, I had some personal shit that I was trying to –'

He suddenly stops because he sees the scorf around her neck.

He's like, 'Whose colours are they?'

He'd focking know if he went to a rugby school.

She's there, 'St Michael's College.'

He goes, 'Did you get it from that rugby boy who's been texting you?'

That rugby boy. Focking Newpork.

She's like, 'His name happens to be Reese.'

He stares at Honor with – yeah, no – *real* spite in his face and goes, 'You're a focking –'

And I'm like, 'Whoa, whoa, whoa – no one speaks to my daugh-ter like that. Look, you've been dumped, Dude. But look on the bright side – you might write a song about this one day.'

Oh, he doesn't like that. Doesn't like that one little bit. He looks at me, then back at Honor. Then he goes, 'Just to let you know, your dad got off with my dad.'

There's, like, silence in the dining room.

'He *what*?' Honor goes.

The dude's like, 'I'm telling you the truth, Honor. Your dad kissed Steve – like he'd never been kissed before apparently. And now Steve's in love with him.'

Everyone at the table – even Sorcha's old pair – bursts out laugh-ing. And I laugh too because, yeah, no, this is one of those rare times when my reputation ends up actually *saving* me?

'If you'd said he kissed your mother, we'd have all believed you,' Sorcha's old dear – in fairness to her – goes.

Honor's there, 'Oh my God, Adam, I didn't realize until now how *actually* pathetic you are? Get the fock out of my house.'

And I'm like, 'You heard the girl, Sheeran. Hit the focking bricks.'

There's a lot of tension in the dressing-room and pretty much all of it is mine. I'm, like, pacing the floor while the players are doing their thing.

Little Grainne Hutton is listening to – yeah, no – her beloved Frank and Walters on her big headphones. Heather Hobson is shouting – I'm presuming – words of encouragement in a Northern Irish accent, although she could be giving out yords for all I under-stand of it. Joanne Wassell scrapes back her hair and puts on her headband, then about thirty seconds later, she takes off the head-band and goes through the entire process again. The famous Nadine is sitting there with her eyes lightly closed, doing some kind of pre-sumably visualization exercises.

I decide that it's time for the big talk. I clap my hands together and go, 'Okay, headphones off, Grainne. Heather, let me do the talking now. Nadine, welcome back to the land of the living. Okay, what I want to say to you is very simple. This is the moment. This is the hour. For you to write yourselves into history. Look, Energia Pork on a Friday night might not have the atmosphere of the Aviva Stadium on a big Six Nations Saturday, but if you beat France tonight, you have the chance to capture the public's imagination in the same way that the likes of Brian O'Driscoll and Ronan O'Gara did back in the day. So go out there – and win!'

It's a real mic drop moment and I'm about to do the whole dramatic turn-and-walk-out-the-door thing when Sive spoils the moment by asking me if *she* can say something?

I'm like, 'Yeah, no, go for it, Sive,' and she walks out into the middle of the dressing-room floor, her Rugby Tactics Book jammed under her good orm.

She goes, 'Okay, lads, just a few things for yee to watch out for. I've been watching Mallory Souply, the French full-back, for a long time now. She's a nervous wreck under the high ball – loses most of her fifty-fifty's – so, Joanne, keep giving her work to do, and the rest of you, make sure you chase the ball down every time she kicks long. The weak link in their pack is their hooker, Hélène Fedèle, who's had a neck injury for the last six months. Hannah, you know what to do at scrum time. Astrid Vial, their scrum-half, has slow hands, so keep harrying her. Nadine, they always charge down the kicker, so be aware of it and don't let it break your focus if they enter your line of sight.'

Holy focking shit.

She's like, 'Joanne, this team likes to hit the ten a fraction of a second after the ball is gone and we have a referee tonight with a history of letting it go. You need to be strong and keep your discipline. Ignore their lineout calls. They're meaningless. Hélène Fedèle, their hooker, has had a weak throwing arm ever since she injured her shoulder against Wales two years ago. The furthest she's going to go with it is the middle of the lineout – to either Jelena Soullard or Karine Ravva. Lastly, get the ball to Nadine on the wing as often as possible. Ross, did you want to say something else?'

Of course, I'm just standing there with my mouth wide open, like the Catch of the focking Day.

I'm there, 'Er, yeah, no, I'd agree with all of that.'

'Well, that's a *huge* relief,' she goes. 'Okay, let's go and beat these assholes. Ross, you're blocking the door there.'

I step to one side and they morch straight past me, out of the dressing-room and onto the pitch.

As we take our seats at the side of the pitch, Sive turns around to me and goes, '*You have the chance to capture the public's imagination in the same way that the likes of Brian O'Driscoll and Ronan O'Gara did back in the day,*' and she does a pretty cruel impression of me, way more hurtful than Honor's or – in fairness to him – Donncha O'Callaghan's.

I'm there, 'I was just trying to make the point –'

But she cuts me off and goes, 'We exist on our own terms. We're not all measuring ourselves against yee.'

Which puts *me* back in my box.

The players stand for the anthems. I'm too nervous to even listen to them. Instead, I'm looking at Nadine and I'm thinking, please don't let me down tonight.

I look over my shoulder, just as the French anthem is coming to an end, and I spot Honor sitting in the main stand, with Reese sitting on one side of her and the old man sitting on the other. They're, like, surrounded by security dudes.

Honor gives me a wave and goes, 'Good luck, Dad!'

I suppose I wouldn't be here if it wasn't for her. I give her, like, a thumbs-up and a smile.

Then my old man, at the top of his voice, goes, 'COME ON IRELAND, BRACKETS, WOMEN!'

I turn around to Sive and I go, 'I just want to apologize for him in advance,' and she actually laughs, in fairness to her.

The match finally gets under way and we end up getting off to *the* worst possible stort. There's only, like, three minutes on the clock when the French number twelve – Valérie Millagou, according to Sive, who's definitely done her homework – cuts right through our midfield and runs the length of the pitch, pretty much unopposed, to score beneath the posts. The crowd – which had been in pretty good voice – is suddenly shocked into silence.

'Jesus Christ, I counted *three* missed tackles,' I go.

Véronique Quérard – the French ten – adds the two and we're chasing the match from the pretty much stort.

We cough up three penalties in quick succession, all of which they manage to kick, the last one – I'm embarrassed to say – when Nadine gets ahead of the play and takes a forward pass from Louise Skeldon at outside-centre.

Ten minutes before half-time, it goes from bad to worse when the same Valérie Millagou plays an incredible dummy pass on the twenty-two to leave us standing flat-footed and pops the ball down between the old breadsticks.

You can actually hear the belief being suddenly sucked out of the crowd. We go in at half-time and we're losing, like, 23–0.

Standing outside the dressing-room, I tell Sive that I'm making changes at the break – specifically, I'm taking Nadine off because she's having an absolute mare.

Sive instantly turns on me. She's like, 'You don't know what you're doing.'

I'm like, 'I don't know what I'm doing? You were the one who told me to pick her. She hasn't made one line break.'

We're suddenly, like, roaring at each other.

She goes, 'She's not in the team to make line breaks. She's in the team to take kicks.'

And I'm there, 'But we haven't had any kicks. And she can't fock-ing kick anyway.'

I haven't had a shouting match with a woman like this since the night in the beer gorden of the Queens when Sorcha said she thought Dave was the best-looking of the Kearneys.

Eventually, Sive goes, 'You take her off and I am walking. And then you can explain to everyone why your Assistant Coach quit just forty minutes into your first match in charge.'

'I'll say it's because you insisted on putting Nadine in the team.'

'Yeah, you've already taken the credit for calling her into the squad, remember?'

Shit, I did – at the press conference the other day. All I can do is just shake my head. She's got me by the short and curlies here. I turn around and I head back to my seat.

She goes, 'What about the half-time team talk?'

And I'm there, 'You give it – since this is basically your team anyway.'

She goes back to the dressing-room. As I retake my seat, I hear the old man shout:

'WHOLESALE CHANGES FOR THE SECOND HALF, KICKER! I'D DEFINITELY TAKE THAT NUMBER FOUR-TEEN OFF! SHE'S CONTRIBUTING NOTHING!'

I decide to just ignore the tool. The team returns and so does Sive.

I'm there, 'What did you say to them?'

And she goes, 'Oh, I took inspiration from you and told them that they could be as big as Brian O'Driscoll and Ronan O'Gara one day!'

Yeah, no, I'm pretty sure she's being sarcastic, though.

The second half gets under way. Quite a few fans have left, judging by the number of seats that are suddenly empty.

Straight away I notice that Megan Barrett, our full-back, and Joanne Wassell, our ten, are doing what Sive told them to do before the stort. They're kicking the ball long to – I think she said her name was, like, Mallory Souply. And Mallory is – just like she said – a nervous wreck under the high ball.

Ten minutes into the second half, she drops one and we attack the French line. After five phases, Rachel Skeldon makes a shape like she's about to pass to her right, but then she checks back and throws a long pass to the left that ends up in the hands of Lisa McGuin, who's an absolute flier. You can hear the volume of the crowd go up as she takes off like a focking gazelle fleeing a pack of lions, lifting her knees high to hurdle over one attempted tackle, then another, then another, before depositing it in the corner.

I punch the air, but it still feels like – I don't know – a consolation, because we're still three scores behind and Lisa hasn't done Nadine any favours with the angle of the conversion, given that Nadine couldn't hit water if she fell off a focking cruise ship.

I watch her shape up to take the kick. She takes her steps backwards and then to the side. Then I'm waiting for her to hit the focking corner flag with it. But she doesn't. She makes perfect

contact with the ball and sends it sailing between the posts from *the*
most horrific angle.

I end up laughing.

'Holy focking shit!' I go. 'Even I would have struggled to put that
kick over.'

I wouldn't, of course. I'd have nailed that kick in purple Crocs.
But even so.

'I told you it'd click, didn't I?' Sive goes.

She's totally calm, by the way, like she thinks everything is in
hand.

Five minutes later, the French inside-centre throws a long, loping
pass across the field and Lisa steps inside to intercept. Off she goes
again – absolutely flying it, her two knees pumping, riding challenge after challenge, feinting one way, then going the other, to
score a second try. This time, she's more considerate to Nadine,
who puts two more onto our total.

It's, like, 23–14 and the crowd is storting to suddenly believe that a
comeback could be on the actual cords here. As am *I*, by the way?

I'm suddenly roaring at them, going, 'COME ON, IRELAND!
THEY'RE GONE! I CAN SEE IT IN THEIR EYES!'

And I'm totally right – about something, at least.

From the restort, we attack their twenty-two like women pos-
sessed. The French try desperately to hold us out. They succeed for,
like, twenty minutes, holding out phase after phase, until the ball is
suddenly whipped wide again to Lisa, who receives it in, like, acres
of space. She's off like a bullet train again and dives over the line for
her hat-trick.

'YEEESSS!!!' I go, jumping all over the place. 'FOCKING
YEEESSS!!!'

Nadine adds the cheese and biscuits – she suddenly can't miss –
and now we're two points behind with, like, five minutes to go.

From the restort, we claim the ball and we go again, the players
smelling blood now. Again, the French resort to desperate measures
to try to hold back the tide. With thirty seconds to go, we win a penalty just inside our own half. It's definitely not within Nadine's
range – and I'm not saying that just to be a dick.

But all of a sudden, she storts calling for the kicking tee.

I'm like, 'No way! No literally way!' but I don't want to tell her that she's making a mistake because – as a kicker myself – I genuinely believed that I could put them over from any angle and any distance and I didn't want to hear any background noise. So I say fock-all.

Silence falls on Donnybrook Stadium as Nadine spots the ball, steps backwards, steps to the side, runs her hand through her hair, looks from the ball to the posts and back again, then from the ball to the posts and back again a second time, before sending the ball high into the sky.

It's moving in the right direction. The only question is, does it have the gas? Halfway through its flight, it storts coming down.

'It's not long enough!' I go. 'It's not long enough! It's not long enough! It's not –'

But then I watch in disbelief as it clears the bor by inches and the flags go up and all hell breaks loose in the stadium. In her excitement, Sive forgets herself and actually hugs me. It's possibly the first time that it feels like we're on the same actual page.

Seconds later, I hear the whistle blow and it's suddenly over. We've beaten France in our first Six Nations match.

I turn around and I look for Honor in the stand. She's jumping up and down with joy.

I point at her and I mouth the words, 'That was for you!'

'ROSS O'CARROLL-KELLY!' I hear the old man go. 'YOU ARE A RUGBY GENIUS!'

And I think – yeah, no – there's a genius here alright. But it's definitely not me.

8.

Win, Glorious Passers

So it's, like, the morning after the night before and I've arranged to meet Sive in the 3fe on Sussex Terrace for, like, coffee and a *debrief*? Which is, like, so random because Ireland are playing England in the *men's* rugby this afternoon and I'd usually be meeting the goys in Dalkey around about now to give them my pre-match analysis over eggs Benedict and whatever else.

She's sitting in the corner when I arrive, polishing off her second coffee, her Rugby Tactics Book open in front of her. She closes it when she sees me coming.

I'm there, 'Sive, how the hell *are* you? I'm not late, am I?'

'No,' she goes, 'I couldn't sleep. I never can after a match. My mind is always –'

I'm like, 'Yeah, no, mine's the same way. I'm, like, constantly re-running plays in my head. What if this had happened and what if that had happened?'

I look around me.

I'm there, 'I have to say, this wouldn't be my usual spot. Full of flat white wankers. What are you drinking, by the way?'

'A flat white,' she goes.

And I'm like, 'Two flat whites coming right up.'

I order the coffees, then I sit down opposite her, putting my own Rugby Tactics Book down on the table beside hers. I can't help but notice that she's added quite a few Post-it notes since last night – we're talking not only yellow ones, but pink and orange ones too. Not only do I notice this, but *she* notices that *I* notice?

I'm like, 'So, er, great result last night, huh? Go, us!'

I hold up my hand for a high-five, forgetting that she's not the high-fiving kind. I put it down again and take a sip of my coffee.

She goes, 'It was far from a perfect performance. We both know that.'

I'm like, 'Yeah, no, but we still won and blah, blah, blah.'

'Thirty-five missed tackles,' she goes. 'If we play like that against Wales, we'll be destroyed.'

We're playing Wales next, in Cordiff.

I'm there, 'Thirty-five missed tackles? Did you, like, record the match and watch it back when you went home last night?'

And she goes, 'No, I counted while the match was going on. You mean you didn't?'

'Er, yeah, no, I did,' I try to go. 'But I thought it was more like thirty-four. I'd be very interested to hear how you came up with a figure like thirty-five.'

She's like, 'Thirty-five missed tackles, seven knock-ons, six line-outs lost . . .'

I'm just sitting there with my mouth open. This is, like, *Rainman* shit?

'Yes,' I go, tapping the cover of my Tactics Book, 'those other figures you mentioned definitely tally with mine.'

She's like, 'So do you have any thoughts?'

I'm there, 'In . . . *terms* of?'

'In terms of how we put things right?' she goes.

I'm like, 'Er, correct me if I'm wrong here, Sive, but the Welsh match is, like, two weeks away – am I right in saying?'

'Thirteen days,' she goes. 'But I *thought* that was why we were meeting up this morning. We're not here to pat ourselves on the back.'

Speak for your focking self, I nearly feel like saying.

I'm there, 'Terroirs sent us down a crate of champagne. Which was decent of them. My old dear would be a regular in there.'

'We've nothing to celebrate. We've achieved nothing.'

'Er, we beat France last night. The first match we've won in, like, three years. The girls – sorry, *lads* – should be allowed to enjoy it.'

'No one's drinking champagne until the Six Nations is over.'

'Just as a matter of interest, what do you think we should do – in terms of our approach to Wales?'

'I think we should move Heather Hobson to hooker and Hannah Fox to tighthead,' she goes. 'I'm going to work on the lineout this week because, if we don't fix it, Wales will crucify us. Also, they'll have seen what Nadine did last night and they'll make sure she doesn't get that kind of space again – so I say we surprise them by switching her from the right wing to the left.'

Jesus Christ, I've got instant goosebumps listening to the girl. Of course, I'm sitting there just nodding like the Barack Obama bubblehead on the dashboard of the cor that Sorcha *isn't* allowed to drive?

I'm there, 'Yeah, no, all of that is definitely where I am in terms of my thinking.'

She knows I'm full of shit, of course.

She goes, 'Did you see the papers this morning?'

I'm there, 'I wouldn't be much of a papers person, Sive. I've no real interest in the world around me. You'll get to know that about me.'

'They're all talking about you.'

'Okay, that I *am* interested in. Give me the highlights.'

'Oh, they're just saying what an absolute genius you are. And what an innovator. How you're not too proud to recognize that rugby can learn a lot from soccer.'

'I feel like nearly suing.'

Her phone all of a sudden beeps. It's, like, a text message. She reads it and sort of, like, sighs to herself.

I'm like, 'Bad news?'

She goes, 'It's my sister.'

'Right – is, em, everything okay?'

'She's giving me a hard time because I didn't go home for Christmas.'

'Yeah, no, I heard you mention.'

'My dad is an asshole.'

'Hey, at least there's something we have in common.'

That puts a smile on her face. I think, in a few short months, she's gone from hating my guts to sort of falling in love with me. She wouldn't be the first to make that journey, in fairness to her.

'I better ring her – see what the story is.'

So – yeah, no – she steps outside to make the call. And it's at that point that *my* phone ends up ringing?

It's, like, Sorcha.

I'm there, 'Hey, how are things?'

But she's like, 'Where are you?' in a really, like, urgent voice.

'I'm in 3fe with Sive,' I go. 'We're having a tactics meeting. There's some unbelievable back-and-forth. We won last night, in case you haven't heard.'

There's no 'Fair focks!' or 'Oh my God, that's fully deserved!' or 'France were the pre-tournament favourites – there's a lot of people in rugby circles who'll be eating humble pie this morning!' and I'm stort-ing to think that maybe she *is* serious about it being *over* between us?

She goes, 'Have you spoken to Oisinn and Magnus yet?'

And I'm there, 'As in?'

'Have you told them that we don't want them using my sister as a surrogate?'

'Your sister?'

'Yes, Ross, my sister.'

I'm there, 'Which sister is that again?' just trying to get her to say her name.

'Oh my God, I only have one focking sister,' she goes. 'And she is *not* carrying a baby for Oisinn and Magnus.'

I'm there, 'Do we really feel that strongly about it?'

'Yes, we do,' she goes, 'because she's only doing it to embarrass me. She will get herself pregnant, then she'll change her mind and fock off back to Australia – and Oisinn and Magnus will be left high and dry. Ross, I want you to talk to them.'

I'm like, 'Fine. I'll see them at the porty tonight.'

She's there, 'What porty?'

'Yeah, no, Christian has bought that idiot girlfriend of his a gaff in Harold's Cross – for her and all her focking influencer mates. They're having, like, a house-warming.'

'Oh my God, this is the collab house porty that Honor mentioned.'

'Honor?'

'Yeah, she follows Lychee on Instagram. I said she could go with you, by the way.'

273

'Ah, for fock's –'

'As long as she's home before midnight, and she doesn't drink.'

She tells me again to talk to Oisinn and Magnus – 'Tell them what an – oh my God – attention-seeking bitch she can be!' – and then she hangs up.

So I'm left sitting there at the table, on my Tobler, and I'm looking down at Sive's Rugby Tactics Book, and I suddenly stort obsessing about it, especially her Post-it notes, and I'm wondering does she have, like, a system – as in, are the yellows one thing, and the pinks another, and the oranges another, or is it just, like, random? – and then I stort wondering generally what's in there? As in, what thoughts and secrets and insights into the game are contained within those leather-look covers?

I reach across the table to open the thing. But suddenly an enormous hand is slammed down on top of mine and it grips my wrist.

'Aaahhh!!!' I go, because it's pretty tight.

I look over my shoulder and Sive is standing there.

She goes, 'Don't . . . even . . . *think* about it!'

Some dude with hair like Louis Tomlinson from One Direction is standing on a skateboard that's balancing on the top of the bannister. And there's a girl with hair like Ariel from *The Little Mermaid* standing at the bottom of the stairs, pointing her phone up at him.

The dude goes, 'Okay, everyone! You READY?'

The hallway of the house is, like, packed with, like, young people. They all go, 'YEEEAAAHHH!!!'

He's like, 'I said, Are! You! READY?'

And they're all there, 'YEEEAAAHHH!!!' and then they stort chanting, 'DAR-I-US! DAR-I-US! DAR-I-US!' which is presumably the dude's name.

He does the two-finger devil sign with both hands, then – I shit you not – he pushes off, careering down the bannister on his actual board. He gets about halfway down when he loses his balance and falls backwards, cracking his head off the wooden stairs and then sort of, like, tumbling to the bottom.

Everyone goes, 'WHOA!!!' although no one seems to know how

274

to feel about what they've just witnessed, at least until they find out whether the dude has sustained a serious head injury or not.

'I feel like I *want* to laugh?' a girl behind me goes. 'But it feels sort of, like, *not* cool – if that makes any sense?'

Her friend is like, 'Totally!'

But then the dude – Darius – suddenly gets to his feet, blood pouring from a cut in the back of his head, and does the two-finger devil sign again. Everyone cheers. I'm storting to get it. He's not dead – so it's automatically funny.

'You want to do it again?' Ariel goes.

But Darius is like, 'Shit, no – post that one! I'm thinking that could be, like, my *thing*, man! I do, like, stunts that go wrong and shit!'

Some nerdy-looking dude with glasses like two saucers – who I feel the overwhelming urge to bully, by the way – goes, 'This is the content we're here for, bro!'

And the chant goes up again.

It's like, 'DAR-I-US! DAR-I-US! DAR-I-US!'

Darius touches his bleeding head and goes, 'Does anyone have, like, a Nurofen?'

I turn around to Honor and I'm there, 'Come on, let's go and find Christian.'

'Oh! My God!' she goes as I grab her hand and drag her through the crowd. 'I just saw Little Orphan Angie!'

I'm like, 'Who the fock is Little Orphan Angie?'

'She's this, like, super-, super-famous vlogger,' she goes, 'who's chorting her psoriasis journey.'

I'm not even going to pretend to understand people of this age, so I don't bother commenting. I just drag her into the living room, where I spot Oisinn, Magnus and Erika standing in a huddle, looking about as comfortable as me at a Holy Child Killiney Class of 1998 reunion.

Erika totally blanks me, by the way. She goes, 'Honor, will we take a wander around the house?' and they fock off, leaving me alone with Oisinn and Magnus.

Word of our heroics in Donnybrook last night has obviously got around because Magnus goes out of his way to say 'fair focksh' to me and Oisinn says he read the report in this morning's *Irish Times*, which described me as a coach who's not afraid to take risks.

He goes, 'Joe Schmidt could do with someone like you on the coaching ticket,' because Ireland were blown away by England this afternoon and they played like focking robots. 'They always do this to us in a World Cup year, don't they?'

I don't get the chance to tell him that Joe Schmidt needs to have the courage to let the flair players do their thing because Christian arrives over to us then. He's with some dude in his, like, mid-twenties, who's wearing cycling shorts, an open dressing-gown and – literally – chains like a Lord Mayor would wear around his neck.

Christian goes, 'Hey, goys – thanks for coming. This is Lychee's best friend, Fernando.'

Fernando's there, 'You've got to give me my full title, man!'

And Christian goes, 'Fernando – the Lord Mayor of Whatever the Fock!'

Fernando just, like, nods at us. He's holding a cigarette-holder that's, like, a foot long and he keeps sucking on it, even though there's no actual cigarette in it.

Christian goes, 'Show them your teeth!'

The dude opens his mouth. He's got a set of gnashers on him like a box of dropped floor tiles.

'Fernando is doing this thing where he hasn't brushed his teeth for, like, two years,' Christian goes, 'and he's tracking their decay on a day-by-day basis on Instagram. It's all, like, photographs of them turning black and falling out. He's got, like, half a million followers.'

I don't know what sort of reaction he's expecting from us, but I'm pretty sure he doesn't get it. When Fernando heads off, I turn around to Christian and I go, 'Dude, I think I speak for all your friends when I say, What? The focking? Fock?'

He's there, 'I know what you're thinking.'

And I'm like, 'You don't, Dude. You definitely, definitely don't.'

He goes, 'These kinds of houses are popping up everywhere, Ross.'

I'm there, 'But who *are* these people? What do they actually do?'

'All sorts of things,' he tries to go. 'Fernando is a mindfulness coach. Rita – she's the girl over there with the black hair with the badger stripe through it and all the tongue rings – she's an e-commerce brand strategist. And her sister, who's rooming here with her, is an imagineer – just like Lychee.'

'I think what Ross means,' Oisinn goes, 'is what do they do here all day?'

I'm there, 'They're sponging off Christian – too nice for his own focking good, as per usual. Been saying it since we were, like, fourteen.'

Christian decides to just ignore this point. He goes, 'They produce content for the likes of TikTok, YouTube and Instagram. Some of them do, like, dance videos. Or they pull pranks on each other and post those. Then some of them produce, like, lifestyle content, whatever they're wearing, or whatever they're having for lunch, maybe a sandwich idea –'

I'm there, 'Dude, I think what we're all wondering here – and these goys are too polite to say it – is who the fock is paying the bills?'

I hear someone go, 'Yeah, great question, Boomer!'

I turn around and it ends up being – yeah, no – Lychee herself. Or focking Leechy is probably more the case.

I'm there, 'I just don't like watching my best mate being taken advantage of. I know a focking freeloader when I see one. I'm pretty much one myself.'

She goes, 'Chrissy, Oliver has just done *the* most – oh my God – *amazing* Boris Johnson lip sync challenge!'

I'm like, 'Chrissy? Are you for focking real?'

She totally blanks me and goes, 'It's, like, Sarah Cooper levels of amazingness! Do you mind if I post it on TikTok?'

And he's there, 'Yeah, no probs.'

'Thanks, Chrissy.'

Seriously?

I turn around to Oisinn and Magnus and I'm like, 'By the way, goys, I was hoping to have, like, a *word* with you about something?'

Magnus goes, 'What ish it about, Rosh?'

I'm there, 'It's about, like, Sorcha's sister.'

'Sorcha's sister?' Oisinn goes.

I'm there, 'Yeah – er, what's her name again?'

But he doesn't bite.

He goes, 'What about her, Ross?'

I'm there, 'Yeah, no, she mentioned that she'd offered to, like, carry a baby for you.'

Magnus goes, 'She hash offered to act ash a shurrogate for ush, yesh.'

I'm there, 'Well, Sorcha doesn't want it to happen.'

Magnus is there, 'The girl ish an adult, Rosh – shurely, she can make her mind up for hershelf.'

'The girl is trouble,' I go, 'and I'm saying that as someone who has – not proud of it – ridden her a good few times. Sorcha has an actual point. There's no guarantee that she'd hand over the baby at the end.'

Oisinn's there, 'She'd have to, Dude. We're going to be using a donor egg.'

'It wouldn't matter to her. She'd fock off back to Australia six months into her pregnancy and you'd never hear from her again. Trust me, Dude. I know what I'm talking about. She's bad news. Steer focking clear would be my advice.'

Oisinn and Magnus look at each other. Then Oisinn goes, 'We'll have a think about what you said.'

Anyway, that ends up being the end of that. We shoot the shit about other stuff for, like, an hour until JP and Delma show up. If *we* feel ancient in this company, I can only imagine how old Delma must feel – about a hundred-and-forty-focking-three would be my guess.

She has this look of, like, quiet disgust on her face – like my old dear whenever she hears the words 'affordable housing'.

JP goes, 'There's a dude outside in the hallway who shotgunned a can of beer and he's got, like, fourteen hundred Likes for it – in, like, an *hour*?'

Oisinn laughs, 'Jesus, if social media had been a thing when we were in UCD, we'd be, like, billionaires by now!'

We all laugh. It's funny because it's true.

I turn to JP and I go, 'Seriously, Dude, what the fock is going on?'

He's there, 'It's just young people, Ross. They're different from us. TikTok is, like, a career path now. There's people in the States buying mansions off the back of having, like, a million followers.'

'I'm talking about Christian,' I go. 'Buying this gaff. And presumably paying all the bills as well. He's being taken for a mug.'

JP just shrugs. He's there, 'He loves her, Dude,' as if that was an excuse for anything.

A few minutes later, Ross Junior tips over to us, wearing a pair of giant, novelty, love-hort glasses.

He's like, 'Hi, Roth!' full of the focking joys.

I'm there, 'Yeah, no, how are you, kid?'

'Roth, my daddy'th girlfriend hath fifthy thouthand followerth on Inthtagram and thirty thouthand followerth on TikTok.'

'Is that right?'

'And she made a vitheo of my brother lip-thinking to Borith Johnthon and it'th very, very funny.'

I'm like, 'Yeah, no, run along now, kid, and let the grown-ups talk.'

So off he focks and I turn to Delma.

I'm there, 'You heard about my old pair getting hitched, I presume?'

She goes, 'Yes, Fionnuala mentioned a spring wedding. I think she said April.'

'Hilariously, I'm one of her bridesmaids – well, a brides*man*.'

'Do you really think she's up to it?'

'In terms of?'

'She's not herself, Ross. I called to the Áras to see her yesterday and she thought I was one of the cleaners. She accused me of stealing fifty euros from her purse and told me she'd have me deported back to my own country.'

'She sounds very much like herself to me.'

'What I mean is, she didn't know me, Ross. I had to leave. Even as I was driving away, I could hear her shouting things out the window about direct provision.'

All of a sudden, some girl with, like, long, grey hair with a tint of pink in it runs into the room and goes, 'Everyone outside! Darius is going to jump through one of the upstairs windows!'

No one even asks why. Everyone just tips outside to see it – including us. There's a dude in the gorden with, like, tattoo-sleeve orms and a topknot, who's pointing his phone at one of the upstairs windows.

The chant storts up again.

It's like, 'DAR-I-US! DAR-I-US! DAR-I-US!'

All of a sudden – I shit you not – the dude comes flying, head-first, through the window and hits the ground in, like, a shower of glass.

He lies there in a heap for about, like, thirty seconds, while everyone speculates about whether he's alive or dead. Then the hand goes up again and he makes the two-finger devil sign while everyone cheers and the dude with the tattoo-sleeve orms and the topknot says, shit, he was filming the wrong window and did anyone else get it?

I decide that I've had enough of millennials for a focking lifetime and I tell Oisinn and Magnus, then JP and Delma, that I'm hitting the road. I spot Erika on the other side of the gorden.

I'm there, 'Erika, I know you're not talking to me at the moment, but where's Honor?'

And Erika goes, 'Honor? I thought she was with you.'

I'm like, 'Er, no, she most definitely *isn't* with me.'

'We were talking to some girl who invented the Chickatees smoothie,' she goes, 'then she said she was going off to find you.'

Oh, fock. Oh, fockety, fockety fock.

My hand automatically reaches for the pocket of my chinos, where my cor keys are – or rather where my cor keys *were*?

I'm there, 'I can't believe she picked my focking pocket!'

I whip out my phone and I ring her number. She answers by going, 'Yeah, not a good time, Dad – I'm here with, like, Reese?'

I'm like, 'What the fock did I tell you about driving my cor?'

She goes, 'See, I *knew* this was how you'd react? That's why I didn't ask for your permission.'

'You wouldn't have *got* my permission.'

'I'm glad I didn't ask for it, then.'

'Where the fock are you?'

'I'm at a porty in Ranelagh. Reese texted me. One of his friends has a free gaff.'

'Drop me a pin – now!'

'I'm not dropping you a pin because you'll only make a focking show of me.'

'Honor, if you *don't* drop me a pin, I'm going to walk through the streets of Ranelagh, calling out your full name at the top of my voice. We're talking Honor Angelou Suu Kyi O'Carroll-Kelly. And don't test me, Honor, I will literally, literally do it.'

She goes, 'Fine, I'll come to you.'

I'm like, 'Honor, don't you dare get back into that cor.'

And at that moment, I hear Lychee go, 'Oh my God, the video of Oliver lip-synching Boris Johnson has already got, like, fifty Likes!'

There's a serious, serious buzz around training all week. Everyone has, like, an extra zip in their step, just off the back of what we did against France.

I'm showing Joanne Wassell and Rachel Skeldon how to do this, like, dummy offload thing that me and Christian – focking Chrissy! – were famous for back in the day.

I'm there 'You're holding the ball like this – in one hand, okay? As the tackler moves towards you, you move your hand backwards to make it look like you're offloading the ball. But then you twist your wrist and – watch! – the ball never leaves my hand!'

They're watching me like I'm a magician at a children's birthday porty – their faces full of just, like, *wonder*?

'Show me that again!' Joanne goes.

And I'm in my element, of course, because this is what I was *born* to do?

'No,' I go, tossing a ball to her, '*you* show *me*.'

She tries it once or twice, but she keeps – yeah, no – dropping the thing.

She's like, 'I can't do it – my hand is too small.'

I'm there, 'It's nothing to do with the size of your hand, Joanne. I could do this when I was, like, thirteen and my hands were a lot smaller than yours. It's all about traction and movement. Watch me,' and I demonstrate it for them again. 'Traction. And movement. Traction. And movement. Let me see the rest of you try it.'

So they all give it a go then – but it's the same result, we're talking balls dropping all over the place like puberty hitting an all-boys choir.

'Keep at it,' I go. 'It's a skill. And, like any skill, it requires practice. We're talking repetition, repetition, repetition.' I love how my voice sounds, echoing around the big, empty stadium.

I notice Megan Barrett – our full-back – is really struggling with it.

I'm there, 'Yeah, no surprise that *you* can't do it,' I go. 'I said I never wanted to see you without a ball in your hands. Yet I saw you coming out of Lyk Nu Dry Cleaners this morning and there was no sign of any ball.'

It's good to send them a message that I'm always watching them – and I hope that doesn't come across as, like, creepy.

She goes, 'I was on my way to show a house.'

Yeah, no, she works as an estate agent with, like, DNG or one of that crowd.

I'm there, 'Doesn't matter. I told you I wanted that ball in your hand at all times. We're not talking half the time. We're not talking some of the time. We're not talking the odd time. We're talking *all* the time.'

She just, like, stares me out of it – not happy at being torn a new one in front of her teammates.

All of a sudden, I hear Sive calling my name. She's over the other side of the pitch, working on the lineout, which – she said it herself – was an absolute shit-show against France.

I walk over to her – even though *she* should technically come to *me* – and I'm sort of, like, spinning a ball in my hands.

I'm there, 'What's up?'

She's like, 'What are you doing?'

'I'm just trying to show them a little trick I learned in my Junior Cup days.'

She can see them all still trying to do it and failing miserably.

I'm like, 'It's a dummy offload – supposed to be.'

She goes, 'And what use is it to them?'

I'm there, 'It's good to have one or two extra clubs in the bag, Sive.'

'But how likely are they to need it in a match situation?'

'I used it once against Belvedere College. Cian Healy saw it. He was just a kid at the time. But he still talks about it.'

'I don't want to tell you how to do your job, Ross, but would you not be better off working with them on their tackling – instead of showing them card tricks.'

'It's hordly a cord trick – it's a skill.'

'Which they're not going to need. But do you want me to remind you how many tackles Rachel and Louise missed against France?'

'I was about to move on to tackling next. I was just about to do it when you called me over.'

'Standing around, just showing off.'

All the forwards stand there watching this exchange with their mouths wide open, even though this kind of tension is, like, normal at elite level. It's actually healthy. It reminds me of some of the pushing and shoving contests I used to have with the likes of Drico and Skids when I was in UCD – although that was usually because the fockers were trying to drag me out of the bor, especially on Morgarita Mondays.

I tip back over to the – yeah, no – backs, who've obviously been listening to our big, stand-up borney.

I'm there, 'Okay, we're going to work on our tackling. Which was a disgrace against France. Where's Megan Barrett?'

'She's gone for a piss,' Rachel Skeldon goes. Limerick girls can be so blunt. 'I actually need to go as well.'

I'm there, 'I think you, of all people, should stick around, Rachel. You might learn something.'

I hear her sister, out of the side of her mouth, go, 'He's only throwing his weight around because he's after getting the bollocks chewed off him by Sive.'

I'm there, 'Yeah, no, you're pretty outspoken, Louise, for some-one who missed – what was it? – seven tackles against France, including one that led to their second try?'

Oh, that softens her cough, because she says fock-all. Tough love – I hate dishing it out, but it's the only thing they understand.

Louise is one of the most fearless tacklers I've ever seen. I'd put her in the same class as Keith Earls in terms of pure courage, and it turns out they're from the same housing estate. But she never seems to get the wrap right and I could say the exact same about her sister.

So I strip it back for them. We return to basics. I arrange them in, like, two lines facing each other. On one side, we've got ball carriers – on the other, tacklers. In slow motion, I demonstrate a textbook tackle for them because it was one of the skills a lot of people would say I totally, totally mastered.

I'm in my absolute element, going, 'Watch me now! The orms shoot out – and wrap! The orms shoot out – and wrap! That's it! You try it now! That's better, Rachel! Better! Remember, left foot, right shoulder! Or right foot, left shoulder! That's good, Louise! Ah, Megan, glad you could rejoin us!'

Anyway, we work on it for, like, an hour and I can see definite improvements by the end. I feel bad for busting their balls, but these are the things that make the difference at this level.

When training is over, I grab a quick shower and I go to my cor, only to discover a surprise waiting there for me. Someone has filled it – and I mean *filled* it – with rugby balls. There's, like, hundreds of them and they're packed in there pretty solidly.

There's no prizes for guessing what Megan was actually doing when she went for her marathon slash.

Behind me, I hear sniggering. The players are returning to their cors and they're looking at mine and laughing their orses off.

I laugh along – you have to be able to take a joke at this level – although I make a mental note to substitute Megan the first time she fumbles a ball against Wales.

'Remember,' she shouts at me from the window of her – yeah, no – DNG-sponsored cor as she's driving away, 'keep those balls with you at all times. Not half the time. Or some of the time. Or the odd time. *All* the time!'

One by one, I stort pulling the balls out of the cor.

Sive walks over to me and goes, 'Megan?'

I'm there, 'Yeah, no, one or two home truths that she didn't like hearing.'

'She's mad as a bucket of piss, that one.'

'Well, she better hope for her sake that she catches every ball against Wales – or she's going to find out what a complete dickhead I can be when I put my mind to the job.'

Literally an hour later, I'm putting the last of the balls away when my phone all of a sudden rings. I check the screen and it ends up being Nudger, Ronan's old mate.

I'm there, 'Nudger, how the hell *are* you?'

He goes, 'Ine gayum-ball, Rosser – but what's all this Ine heardon about young Shadden?'

I'm like, 'In terms of?'

'It's all oaber Figglas, Rosser. She's arthur getting herself a new fedda. Some sham from Blanch called Peadar.'

'Yeah, no, I've met the dude. He works for Hennessy.'

'Is Ronan woyid?'

'Is he what?'

'Does he know abourrit?'

'Yeah, no, I told him when I was in the States.'

'Does he know she's arthur moobin him into the gaff?'

'What? I never heard that.'

'They're libbon togetter, Rosser. It's not reet – Ro has a thaughter libbon in that house.'

'Shit one.'

'So what are you doing abourrit?'

'Er, what *can* I do?'

'Would you not hab a woord?'

'Yeah, no, I tried that – and I got a mouthful of abuse from *her*, then *he* threw me out of the house on my head.'

'What, and you lerrum?'

'The dude is a giant, Nudger. He does, like, mixed mortial orts.'

'*Mixed mortial orts*,' he goes, having a crack at the way I talk. 'Jaysus, Rosser, are you a madden or a mouse?'

'Dude, I've played against some of the toughest men in rugby.'

'We're thalken about putting togedder a posse, Rosser. Meself and Buckets. And Guddle as weddle.'

'What?'

'Guddle as weddle.'

'Okay, I've no idea what you're trying to say, Dude.'

'Ine saying Guddle as weddle. Guddle . . . as . . . weddle.'

'Oh!' I go, the penny finally dropping. 'Gull as well! Jesus Christ, I can't believe you take the piss out of the way I talk.'

He's there, 'Sathordee neet, Rosser, we're godda head out theer to Fox-bleaten-rock and we're godda hab a woord – froyten the bleaten Jaysus out of the sham. What do you think?'

And I'm like, 'Yeah, no, go for it, Dude – if you think it'll do any good.'

'You see,' he goes, 'this is how we sort things on this soyid of the cithy, Rosser.'

I'm like, 'Yeah, no, *we'd* probably go the High Court injunction route – but, as my daughter always says, you do you, Nudger.'

'Fionnuala! O'Carroll! Kelly!' the woman goes.

And the old dear's face lights up like a gorse fire.

She's like, 'Susan! Sykes!' because it turns out that – yeah, no – that was the woman's name, before she was known as Tipper Tynan.

We're in her shop in Milltown, the one that Honor recommended, looking for a dress for the supposed wedding of the year.

'How long is it since I last saw you?' the old dear goes.

And Susan – who, I can't help but notice, is a ringer for Mickey Sumner – is like, 'It must be, what, twenty-five years? Because that's how long I was in the States.'

The old dear's like, 'God, was it really that long ago?' and then she turns to Honor and goes, 'Susan's mother and I were in school together. Poor Amanda – she died way too young, Susan.'

'Forty-four,' the woman goes.

The old dear's like, 'Forty-four. It's no age. Sorry, I shouldn't keep calling you Susan. You're Tipper now, are you?'

'It's just a nickname I picked up in the States. We were in Newport for, like I said, twenty-five years. And Tynan is my married name.'

Honor's just, like, staring at the woman, genuinely stor-struck.

'I love your clothes,' she goes. 'You're one of my – oh my God – favourite Irish designers.'

And this Tipper one smiles at her and she's like, 'Thank you – and who is this *stunning* young lady?'

It's obviously just a turn of phrase. With the greatest will in the world, you couldn't describe Honor as stunning – except if you were referring to her rudeness. And her driving.

'This is Honor,' the old dear goes. 'She's my granddaughter. And this is her father – you remember Ross, don't you?'

She's like, 'Of course I do! You're all over the news at the moment! You're the Coach of the Ireland women's team, aren't you?'

I'm there, 'Yeah, no, that's me – got it in one.'

'Do you remember Susan, Ross?'

'Er, no – I don't *think* so?'

Susan – Tipper, whatever – laughs and goes, 'We used to play together – when you were, like, five and I was maybe *seven*?'

The old dear's there, 'We were living in Glenageary.'

But I'm like, 'Sallynoggin,' because I never miss an opportunity to remind her.

'We used to play brides and grooms together,' the woman goes.

And I'm there, 'Seriously? And who was I marrying – you?' because – yeah, no – she definitely looks like she might have been my type.

'Oh, no,' she goes, 'you had eyes for only one woman! And that was Fionnuala!'

Honor laughs – cruelly, actually.

'Oh, God, yes!' the old dear goes, like it's a somehow painful memory for her. 'You used to get down on one knee in front of me and you'd say, "Mommy, will you marry me?" '

'Oh! My God!' Honor goes – like she *needs* any more material on me? 'Hill! Air!'

I'm there, 'I don't remember that. I'd be very surprised if it actually happened.'

Tipper goes, 'Then you used to dress up in one of your dad's suits – it was so cute, because they were huge on you! – and you'd absolutely insist that Fionnuala walked up and down the kitchen with you while I sang the Wedding March!'

I'm there, 'Sorry, I'm feeling a bit weirded *out* by this story?'

The old dear goes, 'Chorles thought it was a bit creepy. Said I should never have bottle-fed him. That's what created the desire, according to him!'

I'm there, 'Okay, can we maybe change the subject? Can we just tell – I don't know – Tipper what we're actually doing here?'

'Yes,' the old dear goes, 'Chorles and I are getting remarried!'

'I read it in the paper,' Tipper goes, 'and I was so happy. To be honest, I couldn't understand why you broke up in the first place.'

The old dear's like, 'Well, that's all water under the bridge. We've decided to have a theme for the wedding – and it's going to be *The Great Gatsby*!'

Honor goes, 'I was looking at some of your, like, vintage designs online and they're – oh my God – *so* amazing!'

'Thank you!' the woman goes. 'Fionnuala, I am so glad that you mentioned *Gatsby*, because I have something in the back of the shop that I would love to see on you.'

'I hope it's a focking Rottweiler,' I go – although I say it *inside* my head?

Tipper goes, 'I have the most gorgeous cream-coloured Berta dress, with a gold, ort-deco print on it and a plunging neckline. I think it would look fab-a-lous on you!'

The woman disappears into the back of the shop, then returns a few minutes later with the thing on a hanger.

Honor's like, 'Oh my God, it's *so Downton Abbey*!'

The old dear's there, 'What do you think, Ross? Would you like to see me in it?'

I don't give her an answer. Can't think of one.

'With maybe some Mary Jane or T-strap pumps?' Tipper goes.

I'm there, 'Look, I'm just going to come out and say it – I've got the big-time ick after the whole me wanting to *marry* you conversation?'

Honor goes, 'Come on! Try it on, Fionnuala! It's going to look – oh my God – *amazing* on you!'

The two of them disappear into the changing-room with the dress and I stand around outside with Tipper, just shooting the shit.

I go, 'So where do you tend to do your socializing?' trying to subtly suss out whether she's still married.

She's there, 'My husband and I don't get out as often as we'd like to. We've got five kids under the age of –'

And I'm like, 'Hey, I was just making conversation,' cutting her off before she gives me her entire focking life story.

'It's so lovely to see your mum again,' she goes. 'She's the kindest person I've ever known.'

I'm there, 'Is she?' and it's actually a genuine question. She thinks Honor is a lovely girl and the old dear has a gorgeous figure. I'm just saying, she might not be the most reliable judge of anything.

She goes, 'She probably wouldn't want you to know this, but there was a girl in my class in Rathdown who lost her father when she was in First Year. Her mother was going to have to send her to Rockford Manor.'

I'm like, 'Jesus focking Christ,' which I think is the right response.

'That was until Fionnuala stepped in and paid her fees. Not just for that year. She put her through six years of school and did it anonymously. I only knew because my mum found out.'

I'm there, 'That doesn't sound like my old dear, I have to say.'

And she goes, 'Then maybe you don't know her as well as you think you do.'

All of a sudden, I hear Honor go, 'Oh my God, it's *so* nice on you, Fionnuala!'

The changing-room door is opened and Honor steps out, giving it, 'Are you ready? Okay, Fionnuala, come out!'

The old dear steps out wearing the – yeah, no – dress. I'd describe what she looks like except I don't want to ruin a tender moment. All I will say is that the last time I saw a pair of thighs like that, I was slapping Nando's Peri-Peri on them.

Tipper puts her hands up to her face and goes, 'Fionnuala! You! Look! Fab-a-lous!'

The old dear gives herself a twirl in the mirror.

She's there, 'This is it! This is the outfit I'm going to get married in!'

Tipper is thrilled. Two focking grand – you wouldn't blame the woman.

The old dear goes back into the changing-room to take it off. Then Honor – God help us all – storts looking for an outfit for herself. She's pulling, like, dress after dress off the rail, going, 'I'll try on that one . . . and that one . . . and that one . . . and that one . . . and that one . . .'

After, like, five minutes, I realize that I haven't heard a peep out of the old dear for a bit, so I knock on the door of the changing-room and I go, 'Is everything okay?'

I can hear sobbing coming from beyond the door.

I'm there, 'Have you got your hip flask in there?'

She opens the door, just wide enough to drag me through it. She's standing there in her – oh, Jesus – knickers and bra and I'm seeing more of her, in terms of square acreage, than I've ever seen before.

I'm like, 'What's wrong?'

And she says something then that, like, genuinely shocks me.

She goes, 'Ross, I'm *so* humiliated – I've wet myself!'

It's a first. Not her wetting herself. I've put her to bed enough times over the years to know that. But it's the first time I've ever seen her genuinely embarrassed by it.

I'm there, 'What happened?'

She goes, 'It's all port of it, Ross,' and I don't need her to explain what she means by *it*.

I'm there, 'Hey, it's not a problem. Just throw your – okay, I'm struggling to say the word, but *knickers* – into your handbag there. Then put on your trousers. It's called going commando.'

'Is it?'

'Yeah, no, I've done it loads of times. Did you get any on the dress – as in, like, piss?'

'A little bit. Oh, I'm so embarrassed.'

'Don't be. We'll go out there and I'll tell her and Honor that you've got a migraine and you need to go back to the cor. I'll throw the dress on my cord. If she sees that it's wet, I'll just say that I spilled water on it. Then I'll get it dry-cleaned for you. How does that sound?'

She doesn't answer in words. Instead, she just throws her orms around me and gives me a hug, which is very weird because – like I said – the woman is in her smalls.

I'm there, 'Don't worry about it, Mom – okay?'

And she squeezes me even tighter and goes, 'I do love it when you call me Mom.'

It's, like, ten o'clock on a Saturday night and I walk into the kitchen to find Fionn sitting at the table with his head in his hands.

'It's over,' he's going. 'It's all gone. My dream job. My reputation. My future employment prospects.'

Sorcha has her orm around his shoulder and she's telling him that it's not the end of the road – it's just another setback – and that she won't give up trying to clear his name, even if *he* does? She's pretty dogged, in fairness to her. She once spent two hours staring down a cashier in Benetton who told her she could only exchange an item for a credit note. She eventually left the shop with a full cash refund.

Fionn seems a lot more upset than he was this morning. Something has obviously happened.

I'm there, 'What's going on?'

He's like, 'They don't have the fingerprints any more.'

'Fingerprints?' I go. 'What fingerprints?'

'The fingerprints of whoever exposed themselves in the Thomond Bor that night,' he goes. 'I thought if I could show that they didn't match mine, the case against me would have to be quashed.'

I'm like, 'So why don't they have them?'

'They were somehow mislaid,' Sorcha goes. 'I actually think the case against you should be thrown out on that basis.'

He's like, 'They say they're not required to keep evidence forever. I could sue the Gorda Commissioner, but it could take five or six years to get to court, and there's no guarantee that I'd even win.'

I have to say that I'm not enjoying how devastated he is after hearing this news. There's a little bit of me that wants to tell him that it wasn't his orse – it was mine. But that obviously wouldn't be good for *my* career? Then I think, I'll tell him once the Six Nations is over – that's only, like, five or six weeks away.

'I wonder . . .' Sorcha goes, then she just leaves it hanging like that.

Fionn's like, 'What?'

'Okay, it's a long shot,' she goes, 'but what if the Thomond Bor still had the CCTV tape showing what *actually* happened that day?'

Jesus, Sorcha, I feel like nearly saying, would you not just keep your focking nose out of it?

'It's from, like, five years ago,' I go. 'I'd be stunned if they still had it. I think you'd be wasting your time even trying to chase that down, especially with you being a member of the Government and everything.'

Fionn's there, 'Ross is right. And so is my solicitor. I'm just going to have to accept it. I can't keep having my hopes dashed like this.'

All of a sudden, there's a ring on the doorbell. I'm wondering who the fock that could be at this time on a Saturday night?

Sorcha's like, 'Ross, get that, will you?'

I tip outside and I open the door and who's standing there only the famous Nudger.

I'm like, 'Hey, Dude – what's the story?' because I still haven't put two and two together.

He goes, 'Are you retty, Rosser?'

I'm like, 'Ready – as in?'

He's there, 'We're going to Fox-bleaten-rock – to thrun this fooker out on his bleaten ee-or.'

I'm like, 'Yeah, no, when I said I was up for it, I meant I was up for *you* doing it – as in, like, you, Buckets and Gull.'

I spot Buckets of Blood's black van in the driveway, with 'The Attitude Adjusters – Specialists in Debt Recovery!' written on the side.

Buckets is sitting behind the wheel and Gull is in the seat in the middle. I give them a nod.

'You doorty, bleaten coward,' Nudger goes. 'He's yooer sudden!'

I'm there, 'I know he's my son.'

'Then you're cubben wirrus,' he goes. 'Gerrin that bleaten vadden befower I bathor you up and dowun the bleaten geerden.'

I've no idea what he's saying – I only catch every third or fourth word – but it sounds pretty threatening, so I follow him out to the van.

He slides open the back door and I climb in.

Buckets looks over his shoulder at me and goes, 'Alreet, Rosser?'

I'm there, 'Yeah, no, all good, Buckets.'

Gull doesn't say shit – but then he never does.

I'm there, 'I'm still not sure this is a good idea, goys.'

But they all just laugh at me.

Buckets goes, 'We're oatenly godda hab a chat with the fedda, Rosser – and warden him off.'

I'm there, 'So there'll be no actual violence, then?'

'Not udless he wants to leerden the heerd way,' Nudger goes.

I'm there, 'Just to warn you, goys, he's focking huge, this dude – and I think I may have mentioned the mixed mortial *orts*?'

'Mixed mortial orts!' they all go – even Gull – like it's somehow hilarious.

Buckets is there, 'If it's a war he's wanton, it's a war he can hab.'

I don't know how much confidence I'd have in his fighting ability. His nickname might be Buckets of Blood, but it's well known that the blood getting mopped up after he's in a fight is usually his.

Nudger goes, 'Doatunt woody, Rosser – we've mower than enough muscle. He's not the oatenly wooden who knows meertial eerts. I did Jiu Jitsu when I was insoyut. I know how to use a fedda's weight against him. And doatunt forget that Guddle theer was in the eermy.'

'Yeah,' I go, 'the Irish ormy – who never seem to fight anyone.'

'Gib oaber yisser whining,' Buckets goes. 'We'll hab a woord wirrum and it'll be sorted.'

Fifteen minutes later, we're pulling into the driveway of the gaff. There's a black Subaru Impreza with a humungous spoiler on the back porked out front, which I automatically assume belongs to him.

Nudger presses the doorbell.

I'm there, 'You're wasting your time with that thing. She took the batteries to put them into a Santa Claus that plays the drums,' and I hammer on the door with the heel of my hand.

Thirty seconds later, the thing is thrown open and standing there – wearing Ronan's Manchester United dressing-gown and making it look basically skimpy – is Peadar.

We all look up at him.

'What do *yous* waddant?' he goes.

Nudger's there, 'We've come to thrive you howum,' escalating things very early on. 'Hop in the vadden theer and we'll throp you back to Blanch.'

'You widdle,' Peadar goes, 'widdle you?'

Buckets goes, 'You can make it easy on yisser self – or you can make it heerd. The choice is yooers.'

Inside the gaff, I hear Shadden go, 'Who is it, Peadar?'

And over his shoulder, Peadar's like, 'It's nutten, Shadden. I'll be back up to you in a midute – probley less.'

He steps out of the gaff and assumes a fighting pose.

Buckets goes, 'Hab it your way so,' and he storts walking towards him with his fist cocked.

It happens in a blur of movement. Peadar stands on one leg and suddenly spins around, catching Buckets on the chin with the most unbelievable roundhouse kick. The dude is unconscious before his head hits the gravel.

Next, Gull makes a run at the dude – and walks straight onto a punch that snaps his head backwards and puts him to sleep too.

Nudger goes, 'You doorty-looken–' and makes a lunge for him. Peadar picks him up like he's a puppy and turns him upside-down and I'm watching this wondering how Nudger plans to use the dude's weight against him. Peadar slams him down on his back and the last words I heard out of Nudger are, 'Ahhh, Jaaaysus!'

It dawns on me very suddenly that I'm next in the firing line. I stort backing away from him, going, 'Dude, please! It wasn't my idea! It was theirs! I'm actually glad you're with Shadden! I've always said that Ronan was too good for her!'

But it doesn't seem to make him feel any better. He comes after me and I end up having to use my famous turn of speed over the first five yords to put distance between myself and him.

He ends up chasing me around the outside of the house. And I'm not proud of this, but I'm screaming, 'No! Please, don't hurt me! I'm in the middle of a Six Nations campaign! People are relying on me!'

I make a run for one of the trees at the end of the gorden and I scramble up it as he grabs at my legs with his enormous paw-like hands. I manage to kick them away and climb higher and higher into the tree to safety.

He looks up at me, standing on one of the upper branches, clinging to the trunk, my two knees trembling with complete and utter bowel-emptying fear.

'I ebber see addy of youse arowunt hee-or again,' he goes, 'and you'll be leabon in a heerse.'

I'm like, 'In a what?'

'A heerse,' he goes.

'A horse?'

'A heerse.'

'It sounds like horse. Are you saying a horse?'

'Ine saying a heerse.'

It's only, like, an hour later, when I watch the lights in the house go out and I finally summon up the courage to come down out of the tree and wake the other three that I realize the word he was trying to say was hearse.

I've got Sorcha's sister roaring into my ear and I don't even mean that in, like, a *good* way? She's giving out yords to me, calling me every B word, C word and F word under the sun, to the point where I end up having to hold the phone away from my ear.

I'm like, 'Calm the fock down, will you? Will you please let me *speak*?'

She's like, 'I thought you were cool. But you're not. You're a prick. And a wanker.'

I forgot to mention, there's P words and W words in the mix as well.

I'm there, 'Look, I'm not the one who's stopping you having this baby. It's my wife.'

Yeah, no, Oisinn and Magnus have obviously taken on board what I said to them at the TikTok housewarming and told her that the deal is off.

'You said I wouldn't hand over the baby,' she goes. 'You told them I'd go back to Australia and they'd never hear from me again.'

I'm there, 'I'm not sure those were the exact words I said.'

'You're a focking lying prick.'

'I was only passing on a message. Sorcha thinks the only reason you want to carry this baby is to stir the shit.'

'She's just terrified that she won't be the centre of attention. That's all it's about. She'd prefer it if I went back to Australia – so would my focking parents.'

'That's not true.'

It probably is true.

She goes, 'And why are you still doing her dirty work?'

I'm there, 'What dirty work?'

'Your marriage is over.'

'Well, I'm still hoping to weasel my way back in there when the whole thing about me having sex with my old dear's best friend is forgotten. And with my daughter's Irish teacher.'

'You're focking kidding yourself. She has you sleeping in that freezing cold tower.'

'The Dyson has made a big difference.'

'You've focking ruined this thing for me. And I'm going to get you back for this – you *and* her?'

That's when an air hostess tells me that all mobile phones must be switched off for take-off and I tell the girl I have to go.

I notice that Sive, sitting in the seat next to me, is just, like, staring at me. I can only imagine how it sounded to her, even hearing just *my* side of the conversation?

I'm there, 'You were listening to that, were you?'

'The entire flight was listening to it,' she goes. 'And I thought *my* life was complicated.'

I'm like, 'You've no idea, Sive. No idea.'

Behind me, I hear the same air hostess go, 'You're going to have to put your balls away.'

Then I hear this, like, cascade of women's laughter. Yeah, no, Sive even laughs.

The poor air hostess goes, 'Your balls will have to go in the over-head lockers – just for take-off.'

I hear Grainne Hutton – in her thick Cork accent – go, 'The coach said we have to keep them with us. I carried this one up the aisle at my sister's wedding, like.'

The air hostess is like, 'What are you, a rugby team?'

'We're not *a* rogbay team,' Heather Hobson goes. 'We're *the* Arelund rogbay team. We're off tee Corduff to kick the shut ite of Wheels. And these balls are steeing wuth us.'

The air hostess is obviously terrified of her because she goes,

'Fine, you can hang onto your balls – but make sure you keep them between your knees.'

There's a round of cheers and then more laughter. Seriously, when they get together, they're actually worse than me and the goys *ever* were?

No sooner are we airborne than Sive turns around to me and goes, 'Will we do some work?'

I actually think I'm falling in love with this girl.

I'm like, 'Er, yeah, no, why not?'

She takes her Rugby Tactics Book out of the seat pocket in front of her, pulls her tray table down and opens the thing up. On the page in front of her, in red, blue and black ink, is a series of, like, squiggles and circles and arrows and squares that mean literally nothing to me.

I'm seriously, seriously impressed.

'I'm worried about Rebecca Davies,' she goes.

Yeah, no, Rebecca Davies is the Welsh full-back.

She goes, 'Did you see that cross-field kick that opened up Scotland? She did the same thing against England last year. I think we could be vulnerable to it.'

I'm like, 'Good call – yeah, no, we'll do some work on it. So, em, how are things with the family?' and I say it totally out of left field.

Sive's like, 'What?' narrowing her eyes at me.

'It's just that – yeah, no – you mentioned that your old man was a wanker –'

'An asshole.'

'– an asshole then, and I just wondered had things got any better since?'

She goes, 'I didn't think me and you did personal stuff,' and then she goes back to staring at her book.

I'm about to catch the air hostess's eye to ask if they have Pringles when Sive suddenly goes, 'He thinks women's rugby is a joke.'

I'm there, 'Then he knows diddly focking squat about the game.'

'Well, that's not strictly true. He played over a hundred times for Connacht.'

'Fair enough.'

'He just doesn't think women should be playing the game.'

'A traditionalist.'

'That's a nice word for it, yeah. When we got the Wooden Spoon last year, he laughed in my face. He said, "Would you not give up? Embarrassing yourself *and* me!"'

I'm there, 'I'm picking up on the vibe that you haven't spoken to the dude since.'

'No, I haven't,' she goes. 'And I won't either.'

She goes back to staring at her circles and her squiggles and her arrows and her squares.

I look up and I notice Joanne Wassell on her way to the jacks with – I'm happy to see – a rugby ball in her hand. She's, like, flicking her wrist, practising the whole dummy offload thing, when the ball suddenly pops out of her hand, hits the tray table of some random dude sitting next to the aisle and knocks a cup of hot tea into his lap.

The dude jumps up and goes, 'For fock's sake!'

Then there's an announcement that we've storted our descent towards Cordiff. And I stort to get suddenly excited.

'We're a little bit worried,' I go, 'about the cross-field pass – in terms of, like, our *vulnerability* to it?'

It's, like, midday on the day of the match and we're having a tactics meeting in the team hotel after a light training session this morning.

'Yes, *we* are worried,' Sive goes, 'aren't *we*, Ross?'

She's like the proverbial bear with its foot in a trap this morning.

I'm there, 'This Rebecca Daniels is dangerous. You only have to look at what she did against Scotland and then against England last –'

'Davies,' Sive goes.

I'm there, 'Excuse me?'

'Her *name* is Rebecca Davies,' she goes.

Yeah, no, Rebecca Daniels is a girl I know who went to Muckross. I threw up in her old man's aquarium when they were away skiing in Verbs and killed two guppies and a horlequin rasbora.

Haven't been able to stomach Malibu since.

I'm there, 'Rebecca Davies, then. We all know her and we all know the damage she can do from the full-back position. Which is why we have to come up with a plan.'

'I have a plan,' Sive goes, opening up her Rugby Tactics Book.

I'm like, 'Okay – so how do you want to do this?'

'What do you mean?'

'Well, do you want to tell me the plan and then I'll tell them?'

'Not really, no.'

'Okay, you've my permission to –'

'I've your permission to talk, Ross, do I?'

'I'm just saying the floor is yours.'

'Okay,' she goes, standing up, 'we need to neutralize her as a threat. Nadine, you're basically going to mark her – like in soccer, right?'

'Yeah,' Nadine goes, 'that's no problem, Sive.'

'We're going to put you on the other wing tonight. Just to confuse them. But you're the one with the pace. As soon as you see Rebecca shaping up to receive that ball, chase her down and put her under pressure. Don't let her get that kick without getting in her face.'

My phone all of a sudden beeps and it's, like, a text message from Sorcha, telling me to ring her when I get a second. She says it's urgent and the word is in, like, capital letters.

I'm there, 'Sorry, goys, I just have to step outside for a second,' which is what I do – out into the lobby of the old Cordiff Clayton.

I ring the number. I'm wondering is it something to do with the sister.

Sorcha's there, 'Hello?'

I'm like, 'You were looking for me?'

And she goes, 'I got the tape, Ross!'

I'm like, 'Tape? The fock are you on about?'

She's there, 'The CCTV tape – from the Thomond Bor in Cork! I phoned them this morning – I have to admit, I used the whole Government minister thing – and it turns out they still have it!'

I'm like, 'Why? As in, why the *fock* would they hold onto something like that?'

'It was put in a drawer because they thought it might be needed as, like, evidence? But then whoever it was who was pretending to be Fionn pleaded guilty, so no one came looking for it! Can you believe it, Ross? It's been sitting in someone's drawer for, like, five years!'

Why can't you keep your big focking honker out of it, I nearly feel like saying.

I'm there, 'Maybe the, em, footage will be all grainy – or too dork to properly recognize who it actually was. You haven't seen it yet, have you?'

'No,' she goes. 'Kennet's on his way down to Cork to get it.'

I'm there, 'Yeah, no, cool. Sorcha, I have to go, okay? I'll be home tomorrow.'

I phone Kennet's number. He answers on the third ring. He's got, like, music blaring in the background.

I'm like, 'Hello? Kennet?'

He's there, 'H . . . H . . . H . . . H . . . Hag odden, Rosser. Ine godda turden this dowun.'

He lowers the volume.

He goes, 'Just listodden to a birra Ch . . . Ch . . . Ch . . . Ch . . . Christy Mewer, Rosser – shorten the jourdeney, know what Ine saying?'

'I do,' I go. 'Very much. Where are you now, Dude?'

'Ine joost cubben into C . . . C . . . C . . . C . . . C . . .'

'Jesus Christ.'

'C . . . C . . . C . . . C . . . C . . .'

'Cork, right?'

'C . . . C . . . C . . . C . . . Cowurk.'

'Sorcha asked you to pick something up, yeah?'

'That's reet, Rosser – it's a p . . . p . . . p . . . p . . . p . . . p . . . package.'

'Do you have any idea what's in it?'

'Habn't a bleaten clue.'

'Dude, can I ask you for a favour?'

'D . . . D . . . D . . . D . . . Depeddens what koyunt of a f . . . f . . . f . . . fabour.'

'Can I ask you to *not* give Sorcha the package? Can I ask you to give it to me instead?'

'C . . . c . . . c . . . c . . . c . . . couldn't do that, Rosser. She's me bleaten boss, so she is.'

'All you have to say is that you swung into a petrol station on the way home and that you forgot to lock the door. When you went back to the cor, someone had stolen the package off your seat.'

'What's in this J . . . J . . . J . . . Jaysusing package in addyhow?'

'I can't tell you.'

'And why should I do athin to h . . . h . . . h . . . help you? You nebber been athin but a boddicks to me.'

'Dude, look, I know we've had our troubles in the past.'

'Calden me a scumbag and laughing at me bleaten st . . . st . . . st . . . st . . . stuthor. You think I caddent hee-or what's being said in the back of the keer. I can hee-or evoddy bleaten woord.'

'Look, Dude, please do this thing for me – and I'll owe you one.'

'You'll owe me wooden? What does that m . . . m . . . mee-un?'

'Means I'll owe you one – as in, like, a favour?'

He doesn't say shit for a good, like, thirty seconds. Then he goes, 'I'll hab a th . . . th . . . th . . . think abourrit.'

I'm there, 'Dude, seriously, I need to know. We're playing Wales tonight and I don't want this hanging over me when I'm supposed to be thinking, like, *tactically?*'

He goes, 'Alreet.'

I'm there, 'You'll do it? You'll say it was swiped from the cor – when you got out to buy cigarettes?'

He goes, 'Ine vaping the last tr . . . tr . . . tr . . . tree yee-or, Rosser.'

I'm there, 'When you got out to fill the tank, then. Kennet, I wouldn't ask you if I wasn't desperate. Please. I need that package.'

'Alreet,' he goes. 'But remembor, Rosser – you owe me w . . . w . . . w . . . w . . . w . . . w . . . w . . . w . . . w . . . w . . . w . . . w . . .'

I'm there, 'Dude, I've got to go here.'

'. . . w . . . w . . . w . . . w . . . w . . . w . . . w . . . w . . .'

'The match is storting in, like, seven hours.'

'. . . w . . . w . . . w . . . w . . . w . . . w . . . wooden.'

★

There's, like, ten minutes on the clock and we already know that we're in a match. The Welsh players are all built like gorden sheds and they're throwing themselves into tackles like it's the final minute of a one-score game.

Already, I can see that one or two of our players are carrying knocks. Louise Skeldon has a dead leg after taking a deliberate knee in the thigh from the Welsh number twelve, while Heather Hobson is talking gibberish after knocking heads with her opposite number in the front row. The only reason she hasn't been asked to complete an HIA is because no one can understand what she's saying even when she *hasn't* taken a bang to the temple.

We're 3–0 down, having coughed up a soft penalty right in front of the posts, and Wales are storting to grow in confidence after establishing their superiority in the physical stakes.

But then we end up getting a lucky break. Rebecca Davies receives the ball from a ruck. She's about to launch one of her famous crossfield kicks when Nadine – I swear to fock – appears out of nowhere and chorges the ball down. Rebecca turns to try to regather the ball, but, in doing so, she ends up twisting her knee – and badly – because she straight away signals to the bench that she has to come off.

Sixty seconds later, she's carried off the pitch on a stretcher and me and Sive look at each other as if to say, hey, that's possibly all of our good fortune used up for this Six Nations.

It ends up being a totally different match after that. Without Rebecca pinging balls about the place – we're talking left, right and centre – our players stort to impose themselves on the game.

The Welsh are definitely shaken up after losing their best player, but they manage to twice stop us crossing the line when I was nearly sure that Heather Hobson, both times, was going to get over.

As a match, it's not much to look at. Even the crowd is bored shitless. In the absence of anything to cheer, they resort to booing our players every time they manage to put a passing move together.

At half-time, it's still 3–0 for Wales, but the game is anyone's.

I'm looking around the dressing-room and I'm there, 'I've been involved in low-scoring matches before. And I can tell you – it's going to take a mistake or a moment of magic to decide it. So what's it going to be?'

It's a real hairs-standing-on-the-back-of-your-neck moment.

I ask Sive if she wants to say anything and she tells Grainne Hutton that she needs to provide quicker ruck ball, and she tells Heather Hobson to get in the referee's ear more, and she tells Megan Barrett to concentrate on accuracy rather than the distance with the boot.

Yeah, no, we have very different approaches to the game and it's very much a case of horses for courses.

The second half gets under way and the woman who came on for Rebecca Davies – don't know her name – nails an unbelievable drop goal from, like, forty metres out to double their lead.

We don't panic, though. We stort putting phases together and inching closer and closer to the Welsh line. Midway through the half, Heather Hobson crashes over for what looks like a try, but it goes to the TMO, who spends – I shit you not – five minutes trying to see if the ball was actually grounded, before deciding that the evidence is inconclusive and it's back to the drawing board for us.

The time ticks away. Suddenly, there's, like, four minutes left and Joanne Wassell – our ten, remember – has the ball in the middle of the pork. She beats one Welsh player, then another. She has Nadine – with her famous sprinter's feet – haring up the pitch just outside her.

I'm roaring, 'Give it! Give it! Give it!'

And Sive is like, 'She's open! She's open!'

Joanne shapes up for the offload. But then the most amazing thing happens. Two Welsh players go to cover the move. But Joanne just turns her wrist one-hundred-and-whatever degrees. This time, the ball doesn't pop out of her hand and knock tea all over some dude's crotch. This time, it sticks to her hand like glue.

And suddenly there isn't a player between her and the posts. She takes the ball in both hands and she runs like the proverbial clappers, covering pretty much half the pitch, before ducking below the capital H to ground the ball. Me and Sive end up going absolutely ape-shit.

Nadine adds the grappa and breath mints and we're suddenly a point ahead with three minutes to go and I know we're not going to lose it from there.

The final whistle goes and Sive just hugs me.

She's there, 'Okay, I'm sorry,' meaning sorry for having a pop at me for spending so much time teaching the dummy offload.

I'm there, 'Hey, you're a forward – it's understandable that you forget sometimes that, even in the age of seventeen-stone centres, it's still a game of skill,' and – in all fairness to her – she laughs.

We walk out onto the pitch and we hug each and every one of our players. We proved against France that we could come from behind to win and we proved against Wales that we can win an ugly war.

It's an unbelievable feeling. And it lasts about as long as it takes me to get back to the dressing-room and switch on my mobile phone. And that's when I see the message from Kennet.

Well, it's the video attachment that gets my actual attention. It's me – and it's *clearly* me – in the Thomond Bor in Cork, with my orse, taunting a group of Munster fans.

There's, like, a text with it.

It's like, 'You must think I was b . . . b . . . b . . . b . . . borden yesterdee, Rosser.'

I'm not saying he stutters in the text – that's just the voice that I read it in.

He goes, 'You must think I was b . . . b . . . b . . . b . . . borden yesterdee, Rosser. Of course I knew what I was apposed to be c . . . c . . . c . . . collecting. I did what you said, but. I toawult S . . . S . . . S . . . Sudeka that it was lifted ourra the keer. It's mower than one fabour you're godda be doing for me, Rosser. Ine soddy to teddle you this – but your arse is m . . . m . . . m . . . m . . . m . . . m . . . m . . . moyen.'

'Fock,' I think. 'Just . . . fock.'

9.

Prop Friction

It's, like, half-seven in the morning when my phone rings, dragging me out of a deep sleep. I check my caller ID and it ends up being – yeah, no – Sive. I answer and I'm like, 'Hey.'

But Sive just goes, 'What would you think of the idea of moving Nadine to the second row?'

I actually laugh as I'm rubbing the sleep from my eyes.

I'm there, 'No "hello", Sive? No "good morning", no?'

She goes, 'I know we'd lose her pace on the wing, but she's a better jumper than either of our two second rows.'

'Have you slept at all?'

'What?'

'In other words, have you been up all night – thinking about rugby?'

'Not *all* night, no.'

'Most of it?'

'I keep thinking about our lineout. It's still not right.'

'Sive, we didn't lose *any* of our lineouts against Wales.'

'We didn't win any of theirs either.'

That's actually true.

'Okay, let's talk to Nadine later and see how she feels about it.'

'How do you think the front row did?'

I laugh. I'm like, 'What?'

She goes, 'Do you think Heather Hobson is better at tighthead or hooker?'

'Sive, we won – you can let it go now.'

'I think I'm going to watch the match again – and just focus on what Heather and Hannah did.'

Jesus, I thought I was bad in terms of thinking about rugby twenty-four-seven.

I'm there, 'Sive, do you even *have* an off switch?'

And that's when she says *the* most random thing to me. She goes, 'You wouldn't understand, Ross – you're a man.'

I'm like, 'What does being a man have to do with anything?'

'Because women have to work twice as hard as you just to get half the credit. See you at training.'

She hangs up and I think no more of it as I sort of, like, drift off to sleep again. It's, like, mid-term, so I don't have to bring the kids to school this morning. About half an hour later, I'm awoken again, this time by the sound of tyres crunching on the gravel outside. I throw back the duvet, stand up from my mattress and make my way over to the window of the tower. I see K . . . K . . . K . . . K . . . Kennet getting out of the limo in his driver's uniform.

I stort banging on the window, shouting, 'KENNET! KENNET! FOCKING KENNET!' but either he doesn't hear me or he pretends *not* to? He walks up to the front door and rings the bell.

I throw on my chinos, step into my Dubes, then I peg it down the spiral staircase, while at the same time pulling my Ireland training top over my head. I race through the study and into the hallway, where Kennet is standing with a shocked-looking Sorcha and an even more shocked-looking Fionn.

Sorcha's going, 'I can't believe what I'm hearing. I actually can't believe –'

Fionn turns and looks at me. He's there, 'It's like a focking nightmare.'

Kennet's like, 'I thought yous deseerbed to know the tr . . . tr . . . tr . . . tr . . . tr . . . troot.'

I'm there, 'Goys, I can explain everything.'

Sorcha looks at me for the first time. She goes, '*You* can? What are you talking about, Ross?'

I'm like, 'Er, I don't know – what are *you* talking about?'

She goes, 'Someone stole the CCTV tape from Kennet's cor.'

I'm there, 'What?'

He's like, 'For what it's woort, I feel t . . . t . . . t . . . t . . . teddible about it, Ministodder.'

She goes, 'Tell me again what *actually* happened?'

'I puddled into a petroddle station just outside T . . . T . . . T . . . T . . . Tipper Dairy Towun. I fiddled up the tank, then I weddent insoyut to p . . . p . . . p . . . p . . . p . . . pay. I musta leapt the doe-er unlocked.'

'What,' Sorcha goes, 'and someone stole the video cassette?'

He's there, 'I leapt it odden the fruddent passenger seat. When I came back, the doe-er was woyid opent and the t . . . t . . . tape was – like I says to you – g . . . g . . . g . . . g . . . g . . . g . . . g . . . godden.'

Fionn sits down on the stairs, looking totally defeated. He goes, 'That's it, then. It's over.'

Kennet's there, 'I feel teddible g . . . g . . . g . . . giddlety, so I do.'

Sorcha's like, 'It's not your fault, Kennet. It's such a random thing to steal, though.'

'It was probably just kids,' I go.

Sorcha's there, 'Kids would *hordly* know what a video cassette was, Ross. I just don't understand why someone would want to steal *that* of all things.'

'It's a genuine m . . . m . . . m . . . mystoddy,' Kennet goes.

Fionn storts – oh, Jesus Christ – crying his eyes out.

Sorcha's there, 'Come on, Fionn. It's like I said to the Taoiseach the other day when it looked like the withdrawal talks were about to break down without a deal, there was never a night or a problem that could defeat sunrise or hope. Someone said that – it might have been Orchbishop Desmond Tutu.'

He stands up and goes, 'No, Sorcha. It's finished. *I'm* finished. I'm going to go and wake Hillary,' and he walks up the stairs, looking like – yeah, no – a beaten man.

Sorcha shouts after him. She's like, 'I won't give up, Fionn, even if you do,' but she gets nothing back. Then she turns to Kennet and she's like, 'We'd better go. The next round of negotiations are due to stort at nine.'

She heads for the door and he goes, 'I'll foddy you out, Ministodder – Ine joost wanton a w . . . w . . . w . . . w . . . woort wit yisser husbaddened hee-or.'

Out she goes and I'm like, 'Okay, how much do you want for the tape?'

'Muddy?' he goes. 'Ine not arthur m . . . m . . . muddy, Rosser. Doatunt insudult me.'

I'm there, 'So what *do* you want?' feeling like I already *know* the answer?

He sort of, like, chuckles to himself. Yeah, no, he's always dreamt of having this kind of power over me.

He goes, 'You'd a good w . . . w . . . w . . . w . . . w . . . widden the utter neet – beat Wayults, was it?'

I'm like, '*In* Cordiff, yeah.'

'Ch . . . Ch . . . Ch . . . Cheerdles is veddy proud of you, so he is. Says you might eeben widden the Gradden Sladdum.'

'We're not getting ahead of ourselves. At the moment, we're very much taking things one match at a time. Italy are next up and they're nobody's pushovers.'

Okay, I've no idea why I'm suddenly talking to him like he's Gavin Cummiskey looking for quotes. It's possibly nerves because, deep down, I *know* what's coming?

He goes, 'Ch . . . Ch . . . Ch . . . Cheerdles says if you delibber the Gradden Sladdum, the wordled'll be yisser oyster. You could eddend up as peert of the L . . . L . . . L . . . Leddenster serrup.'

I'm there, 'Is that what people are saying behind the scenes?'

'That's accorton to your auld fedda,' he goes. 'Of course, nud of that will happen if it ebber cubs out that you took yisser eerse out in p . . . p . . . p . . . public. You couldn't stay on as the Coach of the Arelunt wibben's tee-um if thee knew that you exposed yisser self.'

I'm there, 'I didn't expose myself. I flashed my orse – big difference.'

'But getting cadencelled would be the least of yisser woodies, Rosser. You let some wooden else take the b . . . b . . . b . . . blayum for you. That's veddy seerdious. That's peerveerton the cowurse of j . . . j . . . j . . . justice. Thrust me – I've severdoddle convictions for it. You're thalken about jaiyult toyum for that, Rosser. You could get banged up for t . . . t . . . t . . . t . . . two or tree yee-or.'

'They won't send me to prison. I went to a good school.'

'You wanth to take that ch . . . ch . . . chaddence?'

'What the fock do you want, you focking scummer?'

'I wanth that young fedda of yooers back from Amedica and back with eer Shadden.'

'Shadden's with someone else – namely, Peadar.'

He chuckles to himself.

He's there, 'Yeah, I belieb you paid them a visit – and he b . . . b . . . b . . . b . . . bathored yous.'

'He didn't batter me,' I go. 'I hid up a tree.'

'Doatunt woody. I'll squeer him off. She's oately using him to m . . . m . . . m . . . m . . . make Ronan jeadous in addyhow. He belogs back hee-or, Rosser – wirr his woyuf and ch . . . ch . . . ch . . . ch . . . choyult.'

I'm there, 'And if I say no? What, you'll send the video to Sorcha?'

'Foget about S . . . S . . . S . . . S . . . Sudeka,' he goes. 'I'll sent it to the Oawult Biddle.'

There's something different about Sive. I can't put my finger on it immediately, but – yeah, no – there's something definitely, definitely different.

'Holy shit,' I suddenly blurt out – we're in, like, the gym in Energia Pork. 'Your shoulder.'

Yeah, no, the strapping has gone.

I'm like, 'When did this happen?'

She goes, 'This morning.'

'You never said.'

'I had an appointment at the hospital. I didn't want to get my hopes up.'

'And?'

'And what?'

'How do you feel in terms of maybe playing against, I don't know, maybe not Italy but hopefully Scotland?'

'I don't know. I suppose I haven't really tested it yet.'

'Well, what are you waiting for? Let's do it!'

So we tip over to the weight bench and she lies down on it.

I'm like, 'Okay, how much do you want?'

She goes, 'Give me eighty kilos.'

Jesus.

I'm there, 'Are you sure?' because I'd struggle to bench-press eighty kilos and I'm not coming back from a serious shoulder injury.

She goes, 'Give me eighty, Ross.'

I'm like, 'Fair enough,' because one thing you'd have to say about Sive is that she has her own mind.

I've never really liked that in a woman but it's definitely *growing* on me?

I load eighty kilos onto the bor and I give it to her. She lowers it down onto her chest. She takes two or three quick breaths, then extends her two orms, at the same time making a noise that's like, 'Eeeuuunnnggghhh!!!'

I'm there, 'Are you okay?' with my two hands poised to take the thing off her.

Except she goes, 'Don't touch it! It's fine!'

I'm like, 'Are you sure?'

She lowers the bor back to her chest and blows a long breath out. Then she lifts again. She seems to find it easier the second time because she storts then having a conversation with me.

'So I was thinking,' she goes, 'that maybe we'll leave Nadine on the wing on Friday night.'

I'm like, 'Er, right.'

'I think we'd miss her pace. It's our big game-changer, isn't it?'

'Yeah, no, cool.'

'Plus, I've been looking at the Italian second rows,' she goes, 'and I think we're more than capable of stealing lineout ball from them. How many's that I've done now?'

I'm like, 'Seven. This is eight.'

'I'll do ten, okay? Eeeuuunnnggghhh!!!'

It's at that exact point that the players stort arriving for training. Grainne Hutton and Joanne Wassell are the first through the door. When they see her with the bor bell, you can actually hear their excitement rise.

Grainne is like, 'Go on, girl! GO ON, GIRL!'

God, I love the Cork accent.

Joanne shouts over her shoulder, 'Lads, lads – look at this!' and the next thing the Skeldon twins walk in and their eyes go wide.

They're like, 'Whoa!'

'Nine,' Sive goes, taking it onto her chest for the last time. 'And – EEEUUUNNNGGGHHH!!! – ten!'

I take the bor off her and the four of them cheer, which brings Heather Hobson and Hannah Fox running into the room.

'What hoppened?' Heather goes.

Grainne's like, 'Sive is back – that's what happened, like.'

Sive sits up, rubbing her shoulder.

I'm there, 'Well?'

She just shakes her head.

I'm like, 'Sore?'

She goes, 'Definitely not ready for full-contact training – not yet.'

'What abite Scotland?' Heather goes. 'Toy soyn?'

Sive goes, 'I don't know yet. We'll see,' and she stands up. 'Okay, let's get outside and train.'

I'm there, 'Yeah, I'll see you out there. I have to make a quick phone call,' and – yeah, no – it just so happens to be the most difficult phone call I've ever had to make in my life – and that includes the time I had to ring Sorcha in the jacks at a Mount Anville Past Pupils Association luncheon and tell her that Sybil Mulcahy had turned up in the Shelbourne in the same Safiyaa crêpe jumpsuit.

He answers on the third ring. He goes, 'Howiya, Rosser?'

I'm like, 'All is good in the hood, Ro. All is good in the hood.'

He's there, 'Yous beat Wayults!'

And I go, 'Yeah, no, thanks for your text. How are things, em, Stateside?'

He's like, 'Unbeliebable, Rosser.'

I'm there, 'Oh, really?' trying to hide my disappointment.

He's there, 'Like yisser self, we'd a big resuddult last week. Do you membor I mentioned the Dearborden Robbedy case to you?'

'Of course I do.'

I don't. I've no idea what the fock he's talking about.

He's like, 'The three of them is arthur being released, Rosser, and

313

they're thalken about brigging cheerges against the cops what
addested them.'

I'm there, 'That's great news. And remind me, which side are you
on again?'

'The feddas what was wrongly convicted – fitted up, Rosser.'

'Yeah, no, I should have known it was the opposite side to the cops.'

'Doorty racist bastards, Rosser.'

'I'm delighted for you.'

'Hazel says thee wouldn't hab had their convictshiddens over-
toordened if it wadn't for me.'

'Again, I'm going to say fair focks. But at the same time –'

'What?'

'I'm wondering was I being unfair to you, Ro?'

'What are you thalken about?'

'You know, when I talked you into going to the States in the first
place. And then staying over there when you've got, like, a wife and
kid at home.'

'I thought you said that Shadden was with suddem cage-fighther?'

'The word I'm hearing is that it's on the rocks.'

'Accorton to Nudger, she's arthur moobin him in. He said yous
weddent out to thry to skeer him off and he kicked the Jaysusin' shit
out of you.'

'He didn't kick the shit out of me – but that's only because he
couldn't catch me and I'm good at climbing. Anyway, I'm just saying that – yeah, no – maybe you should come home after all.'

'Are you seerdious?'

'I think this is where you belong.'

'But Ine doing reedy weddle oaber hee-or, Rosser. Ine apposed to
be steerting in Heervord in Septembor. They're arthur gibbon me
a lubbly appeertment on the Upper East Soyut.'

'What's a lovely aportment on the Upper East Side – compared
to your daughter's happiness?'

He's there, 'Soddy?'

Okay, I officially hate myself.

I'm there, 'I'm just making the point, Ro, that Rihanna-Brogan
misses you. It's killing her not having you around.'

He goes, 'You were the wood who said she'd get used to it. You were the wood who said childorden adjust.'

'I know what I said – but maybe I was wrong. It sounds like you're doing amazing over there, Ro, in terms of work. But how do you feel about – I'm just going to come out and say it – another man raising your daughter as his own?'

'You're arthur saying that Shadden and that cage-fighter sham was on the rocks.'

'Yeah, no, it is, but there's bound to be others. Shadden's a focking slapper, Ro. And – much as it pains me to say it – maybe your place is with her.'

He's like, 'Reet,' and I can hear the sudden confusion in the voice. I'm there, 'I know it's a lot to take in.'

'It's joost you're arthur saying the exact opposite of what you and Edika have been tedding me for the last yee-or.'

'I know.'

'You were the wooden said to cub hee-or instead of taking the appredinticeship with Heddessy.'

'I know what I said, Ro.'

'And now you've chayunged your moyunt?'

'In a nutshell, yeah.'

He sighs.

He goes, 'I doatunt know *what* to do, Rosser.'

And I'm there, 'Come home, Ro. Come home for good.'

The old dear asks me what I think and I tell her I'm no kind of judge. I know fock-all about music – less *than* – never mind jazz.

She's like, 'What do *you* think, Honor?'

'Oh! My God!' she goes. 'I absolutely *love* them?'

Yeah, no, we're sitting in the, I don't know, ballroom in the Áras and we're listening to this band – four dudes, we're talking one on the double bass, we're talking one on the piano, we're talking one on the drums and we're talking one on the saxophone – and the old dear is basically X Factoring them, trying to decide if they're going to be her wedding band.

I'm like, 'What's that one even called?'

'It's *The Sheik of Araby*,' the old dear goes. 'Your father loves this kind of music, Ross. Duke Ellington. Cab Calloway. Fats Waller.'

I'm there, 'Yeah, no, now you're just naming bands I've never heard of.'

She goes, 'I want a wedding at which people dance the Chorleston. I adore the Chorleston.'

Honor's like, 'Oh my God, so do I!'

The old dear suddenly perks up. She goes, 'You know the Chorleston?'

And Honor's like, 'Er, *yeah*? So does Dad! We learned it when we entered the Strictly Mount Anville dancing competition!'

The old dear stands up and asks the band if they know anything by Count Basie. The dude on the piano goes, 'Of course – what do you want?'

She's like, 'My husband's favourite is "Alright, Okay, You Win".'

'No problem,' the dude goes, then the band – I don't know – *strikes up* a new tune and the old dear grabs Honor by the hand and pulls her to her feet.

Honor laughs as the old dear drags her into the middle of the floor, then the two of them stort – yeah, no – doing the Chorleston.

'Oh my God,' Honor goes, 'you're an *amazing* dancer!'

And the old dear is like, 'You're not so bad yourself! Tell me, does your boyfriend dance – the one who wrote the song for you?'

'Er, he's not my *boyfriend* any more?' Honor goes. 'Remember? I'm back with Reese. He's, like, a *rugby* player?'

'Well,' I make sure to go, 'he's not *really*, is he?' because the focker has served his purpose. He's managed to clear Adam off the scene and now he can fock off as far as I'm concerned. 'He's, like, a sub on the Senior Cup team – as in, I'd be shocked if he sees any game time this year, what with him still being in Transition Year.'

'Oh! My God!' Honor goes – this is while her and the old dear are still dancing, by the way, 'did I not tell you? The goy who usually plays number ten – he's called, like, Morcus something-or-other – he got, like, injured? And Reese has been called up for the semi-final against Gonzaga.'

I'm like, 'Seriously?' hating him, yet at the same time respecting him as a fellow kicker who was way ahead of his time in terms of his development.

'He's going to be the youngest player ever to play Leinster Schools Senior Cup for Michael's.'

'I said fair focks, Honor – what more do you want from me?'

All of a sudden, the old dear stretches out her hand in my direction and goes, 'Come on, Ross, your turn!'

And I'm like, 'No, you're grand.'

She's there, 'I want to dance with my bridesman – come on,' and she sort of, like, embarrasses me into getting up. Honor sits down while me and the old dear – yeah, no – Chorleston our way around the floor, the steps coming back to me unbelievably quickly.

'Well, you can really move!' she goes.

I'm there, 'Yeah, no, thanks.'

She goes, 'I shouldn't be surprised, of course. You had wonderful footwork as a rugby player.'

I'm like, 'Yeah, no, that's a nice thing for me to hear.'

The woman doesn't know shit about the game, but I'm a sucker for a compliment.

I'm there, 'I'll take it – and any more that are going.'

She smiles at me.

I'm like, 'So how are you feeling?'

She goes, 'Oh, good – mostly. I think it's helped having this wedding to focus on.'

'Yeah, no, I'm glad to hear it.'

'Gosh, you really are *terribly* handsome, Ross.'

'Am I?'

'Yes – and getting more so with age.'

It might be whatever medication she's on – but, again, I love a boost to the old confidence.

I dance her twice around the room, then all of a sudden I feel a hand on my shoulder and a voice goes, 'Do you mind if I cut in?'

It's the old man.

I laugh. I'm like, 'Yeah, no, she's all yours,' and I hand her over to him.

'"Alright, Okay, You Win"!' he goes. 'It's my absolute favourite!'

She's like, 'Yes, that's why I asked for it.'

'You remembered!'

'Of course I remembered!'

All of a sudden, I feel Honor's hand in mine.

'Come on, Dad,' she goes, 'let's see if the winners of the 2016 Goatstown Glitterball still have the old magic.'

So then we stort Chorlestoning next to the old pair and the band stort the song all over again. I'm not going to get all sentimental here – I'm just going to say that it's nice and leave it at that.

He goes, 'Oh, there's nothing like a bit of music and dance to blow away the cobwebs after another long day telling Monsieur Juncker and his colleagues to wind their bloody well necks in!'

The old dear's like, 'The talks aren't going well, Chorles?'

'No, they're absolutely adamant that, as port of the deal, we agree to pay back all of the money we borrowed in 2010!'

'Who the hell do they think are, Chorles?'

'On top of that, Ross, I've got *your* pals, Messers Varadkar and Mortin, demanding – *demanding*, no less! – that the Dáil be recalled to discuss everything from the withdrawal talks, to the investigation into the burning of Leinster House, to the extent of Russia's involvement in the Malingrad project!'

'What business is it of theirs?' the old dear goes. 'The bloody nerve of these people.'

'My thoughts precisely, Fionnuala! By the way, Ross, Hennessy has persuaded me to have one of these famous *stag* do's!'

I laugh – no choice in the matter.

I'm there, '*You're* having a stag? You have *got* to be shitting me!'

'No, it's just a few of the chaps, Ross, from the porliamentary porty and from Portmornock! We've decided to go to Glasgow for Ireland brackets women versus Scotland brackets women next week! Oh, and you'll never guess who's flying in for it! Only young Ronan!'

'What, my Ronan!'

'Yes, *your* Ronan! Correct answer! The selfsame chap!'

'What, he's coming all this way just for your stag?'

'Well, *entre nous*, Ross – pordon the French – I think poor Ronan is still a tad homesick!'

'Why do you say that?'

'Well, Kennet has mentioned – *in* dispatches – that he and Shadden have been talking on the phone! Kennet is leaning towards the view that young Ronan is in the process of – quote-unquote – healing the breach!'

'Oh my God!' Honor goes, obviously delighted by this news. 'Oh! My actual! God!'

The old man's there, 'Well, let's not get our hopes up yet, eh? But it does look to me like Ronan might be about to end his exile and come home!'

I'm there, 'Are you absolutely sure about this?'

Sive goes, 'I said I was sure, didn't I?'

I'm like, 'Hey, I'm just double-checking, okay?'

Yeah, no, it's half-time and we're, like, 12–0 up against Italy. It's, like, a manky night in Donnybook. It's been pissing rain since about six o'clock this morning and you can sense from the crowd that they're waiting for us to get the next score to kill the game, so they can head to Orthur Mayne's or McCloskeys to dry off.

But we have a problem to deal with, because Hannah Fox banged heads with Angelica Durante, the Italian blindside flanker, just before the half-time whistle. And, while she insists that she's fine to continue, she's asking Megan Barrett if she's interested in going to see the Colosseum tomorrow and it's straight away obvious that the woman thinks she's in Rome.

I'm thinking of different ways we might reshuffle the pack, with Hannah in no fit state to continue. Then Sive says she's going to replace her herself – as in, she's going to play hooker, even though she's a number eight.

I'm there, 'The only reason I'm sounding Scooby Dubious, Sive, is because you've only had, like, one contact session in training and that was, what, yesterday?'

The thing I don't mention is that I thought she was being overly cautious, trying to protect the shoulder, which is understandable.

She goes, 'I have to test it some time.'

Heather is looking at her – yeah, no, I think it's a word – but *doubtfully?*

I'm there, 'It's just the Italian pack is the heaviest in the Six Nations, Sive. If you want to test the shoulder, you're probably better off waiting until Scotland next weekend.'

'Yeah,' she goes, 'there's literally nothing *you* can teach *me* about forward play, Ross – okay?'

'I don't know about that. I actually *played* hooker –'

'For who?'

'It was for, em, Seapoint. In Division 2B of the All Ireland League.'

'There's a big difference between playing for Seapoint and playing for Ireland.'

I'm not going to orgue with that. One of *my* famous moves was to eat, like, a lasagne about an hour before kick-off. Then, just as we were about to engage for the scrum, I'd put two fingers down my throat and throw up all over the shirt of the opposition number two. It would totally fock with his head. Of course, you'd get away with that on a Sunday afternoon in Bruff, but not on a Friday night in Donnybrook.

I'm like, 'Fair enough, Sive, if you think –'

She goes, 'I *do* think,' and that's the end of the orgument.

So out we trot for the second half. And – yeah, no – it's still lashing down. As Father Fehily used to say, it's the kind of rain that'd make you think about going out and gathering two of every animal.

I take my seat. Behind me in the stand, I can hear the old man going, 'COME ON, LADIES! LET'S PUT THIS ONE TO BED AND LET US ALL GET TO DOHENY & NESBITT'S!'

I turn around and look at him. He's sitting with – yeah, no – Verner Ryan, the two of them in their matching camel-hair coats and wanker hats, guffawing away. Honor and Reese are sitting two rows in front of them under an umbrella. Honor gives me a wave and I wave back.

The second half gets under way. It's, like, sixty seconds old when we're awarded a scrum for a forward pass by the Italian centre, Annamaria Bonfantini.

And that's when the match suddenly turns.

Grainne Hutton puts the ball in, then runs around to the back of the scrum and waits for it to come out again. Except it *doesn't*? The scrum goes down and the referee signals for a penalty against us.

When the players get up off the ground, I can see Sive, clutching her shoulder and cursing herself.

'Fock!' I go.

The Italian number ten, Flamini Sabatino, kicks the penalty and I end up getting this horrible feeling of – I want to say – *forbodery*?

Ten minutes later, the Italians are awarded a scrum. This time, it's, like, Rachel Skeldon who plays the forward pass to Louise, and, though Rachel orgues the point with the referee for a good, like, sixty seconds, even jabbing her finger in his chest, the decision stands.

Again, we get penalized. I don't know what it's for. All I know is that it's Sive's fault again because she roars, 'FOOOOOOCK!' and you can hear it echo around what is now a very quiet Energia Pork.

Flamini Sabatino nails the kick and suddenly it's, like, a one-score game.

I know I should make a change at this point, but I *don't*? It's like I'm, I don't know, frozen or some shit.

'Dad!' I hear Honor, behind me, go.

I turn around and she's standing there with Reese, under her – like I said – umbrella.

She goes, 'We're going to head off, okay?'

I'm like, 'Are you not staying until the end? We've got our backs to the wall here.'

'No, we're getting soaked. And Reese has to be up early for kicking practice tomorrow.'

He goes, 'Important match on Monday,' and he says it in a way that implies that this one *isn't* important?

I'm like, 'Yeah, good luck in the semi-final,' although I obviously don't mean it. I hope Gonzaga kick the focking shit out of them.

He puts his orm around Honor's shoulder, then gives me a wink – the cocky focker – and goes, 'I promised this one I'd score a try for her.'

This one? I feel like nearly dragging him over that advertising hoarding and beating him into a thirty-year coma. But then I hear a whistle and I realize that Sive has given away a third penalty.

'Dude,' he has the actual balls to say to me, 'your hooker is going to cost you the match here,' and then off he struts with his big fock-ing Michael's orm around my daughter's waist.

Flamini Sabatino does her thing and suddenly the Italians are only, like, three points behind and the Grand Slam is under threat.

I hear the old man going, 'TAKE OFF GREEN NUMBER TWO! SHE'S A BLOODY WELL LIABILITY!'

There's, like, three minutes left when Marta Cantore, the Italian outside-centre, goes on this, like, mazy run, beating four Irish play-ers to put the ball down under the posts. Suddenly, you could hear, like, a pin drop in Donnybrook. It's, like, all of the energy has sud-denly been sucked out of – yeah, no – Energia Pork.

Flamini Sabatino adds the old jelly and ice cream and from being dead and buried at half-time, Italy are winning by four points with the time nearly up.

I'm like, 'COME ON, IRELAND! LET'S WIN THIS FOCK-ING RESTORT!'

I watch four or five heads go down, but then I notice the Skeldons walking around, telling the other players to cop themselves on, that we're still in a match here.

We *do* win the restort? Nadine leaps high in the air and catches the ball ahead of their full-back, Laura Caruso. And suddenly – for the first time in this Six Nations – we get a maul going. It's, like, pure animal effort that takes them from the Italian twenty-two to literally one metre from the try line. Then, suddenly, Sive has the ball in her hands and she puts her head down and crashes down over the line.

All hell breaks loose. I'm, like, running up and down the sideline with my hands above my head. And even above the roar of the crowd, I can hear the old man going, 'THREE THOUSAND SOULS WERE PRESENT, BUT IN YEARS TO COME, MANY THOUSANDS MORE WILL CLAIM TO HAVE BEEN HERE TO WITNESS THE MIRACLE OF DONNYBROOK!'

In my – I don't know – delirium, I end up not even seeing Nadine miss the conversion. It doesn't matter a fock anyway, because the referee blows the whistle and we've won by a point. The Six Nations and the Grand Slam are still very much on.

I run onto the pitch and I hug Megan Barrett, then Lisa McGuin, then Heather Hobson. I mean, what an effort by them. They're, like, applauding the Donnybrook crowd for coming out on the most miserable night of the year to see one of the most epic finishes to a rugby match that I've ever been involved in.

'Sive!' I go, calling out to my match-winner, who's morching off in the direction of the dressing-room.

I run over to her and I'm like, 'Sive! That was unbelievable!'

But she turns around to me, with a big, angry face on her, and goes, 'I shouldn't have been on the pitch.'

I'm like, 'What are you talking about? You just won the match for us!'

She's there, 'Yeah, right, after I nearly lost it for us,' because she's *such* a perfectionist. 'You should never have put me out there!'

I'm like, 'Er, you *insisted* on playing?'

'It doesn't matter,' she goes. 'You're the Head Coach. You're the one who's paid to make the hard decisions.'

One of the best finishes to a rugby match that he's seen in the last five years. That's Christian's assessment of it.

Even Oisinn goes, 'It took a lot of courage to leave Sive Keenan on the pitch when she was clearly a liability at scrum time,' and he's saying that as a former hooker himself.

I'm like, 'Yeah, no, thanks, Dude. I'll take it.'

Christian has invited us around to the – yeah, no – collab house in Harold's Cross because there's something that him and JP want to talk to us about.

I'm there, 'What is it, goys? How's the whole Malingrad thing going?'

JP's like, 'Yeah, good – we're going to be building a sweatshop in the Philippines, employing more than three thousand people, to fulfil all the orders for beds.'

I go, 'Do I high-five you now? Or is there more good news coming?'

'Well, actually,' Christian goes, 'that's not the reason we asked you here. We're worried about Fionn.'

Oh, for fock's sake.

'Fionn?' I go. 'What about him?'

JP's there, 'What about him? Jesus, Ross, he's been suspended from his job and he's on the sex offenders register.'

I'm like, 'Oh, er, that.'

'Yes,' he goes, 'that. I rang him yesterday and I've honestly never heard him so full of despair.'

'I don't know,' I go, 'I think he was pretty down that time when he had, like, cancer and shit?'

'Ross, he's worse than that now. He said that if it wasn't for little Hillary, he'd move away and try to start his life all over again.'

'There's a lot of countries he wouldn't be allowed into,' Oisinn goes, 'like the States – what with him being a registered sex offender.'

I'm there, 'A sex offender, though? He flashed his orse in a pub – that used to be hilarious, unless my memory is suddenly faulty. Focking Munster fans – that's who rang the Feds, I'm guessing.'

'But he *didn't* flash his orse in the pub,' Christian goes. 'He wasn't even *in* Cork that day.'

JP goes, 'I'm just going to come out and say it. I'm worried about him. About what he might do. We need to keep a close eye on him – especially you, Ross.'

I'm like, 'Me? Why me specifically?'

'Er, you live under the same roof as him, don't you?'

'Well, technically, no. I live in the tower, which has its *own* roof?'

'You know what I mean. Ross, I'm serious. He's in a bad way. I think he could end up doing something really stupid.'

'Principal of Castlerock *was* his dream job,' Oisinn goes. 'And all the things he was going to do. Reintroduce rugby.'

I'm there, 'I think Blackrock would have been too strong for them this year. By the way, did anyone hear how Michael's got on against Gonzaga today?' trying to subtly change the subject. 'Honor's boyfriend was playing for them.'

'They won,' Christian goes. 'They're into the final.'

I'm like, 'Fock them – and fock him.'

'Anyway,' JP goes, 'just promise you'll keep a good eye on Fionn. He's usually pretty strong – but there's no telling how being labelled a sex offender is going to affect him in the future.'

I'm being given the major, major guilts here and I have to say I am not enjoying it. I'm actually – believe it or not – relieved when Lychee, Christian's gorgeous-looking moron of a girlfriend, walks into the room and goes, 'Oh my God, you remember Liosa's video where she shares her sandwich with that homeless man and his dog? It's got, like, five hundred thousand views on TikTok! She's going to, like, monetize the shit out of it now.'

'Wow!' Christian goes – seriously, that's literally how he responds.

She's there, 'Oh, by the way, Chrissy, Darius wants to buy a pair of skis.'

I'm there, 'Chrissy! That will never stop being funny, by the way.'

Christian's like, 'Skis? What does he want skis for?'

'He says he's going to, like, ski off the roof of the house. I know – so random, right? It's just that his followers want him to do, like, more and more extreme stuff?'

'Skiing off the roof!' Christian goes. 'That's pretty extreme alright.'

She's there, 'So can he put the skis on, like, your credit cord?'

And Christian – I swear to fock – just goes, 'Yeah, no worries.'

I'm there, 'You're a focking mug, Christian,' and I don't care what she thinks. 'You're being taken for a major ride.'

She just glowers at me.

'I'm going to the hospital,' she goes, 'to see Fernando.'

I laugh.

I'm there, 'Is he the dude with the daily vlog about how his teeth are rotting in his focking head?'

She's like, 'I'm not even going to give you the satisfaction of answering that question.'

'Why is he in hospital?' I go.

Christian's there, 'He developed septicaemia and his body went into toxic shock.'

She goes, 'Don't tell him anything, Chrissy.'

And it's at that exact moment that Lauren shows up. She

introduces herself – as is often the case – by screaming Christian's name and hammering on the door.

Christian's like, 'Shit – nobody answer that.'

Except it's too late because someone – quite possibly Darius, the focking daredevil – throws open the door to her and she's suddenly loose in the house, shouting, 'Christian? CHRISTIAN?'

I'm actually grinning to myself because Lauren is on the actual warpath and for once it has absolutely fock-all to do with me – as far as I know anyway.

She's going, 'CHRISTIAN? CHRISTIAN, WHERE THE FOCK ARE YOU?'

She steps into the kitchen, where we're all sitting around. Her bottom teeth are showing and she's got eyes like pool balls. It's the angriest I've seen her since the time I borrowed her video camera without asking and it ended up getting stolen from Sorcha's old pair's holiday home in Majorca and a video that she had on it of her having sex with Christian while dressed in the Princess Leia slave girl costume made it onto some porn website – might have even been one of the big ones.

She fixes Christian with a look and she says to him the exact same words she said to me back then. She's like, 'I am going to tear your focking head off!'

Lychee looks her up and down and – brave girl – goes, 'Chrissy, what the fock is she doing here?'

Lauren's like, 'Chrissy?'

And I'm there, 'That's what I said, Lauren. It's what she calls him. Focking ridiculous – the entire thing.'

Christian holds out his two hands, trying to calm the situation down. He's like, 'Lauren, what's wrong?'

'I'll tell you what's focking wrong,' she goes. 'Your focking girlfriend here posted a video of *my* son . . . *on* the internet . . . *without* my permission.'

I'm there, 'Is this the one of him lip-synching to Boris Johnson?'

She turns on *me* then. 'Will you stay the fock out of it?' she goes.

I'm there, 'Hey, I'm here as an observer for once.'

Lychee goes, 'The video has got, like, three hundred thousand Likes. He's, like, InstaFamous.'

Lauren's there, 'I don't focking want him to be InstaFamous – you focking vacuous, brain-dead bitch!'

Lychee turns to Christian and goes, 'Chrissy, are you going to let her talk to me like that?'

He is. He'd be focking mad to do anything else.

'My son,' Lauren goes, 'is not a plaything for your teenage girlfriend.'

'For your information,' Lychee goes, 'I'm twenty-two.'

'I don't care what your birth certificate says. My children are not extras in the movie of your life, whatever your focking name is.'

I'm like, 'Well said! Focking millennials.'

'We are entitled to our privacy. We don't want to see ourselves splashed all over the internet.'

I'm there, 'You said something very similar to me, Lauren, after your video camera was . . . actually, forget I spoke. Focus on the here and now.'

I'm staring through the window into the back gorden, where Darius – I notice – is in the process of setting himself on fire while someone else films it on their phone.

Lychee goes, 'Get the fock out of my house.'

And Lauren's there, 'What the fock kind of a place is this?' because – yeah, no – Darius's entire back is on fire and the dude who *was* holding the phone is now trying to put it out with a fire extinguisher.

'It's a collab house,' Lychee goes, 'you focking Boomer. We make content that people love and happen to want to watch.'

'Well,' Lauren goes, smiling to herself, 'enjoy it while you have it – because I'm going to get it closed down.'

Lychee's there, 'You can't get it closed down.'

And I'm like, 'Oh, yes, she can. If you think that, you obviously don't know who her old man is.'

'Who?' Lychee goes. 'Who's your dad?'

And it's Christian who ends up answering.

He's like, 'Hennessy,' with a definite note of, like, *fear* in his voice? 'Hennessy Coghlan-O'Hara . . .'

*

So – yeah, no – I'm sitting on the Aer Lingus flight to Glasgow and I'm listening to the old man talking in capital letters again.

He's going, 'HE HAS LED THIS IRELAND TEAM FROM THE STATUS OF PERENNIAL LOSERS TO THE THRESH-OLD OF GREATNESS – WOMEN OR NOT!'

I turn around to Sive, who's sitting beside me, and I go, 'I'm sorry about him. He's, em, very proud.'

He's still *going*, by the way?

He's there, 'EXCLAMATION MORK! EXCLAMATION MORK! EXCLAMATION MORK! I SHALL BE VERY SUR-PRISED IF ONE OR TWO CLUB SIDES – EITHER IN IRELAND OR FURTHER AFIELD – DON'T TRY TO ENTICE HIM AWAY WITH A VERY GENEROUS OFFER! I THINK IT WOULD BE VERY REMISS OF THE IRISH RUGBY FOOT-BALL UNION, AT THIS JUNCTURE, NOT TO DO EVERYTHING IN ITS POWERS TO NAIL DOWN HIS SER-VICES FOR THE FUTURE!'

I'm like, 'He's a dick. I'm sorry.'

And Sive just goes, 'So is mine, remember?'

'He's on his stag weekend – he's obviously shit-faced.'

All of a sudden, there's someone standing over my seat. I look up and it ends up being Kennet.

He's there, 'Can I've a quick w . . . w . . . w . . . w . . . w . . . w . . . w . . . word, Rosser?'

And I'm like, 'I don't know. A word from you is never quick, Ken-net. I think it's only an hour-long flight.'

'I *neeyut* to th . . . th . . . th . . . thalk to you,' he goes.

So I stand up and I follow him down to the – I don't know, I think it's called, like, a *galley*?

'Joost so you knows,' he goes, 'Ronan's arribin in G . . . G . . . G . . . G . . . G . . . G . . . Glasgow tomoddow.'

'Right.'

'And he woatunt be going back to Amedica.'

'Has he actually told you that?'

'Toawult Shadden. They're like the cheeks of me eerse,

Rosser – b . . . b . . . b . . . b . . . b . . . b . . . back togetter arthur all that shite, wha'!'

'And Peadar?'

'He's off the s . . . s . . . s . . . scee-in?'

'How can Ronan be sure?'

'You fooken eejit, Rosser – he was on the bleaten p . . . p . . . p . . . pay rowult!'

'You paid a man to have sex with your daughter?'

'How fooken d . . . d . . . d . . . d . . . deer you. I ditn't pay him a peddy. It was Heddessy hantled the muddy side of th . . . th . . . th . . . thigs.'

'So you got what you wanted – now give me the tape, you focking scumbag.'

'Be veddy keerful what you s . . . s . . . s . . . s . . . say to me, Rosser. I hab the vitheo on me phowun, beerd in moyunt. Alls I hab to do is show it to that b . . . b . . . b . . . b . . . b . . . b . . . b . . . bord that's sitting besoyut you. Exposing yissser howult in a fooken pooblic place – you'd be out the bleaten d . . . d . . . d . . . d . . . doe-er, Rosser, especially in the cuddent clibate.'

'So when do I *get* the tape?'

'Soon as he's b . . . b . . . b . . . back libbon in Aerlunt wit he's woyuf and thaughter – and he's f . . . f . . . f . . . f . . . f . . . forgotten all about this civoddle reets ast-me-boddicks.'

Off he walks, focking thrilled with himself. I hear him turn around to the old man and go, 'Will you hab a thrink T . . . T . . . T . . . T.. . Teashocked? It's apposed to be yisser st . . . st . . . st . . . st . . . st . . . stag.'

I hear Hennessy go, 'I don't understand what we're doing on a commercial flight when we could have taken the Government jet.'

And the old man's there, 'AS THE GREAT BERTIE AHERN DISCOVERED, IT PAYS TO STAY CONNECTED TO THE – INVERTED COMMAS – HOI POLLOI! FOR AS LONG AS YOU CAN STAND IT, OF COURSE!'

I tip back to my seat.

Sive is sitting there with her Rugby Tactics Book open on the tray table in front of her.

I'm like, 'Sorry about that. That's my son's father-in-law. He's a focking scumbag.'

She goes, 'What are we going to do about Tarja Andrews?'

Tarja Andrews is the Scottish outside-centre – yeah, no, she's been the player of the tournament so far.

I'm there, 'We get the Skeldons to double-team her – the same way that Drico and Dorce used to deal with Mathieu Bastareaud. One hits her – BANG! – and the other one takes the ball off her.'

'You think that'll work?' she goes.

I'm there, 'I'll talk to them at the team meeting. How do you feel about playing yourself?'

'I rushed back too quickly,' she goes.

'Look, everyone can have an off-day, Sive. I was the same when I came back from my famous rotator cuff injury. I was terrified of banjoing myself again.'

'I'm not ready.'

'What about the last match – against England?'

'Maybe. We'll see.'

It feels like me and Sive are finally a team. There's no doubt we've, like, gelled as a coaching portnership.

The captain announces that we've commenced our descent into Glasgow.

'HISTORY BECKONS!' the old man goes.

I'm actually shaking my head when someone suddenly appears at my elbow. I look up. It ends up being – yeah, no – Verner Ryan.

I'm like, 'Hey, how the hell are you?'

He goes, 'Just, em, apropos of what your father was talking about there – you heard him, I presume?'

'Half of focking Scotland heard him.'

'Well, just to let you know that your name *has* been mentioned in dispatches by, let's just say, several senior people within the Union.'

I notice Sive taking a sudden interest in this conversation.

I'm there, 'In terms of?'

'All I will say,' he goes, 'is that what you've done with this team hasn't escaped the attention of the powers-that-be. I don't think it will be long before you'll be joining the coaching staff of the *actual* Ireland team.'

I suddenly feel my stomach do a somersault. Shit the focking bed, how long have I waited for this moment?

I'm there, 'I'd be happy to talk to Joe Schmidt any time he wants. Obviously, the money side of things would have to be worked out in advance.'

He goes, 'Good luck tomorrow,' and off he focks.

I'm there, 'That was mad, wasn't it?' but Sive doesn't say shit to me. As a matter of fact, she ignores me for the rest of the flight. And even after we get off the plane, she walks on ahead of me, practically sprinting through the terminal to get away from me.

I eventually catch up with her at the *baggage* carousel?

I'm like, 'What's wrong?'

She's there, 'Nothing,' but I've been married long enough to know that when a woman says 'nothing', she often means the exact opposite.

'I never said I was going to stay in the job forever,' I go.

She's like, 'Whatever,' as she watches the bags stort to appear on the conveyor belt.

I'm there, 'I'm on, like, a career path, Sive. I want to coach hopefully Leinster one day – and that's not being disrespectful to Leo Cullen, who's obviously a huge hero to me.'

'Just forget about it, Ross, okay?'

'No, I won't forget about it. It's been, like, an honour to coach this team, Sive. It's been amazing working with this bunch of players. And you – you're incredible, especially in terms of your knowledge of the game. But I was always likely to move on. Like my old man said, there's bound to be interest in me from further afield. That's what comes with success. For instance, I'd be very shocked if the likes of Clermont Auvergne and Horlequins aren't sniffing around me.'

'I don't care who else is interested in you, Ross.'

'Then what's your basic problem? Why are you in an obvious snot with me?'

331

'I'm in an obvious snot with you because Verner said you might get to join the coaching staff of the *actual* Ireland team.'

'Yeah – so?'

'*We're* the actual Ireland team.'

'Yeah, no, what he meant by that was obviously the *men's* team?'

'Because they're the *actual* Ireland team – and we're, what, some poor relation?'

'Sive, he didn't mean that.'

'The ugly sister.'

'You're not ugly – any of you, in fairness to you.'

'You've seen how hard we train. You've seen how seriously we take ourselves as a team. You've seen the sacrifices we make to wear that green jersey. We're as much an Ireland team as any team of men.'

'When he said *actual* Ireland, what he meant –'

'I know what he meant – just as you knew what that asshole meant. My basic problem – as you call it – is that you didn't think enough of us to correct him.'

The atmosphere between us hasn't improved much by the time we reach Scotstoun Stadium, home of the famous Glasgow Warriors. I happen to mention that I've been here for one or two Pro 14 matches and that it looks totally different through sober eyes. But Sive tells me that she has zero interest in my no doubt hilarious stories and reminds me that we're here to do a job, even if it's not the job I really want to be doing.

I walk into the dressing-room and I give the players the talk – and I do it totally freestyle. Yeah, no, it ends up being one of those moments where I automatically know the right thing to say and I say it without having to even look at the notes I've made in my Rugby Tactics Book, except once when I forget the name of the Scottish full-back, who I happen to think is shit. Her name is Isolde Tate. Other than that, I end up just speaking from the hort.

I'm like, 'I am extremely proud of this team. I am extremely proud of what you have achieved. You – the Ireland team,' and as I'm saying it, I look at Sive. 'Because that's who you are. You're Ireland. You're not the Ireland *women's* team.'

'We *are* the Ireland women's team,' Sive goes.

And Heather's there, 'The fock is *he* on abite?'

I'm like, 'Yeah, no, you *are* the Ireland women's team, but you're also just Ireland – as in, like, *actual* Ireland?'

It's pretty stirring stuff alright.

I'm there, 'You're as much Ireland as the team of Stander, Sexton and Stockdale. You're as much Ireland as the team of Ringrose, Corbery and Lormour.'

'Sure, we know that, boy,' Grainne Hutton goes.

I'm there, 'I'm only saying it because not everyone knows it,' and I give Sive a long look.

Then I'm like, 'We are two matches away from doing something that is truly historic. But do *not* allow yourselves to stort thinking about that tonight. A Grand Slam is five matches, each of which is as individual as the fingers on your hand. Each presents its own unique set of challenges and each must be won in its own individual way. We saw that against Italy. You showed you had the mental strength to dig deep and win it at the death. To beat Scotland tonight, you'll likely have to show some other aspect of your character.

'The Skeldons – where are you? Which one is Rachel? Ah, Rachel – remember the plan we discussed at the team meeting last night for neutralizing the famous Tarja Andrews. Rachel, you smash her – and Louise, you take the ball from her. But, bear in mind, you have to be quick. You have to anticipate her receiving the ball in the split-second before the pass is made. Sive, over to you.'

Sive goes, 'Okay, is everyone clear on the new lineout codes?'

Em, *I'm* not? But then I'm not playing – I don't need to be.

The forwards are all like, 'Yeah, we know them.'

She looks at Heather, who's playing hooker tonight, and goes, 'Elspeth Fife likes to shit-talk the opposition front row – don't let her into your head. Jenna Weir on the right wing is their biggest threat to us. She's very quick. Most of their backs have slow hands, so sometimes Julie McLauchlan, their ten, will try to save time by throwing a long pass to Jenna, so be alert to the opportunity of an intercept. Okay, good luck everyone!' and then she shouts, 'Let's win this match!'

The players stand up and they troop out onto the pitch. As I follow them out of the dressing-room, I feel someone tug on my orm.

I'm there going, 'Sorry, there'll be plenty of time for autographs after the match,' but it's only when I turn my head that I see that it's Ronan.

He's like, 'Howiya, Rosser?'

I'm there, 'Ro! It's great to see you!' and I sort of, like, envelop him in a hug.

'Toyum for authorgraphs arthur the match,' he goes. 'You're some fooken tulip, Rosser.'

All I can do is just laugh.

I'm there, 'So where are you sitting?'

'The North Staddend,' he goes. 'With me grandda. And Heddessy. And about thoorty of their securdity geerds.'

'I hear you and Shadden are back together.'

'We're thalken abourrit. The cage-fighter sham is off the scee-un.'

'So you're not going back – to the States, I mean?'

He shakes his head.

I'm there, 'How did your boss take the news?'

'Habn't toawult her,' he goes. 'I'll rig her on Muddenday.'

I'm like, 'I'm sure she'll understand, Ro. Family has to come first and blah, blah, blah.'

He just nods but what he can't hide from me is the, like, *sadness* in his eyes?

He goes, 'Good luck in addyhow, Rosser – I'll see you arthur.'

I'm like, 'Yeah, no, I'll see you . . . *arthur.*'

Then I go and join Sive on the sideline.

I'm there, 'Good speech. I liked it.'

She's like, 'Thanks. You too. For saying what you said. I mean, you made a bit of a hames of it –'

'I didn't have a single note in front of me.'

'– but it's good that you said it.'

The match storts and the first half ends up being *not* a great advertisement for rugby. The two full-backs – Megan Barrett for us and Amanda Jeffries for them – spend a lot of time kicking the ball long to each other, which is what can happen in matches where no one wants to make a mistake.

'They're nervous,' I go.

And Sive's like, 'Yeah, I'm wondering did we put too much fear into them? This is the kind of game that suits Scotland more than us.'

The famous Tarja Andrews has only touched the ball twice and both times Rachel and Louise did a number on her – the Drico and Dorce one-two, although I'm not going to call it that any more. From now on, it's the Skeldon Double.

Nadine Delaney and Julie McLauchlan have each kicked two penalties and we go in at half-time with the scores tied at 6–6.

'What do you think?' Sive goes.

I'm there, 'I don't know – what do *you* think?'

'I think we just say fuck it.'

'In terms of?'

'In terms of the game plan. I think we've given the lads too much to think about.'

'Yeah, no, it's like they're frightened to express themselves.'

She's there, 'Maybe tell them –'

And I don't know why, but I'm like, 'No – *you* tell them, Sive.'

She goes, 'What?'

I'm there, 'Hey, it's your idea – and it's a great idea,' and – again – I haven't a clue why I'm saying it, 'but it doesn't make it any more great just because it comes out of *my* mouth?'

She just stares at me. This is going to sound possibly big-headed, but I genuinely think I'm one of the most amazing people she's ever met in her life.

Into the dressing-room we go. All of the players look at me. But I don't say shit.

Sive goes, 'Tear up the plan.'

They're all looking at each other as if to say, 'What?' and 'In terms of?'

She's like, 'Your only instruction for the second half – is to go out there and enjoy yourselves.'

And that's what ends up happening. We stort playing the free-flowing and – I want to say – *expansive* rugby that we all played when we were kids. And we're rewarded straight away when Joanne Wassell bursts through the Scottish midfield, sidesteps one player, then offloads the ball in the tackle to Rachel Skeldon, who puts the ball down beneath the posts. Nadine does the necessary with the boot.

Literally three minutes later, I watch Rachel and Louise perform the wraparound move that Sive showed them while I was away in the States. It totally bamboozles the Scottish defence, leaving a gaping hole, which Louise exploits to score our second try of the game – and, again, she makes the kick easy for Nadine.

Suddenly, a chorus of 'The Fields of Athenry' breaks out and I can hear my old man's voice above everyone else's, singing completely out of key.

Scotland are desperate now and they know they need a quick response. Julie McLauchlan has the ball in her hands right on the halfway line. She shapes up as if to kick the ball, but then she doesn't. She throws a long pass into the air. Sive grips my orm – I don't think she even realizes she's doing it – and she goes, 'Jenna Weir on the wing!'

But Rachel is alive to it. She leaps into the air – she has *some* focking springs – and manages to catch the ball with just the tips of her fingers. She lands, sticks the ball under her orm, then runs the entire length of the pitch, with Julie in hot pursuit, to score our third try and put the game to bed.

When the final whistle goes, all hell breaks loose. Sive runs onto the pitch and I look up into the stand, where Ronan gives me the two thumbs up and goes, 'Deadly buzz, Rosser!' even though he'd be mostly into soccer and Gaelic football.

By the time I make it onto the pitch, all of our players are standing in, like, a huddle, with their orms around each other's shoulders. And I can hear Sive's voice coming from the middle of the circle.

She's going, 'ENJOY THIS, LADS! BECAUSE YOU'VE EARNED IT! YOU'VE WORKED HARD FOR IT! IT'S ONE MORE VISIT TO THE WELL, OKAY?'

I'm walking around and around the outside of them, trying to find a way in. But there isn't a gap.

She goes, 'TUESDAY NIGHT IS THE START OF ANOTHER WEEK. ENGLAND AT THE END OF IT. WE GO AGAIN.'

And standing outside that circle, looking at the numbers on the backs of their jerseys, is the moment when the penny suddenly drops. This isn't like it was when I coached Andorra, or Pres Bray, or – yeah, no, they all count – the Facebook tag rugby team. It's not like the time when my heroics helped keep Seapoint Rugby Club in Division 2B of the All Ireland League.

The fact is that I'm a total and utter irrelevance within this set-up – and that's a hord thing for a man like me to have to admit. What this team has achieved has literally fock-all to do with me.

It's Sive. It was always, always her.

'A TITTY BOR?' the old man goes. 'I'M NOT GOING TO A TITTY BOR! I'M THE DEMOCRATICALLY ELECTED LEADER OF A SOVEREIGN STATE! I CAN'T BE SEEN IN A TITTY BOR!'

Yeah, no, he's sitting in a shopping trolley, by the way, with an L-plate hanging around his neck, and seven or eight of his mates from Portmormock are pushing it along the street. His security dudes are walking a few feet behind, exchanging looks, wondering at what point do they intervene.

The old man has a cigor the size of Tiger Roll's mickey clamped between his lips and he's absolutely shit-faced.

He's going, 'WHERE'S MY ATTORNEY GENERAL?'

And Hennessy – sucking the life out of a hip flask – goes, 'I'm here, Taoiseach!'

'KENNET HERE IS OF THE VIEW THAT WE SHOULD TAKE THIS PORTY TO ... WHAT DID YOU SAY THIS ESTABLISHMENT WAS CALLED, KENNET?'

'Lap of the Gods,' Kennet goes. 'It's on B ... B ... B ... B ... B ... B ... B ... B ... B ... B ... B ... Blythswood Squayer.'

The old man's there, 'WHAT'S MY LEGAL POSITION, HENNESSY?'

'I don't know about your *legal* position,' Hennessy goes, 'but I think the media would be far more interested in the fact that you've just put away forty ounces of dry-aged Belted Galloway beef!'

Everyone laughs. I notice that it's the members of the New Republic porliamentary porty who seem to find this the funniest.

'OKAY,' the old man goes. 'A TITTY BOR IT IS, THEN!' and they push the trolley onwards.

I'm about nine pints and five shots on the far side of shit-faced myself.

Ronan sidles up to me. He's there, 'You alreet, Rosser?'

I'm like, 'Yeah, no, a bit hammered. Can't drink like I used to.'

'Ah,' he goes, 'you're entitled to cedebrate. That was suddem performance in the second half.'

I feel this sudden urge to tell him the truth, that it had fock-all to do with me – we're talking none of it – but I end up just saying the same that I said to Sinéad Kissane after the final whistle: 'It was very much a team performance – and we've put ourselves in a good position now going into the England match.'

Except I obviously didn't slur my words as much when I was talking to Sinéad.

All of a sudden, focking Kennet storts going, 'Okay, wheer's my s . . . s . . . s . . . s . . . s . . . s . . . s . . . s . . . s . . . s . . . sudden-in-law?' and he comes over and throws a drunken orm around Ronan's shoulder. 'Reet, let's lay dowun the growunt roowults, will we? You're not to t . . . t . . . t . . . t . . . t . . . t . . . t . . . t . . . teddle Dordeen if I end up getting a blowie off a quare wooden. And I woatunt t . . . t . . . t . . . t . . . t . . . t . . . teddle Shadden if you do – are we agreeyut?'

I suddenly stop. I'm about to foocking vom.

Fyodor, the old man's Russian mate, puts his hand on my back and goes, 'Something is wrong? Is food poison perhaps?' and he laughs like this is somehow hilarious.

I'm like, 'Yeah, no, I'm going to definitely spew – you goys keep walking.'

Which they do, pushing my old man up the road and around the corner onto Blythswood Square.

I lean over, with one hand against the wall, and I empty the contents of my stomach onto the footpath – we're talking steak, we're talking chips, we're talking onion rings, we're talking beer. My Dubes end up taking a serious pebble-dashing.

When I'm finished, my face feels hot and my eyes sting. And that's when – yeah, no – my phone rings and I can see from the screen that it's, like, Erika. It's probably, I don't know, delight at seeing her name, even in my gee-eyed condition, that leads me to answer the phone.

I'm there, 'Hey, Gorgeous – are you and me all made up?'

She goes, 'You focking prick,' so I'm guessing the answer is no.

I'm like, 'What's wrong – as in, what have I done now?'

She goes, 'I was talking to Rihanna-Brogan earlier.'

I'm there, 'Oh yeah?'

'She told me her daddy is coming home – for good.'

'Yeah, no, him and Shadden had a chat and it seemed to do the job in terms of clearing the air between them.'

'She said you talked him into coming home.'

'*I* did? It's not ringing any bells for me, Erika.'

She ends up just roaring at me then. She's there, 'DON'T FOCK-ING LIE TO ME! WHAT THE FOCK DID YOU SAY TO HIM?'

'Okay,' I go, 'I told him to come home. I told him that where he belonged was in Ireland – with his wife, the focking slapper.'

'Why? After everything we focking did to get him away from Dad and Hennessy?'

'Kennet has something on me, Erika.'

'What?'

I'm there, 'A secret. About something I might have done in the distant past. It could destroy everything I've been working towards.'

She goes, 'For once in your focking life, Ross, will you own your focking mistakes?'

I decide that I can't listen to any more – don't want to, is *more* the case? – and I hang up on the girl.

Then I stagger to the door of Lap of the Gods. I see the shopping trolley porked against the wall outside. I pay the cover chorge and I head inside.

Jesus Christ, it's a scene of absolute mayhem. The first thing I see when I walk through the door is my old man getting a dance. There's a woman sitting on his lap – reverse cowgirl are two words I never expected to hear myself say to describe my old man's situation – but she's sort of, like, twerking away, with her back to him, and he's talking to her about – I shit you not – the EU withdrawal talks.

He's going, 'I said to Jean-Claude Juncker, "Luxembourg isn't even a bloody well country! It's got a population that's roughly approximate to that of Cork! How DARE you come here and presume to tell us how to run our country!"'

I look over at the bor and there's Ronan standing next to Hennessy, who has his orm wrapped snake-like around his shoulder. I watch Kennet grab a passing girl by the wrist, then he introduces her to Ronan. Hennessy whispers something into his ear and Ronan feasts his eyes on her – yeah, no – yum-yums and laughs.

And if I have to pinpoint the exact moment that changes everything for me, then that's it, right there.

I walk over to Ronan and I go, 'Ro, can I have a word?'

And he's like, 'Ine a bit busy at the moment, Rosser. This is . . . soddy, what did you say your name was, love?'

But she doesn't get an opportunity to answer because I grab Ronan by the scruff of his shirt and I drag him across the floor and outside into the air.

He's there, 'What's the stordee, Rosser? What's this about?'

I'm like, 'I want you to go back – to America.'

'What?'

'I want you to go back. And go to Horvord. And graduate. And work for the law firm. And never, ever have anything to do with my old man and Hennessy and the Tuite family again.'

'Jaysus, will you make up yisser moyunt, Rosser?'

'Kennet blackmailed me into persuading you to come home.'

'He blackmayult you? What's he hab on you?'

'It's a long story. Ro, I should have never talked you into coming back. Erika's right, I should have owned my own shit. But I'm owning it now.'

'But what about Shadden? She's arthur fidishing it wirrer fedda – the cage-fighter what bathored you and the boys.'

'Ro, Kennet was paying him to have sex with her.'

'Soddy?'

'It was all a ploy to try to get you home, Ronan – and it worked.'

'The doorty fooken –'

'Ro, go back to New York. Please. It's where you belong. Not here with these people who'll lead you down a bad path.'

I can tell from the set of his jaw that he knows I'm talking sense.

He nods his little head. He goes, 'Ine godda head for the airpowurt – see if there's a flight out foorst thig in the morden. Will you ted Tasha Ine soddy?'

I'm like, 'Who?'

'The boord I was about to get a daddence off. And give her this, will you?' and he goes to peel a fifty-pound note off his wad.

I'm like, 'Dude, don't – I'll look after that. Just get the fock out of here, okay?'

He stares at me for a long time, then he grabs me in a clinch and holds me tight.

He goes, 'I lub you, Rosser,' and it's probably the drink.

I'm there, 'I love you too, Ro.'

He hails a taxi then and off he goes into the night. I whip out my phone and I dial Sive's number.

She answers by going, 'What the hell?'

I'm like, 'Sive?'

'Ross, it's three o'clock in the morning.'

'Look, I have something to tell you all. Can you get the entire squad together?'

'When, now? How drunk are you?'

'No, not now – first thing in the morning. Actually, no, better make it midday – before we head to the airport.'

She's like, 'What's this about?'

I'm there, 'I'll explain it all tomorrow.' Then I hang up on her.

The next phone call is the hordest of all. I'm not expecting him to be awake. I'm thinking the phone is probably going to ring fifteen or twenty times before it's finally answered, which will give me a chance to decide what I'm going to say. Except he ends up answering straight away.

I'm there, 'Fionn, I have something to finally tell you – and you're not going to possibly like it.'

'You focking . . . ORSEHOLE!' he goes, which obviously throws me.

In the background, I can hear Sorcha going, 'Who is it? Is that *him*?'

I'm there, 'Fionn, I have a confession to make.'

He goes, 'I focking know, Ross.'

I'm like, 'Know what?'

He's there, 'I know it was you who took your orse out in the Thomond Bor!'

'Shit,' I go. 'How did you –'

He's there, 'Sorcha had a blazing row with her sister tonight.'

And I'm like, '*Sister?*' in the hope of getting a name out of him.

He goes, 'She told her the full story.'

I'm like, 'Dude, I'll get you your job back. I'll explain the entire thing to the hopefully Board of Management. I'll tell them that it was my orse.'

'You're going to be explaining it to more than just the Board of Management, Ross.'

'As in?'

'I rang the Gords tonight and I told them everything. They're going to want to interview you when you get home. And I hope you end up in focking jail.'

10.

Once Upon a Time in Donnybrook

They're already waiting for me in Conference Room Three in the Holiday Inn Glasgow, we're talking a group who I've come to know very well over the last, I don't know, six months. And they've no idea of what awaits them – the news that's about to rock their world.

Yeah, no, I'm looking around at this, like, wall of faces, all obviously wondering, what the fock?

I'm there, 'Where's Verner?'

And Sive goes, 'He's coming now. Ross, what's going on?'

I'm like, 'Let's wait until the dude gets here, will we?'

Ten seconds later, he walks through the door, going, 'I just saw your father, Ross, looking the worse for wear, being pushed back to his hotel in a shopping trolley!'

If he's expecting me to laugh along with him, he's disappointed.

I'm there, 'Verner, will you sit please down?' and I realize that I'm quite possibly still pissed.

Heather Hobson goes, 'What are woy doying harr – we're supposed to be in the urport in tee hours. Should we not be in our royms, pocking?'

I'm there, 'What I have to say, Heather, won't take long. And what I have to say is this. I've decided to resign my position as Head Coach of the Ireland women's rugby team – I think it's a word – *forthwithly?*'

All I can see in front of me are just, like, shocked faces. Then the questions stort coming at me. They're like, 'What?' and 'Why?' and 'What the fock?'

I'm there, 'It's a long story. It's probably enough to say that a secret from my distant past has come back to haunt me.'

'A secret?' Sive goes – and it's pretty clear that they all want details.

343

I'm there, 'The long and the short of it is that I took my orse out in the middle of the Thomond Bor in Cork – this was back in the day when that kind of thing was considered hilarious.'

'When *was* this?' Joanne Wassell goes – I think she's learned a lot from me in terms of the kind of things that a number ten should do on the pitch. 'As in, what year?'

I'm there, 'It was 2014. And, before you ask, I was there to watch the semi-final of the Heineken Cup.'

Of course, that just throws up even more questions, like, 'Why did you take your orse out?' and 'Why did you think people would find that funny?' and 'Was it not called the European Rugby Champions Cup in 2014?'

I'm like, 'No, that wasn't until the following year.'

Grainne Hutton – as Cork as they come – goes, 'Was that the year that Denis Hurley scored the try from the little chip over the top by Ronan O'Gara?'

And I'm there, 'No, I'm pretty sure that was against Clermont Auvergne the *previous* year?'

No one can say that I don't know my rugby – sex pest or not.

'So why did you do it?' Sive asks.

I'm there, 'Like I said, Sive, the world was a very different place back in those days. You could get away with saying a lot more and doing a lot more. My big mistake was that when I was arrested, I gave the Feds the name and address of one of my friends, and he – not me – ended up on the register of sex offenders.'

Verner looks suddenly panic-stricken.

He's there, 'We can't have anyone employed by the Union who's involved in exposing themselves in public.'

Jesus, the 1970s and 1980s must be just a blur to this dude.

I'm there, 'You don't have to worry yourself, Verner. Like I said, I've decided to resign – portly because I don't want the issue casting a shadow over the Grand Slam decider against England.'

Grainne Hutton goes, 'Was 2014 not the year that Munster lost to Biarritz?'

And I'm like, 'Yeah, no, I'm pretty sure that was 2010, Grainne. The year I'm on about was the year Toulouse went on to play

Saracens in the final and Jonny Wilkinson gave Owen Farrell a kicking masterclass.'

I can see Sive suddenly looking all serious. It's obviously storting to sink in – what this is going to mean for our Six Nations hopes.

She's like, 'Jesus, lads, the timing.'

And I'm there, 'Couldn't be avoided, Sive. This thing has been hanging over me for months – in fairness, it's a relief to finally have it out in the open. Even though I'd prefer if we could hopefully sweep it under the corpet – at least until I find out if I'm going to be chorged.'

Verner goes, 'So what are *we* supposed to do?'

I'm there, 'In terms of?'

'In terms of, who the hell is going to coach the team against England?'

'Is that not obvious?'

'Not to me it isn't.'

'It's someone you know.'

'Has he coached at international level before?'

'Yeah, no, it's not a *he* – it's a *she*?'

'It's not Benedetta Bonansea, is it? It's just that we sort of messed her around when we decided to give you the job and I think she might be working with the under-18s at Zebre.'

'Jesus Christ,' I go, 'I'm talking about Sive!'

I swear to fock, I have no idea how this dude is in his job.

He's like, 'This Sive?' flicking his thumb at her. 'But sure, she has no coaching experience.'

I look at Sive. Our eyes meet. I go, 'I'm sorry that this is how the world works, Sive, that people like you – namely women – have to work twice as hord as us to get half as much recognition.' Then I turn to Verner and I'm like, 'What we've achieved in this Six Nations so far has had fock-all to do with me. It's all been down to her.'

He's there, 'What?' and it's like I've just told him that I've been, I don't know, picking the team according to the players' horoscopes. 'You can't be serious.'

I'm like, 'Dude, she has a Rugby Tactics Book that's thicker than mine and has more focking Post-it notes sticking out of it than I've ever seen in my life. And forget about what's in her book – what's in her head is even more important. She reads the game better than anyone I've ever known. The hilarious thing is that you put her on a focking interview panel to pick the next Ireland women's coach – and she was the best person for the job the entire time.'

Sive smiles at me. It's a moment – there's no doubt about that.

The dude ends up having to ruin it, of course. He's like, 'Why did you feel the need to take your orse out in a public house of all places?' and he's obviously thinking about the statement he's going to have to put out to the media.

I'm there, 'Like I said, Dude – different times. Anyway, I just want to say to the players that I have had the most unbelievable time working with you. I've learned from you and I'm hopefully a smorter coach, but also a better man for having met you. Sive Keenan is a genius – but then, you all knew that. Listen to her and there's no doubt in my mind that you'll beat England.'

Heather Hobson storts clapping and she's very quickly joined by the rest of the players. I take that as my cue to leave. It just feels like the right moment. As I pull the door open, they actually stort cheering me.

I can still hear the raucous send-off they're giving me when I step outside Conference Room Three and my phone suddenly rings.

I make the mistake of answering it.

'Ross?' a man's voice goes.

I'm like, 'Yeah, no, depends who's asking.'

'This is Steve,' he goes. 'As in, Adam's dad? Don't say anything yet. I just wanted to let you know that I've decided to leave Norma and I wondered if you'd changed your mind about –'

And I'm like, 'Not a good time, Steve. *Not* a good time.'

'What in the name of Hades is going on?' the old man wants to know.

I'm there, 'What are you talking about?'

He missed the Aer Lingus flight back to Dublin, by the way. No surprise there.

'I woke up this afternoon to find out that Ronan has decided to

346

go back to America after all and that you've resigned as the Head Coach of the Ireland – albeit ladies – rugby team! I said to Hennessy, "How long was I unconscious for, Old Scout?"'

And I'm like, 'Yeah, no, it's true – all of it.'

'But why on earth have you resigned, Kicker? Verner seemed to think you were on the verge of landing yourself a proper job!'

'I had a proper job.'

'So why give it up? God, my head hurts this morning!'

'I took my orse out in a pub.'

'What pub? Wasn't the Drum & Monkey, was it? I'm afraid my memory of the evening is as vague as the look on Leo Varadkar's face when he's trying to look like he cares about something!'

'It didn't happen on your stag. It was, like, five years ago – in the Thomond Bor in Cork.'

'Hold on, I'm still struggling to catch up here! You exposed your bottom?'

'Orse, yes.'

'In Cork?'

'The Thomond Bor.'

'Five years ago?'

'It was after Munster lost the famous Wilkinson semi-final.'

'But that's very funny, isn't it?'

'Was at the time. Not so much any more.'

'Good Lord, Ross, if everyone in Ireland had to resign for taking their bottom out at some point in the past, well, our legal and banking systems would cease to function!'

'It's, er, *slightly* different in my case in that I got arrested and – yeah, no – gave the Feds someone else's name. He ended up on the sex offenders register – and blah, blah, blah.'

'That sounds like a job for Hennessy!'

'I don't need Hennessy.'

'He'll get you off, Kicker! What's the point in having the – quote-unquote – Attorney General as your bloody well godfather if you're not going to ask for his help!'

'I focked up in a big-time way – and for the first time in my life I've decided that I'm going to own it.'

'Own it? You're not still drunk, are you, Ross?'

'No, I'm totally sober.'

'You don't sound it! Anyway, I'd better put some clothes on.'

Jesus Christ, I can't believe he's talking to me while still in the raw.

He goes, 'Missed the flight, of course! But it's okay, the Government jet is coming for us! And what about Ronan? What happened there?'

'He obviously decided he wanted to go to Horvord instead of spending the rest of his life doing Hennessy's dirty work and hanging out with scum, scummers, scumfocks.'

I suddenly hear footsteps coming up the stairs of the tower. I'm there, 'I've got to go,' and I hang up on him.

Five seconds later, Sorcha appears at the foot of my mattress. She doesn't even look pissed off. She just looks, I don't know, *sad*?

She goes, 'Fionn said he can't go on living here if you're here.'

I'm like, 'Is he going to move back in with his old pair?'

She just, like, stares at me – doesn't say shit. I suddenly get it.

I'm there, 'Oh, right, *I'm* the one moving out, am I?'

She goes, 'Well, he and Hillary have formed a very strong bond. It wouldn't be fair to break that.'

'Could he not –'

'What, Ross?'

'I don't know, take Hillary *with* him? His old dear could look after him while Fionn goes to work.'

'What, you think the upshot of what you did should be that I no longer get to live in the same house as my son and watch him grow up every day?'

'No, I'm just making the point that maybe if I talked to Fionn and explained –'

'He doesn't want to talk to you, Ross – and I, for one, don't blame him. Have the Gordaí spoken to you yet?'

'Not yet.'

'They're obviously going to want to. You'd better tell Hennessy.'

'I don't want Hennessy's help.'

'What?'

'I'm not going to ask him to get me off – not this time.'

'Are you still drunk?'

'No, I'm one hundred per cent sober.'

'Well, you don't sound it.'

'Did Fionn get his job back?'

'He's meeting the Board of Management this afternoon.'

'If they want me to confirm the story, they can ring me on the mobile.'

'Where will you go?'

'Go? Oh, em, I don't know. Maybe – yeah, no – Christian and JP might find a vertical bed somewhere for me.'

'For what it's worth, I've heard they're surprisingly comfortable.'

'Yeah, no, I've heard good things.'

If I'm looking for pity, it's obvious that I'm not going to get it from her.

'They're very space-efficient,' she goes.

I'm like, 'Very.'

'They're saying that's how everyone in Ireland will live in the future.'

'Yeah, no, I was there that day in Malingrad, bear in mind.'

'Honor will be devastated.'

'I know.'

'I want you to know that you can see her any time you want.'

'Even if it's every day?'

'Even if it's every day. The same applies to the boys.'

'Well, I might make it once a week with them – until they're a bit older and less annoying.'

We end up staring at each other for a good, like, thirty seconds and I can tell that this is – yeah, no – killing her.

I'm there, 'So this is it, huh? It's definitely, definitely over?'

She goes, 'It was definitely, definitely over before this happened, Ross,' and she makes a big point of looking around her. 'I think this tower was just my way of keeping you close until I was sure. I'm sorry if that sounds selfish.'

'Hey, no offence taken. I'll be gone within a week, okay?'

'A week is fine.'

She looks out the window at the sea beyond and sort of, like, smiles – except not in a *happy* way?

'And to think,' she goes, 'when I was a little girl, I dreamt that I would meet my prince in this room. I never thought it would be where I said goodbye to him.'

I'm there, 'Sorcha, for what it's worth, you know absolutely everything now. If you did take me back – and I know it's a big if – there'd be no more, I don't know, secrets crawling out of the woodwork.'

She smiles at me and goes, 'Deep down, Ross, I think we both know that that's a lie.'

Then she turns to leave.

'Oh,' she goes, turning back again, 'Adam's dad called to the house last night, drunk out of his mind. He said he's left his wife –'

'So I heard – focking Newpork.'

'– because he's in love with you and he knows from the way you kissed him and held him that night that you're in love with him too.'

I'm like, 'Eeeeeerrrr, right.'

'He asked me to pass that message on,' she goes.

And I'm there, 'Yeah, no, thanks.'

The dude on the radio says that the Taoiseach, Charles O'Carroll-Kelly, has strenuously denied fresh allegations that he ate meat despite claiming to be a vegan.

'The latest claims,' he goes, 'arose out of a visit to Glasgow last weekend for a stag night, during the course of which it's claimed that the Taoiseach ate a forty-ounce, dry-aged steak while out for dinner with friends. The Taoiseach has called the claims a disappointing but predictable attempt to smear his good name.'

I laugh and I turn to Honor. I'm there, 'He did have the steak. I watched him eat every focking mouthful.'

Honor just laughs. She's like, 'That's, like, oh my God! Hill! *Air?*'

'Meanwhile,' the dude goes, 'the talks between the Government and the European Union over the terms of the so-called Irexit deal broke down this morning, with the Taoiseach saying that Ireland would now leave the EU without a deal. He also said it was his intention to renege on the debt commitments that Ireland made during the 2010 bailout of the Irish economy by the European

Commission, the European Central Bank and the International Monetary Fund.'

I turn off the radio as we pass a sign that says 'Ballinasloe, 10 kilometres'.

I'm there, 'Honor, there's something I need to talk to you about. It's probably going to be the most difficult conversation I ever have with you.'

She's like, 'Are you and *her* breaking up.'

'Yeah, but just let me explain why.'

'I *know* why.'

'Adult relationships are a lot more complicated than, say, teenage relationships.'

'It's because you took your orse out in a pub in Cork in 2014 and you blamed it on Fionn.'

'Yeah, no, that's a slight oversimplification –'

'That's also the reason you had to resign as the Coach of the Ireland women's team – because you're about to be, like, *cancelled*?'

'Who told you that?'

'I heard her and Fionn talking.'

'Well, maybe they should both keep their focking voices down – especially if there's children around.'

'I laughed when I heard it was you.'

'Thanks, Honor.'

'I mean, it's, like, funny, isn't it?'

'Yeah, no, that would have been the general take on it at the time. But the world has changed, Honor. Shit that was hilarious in 2014 is no longer funny in, I don't know, whatever we're up to now.'

'It's 2019.'

'But I want you to know, Honor, that just because your old dear has decided that our marriage is over, it doesn't mean that we don't love you very much.'

'Whatever.'

'Now, I know you're going to be upset.'

'I'm not upset.'

'Aren't you?'

'Not really, no.'

I know I shouldn't say this, but I'm actually a bit disappointed.

'Oh,' I go. 'And, er, do you mind me asking why not?'

She's like, 'Dad, *loads* of girls I know have parents who are, like, divorced.'

'Well, we're not divorced. We're getting – I don't know – re-separated, if that's a thing. And don't you worry, Honor, I'm hoping to chorm my way back in there once the heat goes out of the situation.'

She's like, 'Half the girls in Mount Anville have parents who aren't together. Sincerity's parents are divorced.'

I know. I rode her mother.

'Oh, and by the way,' she goes, 'Adam's parents are separated now as well.'

I know. I rode his mother too. And got off with his dad – although just a little bit.

She's there, 'It's, like, not a major *deal* any more?'

I'm like, 'I'm sorry to hear that. About Adam's old pair, I mean.'

'Oh! My God!' she goes. 'Do you know what the rumour is?'

'Er, no – go on.'

'Everyone's saying that his mom and dad were, like, *swingers*?'

'Swingers? Jesus. That's a shock, it has to be said.'

'Apparently, his mom would go out and, like, hit on men, then bring them home for them *both* to enjoy?'

'Jesus.'

'That's what, like, *everyone* in school is saying?'

'So are you, like, still in touch with Adam?'

'No, he's *such* a focking weirdo – *and* a sap?'

'That's good news. Yeah, no, it sounds like he's got a very focked-up home life. Although I know I'm one to talk. So how's the famous Reese?'

'He's fine.'

'And that's still going well, is it?'

'Why do you sound so surprised?'

'No, it's just a bit, I don't know –'

I do know. It's a bit suspicious. He's the kicker for a school that's about to play in the Leinster Schools Senior Cup final. The dude should be beating them off with a cattle prod, not hitching himself to a girl who – let's be honest – wouldn't be winning many beauty pageants.

I'm there, 'He must be looking forward to Paddy's Day, is he?'

She goes, 'Oh my God, he *so* is! I can't believe he got back with me.'

I'm thinking, you're not the focking only one.

She's there, 'As in, I can't believe that out of all the girls he *could* be with, he decided that he wanted to be with me.'

I'm like, 'It's focking unbelievable – I'm agreeing with you.'

We suddenly pass the Dubarry factory.

I'm like, 'Whoa! Did you focking see that?'

'Dad,' Honor goes, 'keep your eyes on the road, will you?'

I'm there, 'We're calling in there on the way back! Just to pay our respects!'

She goes, 'Who's this man you're going to see anyway?'

And I'm there, 'He's just someone who needs to hear one or two home truths.'

I follow the Satnav's directions and twenty minutes later I pull into the cor pork of Ballinasloe Rugby Club. I get out of the cor.

I'm like, 'I won't be long. Do *not* go anywhere.'

But she's there, 'I'm coming with you. If you're going to punch someone in the face, I want to see it.'

'I'm not punching anyone, Honor. I'm just going to say some things that need saying.'

She follows me into the bor anyway. There's a dude there putting beermats on all the tables.

I'm like, 'Hey, how the hell are you?'

He's there, 'Afternoon.'

'Do you know where Sive Keenan lives?'

'Sive Keenan?'

'Er, the *rugby* player?'

'She lives in Dublin, doesn't she?'

'I'm talking about her actual *family* home?'

'Oh, it's not far from here. Who are you looking for?'

'Her old man.'

'You're in luck – that's him over there.'

There's a dude sitting in the corner and he's writing something in, like, a ledger. I end up doing a double-take when I see him – as does *Honor*, by the way?

'Oh my God,' she goes, 'he's in a focking wheelchair.'

I'm there, 'Yeah, so I see, Honor.'

'Dad, you can't hit a man in a focking wheelchair.'

'I never said I was going to hit him, Honor. You were the one who said I was going to hit him.'

The dude looks up. He's like, 'Howiya?'

And I'm there, 'Yeah, no, hi. That, em, looks heavy.'

'Yeah, I'm just doing the stocktake.'

Shit, I think I remember Sive mentioning that he was, like, the *bor* manager here or some shit?

I'm there, 'The name's Ross – as in, like, Ross O'Carroll-Kelly?'

He shrugs. Means fock-all to the dude.

'I'm the Head Coach of the Ireland women's rugby team,' I go. 'Or *was* – until I resigned at the weekend.'

He's there, 'Oh, yeah?'

'I'm also a friend of your daughter's. As in, like, Sive?'

I watch his face suddenly horden.

I'm there, 'I just want to say a few things here. The first of which is that your daughter is a rugby genius, and I don't say that lightly because I like to consider myself one. She's forgotten more about the game than I will ever know, and I actually fill up when I think about her Rugby Tactics Book and whatever secrets it, I don't know, *holds*.'

He goes to say something, but I'm like, 'Let me do the talking, Dude,' and I suddenly realize that I'm shouting. 'I don't know if you heard the sports news this morning, but Sive has just been appointed as my replacement. And this Friday night, in a certain stadium in Donnybrook, she's going to be coaching and hopefully leading the Ireland team out against England with the Six Nations and the Grand Slam at stake. And you're not going to be there.'

'No,' he goes, 'I won't be there.'

I'm like, 'Why, because you don't agree with women playing rugby?'

'That's right,' he goes.

I'm there, 'Then you're going to miss what might be the greatest moment of your daughter's rugby career and possibly even life,' and – I swear to fock – I suddenly stort crying. 'I focking pity you for that. I focking pity you for it.'

Honor goes, 'Oh my God, Dad, you're making a focking show of yourself.'

I'm there, 'I don't care,' and I'm literally wiping away tears as I say it. 'You see, I used to be like you, Dude. I used to think that women had no right to play the beautiful game. But that was down to my upbringing. I went to a school where we were taught that women didn't even get into Heaven. So I used to watch clips of women playing rugby with the *Benny Hill* theme tune on in the background and I thought it was hilarious. And then this girl here – my daughter, Honor – called me out on my, I don't know, what was the word, Honor?'

She's like, 'Misogyny.'

I'm there, 'She called me out on my misogyny. On my bullshit, in other words. And, because of that, I got to meet your daughter and a bunch of incredible, incredible rugby players who have more skill and more courage and more desire than most of the players I ever played with.'

'Can *I* speak now?' he goes.

And I'm there, 'Yeah, go on – whatever.'

He goes, 'I refuse to watch my daughter play rugby –'

I'm like, 'Yeah, no, so she said.'

'But not for the reasons you mentioned,' he tries to go. 'I'm scared of her getting hurt.'

I'm like, 'Don't give me that, Dude. The chances of sustaining a serious injury in rugby are still –'

And then I suddenly stop what I'm saying. Because I'm looking at the wheelchair and it suddenly all makes sense to me.

'Shit,' I go. 'Dude, I'm sorry.'

He's there, 'All those matches I played for Connacht – do you think it was worth it? Me spending the last twenty years of my life in this chair? *This* is why I can't watch my daughter playing rugby.'

I'm like, 'Dude, I'm sorry. I'm genuinely, genuinely sorry to have bothered you,' and I can't wait to get out of the door.

I'm, like, so shaken up by the time we get back to the cor that I end up going, 'I'm going to need a minute here, Honor.'

She's there, 'Give me the keys. I'll drive home.'

And I'm like, 'Er, yeah, that'd be a *no*, Honor?'

I tell Christian thanks. For the bed that he's promised me. And the Homedrobe. Yeah, no, he said I can stay in one of the investment gaffs he bought in The Antform @ Cherrywood – just until I find something more permanent, or until Sorcha takes me back, which-ever happens first.

He goes, 'I'm doing this because I know you've got nowhere else to go. But I still think what you did to Fionn was pretty shitty.'

I'm like, 'Dude, I know.'

'One of the shittiest things you've ever done on any of us. Maybe *the* shittiest – and that includes having sex with my old dear.'

'I take your point – you don't want to take sides.'

'No, Ross, I'm *taking* sides. I'm on Fionn's side – as are JP and Oisinn, by the way. I mean, we had a meeting, Dude, at which we talked about how worried we were about him.'

'Hey, at least he managed to save his job – there's that.'

'Seriously, Ross, I'm happy enough to give you the keys to the Homedrobe, but don't try to minimize what you did, okay? Because it's not going to work this time.'

'Fair enough.'

'Have you heard from the Feds?'

'They're still gathering evidence apparently. I'm expecting a knock on the door any day now.'

He's there, 'Like I said, you'll get no sympathy from me. Anyway, I have to go. I've got focking Hennessy suing me now for breach of his grandchildren's, I don't know, intellectual property rights or something. I'll talk to you soon.'

He hangs up on me.

I'm sort of, like, packing all of my shit together – my clothes, obviously my Rugby Tactics Book, then one or two keepsakes – for the trip to Cherrywood.

As I'm stuffing it all into my bag, I hear a voice go, 'I can't believe she's actually doing it? As in, like, *actually* throwing you out?'

I turn around and – yeah, no – it's Sorcha's sister standing in the doorway of what will soon be my former bedroom.

I'm there, 'Well, you went and opened your big mouth, didn't you?'

She goes, 'Hey, you told Oisinn and Magnus not to let me carry their baby. I think that makes us about even.'

'I was about to come clean to Fionn anyway. You just beat me to the punch by a few hours.'

'But she's, like, throwing you out of your own home – for, like, *that*?'

'Bear in mind, it *was* pretty bad what I did. I mean, Fionn ended up on the register of sex –'

'But Fionn isn't her husband.'

'I know that, but he's, like, one of her best friends. And the father of her –'

'Exactly. Like, how the fock are *you* supposed to feel? She has the man who cuckolded you –'

'I don't know what that word means.'

'– living in your house with the product of their adultery. It's no wonder you're angry with him.'

'Er, I'm not, I *was* angry with him – although I like the general thrust of what you're saying.'

'Of course you're angry with him. You just don't know it. I did, like, a lot of therapy when I was in Australia – a *lot* of therapy – and ninety-nine per cent of the things we do, we don't even know why we do them.'

'Is that an exact number? It seems like a lot.'

'Ninety-nine per cent, Ross.'

'Well, I'm going to hopefully remember that stat.'

Oh, holy focking shit. She's giving me that look – as in, like, *that* look?

I'm there, 'No way. No focking way.'

She goes, 'What?'

'We are not doing that. We are one hundred per cent *not* doing that.'

She actually *laughs*?

She's like, 'Ross, as if you have any focking choice in the matter?'

I'm there, 'Excuse me?'

She goes, 'You're a total focking slave to your desires.'

I'm like, 'I wouldn't say that.'

She moves closer to me and – oh, fock – grabs the belt of my chinos and unbuckles it slowly while maintaining full eye contact, an old tactic of hers that I remember from back in the day. As per focking usual, I'm powerless to do anything about it. I can hear my breathing go all, I don't know, raggedy and *uneven*?

She goes, 'You're not exactly pushing me away, Ross, are you?' as she presses her mouth close to my ear.

I'm there, 'Shit!'

I'm looking at her bare orms, at the tattoo sleeves that she's had done since the last time I was with her – as in, like, *with* with?

She whispers in my ear, 'You knew this was going to happen, didn't you?'

And I'm there, 'I thought it might possibly, yeah.'

'I saw you looking at me across the dinner table on Christmas Eve. You had a big horn on you.'

'Jesus, you're very blunt, aren't you?'

'Only when I want something.'

She snaps open the top button of my chinos, then untucks my shirt and storts rubbing her hands up and down my abs.

'Oh my God,' she goes, 'it's like playing the accordion. I feel like I'm in focking Mumford & Sons here.'

It's that line – I've no idea why – that sends me over the edge. I make a lunge for her and stort kissing her mouth, her face, her neck.

She's going, 'I told you. I could have you any focking time I want you. And, deep down, Dad always knew that.'

Yeah, no, it's a random thing to hear when you're about to get down to the deed, but I decide to let it go in the interests of not killing the mood. I take her top off over her head, while she kicks off her Vans, then steps out of her skinny jeans like she's morching up and down on the spot.

I push her down onto the mattress, where she removes her – yeah, no – smalls while I do the same to mine, then I sort of, like, fall on top of her, full of the passion, except she rolls me off her and onto the floor, then presses two hands down on my chest and throws her left leg over me like I'm a focking pommel horse.

And there – as the director of this little movie – I'm going to shout, 'Cut!' because it would be, I don't know, unnecessary to go into the details of how she squatted over me like she was taking a shit in an Indian toilet, then how she bounced up and down on me like she was back at pony-trekking school, and how the entire time she had this, like, angry look on her face and kept shouting out random shit like, 'Stupid focking bitch, staring out the window, saying your prince was going to come – well, your focking prince is going to come alright.'

Anyway, mid-deed, I just so happen to notice that she's got this, like, chain around her neck and it's, like, swinging back and forth in front of my face as she's leading me over the jumps. It's got, like, a word on it, and I'm thinking – holy shit – it's her focking name! So I'm lying there, sweat blinding me, panting like a hot dog, my two eyes turned inwards, and I'm trying to read it, except the thing keeps moving – backwards and forwards, backwards and forwards, backwards and forwards.

All the time, I'm trying to, like, *focus* on it? It's got, like, an N in it – and I can definitely see a T. And then, as we both reach the point of – I'm just going to come out and say the word – *climax*, she stops moving, and so does the chain, and I can finally read the name on it.

And it says . . .

Ah, *that* was it! How could I have *not* remembered it for all these years?

I'm there, 'OH, NICOLETTE!' as my two eyes return to their normal positions.

And she goes, 'Excuse me?'

I'm there, 'Sorry, I was just blurting out your name there!'

'That's not *my* name,' she goes, touching her necklace. 'Nicolette was the first girl I was ever with – as in, like, *with* with? – when I moved to Australia.'

I'm like, 'Yeah, no, I, em, knew that. I thought it was random alright.'

As she climbs off and storts putting on her clothes, she goes, 'You do know my actual name, right?'

And I just laugh.

I'm there, 'Of course I know your actual name! What kind of a question is that to ask me?'

This is not how I *thought* the Six Nations was going to end? With me paying fifteen yoyos in to watch the team that I once coached. But – yeah, no – I end up queuing up with all the other plebs.

When I get to the gate, the dude goes, 'Ticket?'

I whip out my credit cord and I go, 'Is there somewhere I can swipe this?'

He's like, 'It's ticket only. Match is sold out.'

I sort of, like, smile to myself. Because I'm remembering the night a few months ago when I took them for a run along Anglesea Road – just to try to put them out there. And even though it ended with their captain and best player on the team getting creamed by a bus, it's lovely to see how they've captured the imagination of the public.

The dude goes, 'Sorry, could you step aside there, son?' because I'm standing there grinning like an idiot and holding up the queue.

That's when Honor produces her phone and goes, 'I've got our tickets here, Dad.'

And I'm like, 'You booked tickets?'

'Of course I booked tickets! It's, like, sold out!'

'Hey, fair focks, Honor. Fair – definite – focks.'

'I put them on *your* credit cord?'

That doesn't even require saying. She puts everything on my credit cord.

So into Energia Pork we tip.

I'm there, 'So, er, how's everything at home, Honor?'

She's like, 'Great,' which – again – sort of, like, stings. 'Oh, the boys got suspended from school.'

'Suspended? What are they, like, five years old?'

'They're six, Dad.'

'Six, then. The fock did they do?'

'Oh my God, it was sort of, like, *my* fault? They were playing a hockey match against, like, Willow Pork. And I was letting them listen to the Hitler speeches beforehand – just to get them into the zone. But they probably, like, overdosed on it. Johnny punched one of the Willow kids in the face.'

'Good enough for the little focker.'

'Then Brian cracked one on the head with his hockey stick.'

'This is how Willow kids roll when they grow up, so it's nice to see them get a taste of it.'

'Then Leo scored a goal –'

'Fair focking focks.'

'– took off his shirt –'

'Jesus, was he watching videos of me back in the day?'

'– and storted shouting that he who doesn't wish to fight in this world, where permanent struggle is the law of life, has no right to exist.'

'In German?'

'In German.'

'Jesus.'

'Mom had to go up to the school – and she was like, "As if I haven't got enough on my plate already what with Ireland leaving the European Union without a deal and now the focking formers sending me testicles through the post, not to mention my sister being a constant bitch." I think she might be going *actually* mad.'

'Jesus, I'm glad I'm out of that situation.'

We go and we find our seats. I can see the players down on the pitch doing their warm-up. It's, like, a cold Friday night in Morch and you can nearly taste the tension in the ground. Like Ireland, England are unbeaten in the Six Nations and they're looking for the Grand Slam too.

I watch as the players go through their own little pre-match rituals that I know so well. Joanne Wassell tying her red hair back in her headband, then shaking it loose again and redoing it at, like, sixty-second intervals. Heather Hobson stretching her neck and shoulder muscles. Rachel and Louise Skeldon sprinting from one side of the pitch to the other while passing the ball back and forth to each other at high speed.

'Holy shit,' I suddenly go. 'Holy focking shit.'

Honor's there, 'What?'

I'm like, 'Sive is down there. Warming up. Means she's going to stort.'

The teams line up for the anthems. First, it's, like, 'God Save the Queen', which always goes down well in Donnybrook, let's be honest, then it's – I don't know – whatever our one is called, followed by 'Ireland's Call'.

I'm just, like, fully focussed on Sive. I only have to look at her face to know that she *has* this?

When the anthems end, the roar goes up. It's like, 'Come on, Ireland!' and I end up shouting it myself.

The players take their positions. It looks like Sive is going to be playing hooker.

The match gets under way. With so much at stake, it'd be understandable if the rugby wasn't exactly vintage, but the two teams stort like they want to give the crowd a show. There's some nice, skilful play from both Ireland *and* England and the tackling is, like, unforgiving. I'm watching Sive and she's not protecting that shoulder. Yeah, no, she's throwing herself into contact like a woman who's never been hit by a bus before and it's brilliant to see. She's also, like, roaring at the others, going, 'Lads, will yee wake up!' and 'Come on, lads, I need to see more from yee!'

Honor is as smitten as *I* am? 'She's *so* amazing!' she goes.

I'm there, 'You'd want to see her Rugby Tactics Book, Honor,' and I use my thumb and forefinger to give her an idea of the thickness of it. 'We're talking, like, three inches, with focking Post-it notes spilling out of it like there's no tomorrow.'

Honor's like, 'Oh my God!'

I'm there, 'If you offered me half an hour with Margot Robbie or with that book, I'd take the book. There wouldn't even be a conversation about it.'

362

She goes, 'No, look!' and I do look – just as the roar goes up. Rachel Skeldon is about to throw an unbelievable skip pass to Nadine Delaney on the wing. Nadine catches it perfectly and gets over the line in the corner. She hits the post with the conversion, but Ireland are still five points to the good with only seven minutes gone.

England roar straight back and they level with a try from their – believe it or not – scrum-half after she takes a quick penalty while our players are half asleep.

This sets the pattern for basically the entire first half. Joanne scores a try, then England score one back. Lisa McGuin scores a try, then England score one back. Nadine Delaney gets a second, then England score one back. It's, like, two cage-fighters going at it – we're talking toe to toe. At half-time, we're winning 40–37, but it's anyone's match.

I look behind me and I spot Verner sitting in the crowd. I give him a wave, except he pretends not to see me. Yeah, no, the reason for my abrupt deporture hasn't hit the papers yet, but I suspect it will once the Feds talk to me, and the dude obviously doesn't want to be seen talking to me.

Which is fair enough.

I turn around to Honor and I'm like, 'So how's the famous Reese?'

She's there, 'I haven't really *seen* him?'

And I'm like, 'Oh?' because I can already tell you where this story is going.

She's there, 'He's, like, really stressed about the final next week and he's asked me if I could give him, like, a little bit of *space*?'

God, he has all the moves. I think the world is going to be hearing a lot more from this kid in the future, just as Honor is going to be hearing a lot less from him.

I'm like, 'Just, em, be careful that he's not messing you around, Honor, okay?'

She's there, 'He's just, like, really, really serious about his rugby, Dad. Once he gets through this match, then we can be together – oh my God – all the time.'

She sounds so like her old dear as a teenager that I want to nearly cry.

But there isn't time for tears because the teams are back out on the pitch again and the atmosphere – I swear to fock – is cracking.

The two teams stort going at each other again. England score a try after stealing a lineout, which doesn't please Sive – 'I'm blue in the face telling yee, lads!' – but then we take the lead again when Megan Barrett slices her way through the England defence to score under the posts.

England push past us again with a penalty try midway through the half, but then Nadine completes her hat-trick after beating three players and selling two England players the dummy before scoring in the corner.

There's, like, one minute to go. We're winning 60–57. It's been, like, exhibition stuff. The crowd are singing 'The Fields of Athenry', but the tension is killing me. Heather Hobson gets the ball in her hand and makes, like, twenty yords before she's taken down. We're, like, porked on their twenty-two and Sive is roaring at her team-mates, telling them not to do anything stupid, which means it's just going to be, like, phase after phase to run the clock down.

The time is officially up. We're, like, two metres from the Eng-land line and Sive suddenly has the ball in her hands. I'm expecting her to just, like, kick the thing out of play, so that the celebrations can stort. She's just about to do it, but then an England player goes to block the kick, which means she has to turn fully around – and when she does, she sees a space in front of her that's, like, a metre wide. She throws herself through it, just as she's tackled and brought down a couple of feet from the line. But, as she falls, she stretches out her right hand, with the ball sticking to it like Velcro, and she slams it down right on the line.

The referee blows for a try and all hell breaks literally loose. Me and Honor are just, like, dancing around going, 'We did it! We fock-ing did it!'

I'm looking at the players, all hugging each other. Megan Barrett is hugging Lisa McGuin. Joanne Wassell is hugging little Grainne Hutton. The Skeldon twins are hugging each other – I could be wrong, but I think I see one of them even smile.

'Dad!' Honor goes, suddenly pulling at my orm. 'Look!'

I follow her line of – yeah, no – vision and I spot something that's so unbelievable that I wonder at first whether I'm, like, *hallucinating*?

Sive has made her way over to the sideline – and she's hugging a man in a wheelchair. All I can see are their two bodies shaking as they hold each other so tightly that it looks like they might never let go. The tears stort spilling from my eyes.

'Her dad!' Honor goes. 'He came!' and then she throws her orms around me and pulls me closer to her.

'Oh, rugby,' I hear myself go as I kiss her on the top of the head. 'Oh, rugby, oh, rugby, oh, rugby.'

The presentation is made on the pitch. The stadium announcer goes, 'Ladies and gentlemen, the 2019 Six Nations and Grand Slam winners are . . . Ireland!'

Sive holds up the trophy, then the fireworks stort going off. It's like, 'Boom! Boom! Boom!' and the crowd goes absolutely bananas.

The players stort doing their lap of *honour* then? And that's when Grainne Hutton spots me in the crowd. I see her nudging one or two of the other players, then pointing me out, then after a short confab, they stort beckoning me down onto the pitch.

Grainne's going, 'Come on, boy!' because they obviously want me to do a lap with *them* and the actual trophy. But I just shake my head and I mouth the word, 'No!' to her and she knows from the expression on my face that I'm serious.

The players set off on their lap again – all except Sive, who stands there just, like, staring at me, the Six Nations trophy in her hand and tears streaking her face. In that moment, we might as well be the only two people in Energia Pork, the only two people in Donnybrook, the only two people in the actual world. We're, like, lost in each other's eyes, as only people who've been on a rugby journey together *can* be?

She points her finger at me. I just shake my head and point mine right back at her. Then she does the most incredible thing. She puts her fingers to her lips and she blows me a kiss. I reach into the air and I catch it, then I put it in the pocket of my chinos.

It's still there.

★

So it's, like, seven o'clock in the morning and I'm standing in bed when the knock on the door comes.

One of the upsides of the old Homedrobe is that you don't have to walk far to answer the door. You don't have to walk at all. You just stretch out your hand and you open it out.

There's, like, two dudes standing there.

'Ross O'Carroll-Kelly?' one of them goes.

And I'm there, 'Yeah, no, I've been expecting you.'

I step off the little footboard at the end of the Vampire Bed and I can see the two dudes looking at each other in just, like, shock.

'What in the name of God is that?' the smaller of the two goes.

I'm there, 'What, this? It's a Homedrobe.'

'And is that one of them beds I saw on *The Late Late Show*?' the other dude goes.

I'm like, 'Yeah, no, a very good friend of mine invented it.'

He goes, 'Is this your home?'

I'm there, 'Yeah, no, for now – until I get myself sorted.'

'No, what I mean is, well, is that it?'

Yeah, no, the entire thing is the size of, like, a Portaloo.

I'm there, 'There is a communal toilet on each floor and a communal kitchen on every second floor.'

'And what if you want to watch the telly?' the first dude goes.

I'm like, 'Easy – you watch it on your phone. There's, like, chorging points for all your devices in there.'

The two of them just stare at me. They're really struggling to get their heads around it. Although I *am* also standing there in just my jockeys.

'And this is how people live now?' he goes.

I'm there, 'A lot of people – but apparently it's going be how everyone lives in the future.'

From the looks on their faces, it's not something that excites them.

I'm there, 'Let me have a quick bogger shower, will you?' and I reach into a pocket in the back of the door and I whip out a can of Lynx. 'No offence, of course. What accent is that I'm hearing?'

'Mine's Leitrim,' the little dude goes, 'and his is Cork.'

I'm like, 'Fair focks,' as I give myself a blast of deodorant under each orm. 'Fair, fair focks.'

I grab my clothes, which are hanging on a rail just behind the Vampire Bed, then I stort throwing them on.

I'm like, 'So, er, which station are you based in, goys?'

'Dalkey,' the smaller dude goes. 'I'm Detective Jimmy Kavanagh and this is Detective Shane Hughes.'

I'm like, 'Good to meet you, Jimmy Kavanagh. And you, Shane Hughes.'

They tell me that they're arresting me on suspicion of public indecency and perverting the course of justice.

I'm like, 'Yeah, no, I thought it'd be more than that actually.'

I think they're surprised to find me in such cracking form, given the world of trouble I'm in.

I'm like, 'You're not going to handcuff me, are you?'

Shane Hughes goes, 'Unless there's a reason you think we should.'

I'm there, 'Don't worry, you won't be getting a fight out of me,' as I finish getting dressed, then I close the Homedrobe door behind me.

'This way,' Shane Hughes goes and I follow the two of them down the corridor to the lift, then into the lift and down to the basement of the aportment block, where the squad cor is porked. I get in and off we head in the direction of Dalkey.

I'm like, 'So how long have you been a Gord, Shane Hughes?'

And Shane – who's driving – is there, 'Er, two years,' still a bit thrown by how casually I'm taking the whole thing.

Jimmy Kavanagh, who's sitting in the front passenger seat, goes, 'You're entitled to have your solicitor present during the interview. Can I ask you who that is?'

I'm there, 'My solicitor is Hennessy Coghlan-O'Hara.'

The two of them just look at each other like it's suddenly dawned on them why I'm being so cocky.

'Jesus,' Shane Hughes goes. 'I don't want to find myself moved to some remote village in the north of the country.'

I'm there, 'You definitely won't. Because I don't want him present. I'm going to make a statement, admitting everything.'

'You know,' Jimmy Kavanagh goes, 'it *is* your legal right to have a solicitor –'

But I'm like, 'Dude, I'm going to make this as easy as I possibly can for everyone now. It's actually going to be a relief to get it off my chest.'

We arrive in Dalkey Gorda Station and I'm shown into an interview room, where I'm asked if I need anything.

I'm like, 'Maybe just a glass of water,' which they get for me.

Then I sit down opposite the two boys and over the course of the next two hours I tell them absolutely everything. I tell them about going on the absolute rip with Shagger Sorenson and The Shit Murphy, who did the Sportsman Dip. course in UCD, even though neither of them played rugby afterwards, except for The Shit, who spent one season with – I can check this – but I'm pretty sure Dolphin's third team.

I tell them about the three of us ending up in Cork and how we were drinking in the Thomond Bor and how Munster were playing Toulouse that day in the semi-final of the Heineken Cup. I tell them about Jonny Wilkinson's inability to miss with the boot that day, and how, as a kicker myself – one who was often favourably compared to Wilkinson – I cheered every single kick as it went over, which didn't go down at all well with the locals.

Shit, I suddenly remember that Shane Hughes is from Cork. Not that it matters now anyway.

I tell them that there was a very strong consensus in the bor that I was a langball and I should fock off back to Dublin and that people became stronger in this view after Munster's defeat was confirmed. Then I tell them about opening my trousers and flashing my hole.

Jimmy Kavanagh laughs, in fairness to him.

I'm like, 'Funny, right?'

Then he remembers himself.

He's there, 'You were arrested in the pub – and you gave your name as Fionn de Barra.'

'That's right,' I go.

'For what reason?'

'He's a friend of mine. *Was* a friend of mine. I often used his name if I was in any kind of trouble, or if I was meeting a bird on Tinder and didn't want her to know my real name, or if I was ordering porno mags through the post before the whole thing went online. Fionn de Barra was sort of, like, my alias.'

'But he was also a real person,' Shane Hughes goes.

I'm like, 'Yes, he was. Is.'

'And you used his address as well?'

'Yes, I did.'

'And you appeared in court *as* him?'

'I wouldn't say I appeared *as* him. I mean, I didn't put the geeky glasses on or anything like that.'

'What I mean is, you allowed the court to believe that the man who was standing there, facing the charges, was in fact Fionn de Barra?'

'Yes, that's true.'

'And not Ross O'Carroll-Kelly?'

'That's right.'

They have the statement typed up for me. I read it back, then I sign it on the line that I'm shown.

I hand Shane Hughes his pen back, then I go, 'Where am I heading now – the cells?'

The dude chuckles. He's there, 'You haven't been charged yet.'

I'm like, 'But I told you that I did it. Fock's sake, my old man hasn't been on the phone, has he?'

'No, we're going to send a file to the DPP. They'll be in touch when the time comes.'

I'm like, 'Er, right, fair enough.'

I'm in the Gorda Station for a total of, like, forty minutes. When the interview is over, I step outside and I stort wondering how the fock I'm going to get back to Cherrywood. I'm not sure if any buses go there, having not been on public transport since around the time that One Direction were still shitting yellow.

But as I'm leaving the Gorda Station, I see a familiar face looking at me. Holy shit. It's, like, Erika.

I just go, 'Hey,' and I don't call her – I don't know – 'Gorgeous' or 'Sexy' or any of the other names she hates me calling her on the basis that I'm a blood relative. 'How did you know I was here?'

'I called to The Antform @ Cherrywood,' she goes, 'just after the Gords got there. I saw them bringing you off in the cor and I followed them.'

I'm there, 'It was me who took my orse out in the pub in Cork and then let Fionn take the heat for it.'

'Yeah, no, Sorcha told me.'

'But I've just made a statement that will put things hopefully right.'

She just nods – taking this on board.

Then she goes, 'Sea-mon was dischorged from the Central Mental Hospital last night.'

I'm like, 'No way.'

'Her parents went to the High Court, seeking a Judicial Review.'

'A Judicial Review? Fair focks. To all involved.'

'They successfully argued that there was no evidence of mental incapacity.'

'So she's out?'

'No, she's in prison,' she goes. 'But at least she's going to have her day in court now.'

I'm there, 'I'm thrilled for the girl – even though she was never my number one fan.'

I must try to remember sometimes that everything doesn't have to be about me.

I'm there, 'So, em, why were you coming to see me?'

She looks away. Whatever she's about to say next is obviously difficult for her.

She goes, 'You can't stay in one of those focking wardrobes, Ross.'

I'm like, 'It's only for a short time, until I find somewhere better, or hopefully weasel my way back in –'

She's there, 'I talked to my mom. She said you can stay with us.'

'What, in Ailesbury Road?'

'Yes, in Ailesbury Road. And, for what it's worth, Amelie is looking forward to having her Uncle Ross around.'

'And what about you?'

'Don't focking push your luck, Ross.'

'Yeah, no, cool. I presume it's going to be separate rooms for us, though.'

'We live in a house with seven bedrooms, Ross.'

'I've been in it.'

'So why would you and I share a bedroom?'

'Good point, Erika. Forget I said anything.'

The old dear looks like a focking –

You know what? I'm not going to say what she looks like. Not tonight. Not on her hen night.

All I *will* say is that she's a seventy-something-year-old woman who's trying to look like a fifty-something-year-old woman – but who *actually* looks like a ninety-something-year-old man . . . in focking drag.

I'll leave it at that.

And that, by the way, is after a day of, like, beautifying herself in the Spa at the Shelbourne Hotel, where she's had, like, her talons clipped and her face sanded down.

Okay, I won't say anything else.

It's, like, a pretty tight group. We're talking me and Honor – who organized the entire thing, by the way – then obviously Delma, three or four of the old dear's mates from The Gables, another three or four from Foxrock Golf Club, then one or two from each of her campaigns to have various things permanently moved, stopped this instant or closed down forthwith.

Yeah, no, we're sitting around in the famous Saddle Room, waiting to have dinner before we all head to the National Concert Hall for an evening of the Music of Michael Bublé played by the RTÉ Concert Orchestra, then a karaoke bor, then – provided the woman can still stand – drinks in House on Leeson Street.

'Honor,' she goes, 'will you have a pre-dinner cocktail?'

Honor's like, 'No, I'm off the drink this week, Fionnuala. Monday is going to be – oh my God – *such* a big day for me!'

Er, it's a big day for Reese, I think to myself. I don't see how it's big for her, although I don't pull her up on it. I'm just relieved to see that she's turning down booze.

The old dear goes, *'You'll* have some bubbles, won't you, Ross?'

And I'm like, 'Yeah, no, just so *you* don't feel like a chronic focking dipso,' and she pours me a glass of champagne, which I knock back in one.

She stands up then and walks around the table, topping up everyone's glasses. And that's when Delma turns around to me and goes, 'She can't get married, Ross.'

And I'm like, 'The fock are you banging on about?'

Delma smells amazing, by the way. I know for a fact that she had the Moroccan rose and Shea butter exfoliating scrub, and that's not me being a pervert.

She goes, 'Ross, I rang her the other day and she was walking through . . . *Smithfield!*'

I'm there, 'Smithfield? So what?'

'She said she was tired of living a life of excess in the Áras and she wanted to see how *ordinary* people lived.'

'Jesus.'

'Fionnuala, Ross!'

'Yeah, no, it might not be anything to worry about. Might be like the time when I was a kid and she just randomly decided that she wanted us to go on the Dort. She got me to ring Iarnród Éireann and try to book us a private cabin.'

'This is different, Ross. She kept saying to me that, as the country's First Lady, she had a duty to get in touch with the common people.'

'She's spent seventy-whatever years putting distance between her and the common people.'

'I'm just wondering is she –'

'What?'

'– is she of sufficiently sound mind to make the commitment she's about to make?'

'Er, it's not like she's marrying some focking randomer she met in a petrol station. She's marrying my old man – who she's *been* with for most of her life.'

'Ross, no one has any idea what she's going to say from one minute to the next.'

374

'She still has good days, in fairness to her.'

'Well, let's hope the wedding day is one of those and that she makes it through it without there being, well, a *scene*.'

The old dear sits down opposite me again. She goes, 'What are you two whispering about?'

And I'm like, 'Oh, just funny stories from the past.'

'Oh?' she goes. 'Do share!'

I'm like, 'Yeah, no, I was telling Delma about the time you decided to go on the Dort and you got me to ring up and try to book a private comportment.'

Everyone at the table laughs.

'It's true!' the old dear goes. 'I thought it had sleeper cabins and private dining rooms with white tablecloths and silver service waiters! I couldn't believe it when I saw it. Pippa, it was like something out of Calcutta.'

Yeah, no, Pippa is Pippa Poppintree, her mate from the campaign to stop the Luas coming to Foxrock. She goes, 'Oh, that's *very* funny,' which is sort of, like, her *thing*? She declares that a joke is either 'funny' or 'very funny' but never actually laughs herself. 'I've a good idea – let's all tell our favourite Fionnuala stories!'

'No, let's not!' the old dear goes, pretending she doesn't like being the centre of attention.

Er, who do you think *I* got it from?

'I'll go first,' Corrine Brady goes. Yeah, no, Corrine soldiered alongside her in the campaign to keep poor people out of the National Gallery. 'I first met Fionnuala in nineteen-ninety-something-or-other. We were both regulars in the National Gallery, but I didn't know her, except just to see. She stood out because she was always wearing something fab-a-lous. Anyway, we were both eating our lunch and a bunch of schoolboys came in – full of sugar and hormones – and I remember Fionnuala caught my eye and she said, "Why can't people like us just have one . . . focking . . . day . . . of peace in this place?" And that was the stort of the One Focking Day campaign.'

'Oh my God,' Honor goes, 'is that where the name actually came from?'

'That's right,' Corrine goes, 'and we've been friends ever since.'

Pippa clears her throat and goes, 'My story *also* relates to her wonderful civic-mindedness and activism. I remember during the consultation process for that awful tramway thing, we were shown a route map at a public meeting and the line – Fionnuala will remember this – went right through Foxrock village. Well, we were *all* up . . . in . . . orms . . . about it. Very calmly, Fionnuala stood up, produced a scissors from somewhere, walked up to the Minister for Transport – can't even remember his name, irrelevant – and cut his tie! She got a standing ovation, of course!'

Yeah, no, the version *I* heard was that the Gords thought she was going to stab the dude and wrestled her to the ground.

That's when Honor suddenly pipes up. She goes, 'Can I tell a story?'

I'm there, 'If it involves her giving you alcohol, Honor, I probably don't want to hear it. I might actually go for a slash.'

'One of my, like, earliest memories,' she goes, 'was when Fionnuala took me to see Santa Claus in, like, Brown Thomas?'

Everyone's like, 'Awww!!!'

She's there, 'She never let me call her gran or nanna –'

'And I *still* don't!' the old dear goes.

Everyone laughs, except Pippa, who goes, 'Yes, that's funny.'

I'm there, 'Yeah, no, can everyone just shut the fock up and let my daughter speak?'

'She was always just Fionnuala to me,' Honor goes, 'this woman who always looked amazing, and smelled amazing, and was always – oh my God – *so* generous with her money. And that's what this story is basically *about*? Because when we got to BTs, the queue was, like, *so* long – we're talking, like, two hundred *people*? So Fionnuala went to the manager and asked was there a separate queue for people like us and he had no idea what she was talking about. He said we'd have to queue up like everyone else. There was no way Fionnuala was doing that. So she gave absolutely everyone in the queue fifty euros each to let us skip ahead of them. That's how, like, *generous* she is?'

'Two hundred people?' Delma goes. 'Fionnuala, did you really have ten thousand euros in your handbag?'

The old dear's there, 'I always have ten thousand euros in my handbag – for emergencies such as that.'

'What a lovely memory to have of your grandmother,' Corrine goes.

And the old dear's like, 'I don't want to hear the G word – not ever!'

Everyone laughs.

She's there, 'Okay, no more stories, because I want to propose a toast – to all of you. Firstly, I want to say thank you all for sharing this very special day with me. There are more than six hundred years of friendship present at this table – some of the dearest people to me in the whole world. And I want to thank you for your years of loyalty and support. I also want to thank my wonderful brides-maid, Honor, who arranged this entire day for us, and my wonderful bridesman, Ross –'

She suddenly stops. She's like, 'What in the name of God is that banging noise? Can anyone else hear it?'

I'm like, 'Er . . .'

She clicks her fingers to summon the waiter. She goes, 'What on earth is that racket I can hear?'

The dude is like, 'Racket?'

'Yes, it's like a thump, thump, thump, thump, thump!'

'Ah,' he goes, 'there *is* some construction work going on.'

'Well, can't you stop it? I'm trying to raise a toast here!'

'I'm afraid *we* can't stop it, ma'am. It's not happening at the hotel.'

'Well, where *is* it happening, then? The Shelbourne Hotel used to have influence in this town!'

He's like, 'They're, em, starting work to rebuild the Dáil, ma'am.'

'*Rebuild* it?' she goes – and I am *not* making this shit up. 'What's wrong with it that it needs to be rebuilt?'

The dude looks around the table at the rest of us – he's obviously wondering, is the woman pulling his wire – and he's there, 'It was, em, burned to the ground?'

'Burned? To the ground?' the old dear goes. 'I have literally no idea what this man is talking about.'

And all I can feel in that moment is the weight of Delma staring at me.

So I wake up in, like, Erika's old bedroom, lying on the flat of my back, I'm relieved to say, rather than standing up. It's, like, the day of the Leinster Schools Senior Cup final – we're talking Michael's against Blackrock – and I'm wondering, weirdly, how Reese's nerves are holding up.

I throw back the duvet and I tip over to the wardrobe. Erika has a shitload of her old clothes in there and I end up – yeah, no – taking a few things out to look at them and I don't mean that in, like, a *sick* way? A lot of them still smell of her.

That's when my phone suddenly rings. I check the screen and it ends up being Sorcha, so – yeah, no – I answer it.

I'm there, 'Have you had a change of hort? Because if you're in two minds, let me speak first –'

But she's not ringing to tell me that she wants me back. There's, like, panic in her voice – as in, like, genuine, genuine fear.

She's like, 'Ross! Honor has taken my cor!'

I'm there, 'Er, *excuse* me?'

'I was supposed to be meeting Claire – as in, like, Claire from Bray of all places – for lunch, because she wanted me to try their new non-ruminant ostrich burgers with hand-pulled beetroot and reawakened hazelnut purée. But when I went outside, the cor was – oh my God – gone.'

'Could Kennet not drop you to Bray?'

'Ross, are you listening to what I'm even saying? Honor is driving my cor. She's thirteen years old. Jesus, how does she even know how to drive?'

'Yeah, no, it's a genuine mystery. So you definitely know it was her who took it?'

'Yes, because Joy Felton just rang and said her granddaughter swore she saw Honor O'Carroll-Kelly driving through Dalkey village when she was coming home from camogie.'

Camogie? Jesus Christ, what's happening to this port of the world?

I'm there, 'And have you tried ringing her?'

She's like, 'Yes, *obviously* I've tried ringing her, but she's not answering. She must be, like, screening me.'

'I wonder is she heading for the RDS? I'm just thinking, she'll find it very difficult to get porking around Ballsbridge today. Unless she throws it in the Merrion Shopping Centre and walks in.'

'Ross, what the fock are you talking about?'

'Sorry, my brain's in rugby mode – the day that's in it.'

'Will you *please* take this seriously? Your thirteen-year-old daughter is driving around in a focking cor! I'm *supposed* to be a Government minister!'

'Okay, chillax, I'm going to go out and look for her. Like I said, I'll try the Merrion Shopping Centre first. I sometimes pork there if I'm going to a Leinster match and I want to have a few scoops.'

'I'm going to go out looking for her too.'

'Er, you've no *cor*?'

'Kennet's coming for me. Keep your phone on – and *stay* in touch!'

As I hang up, Erika walks into the room. She sees all of her clothes laid out on the bed – tops matched with trousers and blah, blah, blah.

She's like, 'What the fock, Ross?'

I'm there, 'It's not what it looks like.'

'Jesus Christ, are you putting together outfits for me?'

'I don't have time to explain it. Honor's taken Sorcha's cor.'

'What?'

'Again, long story. We have to go and find her.'

So we race outside to Erika's Porsche Cayenne. We get into it and off we go. I ring Honor's number, just on the off-chance that she might answer. Weirdly, she actually *does*?

She's like, 'Hi, Dad!'

There's, like, silence in the background. I'm there, 'Are you not at the RDS? The match is storting in, like, twenty minutes.'

She goes, 'No, I'm up at the Sally Gap.'

I'm like, 'Er, what are you doing up at the Sally Gap?' and I mouth the words to Erika, 'Sally Gap. Ring Sorcha. Tell her.'

Honor goes, 'First things first, Dad. I never actually *liked* Adam?'

I'm there, 'Er, okay,' as Erika points the beast in the direction of Wicklow and rings Sorcha with the news.

'As in, he gave me the total focking ick,' she goes.

I'm there, 'Was it the red hair and the bit of wispy beard?' just trying to keep her talking. I don't even *know* why? I just have this feeling that she's about to do something awful. But then, isn't she *always*?

She goes, 'He's just a focking sap.'

I'm like, 'Yeah, no, I said I was a fan, but I thought you could have done better.'

'He's, like, a sad sack. But I knew he was, like, mad about me and I needed someone to make Reese jealous.'

'Yeah, no, that's kind of what your old dear was like with Fionn.'

'I wanted Reese to, like, *want* me again?'

'And, hey, it worked. Because you're with him now – as in, like, *with* with?'

She goes, 'But I don't *want* to be with him.'

And I'm there, 'Why not? Jesus, there's a lot of girls who would kill to be in your position – and I mean that literally when it comes to the likes of Muckross Pork and Holy Child Killiney.'

I motion to Erika to put her foot down.

Honor goes, 'You know he's been cheating on me the entire time we've been together? When he said he needed space to focus on the final, it was just so he could be with, like, three other girls.'

'He's a kicker, Honor – that's how we roll.'

'And he told all of his friends that we, like, did stuff that we never actually did.'

'Again, you should have a chat with your mother about all of this – she's got first-hand experience.'

She goes, 'Dad, you're not listening to –'

But then the signal suddenly cuts out.

I'm there, 'Focking Wicklow,' staring at my phone with, like, zero focking coverage. 'How do they focking live like this?'

Erika's like, 'Why is she in the Sally Gap?'

I'm there, 'All I know is, she found out that Reese was dicking her around again – doing the dirt, left, right *and* centre, in fairness to him. I mean, what do these girls expect, Erika?'

'You don't think she's going to –'

'What?'

'Drive off a cliff, Ross?'

'No, I don't think she'd do something like that? Would she? Jesus, she did sound upset.'

Erika puts her foot to the metal. Fifteen minutes later, we arrive in the – yeah, no – Sally Gap and I'm relieved to see my daughter standing next to the cor, although Sorcha will not be a happy bunny when she sees the front of it all smashed in.

I'm there, 'You're cutting it majorly fine if you're going to make it to the RDS. If you go now, you might catch a bit of the second half.'

She looks at me like I'm off my focking meds.

She goes, 'Seriously, how focking slow are you? Hi, Erika.'

Erika's like, 'Er, hi, Honor,' in a really, like, *cautious* voice?

It's, like, deathly quiet around and our voices sort of, like, echo through the – I want to say – *valley*?

I'm there, 'I'm just making the point that Reese will probably be looking out for you in the crowd.'

'Dad, I've no focking interest in Reese!' Honor practically roars at me. 'It was all about revenge, okay?'

And that's when I hear the banging coming from the boot of Sorcha's cor.

I'm like, 'No! Focking! Way! Honor, please tell me you didn't!'

Honor goes, 'Did you honestly think after the way he treated me in Irish college that I would actually want to *be* with him again?'

'Well, after he made the Senior Cup team, I'm going to be honest with you and say yes.'

'Yeah, focking spare me, will you? I've got more respect for myself than that. I said last summer that I would get him back for what he did to me – and now I have.'

I'm there, 'Honor, he's missed the Leinster Schools Senior Cup . . . *final!*'

Erika goes, 'Ross, why is that your main concern?'

And I'm there, 'I don't know, I'm thinking about it as a fellow kicker.'

Erika's like, 'Can I let him out of the boot now, Honor?'

And Honor shrugs and goes, 'Whatever.'

Erika pops the boot and the poor dude jumps out. He's not so much angry as terrified. He's looking at Honor with, like, genuine fear in his eyes and he's backing away, going, 'You're a psychopath! You're a focking psychopath!'

Honor's there, 'Oh, you missed your big match, did you, Reesey? Boo-focking-hoo!'

I'm like, 'If it's any consolation, Dude, Johnny Sexton got to play in, like, *three* Leinster Schools Senior Cups? Although he never got his hands on a winner's medal, as I never tire of reminding him.'

I feel sick for the dude. I know I shouldn't. But I can't *not* see the world through the eyes of a number ten.

We suddenly hear the sound of a cor approaching. We all turn around and – yeah, no – it ends up being Sorcha. Her and the triplets are sitting in the back of her ministerial cor, which is being driven by the famous K . . . K . . . K . . . K . . . Kennet.

The dude pulls up and Sorcha gets out with a look of just, like, bewilderment on her face. Brian, Johnny and Leo spill out of the back as well. Then she sees the shit that Honor has made out of her front fender.

She's like, 'What? The? *Fock?*' which is not only a fair question but the *only* question in the circumstances.

'*I'll* tell you what the fock,' Reese goes – his confidence suddenly returning. 'Your focking psychopath of a daughter smashed me over the head with a piece of wood, bundled me into the boot of your cor and drove me up here so that I'd miss the Leinster Schools Senior Cup final!'

Again, I can't help but feel that he's somehow the victim in all of this.

Sorcha doesn't know what to say. Her mouth is moving but no actual *words* are coming out of it?

It's actually – believe it or not – Kennet who ends up speaking. He gets out of the cor, going, 'No, no, no, no, no – you're m . . .

m . . . m . . . m . . . m . . . mistaken, Sudden. You woke up this mor-den and you'd a fit of the big-match neerves – oatenly naturdoddle,' and then I hear him whisper to Sorcha, 'I'll look arthur him, M . . . M . . . M . . . M . . . M . . . Ministodder.'

Reese goes, 'I'm going to the focking cops.'

And Kennet's like, 'Mon, I'll thrive you to the Geerda Station so,' putting his orm around the dude's shoulder and sort of, like, steer-ing him towards the cor. He puts him into the back of the thing, then he winks at me and goes, 'Doatunt woody, Rosser, he woatunt be making addy statements. I'll froyten the J . . . J . . . J . . . J . . . J . . . J . . . J . . . J . . . Jaysus our of um.'

I shout at Reese. I'm like, 'From what I'm hearing, Michael's are going to be a force in schools rugby for two or three more years to come,' but I don't know if it's any consolation to him.

Kennet drives off with him, leaving me standing there with Sorcha, Erika, Honor and the three boys. No one says shit – oh, except *them*, by the way. Yeah, no, they're loving the way their voices echo through the valley. They're going, '*SCHEIßE!!!*' and '*ARSCHLOCH!!!*' and '*SCHLAMPE!!!*' and they're laughing their little heads off at the sound of their voices swearing back at them.

Eventually, Sorcha – staring at the front of her cor – goes, 'Did you have a crash?'

Honor just shrugs. She's like, 'I drove into a rock. The focking prick was shouting in the boot and distracting me. I want to live with Dad and Erika.'

Sorcha looks at Erika, who just nods at her.

'I think that's probably a good idea,' Sorcha goes, 'because I can't look at you.'

'*Miststück!*' Leo goes, at the top of his voice. '*MIIIIIIST STÜÜÜÜÜÜCK!!!*'

All of a sudden, we hear *another* cor approaching? This time – oh, focking shit – it's the actual Feds.

They pull up and they get out of their cor. There's, like, two of them, we're talking a man and a woman, who's actually okay in terms of looks.

'Was there an accident?' the woman goes.

And I'm like, 'Er, I would have said that was focking obvious, wouldn't you?' because the front of the cor is – I think I mentioned – totally mangled.

'Who was driving?' the dude goes.

And before I can say a word, Sorcha jumps in and goes, '*I was driving.*'

I'm there, 'You weren't, Sorcha.'

She's like, 'Yes, I was, Ross.'

Brian's going, '*Fotze! Fotze! FOTTTTTTZZZZZZE!!!*'

I'm there, 'Sorcha, I was the one who was driving, do you remember? Maybe you banged your head when I hit that, I don't know, sheep.'

But she goes, 'Don't listen to my husband. I was the one who was driving. I'm, like, a Government Minister, if that helps in any way?'

Johnny's like, '*Ficker! Ficker! FIIICKEEERRR!!!*'

I'm there, 'Sorcha, do you remember I said that there were no more nasty secrets to crawl out of the woodwork?'

And the woman Gorda looks at her and goes, 'Can I see your driving licence, please?'

Epilogue

The old man is chuckling away to himself.

'There's a story in the *Irish Times*,' he goes, as he puts on his cufflinks, 'that I was seen eating one of John Shanahan's *filets mignons* last weekend! *Two* eye-witnesses – no less! – according to the famous paper of record!'

Hennessy's there, 'Imagine running a story like that on a man's wedding day,' as he bends down to tie his spats, with a cigor clamped between his teeth. 'Bastards.'

'Bastards is right,' the old man goes, checking out his hair in the mirror. 'Oh, the *Irish Independent* has a story on *you*, by the way.'

'Saying?'

'That you strangled a turkey with your bare hands in the grounds of the Áras on Christmas morning! You should sue, Old Scout – even though it's true!'

Hennessy stands up again and takes the cigor out of his mouth. 'No,' he goes, 'I kind of like it. It's good for my reputation.'

'This snowflake generation – eh, Hennessy!'

'I know!'

'They have neither the mental nor the emotional capacity to deal with anything! And what they don't realize is that the Russians are coming – and they don't give a damn about your pronouns!'

I sort of, like, clear my throat and the two of them spin around, as if they've been caught doing something dodgy.

The old man's like, 'Kicker!'

Hennessy goes, 'How long have you been standing there?'

I'm there, 'I wouldn't worry about it. Most of what you were saying went over my focking head. Can I have a word with the old man – in, like, *private?*'

Hennessy gives me a long filthy, then he focks off.

385

The old man goes, 'You don't mind that I asked Hennessy to be my best man, do you, Ross?'

I'm like, 'No, I probably would have turned you down anyway.'

'It's just that your mother was rather keen on snagging you as a bridesman! You look rather smort, by the way!'

Yeah, no, I'm wearing, like, a black tux with a white waistcoat and obviously Dubes.

I'm there, 'Yeah, no, thanks. Dude, are you sure about this? About the wedding, I mean?'

He goes, 'The biggest mistake of my life was divorcing your mother, Ross! I'm just glad she's allowing me to put that right today!'

'No, what I mean is . . . Dude, she's not well.'

'Not well?'

'Will you stop focking pretending that you can't see it! Her mind is going – just like her mother's went.'

His expression changes to suddenly serious. Then he nods sort of, like, sadly.

'The next couple of years,' he goes, 'are going to be very, very tough! The woman that you and I love is disappearing, Ross, bit by bit! I know that! The process is already under way! It will probably happen quite quickly now until there's nothing of the old Fionnuala remaining except what's on the outside! I just want to make whatever time she has left as happy as I can! And when we're both gone, Ross – because I won't always be here either – I want our children to know that their mother and father were very happy and brought them into the world out of love!'

'That's why you're getting married?'

'It's why I'm doing everything! Look, I know Erika looks at me and she just sees someone who's been corrupted by power! Believe it or not, Ross, I'm doing what I'm doing because I want to leave not just money for my children – but a better, stronger and truly independent Ireland!'

'Jesus, I didn't ask for a porty political broadcast. I was just wondering are you sure this wedding is, like, totally legal?'

'If Hennessy says it's legal, Ross, then it's legal!'

'Whatever. Anyway, I suppose I probably should say good luck.'

'Thanks, Kicker!'

We stand there, looking at each other awkwardly for a good ten seconds, then we just, like, embrace each other. It's not a big deal. Like Hennessy said, it's his focking wedding day.

I tip back to the old dear's room then. She's already dressed in the Tipper Tynan, cream-coloured Berta dress, with the gold, ort-deco print on it and the – whatever – plunging neckline. She's also wearing sporkly T-strap pumps and a headband with, like, feathers sticking out of it, which Honor is doing her best to sort of, like, primp *up*?

'How's your father?' the old dear goes.

I'm there, 'Yeah, no, he's fine,' and I move over to the window and look out.

The wedding is happening in, like, the gorden of the Áras, by the way. There's, like, four hundred chairs set out and every single one of them has someone *sitting* on it? It's, like, a beautiful, sunny, April day and there's obviously a real buzz down there.

Honor is skulling the champagne to the point where I nearly feel like saying something to her. In the end, I don't bother. It's, like, four weeks since the incident in the Sally Gap and the whole thing has been thankfully covered up. Yeah, no, Hennessy managed to get a hold of the WhatsApp messages that Reese sent to his friends about Honor and three or four other girls he happened to be seeing at the same time. Reese's old pair were worried about the damage it might do to their son's future career in – hilariously – Law if it came out that he was a misogynistic prick, so they agreed to drop the entire thing.

That's Ireland, I suppose. It's why we love it.

So Reese's absence from the Michael's storting fifteen was explained away as an attack of nerves on the morning of the final. Which means he'll probably never play for the school again. I keep saying it, but I can't help but feel sorry for the dude.

I'm there, 'He's down there now.'

'Who,' the old dear goes, 'your father?'

I'm like, 'Yeah, no, he's waiting for you.'

The old dear stands up. Even though she wouldn't be my cup of tea, she looks – I might as well say it – *well*?

I'm there, 'You alright, Honor?'

Honor just nods. I think she's a bit gee-eyed.

We both grab our bouquets. Then we head downstairs – with one of us standing either side of the old dear – to the gorden.

I give the jazz quartet the nod and they strike up the song. It's 'Alright, Okay, You Win'.

Honor walks up the aisle first – two steps at a time, the way we practised it yesterday, holding her bouquet in front of her. I go to follow her, except the old dear sort of, like, hooks my orm.

'No, no,' she goes, 'walk *with* me. I want you to give me away.'

And I'm like, 'Gladly.'

So that's what ends up happening. I walk up the aisle with her, the two of us linking orms. Out of the corner of my eye, I can see Delma bawling her eyes out and JP handing her a tissue to clean up her face. I notice even Sorcha smile, despite the fact that she's been chorged with driving without a licence – a case that Hennessy hasn't yet been able to make go away.

Then I spot my little brother and sisters, sitting on the knees of the front-row guests – we're talking Hugo, we're talking Cassiopeia, we're talking Diana, we're talking Mellicent, we're talking Louisa May, we're talking Emily.

When I reach the old man, I hand over the goods and I go, 'Don't fock it up this time!' which everyone hears and which everyone seems to find hilarious.

The celebrant dude goes, 'Ladies and gentlemen, we are gathered here today . . .'

I whip out my phone and I just, like, FaceTime Ronan, pointing the camera at the old pair, just so he can watch the entire thing from the safe distance of his office in New York.

Half an hour later, after prayers, exchanges of vows, readings of Seamus Heaney's poetry, and a quick update from my old man on how construction work on the new Leinster House is progressing, they are pronounced man and wife.

Yeah, no, there isn't a dry eye in the gorden.

Ronan goes, 'Thanks, Rosser,' and – yeah, no – he's wiping away tears as well.

We all head to the prosecco tent then for a drink. I have my orm around Honor's shoulder and I'm telling her that she did a great job and to maybe lay off the drink now until she gets something in her stomach.

She's like, 'Okay, Dad.'

She really is a great kid.

As I'm walking into the tent, I just so happen to catch Fionn's eye. We look at each other for a good, like, ten seconds, then he turns his head away. I'm thinking, he'll hopefully come around, given time. Blackrock College won the Leinster Schools Senior Cup, by the way. There's no way Castlerock were ever going to beat them. I actually think it would have been an embarrassment, although I wouldn't expect him to take any consolation from that fact yet.

Honor says she's going to go and find Brian, Johnny and Leo. I know she's missed those dudes since she moved out of Honalee.

Hennessy sidles up to me. He goes, 'They want you outside. They're doing photographs.'

And I'm like, 'Yeah, no, whatever.'

'I heard you were charged,' he goes.

'Good news travels fast.'

'What are you looking at?'

'Conspiracy to pervert the course of justice, perverting the course of justice, gross public indecency – blah, blah, blah.'

I watch him eat a cube of cheese off a cocktail stick while he performs a quick calculation in his head.

He's there, 'You could be looking at two years in prison.'

I'm like, 'I'm still hoping the fact that I went to a good school will spare me a custodial sentence.'

'I meant what I said. I can make it disappear, just like your daughter's case, if you talk the boy into coming home.'

I'm there, 'I'm not going to do that, Hennessy.'

'You're happy to go to jail to keep him away from me?'

'If it comes to that, yeah.'

He nods – I think he's, like, quietly impressed.

Across the room, I spot Shadden holding hands with the famous Peadar.

'Besides,' I go, 'his wife seems happy enough now. I better go and tell Honor that these photos are happening.'

It's while I'm walking around trying to find her that I happen to run into Oisinn and Magnus, looking all delighted with themselves.

I'm there, 'Hey, goys, you haven't seen Honor, have you?'

'She's over there,' a voice behind me goes. 'She's trying to stop Brian and Johnny from smashing the double bass over Leo's head.'

'Focking morons,' I go, at the same time turning around. It ends up being Sorcha's sister.

I'm like, 'Hey there – er, you!'

She goes, 'You look amazing.'

I'm there, 'Yeah, no, you do too.'

And it's nice because there's none of the usual awkwardness you'd expect when you've – I suppose you could say – ridden your wife's sister. It's actually totally chill. I suppose I could always say that we were on a break, which is one hundred per cent true.

'So,' Oisinn suddenly goes, 'can we tell Ross?'

Magnus is there, 'I don't think that ish shuch a good idea. We shaid we wouldn't do anything to overshadow Charlesh and Fionnuala'sh big day.'

'He's not going to tell anyone,' Oisinn goes, 'are you, Ross?'

I'm like, 'What are we talking in terms of?'

'Plush,' Magnus goes, 'we haven't told Shorcha yet and I think she ish not going to be sho happy.'

'Fock Sorcha,' the sister goes.

I think her name might even begin with a P.

I'm there, 'Sorry, goys, I'm totally lost here. What the fock are you on about?'

'Well,' Oisinn goes, 'we know that Sorcha had strong feelings about her sister here carrying a baby for us. And, as you know, we took on board what she said and decided not to proceed.'

I'm like, 'Good.'

390

'But then,' the sister goes, 'I had a long chat with them and persuaded them to change their minds.'

I'm thinking, no. I'm thinking, please, please *focking* no.

Magnus goes, 'We have fantashtic newsh, Rosh – even though it is shtill only a few weeksh.'

I'm like, 'Don't say it, Dude. Just do not focking say it.'

'Isn't it exciting, Ross!' the sister goes. 'I'm, like, pregnant!'

Acknowledgements

As always, I owe a huge debt of gratitude to the team of people behind these books. A huge thanks to my editor, Rachel Pierce, for her sound directions when I was wandering around blindly in the dark; to my wonderful agent, Faith O'Grady; and to the genius that is Alan Clarke. Thank you to all the team at Sandycove, especially Michael McLoughlin, Patricia Deevy, Cliona Lewis, Brian Walker, Carrie Anderson and Aimée Johnston. Two real-life people made cameos in this book, Ross's arresting officers – aka, Jimmy Kavanagh and Michael's legend Shane 'Shaney Boy' Hughes. Jimmy, thank you for the title of this book. It's inspired. And Shaney Boy's old man, Neill Hughes, thank you for your very kind generosity to GOAL, which will help them continue to do incredible work in the developing world. Lastly, thanks to my family and, most of all, my amazing wife, Mary.